BLIND

A MASTERMIND NOVEL

LYDIA MICHAELS

BLIND

Second Edition Copyright © 2023 by Lydia Michaels

Print ISBN: 978-1-957573-26-7

*For Carla.
Watch out for rogue trees.
I love your crazy ass.*

Listen to the Blind Playlist!
Click Here to Listen!

Listen to the Blind Playlist here!

PROLOGUE

"ARE YOU COMFORTABLE?"

She nodded in the darkness, unsure if the tumultuous excitement brimming inside reached the realm of comfortable, but this was exactly where she wanted to be—the point she'd waited so long to reach.

This was it, the moment Scarlet Farrow had been anticipating for three grueling months. In the darkness of her mind, colors swirled, forming a tapestry of imagined characteristics for this mysterious man. He was her every hidden fantasy come to life.

Mr. Stone.

Warmth bloomed low in her belly as she breathed in his mysterious presence, savoring every memorized detail of the stranger who'd somehow heightened her passions and laid her bare —all prior to setting eyes on him. There was no way to define the array of emotion he provoked in her.

Her throat went dry as his fingertip ghosted over her larynx, barely touching, utterly titillating. Only *he* could provoke such a reaction, simply whisper one question and call her entire being into compliance.

The cool air of the room chilled her exposed shoulders, yet her skin burned for every long awaited caress. There was something about blindness that awakened the senses, goaded courage, and turned vulnerability into raw hunger. Need.

She had no idea what the room looked like, how it was dressed or furnished. According to her other senses, she imagined it massive, with high reaching ceilings and walls somewhat vacant.

From the beginning he'd claimed to know what she required, but after years of disappointing blind dates and lackluster sex, Scarlet was initially skeptical. She'd been wrong. He knew what she needed, and through many lessons in patience and honesty, a side of her she never anticipated surfaced for him. Every fleeting moment in the company of Mr. Stone was worth the seemingly endless waiting—he was *that* impressive.

Burgeoning trust turned to pure, carnal need. It was the liaison of a lifetime, a masterpiece of emotions tied into this, their last moment of blindness, when all would finally be unveiled.

She'd done everything he'd asked, followed every meticulous command down to the last detail. Unsure of his physique or even the expression he wore, her attraction had nothing to do with his body or the smoldering way his gaze scrutinized her nakedness. Perhaps his eyes didn't smolder at all, but his words, his tone, always spoke of an intensity that went beyond the physical and sent her insides ablaze.

She craved his drugging affection with every aching piece of her soul.

He aroused her, not physically, but with intellect, challenging her, pressing her, and unraveling her until the physical need rivaled the screaming desire for his total possession. Simply put, he *saw* her. Exposed. Vulnerable. Raw.

"I need you present, Ms. Farrow."

Understanding the magnitude of this moment, she reassured him every part of her being was invested in the now. "I'm here, Mr. Stone. Always here."

Her body shivered, as her spine lengthened, pulling her shoulders back as her shins pressed into the cool floor. He'd stripped her of more than her clothing. Stripped away her veils, stripped away her ego, stripped away her choice, and all at her eager consent.

The soft click of his shoes over exposed floor halted her breath, reminding her that he was clothed, holding the upper hand to her vulnerable nudity. The echoes, found only in drafty openness of this place, were now familiar.

Never in her life had she placed so much trust in another, let alone in an absolute stranger. He was an unexpected risk, a secret others wouldn't understand. Coming here was a brave decision and she had no regrets. Never before had she been so proud of her courage.

"You're pleased." It wasn't a question, but a confident observation.

He saw through her facades, unveiled the parts of her the rest of the world never bothered to see. He exposed her soul, her bare need, and her darkest desires.

It would be impossible to lie to him. Lips twitching with a hidden smile, she confessed, "I am."

"And so you should be. It's been quite a journey."

Breath dragged into her lungs with each ragged inhalation as if filling her up like a balloon that would soon pop. Everything they'd built together rested in this final moment of truth.

Eagerness to rush forward had her trembling. His finger caressed the soft pad of her lower lip and the sharp rush of familiar excitement came with the touch of his flesh to hers, rocking her off balance.

"Be still."

Her chin quivered as the backs of his soft nails traveled over her jaw, behind her ear, and down her throat. His touch was always so tender, almost hesitant and slightly reverent. It was revealing in a way, because he embodied confidence, control, and patience, yet his gentle touch sometimes spoke of diffidence.

Those refined caresses resembled unspoken secrets, so worshipful and vulnerable in a way she couldn't comprehend. Whoever he was outside of this room, beyond his power, she believed he was innately kind.

"It isn't fair for a woman to hold such beauty," he whispered.

His thumb coasted over the soft curve of her throat, tripping slowly over each ridge of her larynx, teasing the slight curve of her collarbone. Her nipples tightened painfully as the anticipation breathed like fire in her pulsing veins. Her nerves never rested in his presence.

What he so carefully built between them went beyond mere sexual titillation. It was deep, plunging far past the shallow reality most couples shared. Mr. Stone was a man of few words so she savored every confession, every clue, every query, each one a fragment of the masterpiece of this mysterious man.

"When I read your letter, I knew there was something special about you, Ms. Farrow. While there was courage in your words, I sensed the absolute desperation of your plea. True, you did not ask to be found—only to be heard—but I found you all the same. Genuine courage is not borne of fear. True courage takes action, despite the fear. You, my lady, feared what?"

So much. She feared leaving this world incapable of describing what it felt like to be loved. He was right. She hadn't written the letter because she was brave. She'd written it because she was scared, terrified the life she'd led was all there would ever be.

"I feared always being alone."

"Correct. Yet, you've given months to a complete stranger, trusting me to show you something that changes nothing of your predicament outside of these walls. Why?"

The burn of truth wasn't as severe as it once had been. At this point, she was so exposed there was hardly anything left to hide. "I wanted to know what it felt like to be adored, cared for, placed at the top of someone's priority list, Mr. Stone. You said you could give me that experience."

"Do you feel you've achieved your goal, Ms. Farrow? Have you felt those very things?"

Her heart raced. "Yes."

"And do you have any regrets, Ms. Farrow?"

He never bullied her or even pressured her. He merely offered, and while the entire turn of their correspondence had taken her off guard, it was her decision to go to him—on his terms and her trust.

The moment she agreed, life as she knew it was forever changed. Every instruction, every stipulation, disentangled another part of her. Desire bloomed into reckless curiosity as hidden secrets were slowly revealed.

"I have no regrets."

1

THE LETTER

THREE MONTHS PRIOR...

*C*ondom or no condom? Scarlet moved the little foil square back into her purse as she held the phone to her ear and fussed with her appearance. Leaning into her reflection, she noticed yet another cluster of freckles on her nose.

"You'll have a great time, Lettie," Nicole, her best friend and matchmaker extraordinaire rattled on as she continued to prepare for yet another blind date. "Drew's a great guy."

Scarlet huffed and grimaced at the mirror. Glancing at her purse, she paused then quickly removed the condom from her purse and stuffed it in the drawer of the hall table. *Better.*

"Well, I'm pretty sure you've fixed me up with every eligible bachelor in the tri-state area, so process of elimination tells me we have to be getting closer."

"Ex-*actly*. Now, what kind of underwear are you

wearing? Please tell me they're not cotton with daisies on them or something."

She stilled and frowned. Dashing into her bedroom she shucked her bottoms and tossed her underwear in the corner. "*No. I'm wearing panties.*" *Besides, they had roses, not daisies.* She fumbled in her underwear drawer and found something akin to dental floss. Sliding them up her thighs, she winced as the sling of narrow fabric wedged between her ass cheeks.

This was what some women preferred? Impossible.

"Good. Drew can be a very sensual man, from what I hear."

Her hand stilled on her zipper. "Wait, how did you hear that?"

"Boys talk. Matt tells me things."

"Oh. Right." She returned to the hall table and retrieved the condom, stuffing it deep into her purse. Better safe than sorry.

"Now, don't be nervous. He's really easy to talk to so you won't have to worry about filling any awkward moments of silence."

Taking a deep breath, she sniffed and frowned. Scenting her hands and hair, she inspected her fragrance. Would it always be this much work? Gah, she hated all this primping. Racing to the bathroom she washed her wrists, worried her perfume was a bit strong. For someone who didn't wear perfume regularly, even a spritz came off as pungent.

"And remember, play hard to get. Go back to his place if he asks, but don't go all the way. Leave him wanting more."

"Right. Wanting more." Back at her purse she unearthed the condom and tossed it on the table then froze. That was easy advice for someone having sex regularly.

Lights drifted across the front windows and her heart lurched. "Shit. I think he's here, Nicole. I gotta go!"

"Okay," her friend said, immediately falling into rapid speech. "Have fun and try to relax. It's okay to take risks sometimes, Lettie. Don't sweat the small stuff and just—for once—keep an open mind and enjoy yourself without over thinking."

Blowing off the slight insult to her analytical and methodical personality, she humored her friend. "Got it. Bye."

"Call me when you get home!" Nicole shouted as she ended the call.

Scarlet raced to the bathroom and whipped open the cabinet, shoving the box of tampons aside and reaching into the next box, removing a fist full of condoms. There was nothing wrong with being selective, but hey, if she didn't have sex again soon she feared her lady parts might fall off.

She stuffed the condoms in her purse and frowned when it wouldn't zipper. A knock sounded from the door and she panicked, taking a handful off the top and tossing them in the bathroom drawer. Four should be enough. Did people have sex four times in a night? She rolled her eyes. Not in her life.

Forcing out a slow breath, she shouldered her bag and answered the door. "Hi." Oh, he *was* attractive.

"Hi." He smiled and held out a hand. "I'm Drew."

When will this torture end?

If she didn't get out of this moving car in the next thirty seconds she was going to throw herself onto the asphalt rushing by. Back stiff, gaze fastened to the dark world outside, Scarlet clenched her teeth, praying she'd be home soon.

Kaleidoscopes of flashing lights swirled in her gaze as street lights passed with the oncoming traffic. Envy filled her for every pedestrian they zipped by, as she lamented the time it would take to get home. Drew was yet another disappointment.

Nicole had prematurely promised, yet again, that this one was the man of Scarlet's dreams. Sometimes it seemed her single life bothered Nicole more than it bothered her.

Drew was successful, didn't live with his mother or in his sister's basement, owned his own car, wasn't married, and wasn't attracted to men. These were basic requirements that—as she approached her thirties—became more impossible to find.

Nicole had Drew's credentials right, but as far as being the man of her dreams...No, not by a long shot. Drew was more like the man of her nightmares.

Every sentence he spoke started with *I* or ended with *me*. How he didn't have a permanent palm shaped imprint on his jacket from patting his own back was beyond her. Sitting through an evening with Drew was like witnessing a form of egocentric masturbation as he stroked his inflated ego. She'd never seen a man so in love with himself. It was perverted.

Not once had he asked about *her*. Never did he broach the topic of her career as a middle school teacher or ask her about where she'd grown up. Everything was about *him.*

Sure, she wasn't the most fascinating date, but she at least understood a conversation required two people, and the volleying back and forth of opinions and thoughts. Not Drew. He barely took a breath in his declaration of personal greatness to let her grunt a reply. It was as if she were invisible, a feeling she loathed and experienced all too often.

Throughout dinner she'd sipped her wine to smother her growls of frustration. A headache was in full affect by the first course. She mentally made a list of things less painful than their conversation; Chinese water torture; a manicure with a machete; having her eye against a glory hole; anything was better than what she'd endured.

As she consumed half a bottle of red, she casually phased out his self-important blathering and plotted her friend's execution. What had Nicole been thinking, setting her up with this narcissist?

As Drew pulled the car into her driveway—*finally*—she released a breath she'd been holding in with clenched teeth for the last half-mile. Her hand went to the door as she unlatched her seatbelt and made to escape, uttering a quick thank you—*of course*—interrupted by her insensitive date.

"I had a good time tonight, Scarlet."

I bet you did, you pompous know-it-all. "The restaurant was nice." There was no way she was paying him a compliment. She was shocked he even recalled her name.

"I can call you tomorrow."

Get out of the car. "I have a lot going on over the

next couple weeks. Conferences and report cards are just around the corner."

His brow crinkled with confusion. "Conferences?"

My God, you are such a dickhead! "I guess Nicole didn't tell you I'm a teacher." *Would have told you myself if you ever stopped talking and gave me a split second to participate in the conversation.*

"Oh, yeah. She might have mentioned something about that. I forgot."

Her hand tightened on the handle, loosening the gears and popping the door open an inch. "Well, thanks for dinner." Her foot touched the pavement.

"I don't have your number."

So close! Shutting her eyes on a sigh and counting silently to ten, she turned to face him. She wasn't a bitch, she was actually a very nice person, but she also wasn't a masochist and this entire evening had been absolute torture.

"Listen, Drew, I know we have a mutual friend, but that's all I see this being."

"You...don't want to go out again?" If she listened closely, she might hear the faint blubbing sound of his ego deflating. Like an inflated blimp going down, she imagined people screaming in the shadows of its enormous wake.

"I'm afraid you aren't what I'm looking for. I'm sorry." And she was sorry. The journey to find someone who fit her personality was daunting and depressing and each time she failed, it hurt a bit more.

His confusion contorted to disbelief. "Seriously?"

Easy, tiger. Forcing her expression to remain calm, she breathed. "My life's pretty busy and as much as I appreciate you taking me out tonight, I don't think we're as compatible as Nicole hoped."

He scoffed, reminding her of the assholes from college that made up the arrogant fraternity across from her apartment. "Your loss." His body pivoted in the seat, fingers gripping the steering wheel, as his glare drilled into the windshield.

Right. Time to go. Muttering a quick, "Okay, then." She climbed out and gently shut the door. He nearly took off her toe as he sped out of her driveway and whipped the car, into drive.

Rolling her eyes, she dug out her key. "Moron."

Once inside, she tossed her clutch on the table, rolled her eyes at the condoms scattered on the surface, which had a better chance of expiring than being used, and kicked off her heels. Her fingers plucked the clip from her hair and massaged her aching scalp. Thank God *that* was over.

Her phone chirped. Ah, there was her dear friend. Right on time. Sliding her thumb over the screen, she read Nicole's text.

*How's it going? Call me when you get home IF you go home *wink**

A hiccup of disbelief slipped past her lips. It was as if she'd gone out with a different Drew. Thumbing the call back command, she waited for Nicole to pick up.

"You are *not home* already!" her friend answered.

"Looks that way."

"Scarlet, what happened? It's not even nine o'clock."

Nosing through the freezer, she selected one of the

partially eaten pints of strawberry ice cream and peeled back the lid. "What happened was thirty years ago a man named Drew Archer was born and the continents shifted under the bulk of his ego. The guy's a complete narcissist, Nicole."

"No, he's not." She tsked and let out a whine ringing with disappointment. "You didn't give him a chance."

"I gave him two hours of my life I'll never get back. That's all the chance I can afford."

"Lettie, if you don't broaden your horizons you're never going to find Mr. Right."

"This has nothing to do with broadening my horizons. He was, without a doubt, Mr. Wrong."

"Why? He's straight, independent, never been married—"

Scarlet plopped on the couch and pulled the cold spoon from her mouth. "Yeah, you know why that is? Because no one wants to be married to a guy who only talks about himself. Women and gay men have steered clear for a reason. I don't think his independence, bachelorhood, or orientation is by choice. It's a circumstance that comes with being a bigheaded snob."

Nicole was quiet. Scarlet frowned and checked the screen of her phone. Still there. "Why aren't you saying anything?" Crap. Drew was still Nicole's friend. She probably offended her on his behalf.

Nicole sighed into the phone. "You know what, Scarlet? You have an excuse for every guy you're set up with. No matter what, there's always something wrong with them. Drew was really excited about tonight. Just because people aren't as shy as you and enjoy talking, it doesn't make them narcissists. If there was a snob on the date, I don't think it was him."

Her spoon plopped in the ice cream. "Are you serious? Nicole, I went into this with an open mind. My ass is numb from the underwear I wore thinking someone might actually see them. Just because I have standards doesn't mean I'm a snob—"

"Well, how high *are* those standards, Scarlet? No one seems able to reach them. Maybe you should write them down and really look at them. Chances are even you won't measure up."

It truly hurt that her best friend thought such things. "Where's all of this coming from?"

The frustration in Nicole's voice was so out of left field. It was like drunk fighting fueled with honest confessions. Scarlet was only mildly buzzed and every accusation hit with a sobering sting.

"I'm just tired of hearing you complain that no good men are out there. There are plenty of good men, but you've fabricated this ideal person in your head who, quite frankly, doesn't exist. It's time someone told you to get real."

It took a lot for Scarlet to snap, but Nicole was seriously crossing a line and it hurt. "I am being *real*! I'm sorry I didn't want to *marry* your friend. I didn't know my opinion of him would be the stone to tip the scale on what a stuck up person I am. If I'm so terrible, stop fixing me up with people you like. There's obviously something wrong with me if I have such unachievable *standards*."

"I just think you set yourself up for failure," Nicole said in a small voice.

This conversation had to end before their friendship did. Her aching scalp transformed into a piercing headache. "Whatever."

"Don't be mad, Scarlet. Friends are supposed to tell each other when they've lost their grip."

Funny, she thought friends were supposed to be there with a helping hand when life slipped through her fingers. They were both quiet for several seconds.

Exhaustion seeped in. Not the sort of tiredness that came at the end of the day, but the sort of weariness that crept in over time, unnoticed, and swallowed a person whole.

She was a good person. She paid her taxes, voted, volunteered, worked hard with her students. Why wasn't there a decent man out there that recognized those qualities? And why did people assume standards lowered with age? Didn't she deserve a partner that would meet her needs and love her?

Over the last few years, life became painful as friends moved on and relationships thinned over time. Everyone was past the initial marriage excitement and on to having children. Scarlet had done everything she was supposed to do, and her life was turning into a lonely, pathetic slideshow of repetition with no end in sight.

It was becoming more and more difficult to keep up the façade that everything was okay, when in reality, some days, she felt like she was dying on the inside. "I have to go."

"Scarlet..."

She shut her eyes against the bleakness of her solo future. "Yeah?"

"I love you. I just want you to be happy, but sometimes I don't think you know what it is that makes you happy. We all have to pick and choose our ideals at some point."

She didn't want to pick and choose. She just

wanted the basics of happiness. Someone—*anyone*—to be content with who she was and give her a reason to believe in love. "I'll call you tomorrow."

The phone slipped out of her hand as she ended the call. Resting her head on the back of the couch, she stared at the empty walls of her living room. Aside from the picture of her parents on her end table, there were no photographs of loved ones. Framed posters and generic art from *Home Goods* decorated her empty house. It was all so cliché and hollow, not really a home at all.

Nicole had met her husband, Matt, in college. They'd married immediately after graduation. Eight years after the fact, Nicole had no right to act like she knew what it felt like to still be single and thirty. Scarlet lived it, every day of her lackluster, solitary life.

The calls from friends used to come every day and now only came once a week. Texting had replaced the sound of actual voices. Some weekends she had no one to talk to aside from Thor, her cat.

Every evening was a struggle to heat up her Lean Cuisine and force herself to sit at the table like a normal person. On the days she ran out of papers to grade and laundry to iron, she went crazy looking for something to do.

She and her friends used to go out every Wednesday and Friday night. Now, *their* weekends were reserved for date nights and weekdays were monopolized by cozy evenings at home with a spouse.

Her lips twisted. She really needed to get one of those.

In the beginning she was invited over to her friends' houses for casual dinners, but over time those simple visits started to sting. Loneliness imbedded itself deeper in her heart with every secret glance or stolen touch she witnessed, and soon she was making excuses in order to avoid being the third wheel.

She'd done it all, suffered through countless blind dates, swam in the cesspool of dating sites, regretted the aftermath of too many bar pick ups. She even tried babysitting her friends' kids so she had an excuse to loiter at the park and scope out the single dads. No matter what, there was always an issue with the men she'd met. Perhaps Nicole was right. Maybe she was too picky.

Perhaps it was time to peel back the protective shell she'd encased herself in years ago and take a deeper look at the real her, even the ugliest layers, which she loathed to examine. But the idea hurt too much, a shard of unease causing a near crippling cramp in her belly. She'd always shied away from exposure, like a gaze unable to fasten to the unforgiving sun, so she shoved her self-examination back where it belonged.

Shutting out the lights, she detoured into the kitchen to trade in her ice cream for another bottle of red. As she climbed the stairs she considered actually listing her expectations like Nicole suggested. Her standards couldn't be that far out of reach, could they?

She changed into a nightgown, removed the excruciating thong, and pulled the decorative pillows off her bed as she considered what she truly wanted in a partner. She required someone responsible. The world was infested with middle-aged guys that acted more like her students than actual men.

Money wasn't an issue, so long as they held a job and were independent. All she really wanted was someone to care, care if she came home on time, care how her day went, care about her. She'd like to be able to count on someone other than herself for a change so accountability was a must.

Unlike her date from hell, she mostly wanted to be able to talk to someone, to have another person interested in what she had to say and what she wanted out of life, someone who actually knew how to hold a conversation. A simple, *"How was your day?"* would be nice every once in a while.

Reaching for her laptop, she opened up her document and began the list. These qualities were nothing short of what she expected of herself. So why didn't anyone fit the bill?

She wasn't built for a runway, but she certainly wasn't ugly. Shutting her eyes, she conceded. *You're too late. All the good men are taken.*

But how did other people keep finding love? Where were the good ones hiding? They had to be out there somewhere. Even when she made her profiles on the dating sites she was lenient, adapting her standards in hopes that someone decent might bite.

Maybe I am *a snob.*

Nicole's opinions lingered like unwanted cobwebs in the corner of her mind. Scarlet wasn't blind to her flaws. Like any woman, she was blatantly reminded of them on a daily basis. When others pointed out her shortcomings, it only pressed the blade of self-doubt deeper in her tender self-esteem.

Since childhood, she'd found it easier to hide her unfavorable traits by blending in. She easily laughed at herself and never tried to take life too seriously, but sometimes laughter hid real insecurities, insecurities she believed every one had. When she felt low like this, there really wasn't much difference between the woman she was and the awkward girl she'd once been. The race to fit in was exhausting and she'd expected to be past such emotions at this age.

But as everyone else coupled off and left her, she'd somehow ended up standing alone—her shortcomings all the more prominent through undesirable isolation. Some days she wished she could just stop caring, drop all her guards, and just let go.

"Gah!" She flung her head into her pillows. Nothing like a pity party. She was making her self sick with all this complaining. *I'm better than this.*

Scrubbing her hands over her face, she took a sip of wine and readjusted her attitude. There was no point to going on like this. This was her life and while she might not be filling her days with Hallmark sentiments, she was content. That should be enough. The pressure to find a mate had spun out of control and she needed to find level ground, find peace with her independence.

Ditching her list of tallying qualities for Mr. Nonexistent, she opened up a blank document and placed her faith in the cathartic art of writing. She'd always advised her students to journal when they needed clarity, so why not take a bit of her own advice?

I'm thirty and I seem to be the last single female standing, strange that this tends to bother my married friends more than me. Tonight, a friend told me my standards for Mr. Right were too high, but how could that be? Any woman staring into the endless abyss of disappointing blind dates would surely sympathize with how frustrating single and thirty can be. Nobody gets every-

thing they want in this world, but I've seen some get damn close, so why should we—the single and thirty—have to drop our expectations?

My heart will always pinch at the sight of an older couple holding hands or a man smiling at his wife when she doesn't know he's watching. There are those frozen moments in time when I observe couples laughing, but can't hear their laughter. Their happiness is startling and beautiful no matter how many times I see it. I have no idea what that sort of belonging feels like and I crave it, but only with a partner that truly appreciates me.

I've become invisible. I'm the woman you pass in the grocery store with a near empty cart stocked with the necessities for one. I'm the woman who always gets her car inspected ahead of time because I have nothing better to worry about. How nice it would be to take care of someone else's needs for a change.

I make a modest living teaching middle school, support myself, and have been independent since graduating college. I've always been a comfortable size twelve. My hair is red and yes, I even have freckles. Does that mean I somehow don't qualify for the spoils of love? Am I so ordinary I don't deserve something extraordinary? The truth is, I've never been in love and I wonder if I'll ever know what it feels like to be adored.

I know what it is to sleep with a man, but I've never spent the night with a man, never whispered in the dark, or confessed my deepest secrets and desires. I wish I knew what it felt like to truly be seen, to be adored, to feel things I've never felt before.

Just once I'd like to believe my presence is significant. I'm not talking about physical intimacy. I'm speaking of something greater. I want an intellectual man, someone confident and capable of listening, a man who can awaken a part of my soul no other person has touched. There must be someone out there who would cherish what I have to offer. If only I knew what it was to be adored, even if just for a moment, I might be able to release this envy weighing on my heart and appreciate the perks of being single once more.

Just once I'd like to experience that sharp jolt of antici-pation, knowing there's someone waiting for me at the end of the day, awaiting what I'll say next. Someone I could trust to reach parts of me I can't find on my own. Even just a glimpse of this might suffice, one chance to feel the grass on the other side and decide for myself, which is truly greener.

Scarlet sat back and admired her words. It wasn't a masterpiece of literature by any means, but it was definitely more than a simple list. It was a plea—a plea for single women everywhere! Or maybe just for her.

Tipping back the empty bottle of wine, she grimaced then giggled as she caught her reflection in the mirror. Her lips were stained and her cheeks were a tipsy shade of rose. Setting the bottle aside, she reread her letter, falling more and more in love with the sincerity of her words.

It was a damn good letter—the Jerry McGuire sort, except this time it was about cocks instead of jocks. She was seeking for Don Juan instead of the "kwan". Snorting at her clever drunken musings she sighed, slightly unburdened by her journalistic exorcism, and quite liquored up and loose.

She tweaked the document for no good reason. The wine had made her brain fuzzy and she had to actually pause and consider the grammar in some cases. It wasn't like anyone was ever going to read it, but still, she held herself to a certain standard, being a teacher. Plus, this was good shit.

"You and your standards," she mumbled, hiccupping as she made her way back from the kitchen with another bottle of wine and two aspirin for the morning.

As her eyes became heavy, she flopped back on her pillows and rested. Her laptop slid onto the mattress and she sighed. Journaling was good. It was a therapeutic exercise, a reminder that she was vindicated in holding out for what she wanted. It didn't solve anything, but clarity was there somewhere beneath the haze of Merlot.

She toyed with the idea of letting Nicole read it, but quickly shelved the thought. There was no reason to justify her choices to the married population who would never understand what it felt like to fill her shoes at this age. Beside, this wasn't justification. It was more a matter of clarification.

As a matter of fact, it was time someone stood up for all the single ladies out there, dredging their way through the swamp of unrefined bachelors that would never grow up. It was time someone spoke up for the thirty and single as a whole!

Motivated by her one-woman rally, she lurched from her pillows, waited for the room to steady, and retrieved her laptop. There was a columnist by the name of Roxy who wrote for the opinion section of the local paper on all things involving romance. It was a cheesy column, but that was exactly where epiphanies like this belonged. Cheesy or not, she was about to gift

Roxy with sheer brilliance from the mind of a fed up single woman.

In a matter of minutes she was on the paper's contact page, clicking on Roxy's email. Scarlet copied and pasted her kick ass letter. There was a window requesting a name. After pausing for only a second, it came to her, the nickname she'd had as a teenager, Lettie Red Riding Hood. She shortened it to read *L.R. Riding Hood*.

"Bring on the big bad wolf, bitches." Her finger snapped down on the send option and she grinned with satisfaction just before she fell back and passed out.

***

The weekend concluded with a hangover no good person deserved. Scarlet needed to call Nicole to make sure everything was okay with them, but she couldn't bring herself to take the first step. Her friend's words still hurt.

The truth hurts, Scarlet.

The morning after their disagreement, Scarlet berated herself for drinking too much wine and accepted her penance in the form of a killer headache and blank spots in her memory. In hopes of finding temporary comfort, she wasted a good hour Googling sex toys. That market must be a goldmine, as even the little toys cost close to fifty bucks. And what the hell was a *vagankle*? To think, her friend thought her expectations were weird. There were people out there fucking synthetic feet. *Gross!*

After her disturbing browse through pornographic props, she opted not to buy, and took a break from all thoughts sex and dating related. Saturday passed with long moments of cuddling Thor while watching a Buffy the Vampire Slayer marathon and nursing her aching head. Sunday, utterly fed up with her pity parade, she cleaned—not that anyone was coming over.

When she came across her laptop, she deleted her search history and found her journal entry. Embarrassment over her private little rant left her mortified. It was pure drunken nonsense, a pathetic proclamation of desperation. She deleted it immediately. Good God, what had she been thinking? What if a bus hit and killed her, and friends had to gather her possessions, and stumbled across that drivel? She shivered at the thought.

After showering, she tucked herself into bed by eight-thirty and spent the next few hours staring into dark silence. Maybe she should go on a vacation, someplace exotic and far away. The idea of traveling alone frightened her and if she went anywhere close to the equator she'd turn into a lobster.

On the other hand, she might gain something uniquely empowering by doing something so brave and completely for herself. Her little fishbowl was getting cramped, and she was bored with her surroundings. Sure, she could travel alone.

Mental note...see doctor about sedative for air travel.

But nothing too potent. Don't want to be so drugged you get robbed oversleeping on the tarmac.

Maybe she should visit Europe. She had roughly six months to learn a foreign language. Spanish terms kicked around her head, but she was rusty and out of practice. Mmmm...maybe she'd find a nice cabana boy to distract her for a while.

No! This is about you! *You don't need a man to enjoy life.*

Just as she fell asleep she decided that was what she'd do. She'd choose a country, study the culture, and learn a language. Maybe if she did that, she'd find someone to actually talk to. Not necessarily a man, but maybe a single girlfriend who filled shoes similar to hers. No matter what she decided, she was set on one thing. From now on, she would make herself more available and start taking advantage of life's little spontaneous opportunities. She might not find exactly what she wanted, but she needed a change.

Monday morning, she awoke feeling refreshed and focused. Her new attitude was quite *carpe diem* and all that good Latin stuff that filled a person with optimistic possibility. As Thor fluffed his long white tail around her ankles, she poured a glass of orange juice and settled in at the table with the paper like she did every morning before work.

Her cat let out a masculine meow as she slipped him a piece of buttery toast and she turned the page. "Here you go, you big cry baby." He nibbled the morsel from her fingers and purred happily.

After wiping her hands on the napkin, she sipped her juice and—

Juice sprayed everywhere. Holy crap! Was that her letter?

"Noooooo. No, no, no, no, no, no, *no!*"

Blindly blotting up the juice, her wide eyes scanned the article. They'd titled it *Where Are All The Real Men?*

"Oh, my God!" Her finger rushed to the bottom of the page. Shoot, it was a long letter. Turning the page she found the ending. Oh, thank goodness! She hadn't signed it Scarlet. A sound of disgust left her throat. Wow. She must have been really tanked. *L.R. Riding Hood*? As in Lettie Red Riding Hood? She hadn't heard that name since high school.

Talk about pulling the next Jerry McGuire. What the hell had she been thinking? She *hadn't* been thinking. She'd been drinking! That was it. The camel's back was officially broken—the last straw had struck —*whatever*—She was never drinking again. Ever.

Her head flopped on the table as she groaned. Thor jumped on the chair next to her and nudged her hand. Moaning, she petted his ear. "From now on, I only talk to my students and you. I'm such an idiot."

2

"SOME PEOPLE THINK design means how it looks. But of course if you dig deeper, it's really how it works."

~Steve Jobs
Co-founder of Apple Inc.

*A*sher Roan sat on the leather couch across from his partners Jet, Elliot, and Hunter as they reviewed the preliminaries for the next upgrade to GeekPeek. GeekPeek was the social media network they created after graduating high school, the revenue now keeping all of them quite comfortable. Their business was a natural outcome of their similar interests, which took off once MySpace fell off the map. They also fabricated interactive gaming systems like the state of the art Nexus64.

Some days more than others, it struck Asher as surreal, just how far they'd come. True, they were the same people they'd always been, but on days like this when they reviewed the quarterly reports and took note of their ratcheting value, Ash simply sat back and breathed it all in.

Being an introvert came with a disdain for people in general, but in his building, within his company, he was nowhere near as shy as he'd once been. In high school it was abundantly clear where he ranked in the pecking order. Now, he was at the top of the heap.

At six foot and an acceptable weight, no longer the short kid with pimples and a retainer, it was easy to relish how far he'd come. But the memory of that boy still lived inside of him somewhere.

"Don't forget we have our meeting with the Odd-Squad this week," Hunter said, snagging Ash's attention.

The OddSquad was a youth group they created via the local school districts, a place where socially challenged kids with an aptitude for technology could gather amongst peers with similar interests and let their freak flags fly. It really was a cool group and he had no doubt some would go on to make millions.

"Eugene, the kid from Central, has some really great ideas for a new app. He's supposed to be staging this week and I'd like to see his presentation," Ash said, tossing the solved Rubik's Cube aside. "Mark me down to attend."

Hunter nodded and typed in a note. Asher rhetorically smiled as he took in their group. Not many could claim to still be close to their high school friends twelve years after graduation. They'd gone from an excruciating childhood filled with bullies of all shapes, sizes, and genders, to running one of the most respected companies in the world.

Jet, the company's publicity rep and face, danced in front of the ninety-two inch flat screen while a computerized twin tried to escape a fleet of renegades chasing him through Armageddon on the television. "Will PR be attending?"

It was Jet's duty to show whenever photographers were expected, which put the rest of them at ease.

Elliot checked the schedule. "Not this time. Asher should be enough of a presence. If the kids come up with something impressive, we'll hone it and schedule a release with the press."

As the meeting continued, Elliot called out numbers and pulled up schematics for the new feed layout. Hunter was playing with the hologram simulator as Jet continued with his game. All in all, they were the picture of contentment. So why was there a bite of disquiet?

He was losing interest.

GeekPeek started out as a place for kids to discuss codes for gaming and bullshit with friends, things the four of them enjoyed. But over time, it turned into a brainchild no one had expected.

Now a Fortune 500 company and one of the world's fastest growing social sites, GeekPeek was a household name. None of them were really prepared for the influx of money that had hit their bank accounts after graduating, but over the years they figured out ways to invest and kept inventing new things without a hit to their capital. Slowly, all those worries about being different faded.

When one was born a geek, it was in their DNA. Ash had always been a dreamer, which required only mild interaction with others. When they were kids, he designed hundreds of prototypes to test in his parents' garage.

Sure, there had been a few fires, one remarkable explosion, and a couple trips to the ER, but when it came time to pay back his mom for the damage of too many detonated prototypes, they simply bought her a new house. That was when it occurred to the four of them they should move out of the garage and into an actual office building with labs and other settings conducive to their careers.

They were fresh out of high school and sitting on millions of unexpected dollars. They'd settled on an old run down hosiery mill and turned it into a funhouse factory coined the Think Tank. It was every nerd's wet dream. Of course, the stuffy professionals wouldn't see it that way.

Most of the business world didn't have fire poles where stairs should be. The rest of the world found grays and blues advantageous in an office environment, while their building resembled something more along the lines of the Crayola Factory or Pee Wee's Playhouse. Their corridors were lined with priceless memorabilia from George Lucas's original manuscripts, to Hermione Granger's wand.

"I think that's everything," Elliot said, tossing his tablet on the table. The screen saver came to life. It was Princess Leia wearing the infamous gold bikini.

Ash grinned, knowing where they had to be in twenty minutes. "Should we suit up? Are we going Ghostbusters today?"

Jet shut off the television and the sound of war silenced. "I call Venkman!"

Ash stood. "Egon!"

Elliot grimaced. "You were Egon last time. I'm always Ray."

Hunter shut down the hologram. "Whatever, man. No one ever asks me who I wanna be. It's just assumed the black guy's gonna be Winston. He was the weakest Ghostbuster. Even Rick Moranis had more lines than Winston."

"Quit your bitching. Let's go. Devon's waiting."

Devon was their accountant. He signed off on all their endeavors, not that his opinion mattered. But he kept track of all financial undertakings and kept things tidy for the IRS. It was a tradition of theirs to attend all meetings with Devon in attire that would surely embarrass the professional—call it his penance for all the times Devon took pride in embarrassing them when they were kids.

They went to the vault where the costumes were kept, and zipped into their authentic CWU 27/P Ghostbuster jumpsuits. They enjoyed dressing up as heroes, finding it easier than being themselves—at least that's how Asher translated it.

"I'm driving," Hunter announced.

It was always fun messing with their accountant. Devon had graduated with them, but hadn't been their friend until his mid-twenties, after struggling through six years of college resulting in one bachelor's degree.

When they were kids, Devon Rice was a total dick. He was a star football player and took every opportunity to humiliate them. Now, whenever they visited his practice, they repaid the favor and embarrassed the hell out of him.

They piled into the 1959 Cadillac ambulance and let the sirens rip. Five minutes later they were double-parking in front of Devon's office.

Their old nemesis, now friend, came outside and shook his head. "Seriously? Just once it would be nice if you guys respected that I have other clients, and that I'm trying to project a level of professionalism around here."

Ash grinned. It was nice to be in the power seat every once in a while. Hefting his proton pack on his back, he aimed his ray gun at Devon. "What do you think, guys?"

Elliot stepped forward and scanned Devon's personal space with his PKE pack, the small device chirping wildly. "I'm picking up a lot of psycho kinetic energy on this one. I think we should zap him."

Devon scowled and shoved Elliot away. "Knock it off. Can we please go inside?"

Ash laughed and lowered his weapon. As much as Devon pretended to still hate them, they'd helped him get his firm off the ground, trusting him with their largest accounts. He needed them. And, over his humbling adult years, had actually learned to like them.

They settled in at the conference table and Elliot regaled Devon with a brief summary of their more recent plans for GeekPeek. By lunch they'd signed off on what needed signing and sat around bullshitting for a while.

"Hey, Ash?"

He glanced up from the Rubik's cube he was again solving, using another configuration. They really needed to invent a more challenging waste of time. "Yeah?"

"What was that chick's name in high school you used to follow around like a lost puppy?"

Scarlet Farrow. "I don't know who you're talking about."

"Sure, you do. Red wavy hair, freckles, sort of quiet until you got to know her, cheerleader, cute. We used to call her something like Little Red Riding Hood."

Lettie Red Riding Hood—Lettie being short for Scarlet. Ash played dumb. "I don't remember anyone like that."

Hunter gave him a sidelong glance letting him know he was full of shit. Asher had been obsessed with Scarlet Farrow. She was the most beautiful creature he'd ever set eyes on, with her soft Dana Scully red hair, freckles like Kate Austin from *LOST,* and those crazy chameleonic eyes like Lena Headey that switched from aqua blue to emerald green.

Devon shrugged. "I could have sworn you had a thing for her."

"What brings her to mind?" Elliot asked, not giving away the fact they knew exactly who she was and *what* she was to Ash.

Many garage talks had revolved around Ash's pathetic fondness for the cheerleader who annihilated his heart and made the end of his senior year hell. High school always sucked for him. It took someone special to make it even worse.

The accountant leaned forward and snatched a folded newspaper off the coffee tray. "I think this is her."

Ash swallowed. Dear God, was it the obituaries? Ice filled his veins as he stared wide-eyed at the paper. Unable to draw in a full breath, he wheezed, "What is it?"

"Some opinion section for women to bitch about men."

Hunter snatched the paper out of Devon's hand and scanned it. A dimple formed in the dark shadow of his cheek. "Interesting. Ash, you may wanna read this. It does sound like her. It's even signed *L.R. Riding Hood*. She became a teacher, right?"

Elliot chimed in so Asher wouldn't have to answer. "Yeah. She works at the middle school. Took Mrs. Delanie's place, I think."

What was the article about? Trying not to appear overly anxious in front of Devon, he shot Hunter a look. His friend caught on immediately. "Mind if I keep this?" Hunter asked Devon.

"Be my guest."

Meeting finished, Ash was anxious to get back in the ambulance. As they piled into the Ecto-1, Jet was reading the article in the front seat. A slow, fascinated whistle slipped from his lips, petitioning for notice. "I don't remember this chick. She was a cheerleader? I wonder if I hooked up with her."

Enough. Ash leaned over the front seat and snatched the paper from him. "Give me that."

Hunter snickered. "If that's her, Ash, she's single."

No way. No way was a girl like Scarlet Farrow still single. He quickly read the article. It all added up, the description of her appearance, although his depiction would have been a lot more flattering, mentioning how her hips could make Jessica Rabbit jealous and her lashes were so long they sometimes looked as if they held little fiery stars on the tips. Those eyes...

When they pulled back in to the garage at the Think Tank, Asher was rereading the article for the fifth time. Was it her?

The guys stripped off their suits and hung their packs in the vault next to the Justice League costumes. Ash didn't bother. He went right to his private office and shut the door.

Flashing on his computer, he searched her name. Knowing it was unethical and not caring, he punched her name into GeekPeek's database—something he'd resisted the urge to do a million times before, out of self-preservation.

"Bingo." There she was. His heart gave a slight stutter at the sight of her profile picture, still the same beautiful girl, only now she was a woman. She lived in the same area where they'd grown up and Elliot was right, she taught sixth grade at their old middle school.

He scanned through her statuses, noting the usual, but found it odd she didn't seem the social butterfly he'd assumed she'd be. Taking a deep breath, he clicked on her photo albums and exhaled jaggedly.

She was more striking than she'd been in high school. Those eyes, those sharp green-blue eyes, so many fantasies had been entertained regarding those eyes—and her breasts of course. He swallowed and scrolled down.

Her information claimed she was single. There were no pictures boasting of engagement rings or babies. How was that possible?

There was a knock at his door and he minimized the screen. "Come in."

Jet stepped inside and plopped in the Dr. Claw chair across from his desk. "You looking her up?"

His instinct was to lie, but this was Jet. He was a friend. "Yeah."

"Think it's her?"

"Could be. I'm blown away she's single."

Jet tilted his head, his full black hair falling to the side. "Took me a while to place her, but now I remember. She's the one who stood you up for homecoming, right?"

Stood him up, ripped out his heart, humiliated him, and destroyed every hope of ever knowing her. "I guess you could say that."

Scarlet Farrow was always a little bit quiet, but light years out of his league. She'd been on the cheer squad, hung with all the popular kids, was invited to places his kind were never welcome.

Asher had started crushing on her in sixth grade when she returned from summer break with a fresh spattering of cocoa freckles and a crisp bronze tan to her usually lily white skin. That was also the year she developed boobs. He used to sit behind her and get hard from the soft scent of her hair, then spend the rest of the day praying he wasn't called to the board in front of the whole damn class.

As the years went on her loveliness bloomed. She never wore a lot of makeup and her body always appeared so soft under her *Chic* jeans and those worn-in sweaters.

She had her own sort of style. A lot of girls from his generation went with the grunge look, but not Scarlet. She always looked like she'd just returned from a sailing trip around the Cape, hair a wild tousled mess of copper waves and cheeks always a tinge rosy. Her natural beauty warranted a kind of Kennedy esteem, making her somehow untouchable, like American royalty.

The older she became, the longer her hair grew. Those strawberry blonde curls darkened to the most vibrant shade of red and by the end of freshman year, she'd been nicknamed Lettie Red Riding Hood. She could very well be the woman writing under L.R. Riding Hood.

He could imagine her as a teacher, probably driving the present middle school boys as crazy as she drove him. If what the article said was true, she was incredibly lonely. He knew what that was like. If not for the guys and their joint ventures, he'd have nothing.

"You should call her," Jet said.

Ash's lusty recollections slammed to a halt. "Are you out of your mind? She never had a clue who I was until homecoming, and the times I tried to talk to her were painful enough. No need to relive the disaster that was my pubescent years."

"You're different now, Ash. We all are. You own one of the most successful companies in the world, you're worth millions, and you aren't some pint-sized pipsqueak rocking a retainer and acne anymore. She might be interested."

Funny, all that was true, but deep down he was still the nerd he'd always been. Relationships with women only interested in his money and success held no appeal. It was a little too familiar to his teenage years when the popular kids were nice to him simply because he could do their homework and help them pass. He'd always wanted a woman to appreciate *him*. "I don't think so." Not to mention he hated her.

"Why? What are you afraid of?"

Jet wasn't an original to the gang. He'd discovered them in Ash's garage sometime during high school when Elliot promised to do his science homework for a hefty sum. They'd used Jet's money to help purchase a life-size Storm Trooper—not the smartest investment, but a necessary mascot for every dweeb lair. Jet had paid for at least two legs of that collector's item.

"Look, we love you, Jet. You're like a brother, but you don't know what it was like for us. We were the nerd herd. We never got invited to sit with the cool kids, and we had food thrown at us when we accidentally looked their way."

"And now you're paying those dickheads' salaries. Look at Devon. He couldn't survive if it wasn't for you, Hunter, and Elliot."

Jet wasn't gifted like the rest of them. His SATs scores had been an accumulation of getting his name right and leaving a good deal of the questions blank. But he had something the rest of them didn't. He had the face and charisma people were drawn to.

Over time, they'd stopped charging him for midterm papers and continued to do his homework in exchange for details about his dates with the girls who didn't know that Asher, Hunter, and Elliot existed. Twelve years later and he was still that charismatic guy women couldn't resist.

Ash sighed and flipped around some papers on his desk, knocking a few Lego men to the ground in the process. "You're going to have to make a press release next week about the changes being made to GeekPeek."

"Don't do that. Don't change the subject, Ash. You liked this girl. She's lonely as hell and begging for a nice, smart guy to rescue her from all the losers out there. That guy could be you. We aren't seventeen anymore."

"I'm aware we aren't kids, Jet. But look at me. I'm sitting behind a desk covered in Legos. Anakin's light saber is mounted on my wall and my ring tone screams *By the power of Greyskull!* I haven't changed. Girls like Scarlet Farrow are taught to laugh at guys like me. She laughed then. She'd laugh now. I can do without the kick to my pride." He didn't want to have to hide who he was with anyone.

His friend's expression turned sympathetic. "Man, she really messed you up."

His mind went back to the last time he looked kindly on her. She'd been wearing her Cougars cheer uniform, the short red skirt only reaching to her mid-thigh. It was Homecoming week and they'd been at the pep rally, which turned into the annual bonfire on the field.

Everyone had been scrutinizing the lineups and screaming for the athletes, but Asher's eyes had been glued to Scarlet. When the cheer squad launched her into some crazy flip and she landed wrong, he'd jumped to his feet.

Ash didn't hit his growth spurt until he was nineteen, so back then he was rocking a pathetic five foot one and a quarter. Frantically, he tried to stare over the taller spectators, waiting anxiously for any sign of Scarlet's red hair. The nurse and team medics were on the field immediately and she disappeared before the bystanders returned to their seats.

Slipping through the crowd, Asher had gone to find Scarlet. When he spotted her, she was sitting at a picnic table in the dark, icing her ankle.

"*How's your leg?*" *He winced as his voice cracked at the most inopportune moment.*

She glanced up, her green eyes shimmering through unshed tears. "Do I know you?"

"I'm... Asher. Asher Roan. I'm in your chem class and we've gone to school together for years."

Her brow tightened. "Oh, yeah. I remember. You used to sit behind me in Mrs. Delanie's class."

Yeah and they'd shared numerous teachers since then. It never got old; the pain of realizing the people that made up his world didn't even know he existed. "Right. Are you okay?"

"I sprained it. It hurts pretty bad, but my coach said it's not as bad as it could have been. They're trying to find crutches for me."

"Guess you won't be able to cheer for a while."

She shrugged. "Probably not."

Her hair was in a high ponytail, the waves reaching to her lower back. It was tied to with a thin red ribbon, and he wanted that ribbon more than everything on his next Christmas list.

"Hey, Red, that was a pretty nasty fall!"

Asher turned and shrunk a bit when Bobby Westerman loped from the field gate. Great. This was the guy that taped Elliot to a locker last week. Asher sidestepped into the shadows, praying the guy wouldn't start any trouble in front of Scarlet.

She grinned at the oversized linebacker. "Hey, Bobby."

The two started talking and Asher's presence was forgotten. Skulking away, he didn't return to the bonfire, seeing no reason to be there now that Scarlet wasn't cheering.

After finding his mom's station wagon parked amongst the muscle cars belonging to the jocks, the paneled vehicle as unambiguous as a milkmaid on a battlefield of knights and dragons, he drove home.

Several days later, Asher had been minding his own business at school, searching in his locker for something, *when he was shoved face first into the metal door. His stomach pinched at the inevitable shaming that would follow.*

Bobby Westerman gripped him by the scruff of his neck and painfully twisted his arm behind his back. Certain he was going to wind up crammed inside his locker until he peed his pants or puked from discomfort, Asher was shocked when Scarlet's voice snapped, "Bobby!"

Averting his eyes, unable to face her in such a mortifying situation, Asher's body crumpled like an abused sack of bones as Westerman snuck in a final shot. Forcing back the urge to puke from the direct blow to his kidney, he shut his eyes.

Her silence spoke volumes and when he got the nerve to peek at her, such scorn burned in her eyes it halted Bobby from beating him to a pulp. Perfect. She was coming to his rescue. His shame was complete.

Without saying another word, she stalked away with her chin high and posture severe, despite her crutches.

Bobby cursed and kicked him. "Got off easy that time, dick." The bully loped off after Scarlet, and Hunter and Elliot came out of hiding to help him up.

The following week the inconceivable happened. He'd been returning to chemistry class from the lavatory when he spotted a folded up note on his textbook. Glancing around suspiciously, he opened it.

*D*ear Asher,
     I can't lie. I've been watching you and I think you're really cute. Do you have a date for the homecoming dance? I've been hoping you'd ask, but... you haven't.
     Hugs,

Scarlet

is face burned as he shoved the paper in the pocket of his constricting corduroys. Scarlet wasn't looking at him. When the bell rang, he held his books over his crotch and bolted out of class. That afternoon he'd told Elliot and Hunter about the note, but they were equally skeptical.

Asher spent the night staring at the Wonder Woman poster above his bunk bed and fantasizing about Scarlet, her pretty eyes and long fiery hair. The following morning he picked some flowers from his mom's garden and left them at her locker only a short distance from his.

He skulked around, fumbling with books until she arrived. Watching through the slits of the opened metal door of his locker, he sucked in a deep breath and held it as she picked up the blooms and looked around. A stunning smile took over her face. In the days that followed he'd made her a mix tape, wrote her several poems, and slowly built up the guts to ask her to the dance.

She was so pretty it sometimes hurt to look at her. A few days before the dance, a game was scheduled. Scarlet was cheering again, but not going at it as hard as she usually did on account of her ankle. Asher waited for her by the bleachers until the crowd thinned.

He made his move. "Hi, Scarlet—"

"Yo, Lettie! Come on, we're all heading over to Nina's. Her brother got a keg."

Scarlet's attention was stolen along with her presence as the rest of the cheer team followed the jocks to the parking lot. Asher's shoulders hunched as his opportunity vanished.

The following morning there was a note wedged in his locker. His fingers trembled as he unfolded it.

*H*ey cutie,
     I'm still looking forward to dancing with you this Friday. What do you say you meet me at my house a half hour before the dance?
     Hugs and Kisses,
     Lettie

*S*till not fully trusting the note in his hand, he waited until chemistry class to confront her, but his nerves got the best of him. He decided to write her a note back.

*D*ear Scarlet,
     I would like nothing more than to take you to the dance. Let me know your address and what your favorite flower is and I'll be there. Really looking forward to that dance.
     Love,
     Asher

*O*nce he had the note folded, he volunteered to solve the problem on the board. As he walked down the aisle, Scarlet was digging in her bag on the floor. He dropped the note on her desk, heart racing, and met the teacher in the front of the class. When the bell rang, she was gone, but at the end of the day her reply was in his locker.

. . .

S weet Asher,
      My favorite flowers are lilies.
   Kisses,
   Lettie

er address was scribbled at the bottom.

That evening he'd shocked his parents by announcing he would be going to a dance. His dad dusted off his old suit and his mom ordered the nicest lily corsage she could find on short notice. It took a lot to convince them not to embarrass him by taking pictures, but eventually they conceded.

On Friday he took a cold shower and applied extra deodorant. Holding the plastic case with Scarlet's lily, he drove his mom's station wagon to her house. Parking just before her property, hiding the wood paneled eyesore behind some tall hedges, he took a deep breath and stepped around the corner—coming up short at the sight of half the football team taking pictures with the cheer squad on her lawn.

These were his adversaries, but her friends. He'd do anything for her, so he drew back his shoulders and stepped forward.

Bobby Westerman's arm possessively wrapped around Scarlet's freckled shoulders as he pressed his face into her neck. She was exquisite. Her dress was purple and puffy and—why wasn't she pushing Bobby off?

Asher took another step forward and a roar of laughter came from the guys. The girls turned and Scarlet's head tipped curiously. Her ruby curls were pinned high on her head like a princess. His shaky hand extended as he held out the box with her lily, trying not to let the others detect how intimidating he found their presence.

"You got company, Red," Bobby said, giving her a nudge forward.

Scarlet glared at Bobby then stared at Asher as though it took her a minute to place him. "Asher Roan? What are you doing here?"

His blood went cold, every fear hurdling through his nervous system. "I...I'm here to take you to homecoming."

The girls' chortles joined the uproarious laughter pouring from the jocks.

Scarlet's face turned deep crimson. "What?"

He lowered the hand holding the corsage. His voice, barely a whisper, explained, "The... flowers, the poems, the letters..." His words fell away as he painfully accepted the guys were right and it was all one big prank.

His pride stung as the laughter continued. A nervous giggle came from Scarlet and Bobby roared, "Why don't you come give Lettie a kiss, Roan? Or do you only kiss little boys?"

After years of being persecuted when he'd never been anything but nice, he'd had enough. He'd had his face shoved uncountable times into his lunch, been forced into trashcans, lockers, the girls' bathroom. But this—this— was an all time low.

Mortification swelled, morphing into a dark seething hate, and he snapped. Screeching like a locomotive, he dropped the lily and charged. When he plowed into Bobby's broad chest it was like barreling head first into a brick wall. Asher's ass landed on the lawn with a thud and Bobby was cocking back to hit him. Asher winced and turned his face—

"Hey!" Scarlet yelled.

He squinted his eyes as an enormous shadow fell over

him. Bobby scowled down at him, his thick neck flushing red. Scarlet reached for Asher and he took her hand, a thousand volts of energy sparking through his arm. Her skin was so soft.

Clambering to his knees, it suddenly occurred to him that this was his chance. Shifting, he pulled her hand forward, placing a kiss on the back of her fingers like a true knight.

The girls laughed and she snatched her hand away, her face flushing a deeper shade of ruby and transforming her soft features into a scowl. "What are you doing?"

He rose to his feet and retrieved the corsage from the grass. Opening the plastic package he held it out to her. "I may not be good at sports or know how to dance very well, but I promise I'll be a better date than any one of these jerks."

"Watch it, dickweed, or I'll make that suit even uglier when it's covered in your blood."

"Shut up, Bobby," she snapped and turned to Asher. "Um, that's really cute, but I already have a date."

Cute? He winced. "But...they're all jerks."

Her brow pinched defensively. "They're my friends."

He shook his head. Didn't she see? Those guys walked around like a bunch of Neanderthals. They didn't respect her.

Asher didn't have a lot of experience with girls, but he wasn't stupid. Looking up at her, he whispered, "He's using you."

Apparently that was the wrong thing to say. She blinked, her eyes flashing with resentment. Her flushed breasts rose in time with her labored breathing, pressing tight against the plum fabric of her dress. "I don't know who you think you are, but I want you to leave."

He hadn't meant to insult her, only to protect her from

these animals. "You deserve someone that respects you, Scarlet. He doesn't respect you—"

"Get out of here! You think you have the right to come to my house and embarrass me? You? Some little nerd wearing wingtips that reek of mothballs, who barely reaches my shoulders!"

"And in that suit!" one of the girls chimed in.

Asher's throat burned as he stood there wishing the earth would open up and swallow him whole. "I didn't mean to insult you. I'm trying to protect you."

"Well, then I guess all geeks aren't as smart as I thought. I don't need your protection. Leave me alone and go away, you little stalker!"

His heart cracked. This wasn't how it was supposed to be. He wished he were like Jet, fearless when it came to girls. Scarlet was just like everyone else, incapable of seeing past his appearance or giving him a chance to prove himself. Bobby Westerman was an asshole and she could do way better than that, but maybe that was exactly what she deserved.

Breathing hard, he stared at the group of well-dressed seniors laughing at his expense, mocking him, calling him freak show and loser. He was so tired of being the butt of every popular kid's joke. They were no better than he was.

Rage boiled inside of him as he tried to find some shred of dignity. They'd made a fool of him in front of her.

He met her cold gaze and, in his sternest voice, promised, "One day you'll know exactly who I am and see that I'm better than everyone here. Even you."

Chin trembling, she shrieked. "Get away from me, you loser!"

The blood rushed from his face as his heart pounded erratically in his chest. The look of repugnance in her eyes would haunt him forever.

"You better run, asswipe," Bobby said, stripping off his jacket.

Stepping back, Asher did a quick search of the scowling faces glaring at him and decided that was wise advice. He ran. Fingers trembling, he ripped open the dented door of the station wagon and dove onto the well-worn bench seat, slamming down the lock.

Jamming the key in the ignition, he cranked the gearshift and backed away from the curb. Throwing it into drive, the old wagon backfired and jerked forward, drowning out the others' laughter.

When he reached his house he didn't pull in the driveway. His parents thought he was at the dance and he couldn't face more humiliation that would come with confessing it was all a joke at his expense. No parent deserved to witness his or her misfit kid's shame. It would only crush him more to see them scramble to his aide, their attempts to soothe his pride intensifying his sense of inadequacy.

Jet was at the dance waiting for him and Scarlet to show. He'd promised to save them a seat. They'd all eventually know what happened. Driving aimlessly through the neighborhood, he found himself parking outside of Elliot's.

When he rang the bell Mrs. Garnet opened the door and let him in. He found Hunter and Elliot playing Nintendo on the floor of his friend's room. The moment they saw him they knew, but there was nothing anyone could do to ease his pain and humiliation.

The remainder of his senior year passed much the same as his earlier education, but now with a sting of regret and additional humiliation as word spread. Every day, he'd gone to school with one motivation. Her. He'd fabricated some twisted fantasy in his mind over the years and now he actually called himself stupid.

Scarlet Farrow wasn't the sweet girl he'd assumed. She

was a viper, no better than the rest of the jocks and popular kids. From that day on, she knew who he was.

She no longer interfered when Bobby or the other bullies shoved him around. Rather, she stood idly by as the bullies taunted him. Sometimes she even laughed. He didn't know which was worse, the few times he depended on her rescue, or the times she'd witnessed his shame and never spoke up in his defense. By graduation, his tender affection for her had transformed into raw hatred.

Asher looked around his office, trying to take stock in the success he'd accumulated. It had taken years for him to get over that night. Whoever Scarlet was, she was nothing like the girl he'd imagined, a fabricated fantasy of softness surrounding a gentle heart.

There was no sweetness to her. He wasn't buying her sob story in the paper. She was just another one of those beautiful people in the world used to always getting what they wanted and complaining when things didn't go their way.

That's what that letter in the paper was all about; some spoiled girl who'd missed the mark and somehow wound up single and couldn't accept she might belong alone. The utter nerve and self-importance it must take, to make those complaints and publish them as though the rest of the world needed to know what an injustice it was that Scarlet Farrow felt unloved. It went beyond pretentious.

The size of the ego she must have to think the world cared. Jet was right, he probably could get her, but what was the point when deep down she'd always be the girl who humiliated him and found his presence repulsive? Beneath all the money and success, he'd always be a geek to her.

He finally responded to Jet. "Yeah. I can't do that. Not for her. It's taken a long time, but I've actually proven I'm better than her and her opinions are meaningless. There's no point in proving myself to someone who can't see beneath the surface."

Sighing, Jet stood. "Okay, man. But if you ever want to go out, maybe try to meet a nice girl who likes you for you, let me know. I'll go with you. We could double."

The entire idea made him nauseous and too aware of all his resonating insecurities. "Thanks, Jet."

He'd spent a few more hours nosing through Scarlet's GeekPeek profile and then shut it down for good. Nothing positive could come from this reignited infatuation. Her actions of the past still stung and while he wanted to hate her, it was a waste of time. She was mean, and if she was lonely, that was probably what she deserved.

End of story.

---

*B*ut he couldn't leave it alone. Obsessing over Scarlet Farrow was an all too familiar pastime his mind welcomed, no matter how much his common sense warned him not to think about her.

The next morning Asher entered the Think Tank and dropped a grocery bag full of crap on the coffee table modeled after the original Pac Man grid. Everyone stopped and turned. Elliot was the first to approach the pile and pick up a frayed copy of some romance novel.

"What *is* all this?"

"This," Asher explained, "Is every girlie thing I could find in my sister's old room."

"Why'd you bring it here?" Jet asked, picking up a purple bra with his pinky through the strap and raising an eyebrow.

"Because I want to know how women think. This is the stuff they think about."

Hunter frowned, his dark fingers pulling open a little pink compact. "What is this?"

Asher leaned over. "Not sure, but it was in her vanity."

"Diaphragm," Jet announced.

Hunter dropped the compact and gagged. "Ew, man! Don't bring this stuff in here!"

Elliot sorted through the pile. "Magazines, makeup, underwear... Ash, are you trying to tell us something?"

"I've made a decision—"

"To become a woman?" Jet asked.

"No. I've decided I'm going to *get* a woman."

They stared back at him, all wearing expressions of surprise. Like everyone else, they were aware Asher hoped for a partner in life, but as time went on he'd come to terms with being single and never made any attempt to meet women. One-night stands were a paltry excuse for love and when he did connect with women, they always seemed to love his money a bit more than the man behind it.

Jet nodded and smirked ruefully. "That's what I'm talking about! You're going after lonely Red Riding Hood, aren't you?"

"Scarlet?" Elliot asked, skepticism in his voice.

"Ash, what if she remembers you? You're gonna get hurt. I think that's a bad idea."

Drawing in a deep breath, he leveled with them. "I was up all night thinking about this. At first, I was just going to write the whole thing off, but the longer I thought about it the more it got under my skin. There's a reason that article was brought to my attention. If not for Devon, I never would have glanced twice at the women's opinion column. Women never cared about me until I had money, so why should I care about them? I'm convinced Scarlet wrote the article and I plan to find out for sure. Once I confirm it's her, I'm going to make her want me more than she's ever wanted anyone."

"Why?" Elliot asked.

Asher shrugged, still unsure when exactly his motive became a returned obsession, and not yet willing to voice it.

Hunter gave a sympathetic expression. "Man, you're putting a lot of eggs in one basket. Why don't you try meeting someone new at a bar or something?"

"Because the only bar we ever go to is the one at ComiCon. Besides, I don't know the first thing about talking to girls."

"Then how are you going to talk to Scarlet?" Elliot asked. "You'll end up getting hurt again."

"This time will be different. I know what kind of person she is. I'm not some stupid kid anymore who lets his hormones control his brain." Especially not after sitting up all night replaying memories from his banished childhood, recalling all the instances he'd been trustingly made the gullible fool. It would all be worth it if he could somehow manage to erase any memories she might still have of the bumbling nerd he was. "It'll be an adventure."

Hunter shook his head. *"Adventure. Excitement. A Jedi craves not these things."*

Elliot laughed, giving Hunter a high five. "Nice Empire ref." Turning back to Asher, he asked, "And what if she's just not interested? Don't let bitterness pull you to the Dark Side."

Hunter chuckled, and in a high-pitched voice cried, *"Anakin, you're breaking my heart."*

"Will you two knock it off? We can all work together. We're some of the sharpest minds on the grid. Jet's slept with plenty of women. Hunter's had a couple girlfriends and Elliot, you're not a virgin anymore. I read this book this morning and the main character was a complete jerk to the leading female."

Asher snatched the book out of Jet's hands. "Listen to this. *'He pressed her to her knees and told her to open wide. Fear chased up her spine, her eyes measuring his strength, but part of her desired his rough touch more than her next breath. She'd give him anything, so long as he never stopped being the authority she'd come to need.'"*

"Holy shit! Let me see that!" Hunter grabbed the book and started thumbing through the worn pages.

"This is what girls want. They want the asshole, not the nice guy. They want the Bobby Westermans of the world."

"That's not what her article said," Elliot pointed out.

Asher had practically memorized the entire column. "She didn't ask for a nice guy, she asked for a responsible, independent man. I'm all of that. I just need to work out the sexy part."

"Your mom still buys your underwear!"

"No, she doesn't. Only on holidays because she knows what kind I like."

Jet shook his head. "First step is cutting the cord, Ash. No woman likes a momma's boy."

"I know that. I'm going to have to completely redefine myself if I want this to work. I'm an inventor. I can do this."

"One bag of crap from your sister's bedroom isn't going to tell you what women want," Elliot said. "And wait until she finds out you stole all her stuff."

"It's a start," Asher argued. "Take the guy in the book, for instance. He didn't buy her flowers or write her poems or any of that nonsense we think girls like. He was stern and confident and she fell for him. Hard. I need to learn how to be what women want and, like Scarlet's letter said, they want *real* men." They all stared at him. "What?"

"Uh..." Elliot pointed at the guy on the cover of *Cosmo*. "This is a real man, Ash. None of us look like that except for Jet, but even he isn't *that* good looking."

"So?" He dug through the pile and pulled out a DVD. "See this? It's that exercise video that's always on infomercials. It says in thirty days you can go from this to this." He showed them the back picture of a man with a sagging belly turned six-pack. "To this."

"You have to use your inhaler when we run through the airport!"

"That's only during the spring. I can do this! I know I can." He'd bid farewell to scrawny long ago. His body wasn't anything spectacular, but he was fit in an unremarkable way. With the right motivation he could toughen up and tone.

"I have faith in you," Jet said.

"Thanks." He brushed his palms down his vintage

E.T. silkscreen sweatshirt. "Here's my plan. I'm going to read up on all things female and then I'm going to contact her."

"How you gonna do that?" Hunter asked.

"She has an account on GeekPeek. I'll open up a ghost account and private message her. Once I confirm it's her, I'll work my magic."

"You don't have magic."

"I'll find some. I'll be the modern day Wart, heir to Uther Pendragon's throne and shock the hell out of everyone."

Jet's brow furrowed. "Who?"

"The scrawny kid from *The Sword in the Stone*. He became King Arthur," Elliot supplied.

"What if she asks your name?" Hunter wondered, still paging through the romance novel.

"I'll make one up. Something cool. Something that screams sexual prowess."

"What about that French guy all the women used to be up in arms over. My mom was obsessed with him," Elliot said.

"I'll be better than him, because I'll be real. I need a name that's solid, strong, and alludes to power."

"Fabio?"

"Gray?"

"No and no. Something original. I've never taken interest in reinventing the wheel. Like everything else I create, it'll be innovative, and better than all the rest. I'm going to be the man of *her* fantasies."

"I don't know," Elliot muttered, skepticism clear on his face.

"Stick with the sword in the stone thing," Jet said. "Girls dig a guy with a big dagger."

"Real mature." Elliot rolled his eyes.

Jet shoved him. "Oh, lighten up, Elliot. Maybe if you got your blade wet once in a while you'd re-member how to laugh."

Asher chuckled, but Elliot's expression remained unimpressed. "I'm merely suggesting a name with a bit more class. There's no dignity in a name like Mr. Sword." Glancing to Asher, he tapped his chin. "I dub thee, Mr. Stone."

Hunter looked up from the novel. "Mr. Stone's a pretty cool name."

Ash grinned, liking the sound of that. "I have the means to totally redefine myself into everything everyone said I could never be. I'll find a good nutri-tionist and get a personal trainer. It'll be great. We could all benefit from this."

"Sounds like a lot of work," Elliot mumbled, his sole contribution complete. "I like my style."

"You have no style, Elliot. You've been wearing ties since you were seven. It's time to let the Alex P. Keaton thing go. I mean, why should Jet be the only face be-hind everything we've created? We're major entrepre-neurs. It's about time we started looking and acting the part. No more making fools of ourselves."

"Who you calling a fool?" Hunter snapped. "I'm a bad motherfucker."

Jet shook his head. "Man, don't try to talk like Samuel L. You can't pull it off."

"Sorry."

Elliot removed his glasses and rubbed his face. "I don't like this idea. I like who we are. Who cares what the rest of the world thinks? How many other people can say they have an exact replica of KITT from *Knight Rider* sitting in their garage, complete with a func-tioning artificially intelligent electronic computer module that's more effective than Siri? *That's* cool, Asher. All this other crap...it's not us."

"What we have is a 1982 Pontiac Trans Am that's only a turn-on to nerds like us. Girls aren't into that stuff."

Elliot stood. "Whatever. I'm not changing. And I'm keeping my ties."

Ash looked at Hunter and Jet. "How about you guys?"

"I'm down," Jet said.

Hunter voice was unenthusiastic. "I'll feel it out, but only if you remember that all this was created by being exactly who we are. I'm not gonna regret that, Ash. We're thirty years old. Who cares if we're nerds? If this is something you need to do, fine, but don't do it for some girl who thinks you're not good enough just the way you are."

The following day Asher's house was flooded with boxes of items he'd ordered from the Internet. He had everything expedited and was quickly realizing he might not have thought his plan through.

That morning he'd tried to do the exercise DVD and had nearly broken his ankle. Dexterity and rhythm were immediately added to the list of goals. He decided he was more of a people person after all and took a trip to the local gym, a place he'd never visited in his life.

It was like walking into high school all over again, but if he was going to do this, the excuses stopped now. Every person there had a body bigger and harder than his. He nearly made it back to the exit when some large monstrosity of a man approached and asked if he needed help.

Swallowing back his trepidation, he said, "I'd like to speak to your best trainer."

The man studied him, from his Clark Kent glasses to his Chucks, and nodded. "Right this way."

The trainer he met, Steve, turned out to be a pretty nice guy. Asher didn't go into much detail, but slipped him a business card with his home address scribbled on the back and asked him to meet him at seven later that night. There was no way Ash was returning to that gym. He'd create his own.

He'd spent the day reading romance novels. It was amazing how different women's fiction was from the sci-fi novels he'd grown up on. More than a few times the words made him blush—and other things. Did girls really like hearing words like that? It was a complete contradiction to everything he'd always assumed. It was also the most erotic experience of his life.

Romance novels described some crazy situations. The bestsellers had girls getting their hair pulled, butts spanked, necks bit, and hands bound. It seemed every taboo was on women's most wanted list. The more he read, the more he found his body reacting to the source material.

Princess Leia was always one of his favorite images when it came to masturbation, but this stuff blew those schoolboy fantasies out of the water. Once he imagined wielding that sort of authority over Scarlet, he was done. His inner caveman was born and banging on the walls to give this sort of kink a try.

The problem was, he wasn't exactly sure how to execute his plan. He wanted to contact her soon, but if she saw him now he'd likely fail. He needed to go about this in a surreptitious manner. One novel he'd read, *Master of Mystique,* spoke to him more than any other.

The main character was a scarred warrior that captured the heart of a blind female. If Scarlet couldn't *see* him, it would be a lot easier to seduce her mind—not to mention he'd have a bit of a defense against those enchanting eyes of hers.

The one thing he'd learned from reading so many romances in one sitting was that women could be patient—or conditioned to be patient, like in those kinky BDSM books. He idly thought about his sister's reading material, curling his lip at the distasteful image and forcing it away as his plan took shape.

Later that night, the bell rang. Steve, the trainer from the gym, stood outside his door. "Mr. Roan."

"Call me Ash. Come in."

The giant followed him to the den. He wasn't much taller than Asher, but outweighed him by at least a hundred pounds of lean muscle. Once they settled in, he looked the man in the eye and said, "I'd like to offer you a job."

"I have a job."

"How much do you make? I'll double it and pay for any benefits you need."

Steve frowned. "What sort of job?"

"I want you to change me. I want a body women will notice, a body I can be proud of. I'm doing a little experiment and I'll be hiring a team of people to help me in my transformation. I'm prepared to offer you a place to stay in exchange for your training over the next while."

"How long?"

Asher wasn't sure. "How long would it take to make me look more like you?"

Steve's brows shot up. "I've been athletic all my life. I think you'd see a change in a matter of weeks with the right regimen and diet, but for big changes... maybe three months."

He nodded. "Three months then."

"And what happens after that? I can't just leave my job at the gym—"

"Steve, look at me. If you had to make one assumption about the man I am, it would probably be that I'm intelligent. I know we just met, but I assure you this is an offer you won't want to turn down. Are you familiar with GeekPeek?"

"Yeah. Who isn't?"

"My friends and I invented it."

The man's eyes bulged. "Holy shit."

"Exactly. I'll double your annual salary for a quarter of the time. I'd want you available, so I'd ask for you to stay in the guesthouse. You'd have use of the pool and the rest of the grounds in exchange for your service. Aside from work, I don't have much of a social life, so I'd like to work out as much as possible. My three partners at GeekPeek also might take advantage of your services while they're available. I'll be hiring a nutritionist and personal chef, so your meals would be taken care of. As long as we had an early work out on the weekends, you'd have the majority of your Saturdays and Sundays off. If you can actually pull this off and make me take pride in the reflection I see in the mirror, we can discuss further investments down the line. Perhaps you'd want to own your own gym someday?"

"I don't understand. Why me?"

"Because you were the first person I found, and I don't have a lot of time. You also haven't acted like anything I've asked is impossible or laughable."

"It's all possible. You just gotta want it."

Asher nodded. "I want this. Do we have a deal?"

Steve grinned, showing the slight gap in his front teeth. "When do I start?"

"Now. I'll grab you a spare laptop and you can use the library. I want you to design the perfect personal gym. I want to get started tomorrow morning bright and early. I'll set up an expense account and you can order all the equipment you need. Have it expedited. I'm not worried about shipping costs.

"Tonight I'll show you the basement where everything will go so you have an idea of the size room you're dealing with. Everything should be here by the weekend and we can really get started on our training. Tomorrow you can move your stuff into the guesthouse. I'll have a key made up for you. I'd also like you to sit in on the interviews for the nutritionist. There's a woman named Carla coming for an interview tomorrow at noon."

"This is insane."

It was, but it felt right. Asher was riding a tide of adrenaline and his confidence was flowing. "I'll go grab you that laptop."

"Mr. Roan?"

Asher turned. Steve was likely twenty-five, so he'd have to remind him to call him Asher. "Yeah."

"Thank you."

Asher grinned eagerly. "If you can do this, I'll be the one thanking you."

3

STIMULATION

SCARLET PLOPPED on the couch with Thor and scooped up the remote. "What sort of excitement lays ahead for us tonight, sweet love of my life?" she asked her cat as she thumbed through the channels.

"Ooh, a Harry Potter marathon." Tossing the remote aside, she got comfy and glanced at Thor as he curled into the cushion. "Is it totally pathetic that my Friday night excitement includes young adult movies and my cat? No, don't be offended. You're the nicest guy I know."

Thor's eyes shut in contentment as he curled into her hip. Scarlet reached for her laptop and checked her email. Nada. "Let's see what all the cool people are up to."

Signing into her GeekPeek account, she pursed her lips as she scrolled through the feed. Someone got engaged, so-and-so sold their house, there was a new picture of an ultrasound, blah, blah, blah, blah.

When she saw the post of a newborn from a college friend her vision blurred. *Will I ever hold my own?*

Her knee jerk indifference faded to the honest envy it was and she wrote a heartfelt congratulations below her friend's post. She then jumped over to Amazon and ordered a gift from her friend's wish list for the little one.

"There," she said, checking out. "They should get that in a couple days."

Hopping back on GeekPeek, she "liked" and commented on what she should and was about to log off when a notification caught her eye.

She had a friend request. Clicking on the notification, she frowned. "Mr. Stone?" The profile picture was just a large boulder bathed in a ray of dusty light with a relic sword impaled in the rock. "Do I know you?"

It was probably some spammer. Her notifications chimed again. She had a private message. Her brow lowered when she saw the sender was the mysterious Mr. Stone.

> Good evening, Ms. Farrow. Care to chat? ~Mr. Stone

*R*ather than answer right away, she went back to his profile. There wasn't much, being that his privacy settings were pretty tight and she hadn't accepted his friend request yet. Who was this guy? This was GeekPeek, not a dating site. It seemed odd to chat with a perfect stranger.

Clicking on her messages, she typed.

. . .

> Do I know you?

*H*is message popped up only a few seconds later.

> That's your decision. Would you like to know me? I find myself very curious about you.

"*E*w. Stranger danger," she mumbled and rolled her eyes. The guy didn't even have a real picture. He could be a five hundred pound predator camped out in a shed wearing stained boxers, with Cheetos crumbs sprinkled in his hairy chest.

> No thanks. I don't talk to strangers. Have a nice night.

*H*is response again was immediate.

> Pity. I was hoping to have a
> discussion with you, L.R. Riding
> Hood. My apologies. Enjoy your
> evening.

She froze, lips parted, as her gaze drilled into the name he'd used. L.R. Riding Hood. "What the hell?"

Frowning, and breathing a little rapidly, she returned to his profile. Was this a joke? Whoever this was, they'd obviously read her stupid letter in the paper and pegged her as the author. How, though? She decided to play dumb.

> I'm afraid you have the wrong
> person. I don't know L.R. Riding
> Hood.

Her messages chimed.

Tsk, Ms. Farrow. I assumed a woman brazen enough to ask for exactly what she wants would have the courage to be honest. I'm not interested in games. Enjoy your evening.

*S*he scowled. Who the hell was this? It was creepy, not knowing who he was, but at the same time, his response provoked her to reply, prove she wasn't L.R. Riding Hood—which was bullshit—but he couldn't possibly know it was her. More importantly—

Who are you?

*S*he waited.

You may call me Mr. Stone.

What's your first name?

I'm afraid not, Ms. Farrow. Mr. Stone is all you get. Now, shall we be honest, since we're sharing names, L.R. Riding Hood?

Her heartbeat quickened. She was safe in her home under Thor's protection. Her privacy settings were solid, not giving away her address or too much personal drama. What harm was there in entertaining herself for a few minutes with a stranger? There really was no difference between this and talking to a man she never met on a dating site. Besides, she really wanted to find out who'd figured out she was L.R. Riding Hood and how.

Fine. How did you find me, Mr. Stone?

His reply reeked of arrogance.

It wasn't difficult. I'm quite adept at getting what I want in life. Your letter intrigued me. Care to discuss it?

*H*er eyes shot to his picture.

> How come you don't have a real
> picture up?

> You should never end a sentence
> with a preposition, Ms. Farrow. Why
> are you avoiding my question? I
> expect an answer.

*S*he slouched in her seat. Was he a teacher, correcting her grammar like that? *Oh, my God, does he work with me?* Crap. The idea of someone from work discovering her letter was troubling in more ways than one.

Everything suddenly became too real as she stared at the screen, unable to move or think what to do. After several minutes the messages chimed again.

> Have your fears gotten the better of
> you, Ms. Farrow? Pity. I was starting
> to enjoy myself, hoping we could
> have a stimulating discussion about
> all those delicious needs of yours
> and how I might satisfy them.

. . .

*H*er breath sucked in and she slammed her laptop shut. Her skin prickled with awareness as she fought the urge to close the curtains. It was a joke. Someone was teasing her. Probably a friend that read her article. They'd have to know her well in order to suspect she was the author of such a letter. Someone was screwing with her.

Slowly, she grinned. "Nicole." She chuckled. "You think you're so sly."

Taking a deep breath, she hunkered down and decided to have some fun of her own. The screen refreshed as she signed back onto her page. Pretty impressive for Nicole, making up a fake account and messing with her like this. She almost got her too. A muffled chuckle slipped past her lips as she wrote back.

Oh, Mr. Stone, I'd love to discuss you satisfying my needs. How delicious. Tell me more.

You're not scared?

Oh, no. As a matter of fact, I'm intrigued and eager. Please... stimulate me.

Very well. I'll give you a word and you tell me the first word that comes to mind. Agreed?

You bet.

I'm being quite serious, Ms. Farrow. While the satirical tone of your responses may be cute to some, I have no interest in juvenile defenses. If Ms. Farrow—the woman—would like to step forward, I shall continue.

She snorted, amused and a bit shocked at the response. Her friend had her thesaurus handy. Talk about being chastised. This guy—or Nicole, to be more realistic—was really playing the part. She toned down her mocking attitude, wanting to see where this was going before she called her friend out on her prank.

You're right. I'm sorry. I'm ready now.

Good girl. We'll start with the word, benevolent.

Kind.

Good, Ms. Farrow. Next word. Own.

Car.

Car?

Yes, car. You said the first thing that pops into my head. Most people own a car.

I want you to think about the actual word, not the possessions linked to it. Apply the word to yourself. How does it make you feel?

*S*he chewed her lip. Was this a test? Breathing out an amused puff of laughter, she decided to play the game.

Sexy.

Interesting. Why sexy? Is it that you want to own someone, a part of their soul, or perhaps it's you who would like to be owned, that irrevocable sense of belonging to one person, treasured, cherished? Exactly what makes the word sexy?

. . .

*I*t was an interesting query. She wasn't sure. Forgetting this was possibly her friend messing with her, she gave the question considerable thought and wrote her honest answer.

> He'd have to be quite incredible to accomplish that, knowing how to reach my mind, treat my body, and touch my soul. Any man able to get to that level with me, could definitely have me—own me.

*T*he second she hit send, reality crashed over her and she cursed. Nicole was probably rolling on the floor laughing at that ridiculous answer. Unintentionally wrapped up in the game, she'd betrayed her personal secrets. Her eyes searched for any possible way to revoke the sent message, knowing there wasn't one. As her humiliation spiked, the computer chimed.

> You expressed that beautifully, Ms. Farrow. Indeed, he should be quite a capable male to earn such a gift. The surrender of an intelligent woman is priceless.

. . .

Okay, Nicole didn't talk like that. Something wasn't adding up here. His next message distracted her worry.

Next word, Ms. Farrow. Claimed.

Hot.

The idea of being claimed makes you hot, Ms. Farrow?

Her body heated, nerves coming to life. This *conversation* was starting to make her hot, which was a really bad thing if this was Nicole. Her face tightened as she did what she had to do.

Nicole?

I beg your pardon?

Tell me who you are.

Enough messing around. He'd gotten her attention—whoever he was—and now she was intrigued. If he didn't give her some information she was out.

> I am a man with no connection to your personal life. However, that could change once we've finished our discussion. I find you quite intriguing. You asked where all the real men are. I assure you, I'm real. I'm also very private. I intend to respect your privacy, as this has only to do with the two of us, and I expect you to respect mine. Should that be something you cannot do, we shall say goodbye now.

Her mind rapidly tossed out possibilities of who this man could be. No one came to mind. It could be *anyone*. It didn't even have to be a man.

No longer thinking it was Nicole, she struggled to come up with an answer. The men at work wouldn't do this. Maybe it was someone from her past. But this guy seemed intelligent in a way the men she dated never were. She pushed for more information.

> Are you saying you'd like to go out?

> That depends on you, Ms. Farrow.
> I'd like to learn a bit more about the
> woman who wrote that letter. Should
> your answers please me, we can
> make further arrangements. I'm very
> precise in my comforts and tend to
> be quite demanding. You may not be
> able to help me. But I'm certain I can
> help you.

*H*er body shivered with excitement laced with fear. This could be a serial killer. He knew her name. What the hell was she thinking talking to this guy? *You're thinking he might be the answer to your prayers.* She needed to get real. Someone was yanking her chain. Maybe he worked for the column and hacked her email to get her name.

You're messing with me.

How so?

I don't believe your name's Mr. Stone.

You are correct. Anonymity is important to me. While I can help you, I have stipulations, should we reach that point. For all intents and purposes, you will know me as Mr. Stone. My name carries no influence in the end result.

Help me how?

Why, Ms. Farrow, I thought I made that clear. I'm the man you seek. Should you please me, I'm prepared to show you exactly what you're after.

Which is?

Absolute adoration.

She stilled. The joke was no longer funny. Her breath came out in a shaky exhale as she carefully catalogued what was happening. A stranger—without a face—approached her online after reading her article and now was possibly offering her everything she wanted. Impossible—and scary.

You're being very quiet, Ms. Farrow. Tell me what you're thinking.

I'm thinking there are a lot of crazy people in this world.

Ah. And you're wondering if I'm one of them. Well, while I insist on a certain level of mystique to protect myself, I can offer you this, whether you trust my words is your decision. I am a responsible American citizen, residing close enough to have received your article in the paper's circulation. I own my own company and do well enough for myself. I'm very private in my personal life, due to the fact I don't easily trust people's motives. The last time a woman captured my interest she fell short of my expectations. My desires are quite defined and I'm patient, believing there must be a cerebral connection before a physical relationship can develop. I have never, nor would I ever, physically harm a living thing. I believe most women are gentle creatures and the praiseworthy ones deserve to be cherished.

*S*hallow breaths filled her lungs. The light, teasing mood of the conversation had completely evaporated. In its place was curious caution. He could've just made that whole spiel up. Choosing her words carefully, she responded.

What do you look like?

I'm disappointed if this is a weighing factor. Based on your letter I assumed you were more preoccupied with the intellectual stimulation of a relationship.

You can see what I look like. You have a rock as your profile picture. Fair is fair.

Ah, but appearances tend to make impressions and tempt assumptions. You're a smart woman. Think of how a sightless man's senses are heightened by blindness. I want to provoke your senses, Ms. Farrow. Everything you asked for depends on trust. I require a level of trust in order to proceed. My appearance should be irrelevant. I'm not asking for a physical encounter. Rather, I'm more interested in your mind, as you should be interested in mine. However, I understand the sort of ill-favored images you're probably concocting in that imagination of yours, so I will offer you this. I'm thirty years old. I have a personal trainer, no nasty personal habits. My hair is medium brown and my eyes are blue. I'm a little over six foot tall and have never been overweight. My health is good and I've had two cavities in my life. That should be enough to satisfy your curiosity for now.

Still, he could be lying. If he wouldn't show himself he had to show her something. She needed some clue to put her at ease and know he was trust worthy.

. . .

Where are you now?

I'm sitting in my home office.

"*H*mm...Let's see how honest you really are, Mr. Stone." She typed out her next request.

Can you describe it to me? It'll put me at ease.

Of course. The walls are deep sapphire. My desk is glass. There are floor to ceiling bookcases on either side of the marble fireplace. And my drapes are pale blue. Satisfied?

No. You swear that's where you are?

What purpose would it serve to lie?

*S*he laughed. "The purpose of murdering me in my sleep." She smiled as she typed her next test.

Prove it. Send me a picture of the room you just described.

She waited only a minute before the image loaded and her lips parted. Wow. Talk about lush. The carpet looked super expensive and the woodwork was masterful. It matched everything he described although the picture was even prettier than his description. She'd never seen an actual house with a room like—

"Wait a minute." She responded again.

How do I know you didn't just copy and paste that from Pinterest or something?

I suppose you have to trust me.

Trust is earned.

I see. Would it help if I wrote a word on a piece of paper and took another picture, so you could see the pictures are mine and not premeditated?

Yes. But I get to pick the word.

Fine. What shall it be?

. . .

*S*he considered some choices, but wanted to choose something totally random to make sure he was the one producing the pictures. She grinned cleverly as Harry Potter continued to play in the background. Nothing like a random movie quote.

> You have to write the words: The spiders…they want me to tap dance.

*S*he waited patiently. If he actually did this and proved that was the room he was sitting in, she'd be highly impressed. Anything that looked superimposed or photo shopped and she was blocking him.

The screen dinged. "Holy. Shit."

There was the impressive office and fireplace, and there was a man's hand holding a slip of paper that read:

> I admire your movie reference, Ms. Farrow. THE SPIDERS…THEY WANT ME TO TAP DANCE. I believe the next line is, "And I don't want to tap dance! …You tell those spiders, Ron."

. . .

She laughed. He'd certainly done what she'd asked and proved himself. She analyzed every clue she had at her disposal. His hand looked clean. His wrist was a normal size with a nice looking watch. And his handwriting was very nice, sort of like the kind they used for Sharpie ads. Plus, he liked Harry Potter enough to know one of the quotes. Cool points.

When the screen alerted her to a new message, she minimized the image.

> Satisfied? Shall we continue?

Yes, she was definitely satisfied. However... She didn't want to come off as an idiot, but certain things weren't making sense.

> Yes. Thank you. So…are you interested in dating? I don't understand your intentions.

> Think of it as someone being focused on you—in a positive way, Ms. Farrow. You piqued my interest and I find myself charmed with the idea of being the man you seek.

But you aren't interested in anything sexual?

ot that she'd have sex with a stranger. She was simply trying to understand what this was exactly.

What gave you that idea, Ms. Farrow?

You said you're not interested in a physical encounter.

Ms. Farrow, allow me to enlighten you. The largest sexual organ is in fact the brain. Our bodies are aroused through the mind, erotic imagery formulated by the brain's processing of the senses. Not all absorbed things must be learned on a kinesthetic level. I can take you where no man ever has, without ever laying a hand on you, so long as I can engage your mind.

hoa. He was smart. Maybe he was a doctor or something. The longer she spoke to him the more information she gathered. Brown hair, blue eyes—the trainer was a plus—good with words, owned his own company—company, not practice, so probably *not* a doctor then. But most of all, he was smart! Mr. Stone was adding up to quite an interesting person. To be honest, he sounded like a catch. But it was still strange not seeing him. This could all be bullshit. She wished she had more proof then a wrist shot to know he wasn't plotting her death.

Her laptop chimed. She'd been thinking of a reply but hesitated.

> Shall I give you another word, Ms. Farrow?

> All right.

> Good. Your word is, discipline.

Her nose wrinkled at his selection. Own, claim, and now discipline? Maybe this guy was a little too intense. She responded.

Dog.

Interesting. Why dog?

You say discipline and I imagine a hand rolling up a newspaper and swatting a dog.

Did you have pets growing up, Ms. Farrow?

Yes, cats and dogs, but we never hit them. I love animals.

I'm curious what would make you associate the word discipline with a cowering animal.

I don't know. I don't like that word. I had a different reaction to it than the others.

I see. And what do you call it when you see a person in training running through the rain or a soldier crawling on broken bones and bloodied limbs to save a life? Is that not discipline? What of the guards that stand silently to protect their homeland or the child who struggles through school, despite his learning difficulties? The addict that recovers against all odds and continues to stave off temptation every day for the rest of his life? These are all admirable qualities to my way of thinking. And all require discipline. Do you not agree?

*H*e completely flipped her thinking.

You're right. I suppose I was thinking more along the lines of discipline in terms of modifying behavior. You're interpreting it as an adjective where I saw it as a verb.

And now that we've clarified, how would you respond in one word to the word discipline.

$\mathcal{S}$he thought for a moment and typed her answer.

Strong.

Very good, Ms. Farrow. Your amended answer pleases me and I agree with your choice. Discipline is strength.

$\mathcal{U}$nprecedented warmth spread through her chest at his praise. It was bizarre, having such a reaction to a stranger's opinion. Her skin heated and she found it difficult to look at the computer, which was ridiculous.

Before she could process her reaction, the laptop chimed again and she was analyzing yet another strange result. Anticipation—it bloomed the second her laptop notified her that he'd written more.

Next word. Chivalry.

$\mathcal{T}$hat was an easy one.

Want!

Well, there's some enthusiasm. No need to go on. I understand. Next word. Trust.

She breathed in a deep breath and slowly let it out. That was a big one. Trust was a lot of things. In any relationship it was necessary, especially when getting to know someone for the first time. Trust was weighed, earned, and then maintained. The truth was, trust wasn't something she easily granted.

Cynical.

Are you simply throwing out an antonym, Ms. Farrow, or are you admitting to trust issues?

Trust issues. I used to be optimistic. Then I hit thirty.

I see. And you've applied this newfound pessimism to all future encounters, a sort of blanket approach?

She sighed. She never used to be pessimistic, but over time there had been so much disappointment. She really wanted that hopeful side of her to come back.

I suppose I've become a bit jaded with the selection out there.

It can be quite discouraging.

His response jolted her forward with a sense of camaraderie.

Yes! Some of the dates I've gone on were awful. I could write a book with the characters I've met.

Do you enjoy reading?

Yes.

What genres?

All of them. I like romance and science fiction best, though.

Tell me your favorite male character from fiction.

Their conversation picked up pace, a quick volleying of Q and A that required minor contemplation and had her smiling. It was nice to have a conversation with someone other than her cat. Pair this with a nice dinner and one had themselves the perfect date.

Hmmm… Jordan Rider.

Tell me about Jordan. What appealed to you?

He was a pirate in an old romance I read when I was young. It was my first romance novel and my mother would have flipped if she knew I was reading it. Compared to what's out now, it wasn't even that bad, but Jordan Rider was the sexiest man I'd ever come across. I loved him. I still do, over a decade later. Just his name gives me chills.

What was it he did that was so remarkable?

It wasn't what he did, but how he did it. He carried himself in a way real men can't pull off. Everything about him was unapologetically masculine. Sometimes he could be rigid and demanding, but he never lost his temper except for this one time when any man would have done the same. But other than that he was perfect. He treated the heroine with such esteem, adored her, possessed her, handled her with the perfect amount of tenderness and strength blended into one.

You want a fairytale.

She laughed. What girl didn't? Shifting on the couch, she bounced her foot and Thor gave her a disgruntled look for disturbing his catnap. They'd been chatting for quite a while. She had to use the bathroom, but didn't want to miss a reply.

Of course. I'm a woman after all. We're all hoping to someday find our happily ever after, our knight in shining armor. BRB

She scooted Thor off her lap, rushed to the bathroom and her computer chimed as she was washing her hands. Running back to the couch she snatched the laptop off the coffee table and quickly read what she missed.

> What does your happily ever after include, Ms. Farrow?

Her lips twitched in a secret smile. Every incoming response added to the strange sense of giddiness filling her.

> I think happiness is contentment.

He wasn't doing more than asking her questions, yet his words stimulated some side of her brain that flourished under such personal attention. He made her seem interesting and that felt nice. Completely engrossed in their conversation, she anxiously awaited his every reply.

Are you not content with your life, Ms. Farrow? Scratch that. Of course you're not. A content woman would not write such a letter to the local paper. I've read your letter several times and, after talking to you, I believe I can definitely help you.

What does that mean, exactly? Help me…?

You wanted to know what it feels like to be completely adored, if even for a short time. I'd like to get to know you, Scarlet. I believe you'd be quite easy to adore.

Her arms prickled with goose bumps. She liked when he used her first name. They were becoming more intimate with each other. Strangely, she wasn't as freaked out as she had been earlier in the evening.

What did you have in mind?

The intoxicating build of anticipation flooded her as she waited for his reply.

. . .

First, I will require one thing from you. I'm not sure you're capable of providing it at this time, but once you are, I think we should meet in person.

Oh, God. This was the point where he announced some ridiculous fetish that would surely be a deal breaker. Even with the elements of mystery, he seemed a bit too perfect.

She cringed as she typed her next question, dreading he might suggest she join him to sacrifice a goat or come to dinner wearing a strap-on. There were tons of freaks out there. Chances were he was one of them. Holding her breath, she hit send.

What's the requirement?

Her breath left in a rush when his response appeared.

Trust.

. . .

rust? That wasn't weird, although it asked a whole lot. Relief came so swiftly, skepticism reflexively followed.

That's it?

For now, yes, that's it, though I don't regard trust as a minimal entity. I don't want us to meet until you've developed some level of trust. I'm not concerned with the time this will take. I'm typically a trustworthy person and I believe you'll realize that. However, my endorsement of my own honor is worthless. You must decide if and when you trust me and at that point we can proceed.

ow. Maybe there wasn't anything impressive about his conditions, but for some reason his logic impressed the hell out of her, removing some lingering apprehension. His confidence influenced her decision as well. Perhaps that was the motive behind his spiel and she was just gullible.

> Okay.

> I'm pleased we agree. Trust is necessary to proceed. We'll start with this, Ms. Farrow. What are your plans tomorrow?

She grimaced with self-disgust. Her schedule was, of course, wide open.

> I have some work to catch up on, but I'll be around most of the day.

As the message sent, a nip of panic crawled up her spine. What if she was the easiest target in the world and she just gave him enough information to find her, kill her, and get away scot-free?

> Perfect. I will message you here tomorrow at 12:00. We can have lunch together.

he laughed—a cyber lunch. They were taking the term online dating to a new literal level.

Okay.

I look forward to it, Ms. Farrow. Enjoy the rest of your evening. Sweet dreams.

isappointment swamped her as the abrupt conclusion of their conversation took her by surprise. Maybe he worried he was keeping her from something.

We can talk a little longer if you'd like.

True, but I'd rather leave you to think on what I've said for the night. It brings me great pleasure to imagine you in bed thinking of me. I'll be doing the same, in my bed, pondering you and all the ways I intend to adore you. Goodnight, Scarlet.

She shivered. There had to be something wrong with a person who could get turned on by an absolute stranger. Her mind was so lost in the fantasy of Mr. Perfect, she didn't want to consider reality.

In reality, she'd likely never meet him. He'd move on to some other girl and she'd be forgotten. Or she might come back and find his profile deleted like it was never there. Either way, she was certain they'd never really meet.

Most likely he'd just bullshitted the hell out of her, but hey, if this was role-playing it had the desired effect. She felt better than she had in weeks, wanted and attractive. Pretending online for a few hours on a lonely Friday night beat the hell out of watching Harry Potter with her cat for the twentieth time.

4

ENCHANTMENT

THE FOLLOWING MORNING, Scarlet awoke a bit lighter. Lying in bed, she grinned to herself, recalling the interesting man of mystery from the night before. Mr. Stone.

Her mind played over various shades of blue, trying to decide which was closest to the color of his eyes. No matter how much she tried not to get ahead of herself, every time she imagined him he was gorgeous. The temptation to run to her computer and check if his profile was still there was only belied by her fear he'd be gone.

Last night was such a breath of fresh air. If anything, Mr. Stone broke up the monotony of her weekend and she liked him for that simple fact alone. So what if it was all talk and they never actually met? It wasn't like he was keeping her from living a real life.

Playing over their conversation in her mind, she grinned then groaned into her pillow. "You're living in a fantasy world," she mumbled to herself as Thor pounced on her butt and began kneading as if her were a baker making fresh bread.

Was it strange that she missed him? Her curiosity was increasing with every speculation. Unable to resist another minute, she climbed from bed and found her laptop.

Thor impatiently nudged her knee in a plea for food. Her heart raced as she waited for her computer to load. Passing the time, she opened a can of Fancy Feast—only the best for her beast—and quickly fed the cat.

The excitement running through her veins made it difficult to type as she logged into her GeekPeek account. As soon as the page opened she went right to her messages. There it was, their entire conversation.

Carrying the laptop to the table, she doctored up her coffee, distracted by his curious words and getting sugar everywhere. Reading over the exchange was as exciting as it was the first time round. Maybe more so, because now she wasn't as afraid of him and no longer assumed it was Nicole trying to punk her.

Sipping from her mug, she grinned as she continued to read, intrigued all over again. When she reached the part where he said goodnight, the same disappointment from the evening before swamped her.

Glancing at the clock, she noted there were still several hours until noon. Damn it! She wanted to talk to him again, but she didn't want to come on too strong or too desperate. Snooping around, she went to his profile. Without accepting his friendship request there really wasn't much to see.

Taking a deep breath, she clicked accept. Whatever she was expecting, it wasn't this. Her mouth pulled to the side as she scoped out his profile. The sword in the stone picture was the only photo. He'd joined Geek-Peek only a week ago, which meant he was probably full of shit.

Overwhelmed by the sense of disenchantment, she drooped back in her chair. "You're an idiot, Scarlet."

She was so gullible. She knew it. No matter how much she warned herself it was a joke, she still got carried away.

As she prepared to log out, a notification pinged. A strange cross of skepticism and longing filled her when she read his name. If she let this continue she'd likely wind up more disappointed than she already was.

He isn't real.

Sighing, she—a glutton for punishment—clicked the notification and was taken to a post on her profile.

I THINK THIS IS THE BEGINNING OF A
BEAUTIFUL FRIENDSHIP.

S carlet rolled her eyes. "Oh, okay, Humphrey Bogart. Now you're just being lazy." He could at least make up his own lines.

Disgusted with how hopeful she'd allowed herself to become, she backed out of the page, accidentally hitting the key that took her to the page last visited. His page. But now it was updated.

"What the—" The post was to her.

GOOD MORNING, MS. FARROW. I
TOLD YOU I TOOK MY PRIVACY
SERIOUSLY. NO ONE CAN SEE THIS
PAGE BUT YOU. STOP WASTING TIME
ON GP AND GO START YOUR DAY. I
DON'T EXPECT YOU TO BE
DISTRACTED WHEN WE HAVE LUNCH.

Scrolling down to his friend list she, again, noted more peculiarities. She was it. This was such crap. She should de-friend him and block his lying ass. But *she'd* be lying if she said his flirty post didn't excite her. God, she really was desperate, settling for a pathetic puppet profile rather than having the dignity to move on.

She scowled at her laptop. She should shut it. Just walk away. Forget he existed—which he didn't—and go interact with some real people in the real world. Funny, that was easier said than done. And maybe that was partly her fault.

She growled. Her dating life was a disgrace due largely to inner monologues like this. The games, the facades, it was all bullshit, nothing but smoke and mirrors leading people to destinies they probably weren't meant to find. She could be mysterious too, she decided.

Leaning forward, she quickly commented on his post.

I'm not wasting time. I was talking to friends. A little arrogant of you to assume I came here for you.

Her finger snapped down on the enter key and she waited...and waited...and waited as doubt slowly corroded her bravado. What if she pissed him off? She shouldn't care. He wasn't even real. Stone indeed. She desperately needed to adopt a nothing to lose attitude where this guy was concerned.

The computer chimed and she refreshed her screen in a demeaning display of hopefulness. Oh well, it wasn't like anyone was around to witness it.

Noon, Scarlet. Noon.

She pouted, actually pouted. What was happening here? He'd somehow taken control of the situation and now she was pressed to do—what exactly? Housework? Grade papers?

There were three hours until lunch. Her schoolbag was in the hall. Retrieving the tests from last week, she settled in at the table. Thirty minutes later they were marked and she was adding the scores to her grade tracker.

Once she finished with the paperwork, she put everything back in her bag and tapped her foot impatiently. What the hell should she do now? She glanced at her laptop. *Don't do it.*

Shaking her head she went to the broom closet and retrieved the furniture polish and a rag. As she dusted, her mind wandered. Why was she listening to him? Who was he to tell her what to do? Yet, for some reason, she wanted to do as he asked, liked the subliminal link to someone other than herself.

Attention that had to be begged for, only held a fraction of the value of freely given attention. If she waited and kept herself busy, it would be worth more in the end. It would also be more exciting.

Wow. She *was* excited. But her empty availability shined a bit too much light on her lonesome circumstances. Once the furniture was clean and her house smelled like soft lemon, she tossed the rag in the laundry and went to take a shower. As the water poured over her body, her mind wandered. Visions of blue eyes and broad shoulders filled her head. What would his voice sound like?

Oh, she imagined that horrid episode of *Sex and the City* when the girls were checking out the pool boy who turned out to have an unbearably high-pitched voice. That wouldn't be good.

There had to be something wrong with him. Eventually she'd discover his flaws and that would be that, alone again. Wait. What was she saying? She was alone now.

Shaking her head, she dried herself off and tried to get a grip. She was really getting ahead of herself.

Slipping into soft lounge pants and a hooded sweatshirt, she grabbed her purse, and headed out the door on a whim. She drove aimlessly for several minutes, her pointless wandering irritating her more with every passing second. *Go buy something.*

There really wasn't anything she needed, but— Her gaze caught on the new boutique on the corner. It looked like something of a perfume imperium, but she wasn't sure. It also looked expensive. Sliding into a metered space, she stared at the storefront, noting the well-dressed woman entering.

Her gaze dropped to her lap, scrutinizing her yoga pants and flicking a tuft of Thor hair off the knee. A sense of empowerment slipped through her. She could be a woman like that, couldn't she? She shut off the car and grabbed her purse before her introverted nature got the better of her.

She hadn't always been such a homebody. As a matter of fact, she wasn't exactly sure when she'd decided to shut the world out and make her own. It wasn't something she excelled at—world building. If anything, hers was bleak and littered with conversations between her and her cat. Yeah, she was doing this.

Pushing through the heavy glass door of the boutique, her senses were assaulted with feminine fragrances as her eyes adjusted to the lush displays and white lighting. "Good morning," a woman adjusting a display of necklaces crooned.

Scarlet smiled. "Good morning."

"Can I help you find something?"

When she didn't scoff at her attire or sloppy bun, and Scarlet's anxiety faded a notch. "You know, I'm not really sure what I'm looking for. Something for myself, I think."

The woman smiled, placing the last of the necklaces on the display and coming around the counter.

"Well then, we should find something great. Do you like jewelry? Or perhaps one of our signature fragrances? We also have a new makeup line. Do you have time for a consultation?"

Her awkwardness might as well be body odor, because it seemed to be emanating from her pores. "Um, like you do my makeup and show me how?"

The woman laughed. "Exactly. Come have a seat."

Scarlet followed her to a plush violet stool and stashed her purse on the floor. She fidgeted as the woman gathered pallets and enough brushes to paint the Sistine Chapel.

"My name's Fiona."

"Nice to meet you. I'm Scarlet."

Fiona used a soft cloth with something moist to wipe down her face. Whatever she was using smelled so good if it was food, Scarlet would have eaten it. "What sort of regimen do you use, Scarlet? Your skin's beautiful."

Having the other woman so close gave Scarlet ample time to appraise her beauty and it was astounding. "Um, I don't really have one. I put lotion on my face when it's dry and I'm a big fan of chapstick."

Fiona smiled. "Are you going somewhere? Looking for a new look?"

"Not really. I guess I just figured a change might be nice."

She combed her eyebrows with a dainty bristled wand. "Change is fun. A woman needs a good change now and again. Are you married?"

Why? Why did this personal inquisition happen with every stranger? "No."

"Boyfriend?"

"Not at the moment."

"Well, lucky you. I sometimes wish I had a chance to go back to your age and do it all over again, single, without all the dating nonsense."

She frowned. It was so rude, but she had to ask. The woman looked fresh out of college, if that. "How old are you?"

Fiona winked, as if the illusion of youth was intended and Scarlet's uncertainty flattered her. "I'm forty-six."

"Wow."

She nodded and applied a silky beige cream to her cheeks. "The products we sell are amazing. You'll see. What do you do for a living?"

"I'm a teacher."

"So you'll be wanting a subtle look, I assume. Something easy for those early Monday mornings?"

"Sure." Makeup was a foreign concept to her. On fancy occasions she sometimes swathed her lashes with drug store mascara, but that was the end of her knowledge on facial products.

As Fiona brushed her face with various powders, Scarlet developed a strange fondness for all the fancy vials and compacts, finding them ultra feminine, but nonetheless intimidating.

"You have gorgeous eyes. They're such a fascinating shade of blue-green."

Her skin heated. "Thanks. Yours are pretty too."

Fiona winked. "Contacts. Mine are actually brown."

Her lips parted. "I never would have guessed."

The woman smiled again. "Part your lips. This shade of gloss will compliment your complexion."

As she worked, Scarlet lost herself in her surroundings. When the thought of Mr. Stone suddenly popped in her head, she was pleased to note the lapse of time since she'd last thought of him. Mission accomplished. Maybe Fiona was right and there was something about being thirty and single.

"Take a look."

The woman in the reflection was almost unrecognizable. It was her, but the prettiest version of herself she'd ever seen. "Wow."

Her eyes were defined in an understated way that gave them a naturally dramatic appeal. Her skin tone was perfectly even, looking like it had years ago. She hadn't taken note of the exact time that youthful glow faded, but Fiona had magically restored it. Her cheeks and brow bones were perfectly defined and for the first time in a long time, Scarlet saw herself genuinely smile.

"You like it?"

"It's amazing." Her fingers lifted to her cheek and feathered over the soft makeup, not finding it heavy or thick.

"It didn't take much. You're a natural beauty."

Her reflection tinged with a sharp blush. "Thank you."

She described all the products she'd used and where she applied them. In the end, Scarlet bought everything she suggested. Who knew if she'd ever look that way again? Her ability to replicate Fiona's work was a lot to hope for, but she appreciated her time and effort. The cost was minimal compared to the jolt of confidence she found in that boutique.

As she returned to her car, her cheeks pinched with an unbending grin. At a traffic light on the way home, a man in the car beside her smiled in her direction and Scarlet nearly got in an accident as the light turned green she was so taken off guard.

Recognizing how low her self-esteem had plummeted was upsetting. Whatever provoked her to enter that boutique, she was grateful she did. The experience showed her there was a salvageable spirit hiding inside of her, beneath all the jaded, Debbie Downer garbage that had been weighing on her shoulders since her thirtieth birthday. No more—she decided.

As she plucked the keys from her car and walked into her house, she made a vow. This next chapter of her life would be a happy one. She was going to try new things and force herself to take risks. She would not let the next year pass like the last one. She made the resolution to take advantage of every exciting opportunity that came, promising to start this decade off right. It was a *deca-lution*, she decided.

She was done waiting for a man to give her purpose or a reason to live. From now on, she would live and let the men wait for her. If they wanted her to notice them, they'd better up their game, because she no longer had time for little boys.

Speaking of which, her eyes glanced at the clock. The morning had passed a lot faster than she'd expected—which was what usually happened when one stopped sitting around waiting for the phone to ring, or in her case, the laptop to ding.

The closer the hour came to noon, the more her tummy twisted with fluttering excitement, but there wasn't the sense of dependency she'd woken up with. This time, she was curious, but no longer hanging her every hope on one guy. However, she was definitely giddy with anticipation. There was no denying that.

In the kitchen, she poured herself a glass of water,

and grabbed her laptop. Six minutes. Anticipation had her breath quickening. Shit. She was supposed to have lunch with him. In a matter of two minutes she made a PB and J sandwich and grabbed a banana for dessert. Perching on the couch, she opened her laptop.

It chimed and she let out a breath she'd seemed to be holding.

Good afternoon, Ms. Farrow.

Good afternoon, Mr. Stone.

Did you enjoy your morning?

Yes. I graded some papers and did a little shopping.

*P*roud she could honestly say she didn't spend the morning sitting around waiting, she grinned.

What did you buy?

Just a few things from a little boutique that opened in town.

*I*t seemed wrong to tell a man she spent over a hundred dollars on makeup, so she kept that little tidbit to herself. He didn't seem overly interested in her shopping excursion anyway.

What subject were you grading?

*S*he smiled, finding his interest in the fundamentals refreshing.

Math.

Is that what you teach?

*S*he hesitated. Last night they'd sort of flirted and discussed inconsequential things. Now his questions were getting personal.

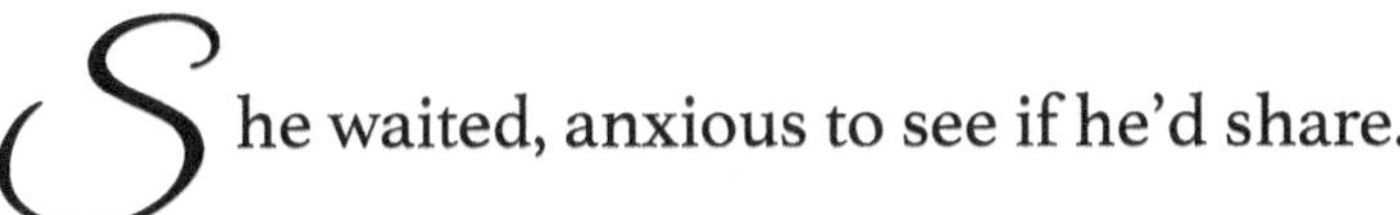

*S*he waited, anxious to see if he'd share.

I'm a designer of sorts.

As in interior design?

*F*unny, that didn't fit with what she'd assumed about him. It wasn't disappointing information, just unexpected.

It's a bit more technical than interior design. My career focuses more on digital design. What are you having for lunch?

*H*e always tended to give minimal information about himself and deflect the conversation back to her. Was he shy or literally that private? Or perhaps the better word was secretive.

Peanut butter and jelly sandwich with a banana.

Ah, the lunchroom special.

What are you having?

. . .

*F*inishing her sandwich, she crumpled the napkin and peeled her banana as she waited. Her heart pounded as she considered how curious she was about this man, not just about his lunch, but everything.

Her eyes continuously checked the time, fearing the moment he'd conclude their conversation. Her phone suddenly rang at the same time the computer chimed. The caller ID said Nicole, but she hesitated, too drawn to Mr. Stone's reply.

I'm having seared ahi tuna, fingerling potatoes, and green beans mixed in a balsamic vinaigrette.

"*H*oly shit." She distractedly reached for her phone. "Hello?"

"Hey, what are you doing?" Nicole greeted. There was an echo on the line, telling Scarlet her friend was in the car.

"Um, I'm having lunch."

"Are you home?"

"Yes," she answered slowly, not wanting any interruptions.

"Perfect! I got a dress for that get together at my work. I wanted your opinion. I'm going for thirty and owning it, but I'm afraid this might scream trampy desperate. I'll be there in ten minutes."

She should have never answered the phone. Sighing, knowing her BFF duties couldn't be overshadowed by a guy she barely knew, she said, "I'll be here."

"Great. See you soon."

Call ended, she tossed the phone aside. There were several messages waiting for her.

> What else did you do this morning, Ms. Farrow?

> Scarlet?

> Did my lunch offend you?

She quickly typed out a response before he assumed she'd left.

> Hi.

> Sorry. I got a phone call. I'm going to have company very soon.

His response wasn't immediate this time. Damn it. Why did Nicole have to come over now? All she wanted to do was talk to Mr. Stone. They'd only had a few minutes and Nicole would likely be walking through the door in the next five.

> I assumed we would have longer to chat.

$\mathcal{I}$t was amazing how disappointed she was over the same thing. Interesting that they both seemed to be experiencing the same frustration.

She could've told Nicole she was talking to a guy. She could even continue to talk to him while Nicole tried on her new dress, but for some reason she wanted to keep Mr. Stone a secret—at least until she got to know him a bit more.

Huh. It suddenly occurred to her that if Nicole was in the car driving to her house, she definitely wasn't pretending to be the mystery man occupying her time. Strange, her suspicions of such a charade had disappeared sometime in the last eighteen hours without her realizing. The more time that passed the more real he became.

> Scarlet, you're developing a habit of making me wait for replies.

> Sorry. I was hoping we'd have more time to talk too. I could come back after she leaves.

I'll admit I'm relieved you said she. I had wanted to speak to you about my expectations, but it isn't a conversation that should be rushed. How does 7:00 work for you?

*T*hat was seven hours away. Wishing he'd suggested a closer time, she pursed her lips and agreed, not wanting to come off too needy.

That works fine. I'll talk to you then.

I look forward to it, Ms. Farrow.

*H*er mouth tightened with a smirk. The Ms. Farrow thing was growing on her. It was totally different, reading her formal title from a man, than hearing it from her students.

Me too. Bye.

*S*he shut her laptop and tucked it out of sight. Two seconds later Nicole walked in. Scarlet put on a happy face and embraced the situation. She had six hours and thirty-eight minutes to kill.

As Nicole rounded the corner, Nordstrom's garment bag in hand, she came to a jolting halt. "Whoa. You look fabulous! Did you have a date last night or something?"

Scarlet had been very cautious, avoiding all dating topics with her friend since their disagreement, but she could never stay mad at her forever. "Nope. But I took myself out this morning and got a makeover."

"All by yourself?" Her friend's expression of disbelief was a testament to just how closeted Scarlet had allowed herself to become.

"Yup."

"Well, look at you!" Nicole smiled. "That's awesome. Where did you go?"

"That little boutique on Main."

"Stelluna? I love that place! I always go browsing, but never know what to buy. It's so fancy and pristine. I can't believe you went there by yourself!"

Scarlet laughed. "Well, I've decided to try new things. Today I tried makeup. I can't believe how expensive that stuff is."

Nicole draped her dress over a chair and disappeared in the kitchen, the clink of glasses preceding the rush of the faucet. A moment later she returned sipping a glass of water. "I know, but aging sucks. If I go out without my eyes done everyone asks if I'm feeling okay, like, I look ill without makeup. Fucking people. Do you think I look old?"

"God, no! Nicole, you look the same as you did in high school. People are idiots."

She sighed and sagged against the wall, her mouth screwing to the side. "I'm really sorry about what I said the other day." Her hand waved in her general direction. "You don't need to change who you are to get a decent man, Lettie. I never meant for you to go out and get a makeover."

She appreciated the apology, but had to laugh. "I didn't do this for a man. I did it for me. I wanted to buy something at Stelluna that was solely mine and I did."

"That's really great. And listen, Mr. Right is out there—"

She held out a hand. "Stop. I love you for trying to find me a husband, but the search is making me insane. No more blind dates for a while. I'm taking some time for me. I'm going to let life lead me where it will and if an opportunity comes along, great, but I'm not sitting around waiting for it."

Nicole smiled, her eyes dancing with surprise. "Okay. You go get yourself a big old bite of life."

"I plan on it. Now, go try on that dress so I can gush over you for a while."

"Okay, but if I look fat, lie and blame it on the design. I'm a bottle of Belvedere away from going all elastic and living off Oreos. Why the hell are they making dresses so short now?"

"Because the fashion industry is evil and that's exactly why I stick to more conforming brands."

Nicole laughed. "You don't have a brand. You bought that sweatshirt at Sam's Club."

"Sam's has nice clothes!"

"It's a grocery store, Lettie!" She grabbed the dress and sashayed up the steps.

Scarlet admired her sweatshirt.

A lot happened over the course of six hours. Scarlet experienced a myriad of emotions, not all of them pleasant.

Once Nicole had finished modeling her dress, they'd had coffee and talked for a bit. Every time Scarlet was tempted to tell her friend about the mysterious Mr. Stone something held the confession inside.

Mr. Stone was a small personal joy, one she wasn't sure other—married people—would understand. *Why* his presence wouldn't be understood left a lot to examine.

Over the years there had been many debacles in the dating arena. There were the headliners Scarlet hoped would work out, the good guys she wished triggered a spark of chemistry, and those she couldn't get away from fast enough.

But there were also the so-called "duds" she'd been interested in for reasons her friends couldn't comprehend. Protectively, she didn't want Mr. Stone to be labeled a dud.

She wasn't sure what ingredient he brought to the table, but he captivated her. Something about this man was different and she had yet to figure it out. She didn't want Nicole stepping in with warnings and disapproval.

Sure, he was a stranger and the world was a dangerous place full of dangerous people, but what harm was she putting herself in if she only talked to him online? Okay, fine. There were definite risks to proceeding with an online relationship. Hell, she warned her student's of the dangers all the time, but there really was no difference between what she was doing with Mr.

Stone and what she did when people contacted her on dating sites, so in the end she justified her actions. It was all part of her new *deca-lution* to seize the day.

Of course, there was the slightly creepy factor that he'd identified her from her letter, which she needed to investigate, but still... All of her trepidation was overridden by the hopeful idea that this could be destiny stepping in.

What if he was *the one?* She didn't want to dismiss the possibility too soon and miss out on something exciting and possibly wonderful. As much as she declared not to be searching for Mr. Right at the moment, she also didn't want to miss the door should he come knocking. And even if he wasn't Mr. Right, he might be Mr. Fun or Mr. Really-Good-in-Bed or Mr. Distraction. They were all worth meeting.

The reactions Mr. Stone provoked were definitely worth investigating. She couldn't figure out how much of what she felt was due to her own desolate existence or to the actual man behind the name.

The one thing she could admit was that she was enjoying herself. Her apprehension had faded into manageable caution and her usually guarded self was prepared to take considerable risks in order to see where this led.

Is this how people end up dead? Oh, stop being Captain Panic! You're only talking.

She didn't think he was a dangerous person, but she wasn't certain. If only she could find out a little bit more about him.

At six forty-five she was anxiously pacing. Her laptop sat on the edge of her bed, the screen slowly fading to the sleep setting, which she would repetitively interrupt with a brush of her finger over the mouse pad.

By ten-of she was nervous he wouldn't contact her. The ten minutes leading up to seven were filled with a ricocheting tangle of hopes and fears until finally, at precisely seven o'clock, her computer chimed.

Good evening, Ms. Farrow.

Her heart erupted with numerous sensations she hadn't felt since high school. His punctuality earned a small measure of trust. Falling to her bed, she slid her computer close and smiled.

Good evening, Mr. Stone.

I assume the rest of your day was pleasant.

Breathing in a sigh, she poised her fingers over the keyboard to type out a response just as her phone rang. "Damn it."

Reaching to her nightstand she set it to vibrate. There would be no interruptions this time. Her brow lowered when the caller ID read *Restricted.* Freaking telemarketers.

.   .   .

> My day was very pleasant. And yours?

The phone silenced and abruptly started buzzing again.

> Very pleasant. Pick up the phone, Scarlet.

She froze, her gaze devouring his command on the screen and slowly drifting to the buzzing phone on her bed. Her heart thundered heavily in her chest. No, he couldn't be calling her. How did he get her number?

> Are you calling me???

> Your privacy settings need to be amended if you intend to set your contact information as unavailable to the public.

Still not picking up the phone, the buzzing continued a few more times then stopped only to start again.

. . .

> I have my number listed for my students' parents to get in touch with me.

> Understandable. Now, answer the call.

*S*he stared at the phone, her body shivering with fears of the unknown. Inevitably, she knew she'd answer, but this was a big deal. He was *calling* her. She'd finally hear his voice. A voice could tell a lot about a person.

Her fingers slowly closed over the phone as she drew in a steadying breath. What if he didn't like *her* voice? Closing her eyes she swallowed as the phone rattled in her grip.

"Please don't have high pitched pool boy voice," she muttered under her breath before sliding her finger across the screen and bringing the phone to her ear. "Hello?"

"Hello, Scarlet."

Oh, thank God. His voice was deep, masculine and gravelly, rich with maturity. Hers, on the other hand, had turned pinched and falsetto. "Hello, Mr. Stone."

"It's lovely to finally speak to you."

She remained silent, unsure what to say and still processing the appeal of his voice, his words pitched low as though he were whispering dark, dirty secrets. "Are you comfortable speaking on the phone?"

Uhhh...her senses were on high alert, definitely not a relaxed feeling, but certainly not an unpleasant one. Getting a call from him was so unexpected she was still analyzing the experience.

Adrenaline pumped through her veins. Gone was the ability to think out her responses. They were live, in the moment. What was already strangely cozy transcended to unusually intimate.

"Yes," she rasped.

"You sound a bit breathless. Is everything all right?"

Needing to take a moment to regroup, she jaggedly sucked air into her lungs. She could do this. She could talk to him. "I'm okay. I wasn't expecting you to call."

"The messaging was becoming tedious. I find this method of communication a bit more personal, wouldn't you agree?"

"Yes." Jeez, did she know any other words?

"What were you doing before I called?"

Waiting for you. "Just tidying my room."

"Tell me about your room."

She glanced at the furniture filling the space as though seeing it for the first time. "It's small. The walls are pale purple. My furniture's black." No need to mention the plum satin dragon scale pillows or the wall art that said *I'm not a princess I'm a Khaleesi.* Sure. She was a grown-up.

"And what of your bed, Scarlet? Is it large?"

"No. It's a double." Why did everything she say sound so unsophisticated while his words sounded eloquent, and chosen with a refinement she lacked?

"Is it soft? What color's the coverlet?"

She blinked, finding his attention to detail different. Maybe he really was into interior design. Maybe he lied. Oh, God, maybe he was gay. It became clear she was more than curious. She was becoming attracted to him.

"Um, it's sort of a dusty olive color."

"After seeing your pictures online I think those colors suit you. I can imagine you there."

It was still off-putting that he'd seen her. Sure, it was only in stills shared through her GP profile, but that was more than she'd seen of him.

"Can I see what you look like?"

"I've told you my features."

"But you've seen pictures of me."

"Yes, and they're lovely."

Hedonistic gratification crowded her frustration. Being introverted didn't usually garner compliments, but his praise seemed more valuable than the few she'd received. He was adept at knocking her off balance.

"What is it that worries you, Scarlet? I have no remarkable scars. I'm a fairly average man. You continue to fixate on my appearance. What holds more relevance here, my words or my physical attractiveness? I personally find intelligence the more alluring attribute."

Well, yeah, she didn't want to date a beautiful idiot. Everything about him so far seemed incredibly attractive. There had to be something hideous she wasn't seeing, and she wasn't seeing him.

"I'm not superficial. I guess it doesn't matter."

"Good. Should we ever come face to face, I would hope my appearance is pleasing to you. I certainly find you attractive. However, I wouldn't want it to be an interfering factor in getting to know one another."

There was no ignoring that he'd established the

upper hand, but she didn't want to get too hung up on looks alone. She decided to investigate other facets. "How old are you?"

He didn't sound too old or too young. His profile said he was thirty. This was more fact checking, in case there were holes in his story.

"I'm thirty."

His response to her gentle interrogation was solid so far. "And you own your own company?"

He tsked three times slowly. "I find it exasperating how social interactions have turned into a sort of practiced interview. How much did you make at your last place of employment, Ms. Farrow? What's your opinion on the recent amendment to the Individuals with Differences in Education Act? Let's press beyond the credentials of our resumes."

She chuckled. "Point taken. So...what should we talk about?"

"Let's discuss your letter."

She groaned. "That letter. It wasn't meant to be read by anyone but me."

"Yet it was published in the paper. Care to explain?"

"Too many failed blind dates and too much wine."

"Ah, so you plead unaccountability by liquor."

"Yes," she agreed emphatically and giggled. She could appreciate his dry sarcasm.

"Some would say intoxication leads to truth. Drunken words are often sober thoughts. Alcohol lowers inhibitions, those pesky little walls we erect to protect our most vulnerable feelings—as does sex."

Her mouth went dry at the mention of sex. She laughed off her nervousness. "I've had more luck with booze than the latter."

"Interesting, and so I gathered from your letter. Let's examine some of those thoughts, shall we?"

"I'd rather not."

"Because you're in a state of awareness, weighing the consequences. Too many times people alter their actions in fear of consequence, when some consequences to our actions can bring about rather pleasant results. My personal experiences have taught me to invest less in others' opinions and focus more on satisfying my own personal desires. I've achieved many things I've wanted in life, but none of that would have been possible if I let my fear of consequence stop me from traveling paths untraveled. I intend to help you push through those walls, Ms. Farrow, among other things. But you must be honest."

"No one likes their flaws exposed," she commented, searching for empathy.

"I agree, however, revealing our deepest desires and fears can liberate us from emotional bondage. Let's begin with your standards. You stated that others have accused you of setting your standards too high."

"I can't help what I want."

"True. Our emotions dictate themselves. *We* are only responsible for how we react to our feelings. What is it you want, Ms. Farrow?"

Her eyes closed as his voice lulled her into a state of intimate secrecy. They were entering some sort of metaphorical confessional and she suddenly longed to unburden herself. "What everyone wants. Love."

"That's quite an assumption. Some could argue other motivators in life; greed, power, or even lust."

She rolled to her back and stared at the ceiling. His voice was intoxicating, lowering her inhibitions as though it carried the headiness of wine. "But it's a love for those things that moves people."

"Very true. And what is it you love?"

"I don't know."

"Have you ever been in love?" His whispered question rolled over her, thick and tempting.

"No, not by any mature definition. I love my parents and my friends, but I've never had an impassioned need for someone else."

"And that's what you want." He posed it as a statement, not a question, as though he were gathering facts.

"Of course."

"And your definition of love is impassioned need?"

"Among other things. It has to be mutual."

"You want to feel needed with a passion so bold it requires action."

"Yes." That was exactly it. No one had ever summed up her feelings so accurately.

"Tell me about the other standards."

"I don't think they're unreachable. I want a partner, someone who holds my hand through the ups and pulls me from the downs. I want to be that person for someone as well."

"That's lovely, the way you phrased that. I can't see many disagreeing with you, which leads me to believe those are not the standards your friends criticized. Care to expand on your answer?"

She sighed, fearing he'd see her as high maintenance. "I don't think it's too much to expect a guy to have a job, be independent, know how to hold a conversation, and own a car."

"I'd have to agree with you, but I'm curious why you felt the need to qualify your expectations with an excuse. If those are your expectations, you should stand by them. Leave the justification out."

She smiled. "Thank you. You seem to be the only one who agrees those are reasonable ideals."

"I wouldn't want a relationship with a woman incapable of having a sophisticated discussion. Nor would I be interested in a person dependent on others. I understand the comfort of reliability, but to be completely reliant on someone else at this age...no, I'm afraid that holds little appeal. A vehicle is somewhat necessary, especially in this area. And I think working is healthy. Even the richest man needs to serve a purpose."

His words stirred something inside of her. Not only had he listened and agreed with her, he took the time to clarify his comprehension and verify that he understood her reasoning.

Having such an open conversation curbed fear of judgment. Mr. Stone appeared to be a very impartial man.

"Tell me about your worst date," he said.

The way he didn't ask, but confidently directed her to continue was arousing on a psychological level. It showed a desire to learn more about her, but at the same time gave him authority over the flow of conversation. Surprisingly, she found that attractive. She became a passenger in the journey of getting acquainted, which was easier than driving the conversation on her own.

"There've been so many. I'm not sure I could pick the worst. Too many bad experiences vying for the title." She laughed.

"Your most recent then."

"Hmm... The last date I went on the guy did nothing but talk about himself."

"Did he have a car?"

"Yes."

"A job?"

"Yes."

"Was he dependent on someone other than himself?"

"No."

"Yet he didn't meet your standards."

"Well, yeah. A conversation requires two people. He wanted me to just sit there and listen to all his wonderful qualities."

"I see. So perhaps you should amend your standards and add that the man must take a personal interest in you."

"Well, that's a given."

"Not necessarily. Had you clarified this, perhaps your friends could understand your aversion to this man."

He was right. Funny, with all of her standards, none of them had to do with her personally.

"What are you thinking?"

The sudden revelation made her sit forward. "I'm wondering when I took myself out of the equation."

"And have you found an answer?"

She blinked, unable to pinpoint when exactly that happened. "I don't know. Over time, the likelihood of finding a decent partner became so implausible, I guess I sort of lowered the bar."

"We should never lower our standards, Ms. Farrow. The world is full of people who accept what *is* and don't expect anything different. Those that truly believe life can be better and dedicate their energy to proving the naysayers wrong are the people who improve life—for more than themselves. Never negotiate your personal ideals. *Fight* for them."

"Are you like a life coach or something?"

He chuckled, the sound deep and gravelly. "No. I'm just a person who had to fight for his happiness. It took a lot for me to find contentment, and I'm conceited enough to pride myself on not giving up. Let's discuss envy. In your letter you mention feeling like an outsider looking in. Have you always felt that way?"

"Pretty much."

"Even as a child?"

She thought for a moment. "Well, no, not when I was really young. I was an only child, so for a while I was the center of my parents' universe. I guess I started feeling like that when I became a teenager."

"Give me one word to describe your adolescent years."

"Fun."

He was quiet. She wished she had a more familiar name for him. "Mr. Stone?"

"Yes, I'm here. I was recalling my own teenage years. My apologies—"

"How would you describe yours?"

He didn't answer right away. "Tiresome. I started my business right out of high school, and found the entire public education experience to be an obstacle I was forced to endure. I had to walk through an experience I would have preferred to climb over. Tell me a fun memory from your teen years."

He didn't seem to recall high school as a favorable time, so she tucked his comment away for later. "My friend, Nicole, she and I were on the cheer squad together. One time, after a game, we ended up at a party for the rivaling team. We were there for almost an hour before we realized the house didn't belong to one of our classmates. Once we realized, we couldn't get out of there fast enough. On the way out I tripped and knocked over an entire table, and drinks went flying everywhere. That was likely the moment the other school realized they had rivals on their territory. We couldn't stop laughing, even though we needed to escape. When we made it to the car, Nicole was hysterical. She'd stolen the head of their mascot costume."

"Sounds like quite an adventure."

"The jocks from our school were in our debt for a long time. The head's probably still mounted on the wall of my high school locker room."

*A*sher's stomach tightened as he visualized the mascot head, recalling exactly where it had been mounted, unseeing eyes to every brutal attack he'd suffered in that locker room. Discussing high school with Scarlet and detecting the fondness in her voice was difficult. It reminded him how different they were.

This was not someone new, but someone he'd known in a previous life, someone who'd hurt him. The more she intrigued him the easier it became to overlook their painful past interactions, but he wasn't sure if that was a good thing.

His sole focus remained to rise above the boy he was to the sort of man a woman like Scarlet Farrow could appreciate. If he could accomplish that, those painful memories might not sting as much as they once did, because if she saw something strong and noble in him, he might actually be able to recognize such qualities in himself.

He forced his voice to deepen, speaking in a tone lower than his usual octave. "What did you feel the moment you were spotted at that party? Do you remember?"

She didn't answer right away and he was establishing Scarlet Farrow was a woman who chose her words with careful consideration. "Excitement. Adrenaline. It wasn't like they would've hurt us, but there was definitely fear of being caught, which we sort of were. It was... a rush."

"You like being seen," he provided, recalling her confession about feeling invisible.

"Sometimes. I think everyone goes through embarrassing moments they wish no one else saw."

"Indeed. Tell me a memory when you felt embarrassed."

The soft sound of her breath caressing the phone met his ear. "I tripped the day I interviewed at the school. I can be such a klutz at times. I'd just finished my interview with the board and packed up my portfolio. I thought everything, up until that moment, went well. As I was leaving my shoe caught on nothing at all and I went down with a bang."

"Describe the feeling."

"Well, there was the sensation of my knees crashing into the floor."

"But that's not what hurt."

"No," she said quietly.

"Tell me the emotions. Describe how they affected your body and mind."

"My heart stopped, only for a second, but when it started again it did so with a punch strong enough to knock the wind out of me and flood my blood with adrenaline."

"Did you shake?"

"Yes, more so in the minutes that followed."

He'd had that sensation many times. "That's your survival skills kicking your pain receptors into overdrive. It's a coping mechanism our bodies reflexively trigger when the brain experiences fear."

She laughed it off. "I don't know why we react like that. Everyone trips from time to time—me more than most."

He didn't want her to minimize it. It was important they address her vulnerabilities, imperative he understand how her mind processed her shortcomings, in order to better grasp her interpretation of self. "Perhaps it isn't about the cause, but the effect."

"Well, yeah. I was on an interview. I was hoping to make the best impression and I ended up humiliating myself like a clod."

"Do you blush, Ms. Farrow? I imagine with your fair skin and red hair your pigment can be quite telling of your emotions."

"Oh, yeah. I blush, get hives when I cry, burn in the sun, it's all part of the joys of being a redhead."

"I find your coloring exquisite."

Her voice turned small. "Thank you."

"You're welcome. There's a paradoxical component to embarrassment. While there's the reaction our body has in situations like the one you just described, there's also similar sensations triggered by positive attention. Our physical reactions mimic those of dreaded exposure; only the shame of failing social expectation is replaced with the pleasure of meeting it. Our bodies show the same symptoms, such as blushing and accelerated heart rate, yet we process them differently."

"Oh."

Simplifying his point, he went on. "Blushing's the release of hormones into the bloodstream. Adrenaline touches the nervous system, widening the capillaries touching the skin. Do you blush when you're aroused, Ms. Farrow?"

Her laugh was soft and nervous. "I'm probably blushing now."

He eased back on his bed, his body tightening with desire as he imagined her doing the same. "Do words relating to sex embarrass you?"

"I don't think so. Not really." Yet a nervous laugh escaped her anyway.

His hand rested on his belly, unconsciously traveling lower as he whispered, "Sometimes we aren't fully aware of our internal reactions and the emotions that stimulate them. I imagine discussing sex does embarrass you on some level. Thus your blushing. Sex equates to exposure. Exposure equals fear, which releases adrenaline, and thereby causes the capillaries in your cheeks to dilate." There was no denying the effect the conversation was having on him. Realizing he was on the cusp of touching himself, he redirected his hand, trapping it under his head. "Would you agree?"

"Yes."

He grinned. By her voice it was clear he was setting her off balance. "So the question remains, is sex something that triggers a pleasant form of embarrassment or an unpleasant one?"

"Well, I'm not frigid. I find sex pleasant."

He noted his own physical symptoms. "Is your heart beating fast, Ms. Farrow?"

Her shallow breaths rasped against the phone. "Yes."

"Why do you think that is?"

"I don't know."

"Do you still feel invisible?"

"No."

A grin slowly spread over his lips as his eyes closed at the small victory. He was doing this. He was actually speaking to Scarlet Farrow and—*perhaps*—arousing her. He continued to push. "Would you say you feel exposed?"

"Yes."

"And yet we're merely having a discussion about physiology." He paused for a moment, allowing her to savor the effect of their discussion. "Pour yourself a glass of wine, Scarlet."

She laughed. "I've recently given up drinking."

"Only as a way to protect yourself from divulging too much personal information. One glass will calm you down without threatening your defenses."

His chest swelled with satisfaction at the rustling of movement. Never had he imagined he could dictate to a woman in such a manner, yet so long as he kept his voice calm and even, she followed every command. It was intoxicating. Such an intangible implication of power seemed to satisfy a need deep inside of him he hadn't realized he possessed. The more she filled the void, the more aware he became of the hollowness he'd learned to ignore. Suffice it to say, he liked being in control very much.

He chuckled as the pop of a cork sounded. "Assuming you still have wine in your home, I gather your vow of sobriety wasn't intended for the long haul."

Her laugh was a throaty melody, rich with of

amusement. "I guess not. There's that pesky discipline you mentioned."

"Or lack thereof," he teased. The soft tinkling of liquid filling a glass carried over the line. "What are you drinking?"

"Merlot."

"Again, interesting that it was at the ready, not even needing a corkscrew from what I could hear."

She chuckled. "My convictions are weak in the face of my love for red wine."

He smiled, enjoying the light banter, and surprising himself when he impulsively gave into the playful teasing. "We'll have to work on that."

As if suddenly realizing he was enjoying himself too much, he sobered. It was too easy to feel tenderly for her, those apparently hibernating emotions announcing themselves with an all too recognizable familiarity. But he needed to protect himself. It was time to say goodnight.

"Before I say goodnight, I want you to do something for me." She didn't object so he went on. "I want you to contemplate your desire to no longer be invisible. Truly weigh what it is you're asking. Being seen, exposing vulnerable parts of oneself, can often provoke unprecedented emotions. Be careful what you wish for, Ms. Farrow."

"Okay." Her agreement came without pause. "I enjoyed talking with you tonight."

"I enjoyed myself as well. I'll call you tomorrow evening at the same time."

He didn't want to end their discussion, but in all his research he'd learned that the moment a romantic situation became predictable, the spell was broken. He needed to keep her guessing in order to keep her interested. "Goodnight, Ms. Farrow."

"Goodnight, Mr. Stone."

He disconnected the call and collapsed back on the bed releasing a long held breath. "Holy. Shit." He'd done it. He'd actually talked to her and somehow managed to draw her interest. He couldn't wait to tell the guys.

5

DISCIPLINE

"No pain no gain, Asher. Move it."

"I fucking hate you," he hissed, oxygen pumping through his burning lungs like fire.

Steve chuckled. "You wanted this." The incline of the treadmill elevated as Steve reached over and increased the speed. "No one said beauty was painless."

Sweat burned his eyes behind his glasses as he mopped his brow with the back of his hand. His shirt drooped off his frame, saturated with perspiration. They'd been at it since six in the morning. Two hours later and he was amazed he still stood.

His legs were jelly and his fingers tingled from exertion. The day started with a warm up, thirty minutes on the elliptical. From there they hit the weight bench and worked the upper body. Asher tried not to think about what other men his age could lift. He was slowly building up his strength and endurance, personifying the quintessential hare that would win the race.

"One more mile."

Sure, one more mile, then his mid-morning meal,

a short respite, and onto laps in the pool. When he asked Steve to totally redefine his physique, he hadn't quite considered the pain that would come with such an undertaking.

Having read numerous shapeshifter novels, his mind dwelled on the descriptions of bones snapping, ligaments popping, fluid muscles unraveling, until the body transformed into something animal. No author ever described it as painless, and he was certainly experiencing his fair share of agony.

"So," Steve said, balancing an elbow at the head of the machine. "I noticed you have a lot of romance novels laying around. Is that like a thing you're into?"

His body and mind were too tired to register embarrassment. "I'm doing some research," he panted.

"That's cool. On what?"

"Women. It's sort of an experiment. This is all part of it." Jesus, his legs were gonna fall off.

Several times he'd considered giving up, but he'd never been one to back down from what he wanted—except with Scarlet, that is, but even then he'd gone after what he desired as avidly as he knew how. Too many times in life he'd been made to feel he wasn't good enough, and had his physical limitations thrown in his face. He was sick of it.

Growling with renewed determination, he grit his teeth and ran harder. Heat bathed his knees as he trudged on, the heavy footfalls over the racing band of the treadmill echoing through the exercise room.

Only half a mile left. Then would come the high of having pushed himself a little further and a little harder than the day before. Slowly, but surely, he was improving.

It might not seem like much to outsiders, but he

could already sense a difference. The running was probably the easiest. Those damn mountain climber lunges Steve had him do yesterday, though...they were enough to drive a man insane.

Every time his trainer demanded he drop into another burpee, Asher wanted to punch the guy right in the dick. He would have, too, if Steve wasn't three times the size of him and capable of killing him with a flick.

He was tired of being weak. It was time to be strong. Maybe not as strong as Steve, but he'd settle for an early Peter Parker post-bite build. Bruce Wayne would be his next goal. The dream was Wolverine, but he had to keep things realistic.

The pace of the treadmill chugged and slowed as his cool down started. Sweat poured out of him as he slowly caught his breath. Steve was there, handing him a bottle of water, which he demolished in seconds flat.

It turned out Steve was a decent guy. Asher was happy he hired him. He pushed him harder than anyone ever had, but when they weren't working out and simply speaking, Steve was a nice person to talk to.

It was a strange relationship. For as in awe as he was of the other man's physique, Steve was equally in awe of Asher's success.

He asked lots of questions and confessed to finding Asher's story inspirational, which gave him total confidence that Asher could successfully redefine his physical form. That helped because there were definitely moments Asher thought he was attempting the impossible.

The machine beeped. "Awesome job, Ash. Take a load off."

Asher stumbled off the machine and collapsed on the matted floor. His chest heaved with each enormous draught of breath. Steve wiped down the machine and tossed him a towel to mop up his sweat.

"Ash?"

At the sound of company Asher mumbled gibberish. His brain was as fried as his body. "He's down here," Steve answered, laughing.

Elliot entered the gym. "Holy crap. What did you do with all your stuff?"

Lifting a hand and letting it fall weakly to the floor, he whimpered and pointed like a cadaver in the direction of the closet. Elliot frowned at him then asked Steve, "Is he all right?"

"He's fine. He's just being dramatic. I'm gonna go see about getting you some food. You want me to tell Carla to set it up in the dining room?"

"Yeah." It was too difficult to speak in complete sentences.

Steve left them alone and Elliot awkwardly sat on the seat of the butterfly press. "Where'd you get all this stuff?"

Asher unscrewed the new bottle of water Steve left and took a swig. Easing into a seated position he faced his friend. "I had Steve order it."

Elliot laughed. "I can't believe you're actually going through with this. Seems a little extreme."

Maybe it was, but it was also necessary. "Don't you ever get tired of it?"

"Of what?" Elliot asked.

"The looks, the sense that we don't count as much as everyone else."

Elliot's face twisted with disagreement. "No. Who are we supposed to be like? Those idiots on reality TV everyone's obsessed with? Look at the people being idolized by society, Ash. I'd rather be me."

"You say that because you've never been given the opportunity to be someone else."

"No, I say that because I don't care what other people think. I put on a tie every day because I like to. I don't do those things to meet some standard. I own my own company. I could come to work in footy pajamas if I wanted to."

"Please tell me you don't still wear footy pajamas."

"Whatever. Your mom buys your underwear."

"She does not!" He'd put a stop to that. He just hadn't told her yet. "I have a stylist coming by this week. You and Hunter should come over, get yourself some new ties."

"Maybe. You're investing an awful lot into a plan that might not even get off the ground. Who says she'll even talk to you?"

He grinned. "I do. I talked to her last night."

Elliot's eyes went wide behind his glasses. "You did? Where? How?"

Wincing, he pushed himself off the ground. His limbs throbbed, but the pain was giving way to a pleasurable burn. "On the phone. Her number was listed on her GP profile."

"What did she say?"

He shrugged and chucked his water bottle in the recycling. "Come eat."

Elliot followed him out of the gym and through the house. "I don't understand. You just called her?"

"Yup. We talked a little bit online first, but that was getting old."

"What...what's she like? I mean, now that she's older."

He peeked over his shoulder, assessing his friend. There was hope in his expression that wasn't there two minutes ago. No matter how much he denied it, Asher knew Elliot's life was lonely hell. There was no need to beat a dead horse. He'd raise the bar for all of them. Elliot would eventually appreciate Asher's hard work, especially if it proved women weren't always their kryptonite.

They were all lonely and—aside from Jet—overdue to get laid. But prior to his finding out about Scarlet, those topics were off limits, even with his closest friends. Elliot did a good job at pretending in-difference, and Asher could sympathize with his fear of the opposite sex. He didn't harp on the subject, because too much attention given to his friend's non-existent love life could make Elliot snap.

All of their lives people had doubted their abilities. If not for having such supportive parents, none of them would have believed in themselves.

There were plenty of people in their past that swore they'd never amount to anything, but they proved them wrong and accomplished the impossible. While people accepted the world as it was and close mindedly refused to imagine anything better, he, Hunter, and Elliot invented the next best thing.

How was improving his body and health any different?

They settled in at the table where Carla, his personal chef, had laid out a spread of fruit, eggs, and protein shakes. Asher answered Elliot's question. "She was normal, I guess. More mature, kind of vulnerable."

"What did you talk about?"

Asher smiled, thinking back on their conversation. "School, believe it or not."

Elliot's eyes, again, widened. "Does she know who you are?"

"No. I told her my name's Mr. Stone."

"*Mr.* Stone? No first name?"

He shrugged. "It wasn't necessary."

"Sounds a little impersonal. How did you talk about school without her figuring out who you were?"

He swallowed a bite of eggs. "I asked questions, she talked. I didn't mention that we attended the same high school." He chuckled. "Remember the beaver head in the locker room? Her and her friend stole it."

"Seriously?"

He laughed. "Yeah, totally by accident, but yeah."

"Man, high school must've been a completely different experience for people like her."

"You aren't kidding. She described it as fun."

Elliot snorted. "Definitely different. You know, I heard Westerman lost his job at the steel mill."

"Good." Asher typically didn't wish people to fall on hard times. Devon, although a foe from their past, had actually become somewhat of a friend over the years. But Bobby Westerman was different. He'd tortured every single one of them and made their lives a living hell. Not to mention he'd dated Scarlet, something he still couldn't fathom. Every time he imagined their dates, Asher lost his appetite, so he didn't entertain such imagery now.

As they ate, he told Elliot a bit more about his discussion the night before, but kept a good amount of personal detail out of his synopsis. For some reason, he felt the need to protect her confessions.

After brunch, Elliot left. Asher wished he could convince him to share some of the modifications he was making in his own personal life. It was work, but it was the kind of work that came with great personal rewards, things money couldn't buy, like confidence and pride.

Maybe his friend needed to see that the physical transformation was possible first. If that were the case, Ash would gladly be the prototype. He wanted to be happy with himself, but he also wanted that same level of contentment for his friends.

Who knew? Maybe after this whole thing with Scarlet was over, he'd actually be secure enough to attempt dating someone in a traditional sense. He'd always wanted a family and children, but most of the women he met were either way out of his league or too weird for even him. Time would tell, but he certainly was experiencing the dawn of a new hope.

Cue *Star Wars* score.

"*T*ell me something from your childhood that changed you."

Her voice was soft and he imagined her reclining on a bed or a sofa. They'd been on the phone for over an hour and Asher's heart hadn't slowed down once. He was quickly becoming addicted to the excitement that preceded everything she said.

"When I was in high school I dated someone who wasn't very nice. I don't know why I went with him, but I did. Peer pressure I guess. We dated on and off throughout my senior year, mostly for dances and stuff. I don't think I was ever the same after dating him."

His mind immediately recalled Westerman, his arm draped around Scarlet's freckled shoulders peeking from her purple homecoming dress. "What did he do that made him not nice?"

She sighed, the sound soft and seemingly tired. "He was a jerk, always obnoxious and garish. I hung around with a lot of athletes, so no one was really quiet, but he never quit with the high energy. He was also a big guy, so he had no problem demanding everyone's full attention."

It had to be Bobby. "Was he ever not nice to *you*?"

"Sometimes." Pressure built in his chest as he awaited her answer, a true glimpse of the girl he loved many years ago.

He wasn't sure which side of the coin he favored. So many times she'd stood there, allowing Westerman to humiliate him. Perhaps she'd earned a share of his cruelty because she allowed it to continue, even when he'd taken things too far—far enough to cause a seventeen year old to piss his pants, far enough to disgrace them until they begged with tears in their eyes. All while she simply stood there.

But to imagine Scarlet being victimized by that same tyrant filled him with a sort of impotent rage. She was a girl. It was one thing for Westerman to brutalize them, but not her. Never her. He couldn't understand *why* Westerman would be mean to her. She was his girlfriend and better than he ever deserved.

Because some people are just bad people.

Trying not to lose himself in unpleasant flashbacks, he whispered, "How did dating him change you?"

"I lost my virginity to him."

Whoa. All recollections stopped as he gave her his full attention. Scarlet. Scarlet Farrow having sex. All good images. Scarlet Farrow having sex with Bobby Westerman. Oh, dear God, no. He cleared his mind. "Was he a disappointment in that aspect?" *Please say yes.*

She laughed, but without humor. "I think he was exactly what I should have anticipated."

What did that mean? She'd dated him, so there had to be some redeeming qualities to the guy that Asher and the rest of the world had missed. "What do you remember feeling, emotionally speaking?"

"Scared."

His stomach plummeted and his jaw went slack. Her confession was raw, her disquiet contagious. "Why scared?"

"I always assumed we'd eventually do it. I just didn't expect it to be that night. I wasn't ready, but that didn't seem to matter to him."

Oh, God. Why had she ever involved herself with that asshole? "Did you tell him no?"

"Not the way I should have. We were at our senior homecoming dance."

The story suddenly turned personal. He recalled exactly what she was wearing, even how she had her hair.

"All night he'd been acting a little more possessive than usual. After the dance we went to the cliffs to drink with some friends and I ended up in the back-seat of his car. I remember thinking it wasn't supposed to happen that way, in a car with our friends only a few feet away. I didn't want to make a scene, so I wasn't really firm when I told him to slow down."

His stomach hurt, unexpected nausea forcing him to breathe through his mouth. Imagining that sweaty animal touching her was grotesque. "Did he hurt you?" He wanted to ask if she remembered anything from earlier in the night, but this was more significant.

She laughed, the sound hollow and cold. "*It* hurt. It was my first time and we weren't in the most comfortable place. But most of the pain came afterward. When he was done, my dress, that I had so painstakingly chosen, was wrinkled and split at the seam. He left the car as soon as he'd finished and I could hear him bragging to everyone. I just sat there and cried for the rest of the night. Never once did he come check on me. I felt so used and the worst part was..."

He'd warned her. He'd told her Westerman was only using her. The culmination of his prophecy brought no comfort in the end. He hated knowing she'd been hurt, which was exactly why he had warned her in the first place. "I'm sorry, Scarlet." She'd never know how true his sentiment was in that moment.

She drew in an audible breath and released it slowly on what sounded like a cleansing sigh. "It was a long time ago." He gave her a moment to recover. "Wow. I haven't thought about that night in years."

"Some days are just all around bad." That day had been a defining nightmare for him as well. "Why didn't you—" His words abruptly cut off as he'd almost slipped. Rephrasing his question, he said, "Did you break up with him?" He knew full well she hadn't, but wanted to know why.

"Yes."

He frowned. That was a lie.

But then she said, "It didn't stick. We were always

with the same friends and he'd never let anyone else speak to me. If he saw another guy flirt with me, he... It just wasn't worth it."

Asher swallowed, never imagining she might have been with him against her will. "I assume there were other times. Did it get better?"

"No. Sometimes it got worse. Graduating was my only escape. Sometimes I think back to how much I endured and I wonder how I did it." She was quiet for a moment. "Are you still there?"

"Yeah. Sorry. I was...thinking." He'd been so wrong. His perspective was suddenly skewed in a way he couldn't grasp.

She distracted him again as she said, "Tell me a moment from your childhood that changed you."

Jarred by her request, he took a moment to regroup. She'd earned some of his empathy, which was unexpected. Having no intention of sharing his personal business, he quickly scrambled for a defining moment in his life, searching for one that could be generalized without giving away too much.

"My mother had breast cancer."

"Oh, I'm so sorry."

Her compassion tempted softer emotions, but failed. It had been a terrible time for all of them. "I've always been extremely close to my mother." *Still am.* "When she was diagnosed I thought my world would end."

"That's terrible."

He nodded, even though she couldn't see him. Swallowing, he confessed, "I didn't have a lot of friends growing up, but my mom always acted like they were waiting just around the corner. No matter my shortcomings, she'd always assured me things would get better. She always believed that too. She was my best friend for most of my childhood. Every dream I had, I never had to worry that she might mock me for it. She was always right there, supporting my goals."

"She sounds like an incredible mom."

"She is." Stifling the surge of relevance, he said, "It took her three years, but she eventually beat it. She had a mastectomy and came back like a prizefighter. She's incredible."

"How did your dad handle it?"

His dad was incredible too. "It was difficult. We all feared losing her. He stuck by her side and never lost faith she'd overcome that just like she overcame every other challenge dropped at her door. You'd never know she had a mastectomy. She'd lost her hair, her breasts, and half her body weight, but to us she was always beautiful."

"Wow. I can't imagine being loved so unconditionally."

They fell into a weighted silence. He was losing himself. Asher was surfacing when he should be performing as the impenetrable Mr. Stone. He turned the conversation back on her. "Did your parents have a pleasant marriage?"

"Yes, but nothing like that. My parents aren't very expressive when it comes to affection. I don't think I've ever even seen them kiss."

"Really?"

She laughed. "Yeah. It's kind of sad. I mean, they love each other, but with a quiet commitment instead of a lurid passion. I've never seen them fight either, that I can remember. They've always been sort of private, I guess."

Things were getting very comfortable. The progression of their relationship was moving faster than he'd expected. Things either had to slow down or he needed a back up plan, because she wasn't the only one getting lost in their connection.

"Would you like to grab a drink this week?" she surprised him by asking. "I mean... we don't have to. I don't want to rush things. It's just... I feel—"

"Scarlet." He said her name because she sounded flustered. "Take a breath." The sound of her drawing air into her lungs echoed softly over the line.

"Sorry. I just thought...I'm really enjoying talking to you."

God, me too. Maybe too much. "I'm enjoying it as well, Ms. Farrow, but I'm not sure we're there yet." He needed to protect himself.

"Oh."

Her evident disappointment filled him with regret, but he had to play this smart. She couldn't discover who he was, especially after talking so much about a school they'd both attended. It would be a betrayal of trust for her to figure out who he was, something he wasn't sure he wanted her to know, but the temptation was there, begging for him to have faith in their chemistry and come clean. Yet, he lacked the courage, fearing her reincarnated rejection. "We'll give it a little more time."

"Okay. That's probably wise."

Smart or stupid, he needed more time. Her willingness to meet him was a shock. He never earned this sort of reaction from women. He needed to think. "I'm going to say goodnight now."

"Is...is it because I asked you out?"

Was she insane? He kept his tone even. "No. It's because we've spent a lot of time discussing some heavy topics and I think we should both sleep. I'll call you in the morning around nine."

"Okay." Her voice was tinged with relief. "Oh, wait. I have work."

"What time do you get home?"

"Four."

"I'll call you at four-thirty."

"Okay." He detected a smile in her voice.

"Goodnight, Ms. Farrow."

"Goodnight, Mr. Stone."

Ending the call he fell back on his bed. How the hell was he going to meet her when he was still the lightweight waif he'd always been? She'd recognize him—unless that was putting too much emphasis on the impression he'd left over a decade ago. Still, he knew enough about women to know that his appearance was lacking, especially in the light of her beauty.

Steve was doing the best he could. Monday was the appointment with the stylist, but new attire and a fresh haircut wouldn't be enough to transform him from geek to god.

He glanced down at his shirt. It had the binomial theorem printed on it. Dear lord, he was a mess.

6

ANTICIPATION

ASHER DECIDED it was time to see Scarlet. However, he still wasn't ready for her to *see* him. He'd laid out a fair plan and the truth was she would either go for it or tell him to get lost.

He didn't want to end their relationship, but he had nothing if he didn't maintain control. After further research, and compiling an ongoing list of traits he hoped to portray, an idea took shape.

First, he always said goodbye before she had the chance. This added to the mystique and left her curious. When they spoke it was according to his decision. Telling her when to expect him stimulated anticipation. Anticipation was one element her letter claimed she was lacking in her day-to-day life.

So far, she hadn't objected to any of his stipulations. On the contrary, she seemed to get a thrill from the formal way they interacted under his direction.

When he spoke, he always kept his voice low and even as if he were softly speaking in an ancient language that required her full attention. It was quite different from the way he casually spoke among friends. But he always had her attention.

Scarlet wasn't the only one benefiting from their relationship. Asher was discovering sides to himself he'd never anticipated, sides he truly enjoyed. Every interaction boosted his confidence. He was clearly being stimulated by their relationship as much as her.

He gave her his undivided attention and she reciprocated, hanging on his every word. It was euphoric having the woman he spent the first half of his life idolizing suddenly under an enchanted spell. But what was most enchanting was that she honestly seemed interested in him. Sometimes he even made her laugh, not at him, but with him.

Prior to this, he didn't have spells. He didn't have moves. And he certainly didn't have mojo. But all of these things, he discovered, were teachable and he was aptly learning how to play a game that always intimidated him—a game that now provoked darker yearnings for tendencies he never considered unearthing or even knew existed within his psyche.

If they were to meet, it had to be on his terms. Monday, he contacted his realtor about a property just outside of the city. It was important they had a secluded place to get acquainted that was within reasonable driving distance.

The mansion wasn't necessarily his style, being he favored more simplistic ergonomic designs with clean lines and functional layouts. However, it had potential.

Boasting four floors, a dozen bedrooms and two towers, the old stone house could definitely be an asset at some stage of his life. The windows were original, complete with metal glasswork and custom made hardware. It was drafty, but had a plethora of working fireplaces.

The white elephant had been on the market for years, and the realtor was more than eager to answer questions about the property. In the end, Asher signed the deed for a steal. He could have simply taken her to dinner, but that wasn't how he operated. Besides, he had other conditions that needed to be met.

Once the house was his, the place was overflowing with contractors. He had a very small window of opportunity to get things accomplished if this was where their first meeting would be, so Asher used every resource at his disposal to get the job done as quickly as possible.

A maid service scoured the mansion from attic to basement. Chimney sweeps cleaned every vent and inspected every flue. Wood was delivered and stacked neatly by each hearth. An interior designer named Sven, recommended by his stylist, was responsible for furnishing the entry, ballroom, and lower bathrooms.

The other rooms were of no concern. Should they need them, he'd make arrangements to have them dressed appropriately. For now, they had a space to use. What started less than two weeks ago now seemed a firm investment. He wasn't sure what would come of his time with Scarlet, but he'd basically purchased the mansion for one purpose—her. His friends were convinced he'd lost his mind.

While he'd been working on the house, he remained in contact with her, but careful not to let his control slip. She didn't ask him out again and he wondered if she was embarrassed because he'd said no the first time. He didn't want his response to discourage her, so he reassured her they would meet soon. This seemed to please her.

As he pulled into the rounded driveway of the mansion, he grimaced at the work still needing to be done. The flowerbeds were horrendously overgrown and in serious need of some new shrubberies, but this wasn't the time of year to plant. Reaching in his pocket, he removed his key, and took the ten steps to the entrance.

Two double doors stood the height of two men. A truck pulled in behind his car and he waved at Bruce, the contractor. As his key clicked in the lock the door let out an ominous howl.

"Mr. Roan," Bruce greeted as he climbed the porch, his large build filling out his denim shirt.

"Hi, Bruce. Call me Ash." The contractor nodded and Asher gave the knob another turn, frowning at the whining hinges. "Can something be done about this squeaking?"

Bruce produced a clipboard from under his arm. "That's why I'm here. We'll do a walkthrough and I'll make note of all your concerns. When we're done inspecting the grounds, I'll send out my guys with a prioritized list."

Asher nodded, pleased with his sense of urgency to get the mansion up and running as soon as possible. "Eventually I'll need a landscaper, but that can wait until the weather breaks."

"I have a few contacts I can recommend."

They entered the foyer. The fireplaces were unlit so there was a chill to the open space. There were two wingback chairs and a small table at the foot of the twin staircases. The floors were polished and he was pleased with the progress his staff had made.

"I'd like to order a water cooler. I'd also like a fridge brought in."

"For the service kitchen or the master kitchen, sir?"

"Neither. I want it right here in the foyer for now. I assume you'll have to fiddle with the electric. The fridge will be an insulated cabinet with a humidifier used for wine. Will you need to see the model?" Money came with eccentricity outsiders tended to easily accept.

"It should have the same standard wiring requirements. I'll check with the supplier once you have a model picked."

They entered the ballroom. Asher smiled nervously as Bruce's eyebrow lifted at the sight of a massive four-poster bed in the center. Grand fireplaces, tall enough to fit five men, anchored two of the four walls.

"Both fireplaces passed inspection?" He asked.

"Yes, sir."

Another seating area filled the empty space. A tall armoire stood against the far wall. He'd be placing necessities there. Taking a moment for himself, he approached the bed.

The coverlet was lush, nothing like the one on his bed at home. He'd purchased new furniture when he bought his house, but his home was filled with personal touches and items his mother had suggested. He never gave much thought to beauty, always putting comfort first, but this was definitely a stunning bed.

His throat tightened at the possibilities. Scarlet Farrow might someday rest here.

The inspection continued for over an hour. As the contractor pulled away, he held a list of last minute details needing to be addressed. Asher settled into a chair in the ballroom, his stomach tight, and his breathing restricted.

He was actually doing this.

Once the restoration of the old home was under-way, he'd found himself distracted. Things had moved quickly and in that sudden moment of silence, where all details seemed complete, reality sank in for the first time.

If she agreed to see him—a big *if*—she would come here and they'd start the second phase of their relationship. His mind drifted over his experiences with women, voiding out every horrible encounter from his earlier years and remembering those rushed and surprising moments of his adulthood.

There had been his first, a young woman by the name of Crystal. It was at her house and no matter how much she'd tried to convince Asher her feelings were sincere, the disappointment in her eyes had proved he was a regretful trade off for the money he possessed.

After Crystal he'd become a bit more guarded. From time to time he'd invited a curious female back to his hotel room while on business trips. Suits worn for meetings usually disguised his unimpressive body more than street clothes. They were more generic, making it easier to speak to strangers.

All in all, there had been three women. He'd like to think the last was the least embarrassing. But nothing took away the nervousness he always experienced while dealing with the opposite sex. How would he ever deal with Scarlet?

There was so much emphasis tied to her. She epit-omized his shortcomings and was a bank of painful memories, yet she also represented his greatest desires. The pressure to perform with other women was nothing in regards to her.

Breathing in a deep, calming breath, he forced himself to relax. So long as he continued with the pattern they'd started, everything would work out. Who knew how intimate they'd become?

His objective was to show her everything she'd wanted—be everything she needed—if that was at all possible, he'd be more surprised than anyone. His intentions were blurred. She clearly had something invested in them, leaving her vulnerable in some immeasurable way. If she proved to be the girl he hated, he wouldn't hesitate to vanish. But deep down he was strongly starting to hope she'd prove to be the girl he loved.

That was the terrifying truth he'd yet to share with his friends. God forbid she scorn him again. Keeping his evolving emotions to himself would ensure any pain would remain private as well.

Swallowing hard, he glanced one last time around the room. He could do this. He just had to keep his calm and not lose his head. Hopefully, all his careful planning would aid him when it came time to encounter her face to face. His greatest undoing rested in those enchanting eyes. He needed to make sure she saw something in him before she actually saw him.

"Tell me about a time you were proud of yourself."

Scarlet savored the rush of excitement that filled her as she settled onto her bed and welcomed the long awaited sound of his voice. Their nightly conversations had become something she looked forward to, anticipated with intoxicating excitement, and when they finally started she became drunk with a sort of steady euphoria.

Her voice was low and relaxed. "Hmm... I'd have to think about that one."

"Are there not a lot of proud moments in your life?"

"No, there are. I could tell you the generic ones, graduation, honor roll, buying my house, but I don't think that's what you're after."

"Correct."

She sighed, her mind drifting over a flow of pleasant memories as she tried to select the perfect one to share. "I have it."

"Tell me."

She swallowed. "I teach sixth grade and a lot of my kids are considered remedial. At this point, they've unfortunately been labeled, not just in their paperwork, but by their peers, and even some of the faculty. There was this one student a few years back. His name was Justin.

"He wasn't a bad kid, but he always seemed to find himself right in the middle of trouble and, because he was tall and broody, a lot of times he was blamed for things he didn't orchestrate. After a while his attitude deteriorated, because even when he made the right choices, he somehow always had to answer for everyone else's misbehavior."

Mr. Stone let her set the background for her anecdote and patiently waited for her to make her point. She loved the rhythm of their discussions. It was different from the way most people conversed, always racing to assume the moral of a story before the narrator had the chance to deliver. Their slow paced dialogue was pleasantly refreshing.

"When Justin was in my class, he started flunking. His answers were there, but so outrageous I knew he wasn't even trying. I spoke to my team about my concerns. Justin was a bright kid and he shouldn't have been struggling with the material to that degree. None of my team teachers seemed to care, assuming it was expected from such a kid. I knew if I was going to get to the bottom of his behavior I had to do it myself.

"One day, we had a test. The students were all gone for the day and I stayed after to grade the essays. The class did all right, until I got to Justin's. His test was completely blank. I couldn't sleep that night, wondering how such a bright kid could simply give up. I hate how cruel life can be at that age for children. My greatest fear was that Justin had heard enough people's assumptions, and decided to give them exactly what they expected of him—nothing.

"I refused to believe that was all he had in him. The next day I asked him to stay after class. I showed him his paper and tried to remove all assumption from my expression. I asked him to tell me why he didn't try."

"What was his excuse?"

Her eyes closed, recalling that moment so clearly. "He said, 'Ms. Farrow, I haven't had breakfast. Last night I didn't eat dinner. Aside from a few chips, I haven't eaten in days. I'm so hungry, I don't give a fuck about this test.' Some teachers would have penalized him for his language, but I saw his hunger the moment he made the confession.

"I went to my desk, opened my lunch, and gave him my sandwich. He hesitated only a minute before devouring it. I gave him my juice and grapes and went to the vending machine to buy a Tasty Cake for dessert. I told him to come to my room every morning."

"Did he?"

"Yes, it became customary for us to share breakfast. After breakfast I'd hand him a brown-bagged lunch, just like mine, but with an extra snack since he was a growing boy."

It was nice, recalling her kind deed. Rewarding. Telling the story made her appreciate herself in a way she sometimes lost sight of in her normal day-to-day life.

Smiling, she explained, "You see, our job is to teach, but students aren't always prepared to learn. Sometimes we're the ones who have to learn a new approach. I may not be the best teacher, but I think those moments with Justin made me a damn good one. We learn from example and I think I showed him —an already jaded thirteen-year-old kid—what compassion is. He's in college now and earned a pretty great scholarship."

"That's a lovely story, Ms. Farrow."

It was one of her favorites.

"Did your team ever learn what you were doing?"

"No. Out of respect for Justin, I kept his situation between us, only letting my principal know so that he could advise the parents about student aide."

"Interesting. Many times people are motivated to do good deeds because of the impression it leaves."

"I just wanted to help him. I wasn't looking to impress anyone."

"Very nice."

They continued talking, always with her lingering

hope that Mr. Stone would suggest they meet in person, but she lacked the courage to ask when. He'd tell her when he thought it was time and she liked that she could depend on his direction, seeing it was natural for him to lead.

Pressing for more than he wanted to give would be like asking for flowers. No one wanted flowers they'd asked for. She'd much rather receive such tokens as a true gesture of affection. She only wanted to see him if and when he truly wanted to see her. So when he announced his desire that night, she was slightly shocked and thrilled.

"I think it's time we take our relationship to the next level, Ms. Farrow."

Immediately breathless, she agreed, "Okay."

"I need you to understand a few things first. One, I'm a very private man. Two, this won't be like any other relationship you've had. I intend to give you exactly what you asked for and I plan on doing so on my terms. If you can't accept that, you need to say so now."

Her heart raced. "I respect your need for privacy."

"Can you agree to my terms?"

Shallow breaths filled her lungs. They'd moved ahead so cautiously, yet things also seemed to be moving fast. "You haven't asked anything too outlandish so far. I guess it depends what your terms are."

She swallowed, struggling to calmly wait out his reply.

"Next Friday I will have a driver come to your home and pick you up. He'll have instructions for you. At anytime should you feel uncomfortable, you will only need to say the word and you'll be safely returned home. I prefer to work with objectives, Ms. Farrow, and my objective is to show you what utter adoration feels like. Is that still what you seek?"

Her voice was a mere rasp, full of longing and curiosity. "Yes."

"Very good. I've decided we shall form a liaison of sorts, fourteen encounters spread over the course of our association. Never at any point will you be expected to tolerate anything outside of your comfort zone, but I do intend to push your limits, Ms. Farrow, in order for you to experience the full degree of desire. Still, everything will be consensual or it will cease immediately."

Her throat went dry. Already, without even having set eyes on this man, she desired him with an unaccustomed fierceness. "Why fourteen?" What happened after that?

Pausing for a moment, he spoke his answer quietly, again jarring her with his eloquent handling of language. "It takes fourteen days for the moon to wax enough for its beauty to be bared to the human eye. In astrology, fourteen is the number representative of temperance, the established quality of self-control needed to clearly resolve inner turmoil. Fourteen lines are in a sonnet. There's no one reason I chose fourteen, only that it seemed appropriate and suitable."

Everything about him was unexpected, and she wanted to see him with a yearning so potent it went beyond her previous definition of need. Swallowing in an attempt to quell her excitement and nerves, she whispered, "Okay."

"Very good. I won't be calling you over the next few days." Disappointment immediately flooded her. "If I need to reach you it will be through private message. I want you to take that time to think about where this is going, contemplate your desires, and commit to them. When you come to me I want you to be absolutely sure you're there of your own free will. Do you understand?"

She didn't like the idea of silence between them, but accepted his logic. "Yes." Her chest was tight with anticipation, which would only intensify as the days went on. The time between now and then would be cumbersome and torturous, every minute ticking by at the pace of a year. How would she survive until Friday?

Her mind was already made up. She was going to him, no matter what the risk. This was simply something she had to do.

"And, Ms. Farrow, I expect absolute discretion."

She could never explain Mr. Stone to her friends. "I promise."

"My rules, but you have the power to say when you've had enough."

"I understand."

"I look forward to seeing you Friday, Scarlet."

"Me too."

"Goodnight, Ms. Farrow."

Her stomach flipped with longing to move forward and the reluctance to say goodbye. She wanted the future to be now, but she'd first have to let go of the present in order to get there. That and shave her legs. "Goodnight, Mr. Stone."

The line went dead. Let the torture of anticipation begin.

7

———

SENSORY

Never in her life had Scarlet suffered such poignant anxiety. There was nothing, aside from a vortex of suspicion tangled with unprecedented excitement, swirling inside of her.

For days she'd been a ball of nervous energy. When the bell rang marking the end of the last class on Friday, she'd rushed to her car and was so restless to be in the final stretch of the week, she had to mentally force herself to regulate her breathing.

As soon as she got home there was a subtle sense of disappointment. She'd hoped he'd have called or messaged her by now, but there was nothing. Fear that he'd changed his mind was so encompassing she had to pour a glass of wine to calm her nerves.

As a distraction, she carefully went over her outfit for the evening, which she'd painstakingly selected two days prior, and then she took a shower.

There was no way she was sleeping with him. He was a stranger. Still, she took the most meticulous shower of her life.

Once every inch of skin was exfoliated and every unwanted hair removed, she let the last of the hot water soothe her tense muscles. Afterward, she carefully moisturized her body with a subtle apple scented lotion from Stelluna, a place she now frequented. It took every bit of self-control not to continuously check her phone and laptop to see if he'd contacted her. When she almost lost her last shred of restraint, she painted her nails, filling twenty extra minutes in order for the polish to dry.

Onto her second glass of wine, she fanned her hands while sitting on the edge of her bed in a bathrobe. That was when her computer finally chimed.

Her heart jolted as she lunged for the laptop. Shutting her eyes, she drew in a breath of relief as she opened the message.

> Good evening, Ms. Farrow. I assume your week went well. If we are still on for tonight, my driver requires your address.

This was it. Fully aware of the personal information she was about to divulge, she waited for her survival instincts to kick in. Nope. Nothing. She was definitely doing this.

. . .

I missed you.

She quickly deleted the confession, not wanting to come off too needy, but deleting those ten letters did nothing to alter the truth. She'd missed him like crazy this week. Her fingers quickly typed out a greeting and her address.

> My week went very well, although slower than I would have liked ☺
>
> My address is: 33 Rose Court, Floral Vale, PA

> Very well, Ms. Farrow. My driver will pick you up in one hour. You may address him as Mr. Pennyworth. I trust him completely, and therefore you may speak freely in his presence. Should you, at any time, wish to return home, Mr. Pennyworth will be at your command. Do you understand?

Mr. Pennyworth. Her brow tightened as the name sounded slightly familiar despite its uncommonness. This was crazy, but she wasn't backing out now.

Okay.

I will see you soon, Scarlet.

*S*he squealed and rolled onto her back, her hand pressing to her chest as her heart thundered behind her ribs. "Oh my God."

Her cheeks pulled tight with a smile as she forced out a deep breath of air. She needed to calm the hell down. Biting her lips she slowly stood, and then flew into overdrive, stripping her robe and dressing. Not wanting to make the wrong impression, she had opted for brown suede boots, fitted dark jeans, and a loose ivory sweater.

At first she'd considered dressing up, but this was *her* and she wanted Mr. Stone to meet the real her so he'd be more likely to divulge things about the real him. She had no idea if that would work, but it was the only plan she had.

There was no quelling her nerves. Moisture gathered on her palms down to the last second. Her stomach turned from jittery energy to painful tightness as the time passed.

She was going to vomit, but that was impossible since she hadn't been able to swallow a bite of food all day. The only thing in her stomach was wine and her body was burning off the effects too fast for it to matter.

When lights slowly cut down the dark street she gasped. "Oh God."

Her fingers trembled as she collected her purse and shut out the lights. Her shoulders knotted with tension. Never before had she wanted something to commence and conclude so much at the same time.

The car was a luxury sedan, black with tinted glass. Mr. Stone definitely wasn't living in the poorhouse—he'd said as much, but this was proof. Although it could be a rental.

Don't be cynical!

Stepping onto her porch, she pulled the door shut and locked it. A man—a very large man—stepped from the car and approached the sidewalk. "Ms. Farrow?"

"Yes."

"You can call me Mr. Pennyworth. I'm here to take you to Mr. Stone."

Of course she had to pee. She was nervous and whenever she got nervous her bladder turned into a peanut. Her footing turned unsteady under the heady realization that she was putting herself at risk.

Mr. Pennyworth held out a thick white envelope, sealed with a dab of wax. Holy crap. Who was she dealing with? Wax seals were categorized in her mind with *The Tudors* and mysterious characters in fiction.

"Mr. Stone requires you read this before moving any further."

The chauffeur's voice was calm and friendly, relieving a tiny bit of her anxiety. Taking the envelope in her trembling hands, she popped the seal. The note was written in dark calligraphy, but not the sort generated from a computer. This was definitely done by hand.

The choice is yours, Ms. Farrow. Should you choose to continue, it will be on my terms and your trust. If you consent, place the mask over your eyes and my chauffeur shall deliver you into my care. I hope to see you soon.

~Mr. Stone
A.R.

"He wants me to wear a blindfold?" And what was A.R.?

"I'm afraid so, Ms. Farrow." Mr. Pennyworth held out a strip of lace. It was lovely, delicate, but altogether concerning. Her fingers turned the mask, her gaze examining every detail. Although it was embellished with lace, there was a thick, soft fabric on the inside, assuring she'd be completely blind. Her throat constricted.

"Will I be able to take it off?"

"That's up to Mr. Stone. I was instructed to proceed only if you agree to wear the blindfold."

She swallowed. Okay, this was definitely unexpected. "Why?"

"You'd have to ask Mr. Stone."

She weighed her options. "Can you call him?"

"No, ma'am. You either place the mask over your eyes or I say goodnight."

Just like that? All or nothing? Stepping back, she quickly paced, wishing she had some sort of leverage. Her sly regard scrutinized the chauffeur. He was enormous, but had a sort of gentle set to his broad shoulders. As if he understood his size could be threatening, he hunched by the slightest degree so not to intimidate her more than he already had.

No one was forcing her. She could say goodnight and this would all be over. Mr. Stone would never contact her again and she'd go on living her uneventful, boring life.

Fuck.

"Would you mind giving me a moment? I forgot something inside."

"Of course."

He folded his hands at parade rest and she slowly backpedaled toward the house, trying not to appear too anxious. Her hands shook as she unlocked the door. The second she was inside with the door closed, she dropped her purse on the hall table, and dug out her phone.

Her thumb pressed speed dial and she rushed to the bathroom, quickly unbuttoning her jeans and dropping to the seat.

"Hello?"

"Nicole, listen, I'm in a hurry, but I need to ask you something."

"Yeah?" Her friends voice left Scarlet imagining her sitting at home on an otherwise uneventful night in the world of married life.

"Do I take risks?"

Nicole snorted. "Um, no. Not unless you consider getting your nails done in a color outside of the pink family risky."

"Do you think I should?"

"I don't know, Lettie. It depends. I don't want my best friend to jump out of a plane or anything dangerous, but I think baby stepping out of your bubble wouldn't hurt matters either. What's going on? And are you peeing?"

"Yes, sorry. I told you I was in a rush. Okay, here's the deal. I sort of met someone and I'm wildly attracted to him and he wants me to go back to his place—"

"Is he married?"

"No."

"Gay?"

"No."

"Have any noticeable symptoms of STDs?"

"Ew, no!" At least she hoped not.

"It's a fair question. Do you have condoms?"

"I'm not having sex with him!"

"Oh, well, then I guess it's fine. Who is he?"

"You don't know him."

"How'd you meet?"

She hiked up her jeans and wedged the phone between her shoulder and cheek as she washed her hands. "I don't have time for all of this right now. But listen, if you don't hear from me by two a.m. call the cops. Come to my house and all the information I have will be there."

"This is weird, Lettie. What the hell's going on?"

"I'm taking a risk and doing something for myself. I have to go. Two a.m., got it?"

"Not really. Scarlet—"

She ended the call. Her mind was made up. Dropping the phone back in her purse after silencing the ringer, she made a quick detour into her kitchen and flung open her knife drawer. Scrutinizing her supply, she selected a small but very sharp paring knife and slid it into her purse. She then left a note on the kitchen table.

> *Mr. Stone. Chauffeur's name is Mr. Pennyworth. This is the letter I have which may hold possible fingerprints. More info on my laptop IP page. Password: Thor_loves_bacon!*

She dropped the pen and wiped her hands down her jeans. Creeping to the front window, she dug out her phone and zoomed in on the license plate. The flash reflected off the glass, nearly blinding her, and when her sight came back Mr. Pennyworth was scowling in her general direction. "Shit. I suck at sneaky."

Go time.

Leaving the house again, she was relieved to find Mr. Pennyworth still waiting. Locking the door, she met him on the sidewalk and smiled nervously.

"Are you ready, Ms. Farrow?"

"Um, one more thing. Since I'm sort of putting my life on the line and all, do you think we could take a selfie, just an act of good will proving you're not going to drive me to an abandoned warehouse and chop me up into little bits?"

He chuckled. "Sure."

As he stepped beside her, she held out her phone. "Damn you're big."

"Let me." He took the phone and snapped the shot. It all seemed so normal when he handed it back and waited for her to examine it like women often did. "Good?"

"Perfect. Just let me send this to my wingman."

"Take your time."

She sent both pictures off to Nicole and her phone immediately vibrated with a responding text.

> Oh my GAWD, is that him? YES!! Go to his house and climb all over that mountain of muscle! And WTF is this other picture? It looks like a distorted reflection of your face and a car? Did you mean to send that?

*G*ood enough. She turned her phone off, knowing Nicole's questions could get relentless. Stuffing it in her bag, she nodded at Pennyworth. "Let's do this."

Again, he handed her the blindfold. She carefully pulled it over her eyes, blacking out the world. Her arms extended as she worked to tie it without pulling her hair. Once it was in place she was immediately disoriented.

Mr. Pennyworth placed a gentle hand on her upper arm. "I'll guide you to the car." It was strange, this man could have been Mr. Stone, but something told her he wasn't. Still, she noted his cologne to make sure. Lots of tricks could be played on a woman in a blindfold.

As the door clicked open she had the sudden thought Mr. Stone might be in the car. "Is there anyone else in the car?"

"No, ma'am. Just us."

She wasn't sure if that was a relief or made things worse.

"Watch your head, please."

Ha. Ha. She couldn't watch anything. She was freaking blind!

As though she were being fed into the backseat of a squad car, she unseeingly fondled her way over the soft leather seat. The door shut with a quiet click and the temptation to peek while she was alone intensified. Before she'd decided to take the opportunity, the front door opened and the car slightly shifted with the weight of the driver.

The front door shut and the sound of fabric brushing over leather met her ears. "If you reach your hands out in front of you, I left a bottle of water for you. Mr. Stone suggested you drink it to calm your nerves."

She reached out, finding Mr. Stone's thoughtfulness comforting, as though he were there with her. Cool plastic met her fingers as her hand closed over the offering. "Thank you."

"Do you think you can find the seatbelt on your own?"

Her mind was so overwhelmed she found his question incredibly difficult to answer. Gripping the water bottle between her knees, she patted around for the buckle and glided it over her chest. Her other hand located the cool latch as she directed the seatbelt into the hole. Mr. Pennyworth must have heard the click.

"Shall we?"

"Yes," she rasped, her belly turning as if the car were a roller coaster cart on the cusp of a drop off.

"If you want to return home at any time, just say the word, Ms. Farrow. I'm at your service."

"Thank you."

"Please keep the blindfold on or I'll have to turn the vehicle around, okay?"

"Yes."

The car slowly lurched forward and her stomach lurched and dropped. The soles of her feet tingled as they picked up speed. This was it. Retrieving the bottle from between her knees, she inspected the cap with her fingertips. It was difficult to tell if anyone had tampered with it.

Holding it close to her ear, she gave it a turn, the resistance of the seal broke with a snap as the tiny plastic teeth separated. Chances were the water wasn't rigged. Thank God because she was thirsty as hell. She was being extremely paranoid, but in a situation like this, who wouldn't be?

The plastic crunched as she chugged several deep swallows, sounding obnoxious and loud in the silence of the car. Maybe it only sounded loud to her because she was blindfolded and her other senses were heightened.

The car was the perfect temperature, not too cool and not too warm, though she'd started to sweat. The air held the scent of leather, Armor All, and traces of Mr. Pennyworth. The memory of the driver's appearance was already blurry and she regretted not taking a longer look at him before he drove her God knew where. Later on she'd go back to his picture and *really* study it.

Shit. She was sitting there playing with water and classifying the car rather than trying to track where they were going. Her body swayed with each carefully steered turn and her mind grew frustrated trying to decipher where they were headed.

Why was she being so quiet? Mr. Stone had said she could speak freely to Mr. Pennyworth. Deciding to take advantage of the opportunity, she sat forward. "Do you drive for a company or are you only Mr. Stone's chauffeur?"

She was surprised how easily he answered. "I only work for Mr. Stone, but this is the first time I've acted as his chauffeur."

"Oh. What do you normally do for him?" *Hit man? Thug? Hole digger?*

"I'm also his personal trainer."

"Oh." That made sense, since he was enormous. Also, Mr. Stone had mentioned having a trainer, so that added to his credibility.

She tried to figure out a way to politely phrase a question regarding Mr. Stone's appearance. "Do you train him often?"

"Three sessions a day."

Wow. Mr. Stone was likely as enormous as Mr. Pennyworth. She barely exercised. "Are we going to a restaurant?"

"I'm taking you to a private residence."

"Mr. Stone's?"

"One of them." *Interesting.*

"How far is it?"

"Not much farther. We should be there in about twenty minutes."

"Has Mr. Stone ever been married?"

"I'm afraid all questions regarding his personal life must be directed to him."

"Oh. Sorry."

"Not a problem. No harm in asking. I'll let you know if I'm unable to answer."

It was like twenty questions. She could get an answer—or at least some helpful information—if she phrased the question properly. "Does Mr. Stone usually have guests like this?"

"I can't disclose that information."

Damn it. She tried again. "Do you have any sisters or a wife or girlfriend?"

"I'm single right now. Why? You have friends?" He laughed. "I have a younger sister."

She licked her lips. "Can I ask you something?"

"You just did."

"Do you think I'm in danger? I've never done anything like this before. I'm a little out of my element."

He was quiet for only a few seconds, but it was enough of a pause for her to panic. "Since meeting Mr. Stone, he's never shown me an unkind side of himself. My experience with him has been... inspiring. He's a very driven man, resolute, and dedicated to getting what he wants, but he isn't a cruel person from what I've seen. As a matter of fact I find him refreshingly humble, but that's just my personal opinion, ma'am."

Humble? She wasn't sure how that word applied to the Mr. Stone she knew. "Would you let your sister do what I'm doing?"

He laughed. "I may be driving you, Ms. Farrow, but I don't know what your or Mr. Stone's intentions are for the night. He's a very private man. All I can do is assume. I'm extremely protective of my little sister and involving her in any sort of hypothetical having to do with my assumptions doesn't make me happy. I prefer to think of my baby sister as a completely non-sexual being, if you know what I'm saying."

She wasn't having sex tonight. The confession nearly slipped out, but she understood what he was getting at. Mr. Pennyworth had obviously picked up on some sort of sexual intent from his employer. Her body shivered with new curiosity.

"Do you think I'm crazy for going to a stranger's house blindfolded?"

He chuckled again. "People do all sorts of wild things. Who am I to judge them? We're here."

The car slowed and every muscle in her body tensed. "Can I remove the blindfold?"

"I'm afraid not. Are you ready?"

No. She nodded yes anyway.

"I'll escort you inside."

The door opened too soon and her heart pounded with a need to rapidly decide if it would be fight or flight or enjoy the night.

"If you reach forward, you'll find my hand."

Her body went on autopilot. Her fingers touched the calloused palm of Mr. Pennyworth and she quietly blurted, "Will you be here the whole time?"

Stupid to look to a stranger as a possible protector from another stranger, but he was all she had. However, she could rip off the blindfold if she felt cornered or threatened. But that would end everything and she wasn't ready for that. Still, it was an option.

"I'll be parked here the entire time. If at any time

you express the desire to return home, I will happily and safely return you to your house, Ms. Farrow."

She stood, nodding. Transferring his hold to her upper arm, he announced, "There are stairs. I'll let you know when to step."

She awkwardly shuffled her feet in the direction he led. When he told her to step, she did, following his direction carefully. Lacking sight left her unbalanced.

"Only a few more steps to the door, Ms. Farrow. You're doing great."

His vote of confidence was oddly comforting.

"Here we are. I'll let you in and once Mr. Stone greets you, I'll return to the car where I'll be waiting to escort you home."

"My purse!"

"Did you need it?"

"It has my phone and..." Her weapon.

"If you want, I can run and get it."

"Please."

Fingers closed around hers, guiding her hand until it rested on something cold and solid. "This is the railing. Hold on so you don't lose your balance. I'll be right back."

She gripped the railing as the sound of his heavy steps faded and the car door opened and closed. A second later his hefty footfalls were approaching again. "Here you are, Ms. Farrow." The purse slipped over her shoulder.

"Thank you."

"Shall we?"

She blew out a calming breath that really did nothing to settle her edginess. "Yes, please."

The moment the door opened her front was bathed in heat, and her mind registered the sweet scent of wood burning in a fireplace, a fragrance she always found charming. Mr. Pennyworth guided her inside and just as she was certain she'd have an anxiety attack, the door closed with an ominous thud. *It must be a large door.*

"Good evening, Ms. Farrow."

Her shoulders unknotted as his voice washed over her. Her belly swooped with excitement as his slow steps approached, echoing, pronouncing the room's enormity. *That* was her Mr. Stone.

Her voice shook. "Good evening, Mr. Stone."

Her breath sucked in as her body jerked at the quick brush of his fingers along her jaw. "You look beautiful this evening."

Unable to form a reply, she fought back every fear hitting her with the gravity of a falling planet. What if Mr. Stone was some Bram Stoker type with Hannibal Lector tendencies? She couldn't do this! How had she ever believed she was brave enough to go through with this?

He chuckled. Her hand was lifted as a foreign object was placed in her palm. He gently closed her fingers around it. "A telephone, Ms. Farrow, should you need to call the police. Take a deep breath, Scarlet. I mean you no harm. Would you like to go home? You're my guest, free to leave whenever you choose."

Okay, she needed to chill the hell out. She was making an ass out of herself. Still, she gripped the phone like the lifeline it was. "Sorry. I'm nervous."

"You'll stay then." It wasn't a question, but rather a supposition. "Mr. Pennyworth will be leaving us to return to the car, but he's available whenever you're ready to say goodnight. Understand?"

"Yes." She couldn't seem to find the breath to back her words.

"Very good. We'll see you in a bit, Pennyworth."

The chauffeur didn't say goodbye. The only indication that he left was the sound of the heavy door closing followed by the brief draft of cold air mingling with the warm interior of the house.

Silence.

She trembled as what felt like the back of a knuckle slowly dragged down her sleeve and fingers gently closed around her hand. His touch was warm, his hand large and soft with a slight callus on one finger.

"May I? There are chairs a few feet away where we can sit and talk. I think you'd be most comfortable near the presence of the front door tonight."

Her hand tightened around his, oddly drawing strength from the source of her fear, and he led her deeper into the room. His other hand touched the backs of her fingers, signaling her to release him. A gentle touch pressed into her shoulders. "There's a chair behind you. Have a seat."

Carefully, she reached out and lowered herself into the chair.

"Are you warm enough?"

"Yes."

"Would you like to remove your coat?"

"Can I take off the blindfold?"

"If it is imperative for you to remove the blindfold, I'll call Pennyworth back in to escort you home. Is that what you want?"

"I don't understand why I can't see you."

"We're here on my terms and your trust, Ms. Farrow, just as I stipulated in my note before you consented to come here. It's imperative, in order for me to give you what you want, that we ascertain that level of trust. Have you changed your mind?"

"No."

"Good girl." Why did that phrase have such a pleasantly tingling effect on her? "Tell me what you're feeling?"

She swallowed. "Nervous. Scared. Excited."

"I see your excitement in the heightened color of your cheeks. It's a stunning blush."

Her face heated even more.

"Tell me what's making you feel afraid."

She laughed nervously. "Basically the fear that I'm going to die."

He chuckled. "You have nothing to fear, Scarlet. I assure you, I'm not a murderer and have no intention to cause you harm."

His assurance wasn't all that comforting. Anyone capable of killing would certainly be capable of lying. Her hands gripped her purse on her lap. He wasn't saying anything. "Why are you being so quiet?"

"Does my silence unnerve you?"

"I can't see, so yeah. I don't know what you're doing."

"I'm watching you."

Her breathing slowed. "Oh," she whispered in a small voice.

"I'm trying to figure out what it would feel like to voluntarily place yourself in such a vulnerable predicament. Explain it to me."

"Um, I'm totally freaked out right now."

He chuckled again. "I'm going to pour myself a glass of wine. I think you should have one too, to help calm your nerves."

Could be poison. "Jesus, what am I doing?" she mumbled under her breath.

"You can call me Mr. Stone."

She stilled. Was that a joke?

He sighed. "Scarlet, I want you to listen carefully to what I'm about to say."

She turned to hear him clearly.

"We've had several discussions on the phone pertaining to what you want in your life. While I can't predict the future, I do believe I can give you what you desire, a glimpse, a moment of experiencing the adoration of a completely focused male. The choice to proceed is yours. However, if you can't trust that I'm not out to physically harm you, I see this as pointless. You're emotions are, of course, welcome, but in order for us to make any progress, you'll have to grant me some level of trust. You're here. That's a step in the right direction. Tell me now if this is too much for you and we'll stop."

She couldn't breathe. She wanted to do this, for herself and for him, but maybe this was simply too overwhelming. Her eyes pressed tight behind the blindfold as she tried to catch her breath. She'd never hyperventilated before, but claustrophobia was suddenly choking her.

Her heart rate accelerated as she sucked in breath after breath. She was going to pass out. A hand slid under her hair, and she whimpered.

"Open. Take a sip. It's only water."

A cool glass pressed to her lower lip and her hands reached for the offering, closing over his.

"Good girl. That's it. Now take a slow breath." He pulled the glass away. "Breathe. You're in no physical danger. We're just talking."

A jagged breath pulled deep into her lungs and she let it out slowly.

"Do you suffer from panic attacks, Ms. Farrow?"

What? Her mind was lost in a haze.

"Answer the question, Scarlet."

Panic attacks... "No. This is just a bit overwhelming for me."

A snick sounded to her left and she flinched. "That was me setting the glass down on the table. Tell me how you picture your surroundings. It will help you feel more in control."

"Large. I smell a fire burning. The room has a slight echo and the floor's bare."

"Very good, Ms. Farrow. See how your senses are heightened when the luxury of sight is deprived?"

She nodded. This was Mr. Stone. All week she'd thought of little else but how excited she was to meet him. Her fear was spoiling everything. "I've never done anything like this before."

"You're in control, Ms. Farrow. Say the word and we stop and you return home."

Pressing her lips tight, she shook her head. "I don't want to stop."

"Very well. Would you like to remove your coat now?"

She could do this. She wasn't a ninny. Shifting her purse to her side where she could grab it in an instant, she proceeded to unbutton her coat. Once she slid her arms out, she folded it on her lap.

"May I? There's a coat tree by the door."

She loosened her grip and the wool slid from her lap. Amazing how much security radiated from that coat. Stripping it away and being relieved of the garment was like having another layer of her soul exposed.

His steps echoed as he returned to the other chair. His strides were slow and measured. "How about that wine now?"

Screw it. She needed wine. "Wine sounds great."

He stood and she registered the sound of a cabinet opening, the familiar pop of a cork unplugging a bottle, and the soft trickle of glasses being filled. The upholstery rasped as he returned to his seat. "Reach forward."

Her arm slowly extended and the weight of a goblet filled her hands. It was room temperature, telling her it was of the red variety.

"Cheers, Ms. Farrow."

"Cheers." She sipped the wine, its tart flavor coating her dry mouth and quenching her thirst.

His glass clicked against the table. "Would you like a grape?"

A grape? "No, thank you."

"When did you last eat?"

"Breakfast." She'd been too nervous to eat.

"Have a few grapes, Ms. Farrow."

"No, thank you—"

"Open."

Her lips parted and the small, round ball popped into her mouth. Her teeth bit down and juice spurted over her tongue.

"Take another sip of wine."

She did as he directed. He fed her a few more grapes and instructed her to sip her wine. When her glass was empty and her stomach a bit settled, she was marginally calmer.

He relieved her of her glass. "Your water is still here if you get thirsty again. Are you feeling better?"

"Yes."

"Good. Tell me about this week. I imagine your mind was busy."

She smiled, easing her posture a bit. As busy as her week seemed, it was dominated with anticipation for this very moment, no matter how different she'd pictured their meeting. "I thought a lot about you," she admitted.

"Ditto. Are you ready to hear my other conditions?"

There were more? How many more conditions could he have? She was already blind! Yes, she needed to know what else she should expect. Maybe if she'd had a little warning about the mask it wouldn't have been so jarring.

"Yes. I'm ready."

"I can offer fourteen nights, Ms. Farrow, as I mentioned on the phone. I believe, in that time, you will truly understand what it is to be adored. After that, I can't make any promises, and I wouldn't want you to commit to anything presumptuously. Fourteen nights over the course of time, during which our progress will be dictated by your established trust."

So it wouldn't be fourteen nights in a row. She could probably do that. "What happens after fourteen?"

"Only time will tell."

"Will I be blindfolded the entire time?" Did he have scars? Maybe he was a veteran or in some sort of accident. She didn't care about that. She just wanted to see him, look in his eyes. There was so much a person could discern from eyes.

"Would you object if I said yes?"

"No, but I can't promise I won't complain." That was the truth. Too invested in his personality to care much about superficial flaws, there was no walking away.

"Good enough. I don't have any notable scars aside from where I got stitches in the second grade after bumping my chin on the monkey bars, if you're worried about that."

Her thoughts jolted, as he seemed to read her mind. They were so in-sync.

Trying to imagine him as a child was too difficult, being that she was still trying to piece together the image of him as Mr. Stone. "Are there other conditions?"

"Yes. I will let you know when I wish to see you and Pennyworth will handle all transportation. Each encounter will start with a note, detailing my instructions. You should know that every request will serve a purpose. I intend to show you a side of yourself no one else ever has. I'll press your boundaries, but never force you to do anything without your full consent. The moment you feel I've asked too much, you simply say no and the liaison is over. You will always have the final say so long as we are both invested."

He'd set things up so she would never know what to expect. Maybe the next time the blindfold wouldn't even be mentioned. Perhaps leaving it open was a test. Eventually he had to show himself. Her fingers squeezed the phone still in her hand, the device warm from her hold.

Maybe he sincerely wanted to give her this experience. Realizing she had so many trust issues was unsettling. Perhaps that was why she was single.

Although this wasn't a typical situation, any woman would be out of their element with such expectations.

That realization had her sitting a little straighter. She was here, with Mr. Stone, and not running scared.

"Tell me what has that little smirk on your mouth."

"I'm here. I was scared, but I'm still here."

"An indication that trust is developing. Will you continue to trust me, Ms. Farrow? Do we have a deal?"

It could all end whenever she wanted it to stop. Where was the danger? "Okay."

"Very good. Consider tonight the first of fourteen. We've broken the ice and you survived."

Well, she wasn't out of the woods yet.

"Last we spoke," he continued, voice level and calm as always. "You told me about a moment that you were proud of yourself. Tonight I want you to tell me a memory of failure and what you learned from the experience."

She stiffened. Somehow, divulging such information in person rather than over the phone was a lot more intimidating. She still couldn't see him, but there was a fresh level of judgment to consider. He could see *her*. "Why?"

"Because I asked. If you can't think of a failure, you're either lying to yourself or purposely trying to deceive me. Trust does not tolerate deception."

Oh, she had plenty of failure in her life. "I failed my certification exam."

He tsked. "Go a little deeper, Ms. Farrow. Share something personal with me."

She swallowed. "I see my unmarried status as a personal failure."

"Interesting. Why?"

She scoffed. "Isn't it obvious?"

"Not at all. I'm single, yet I don't see it as a personal shortcoming. It's more of a predilection."

"Well, maybe it's different for men. All of my friends are married and onto trying to have children. I can barely have a successful date."

"You're here now."

"Yes, but this is far from ordinary. I don't even know what you look like."

"Are dates defined by your partner's appearance?"

"No."

"Then I don't see how that applies."

She sighed. "I always expected I'd be married with a family by now. I'm thirty years old. Risks begin to present themselves for women who have children late into their thirties."

"You have a decade of being in your thirties ahead of you. I don't think those risks apply just yet."

"Ah, but you're forgetting the time it takes to meet someone, form a relationship, establish a mutual desire to take things to the next level, finagle a proposal —something totally out of my hands—have an engagement, enjoy a bit of being married, and the time it takes to conceive *if* there are no unforeseen complications."

"So, if I understand correctly, you're stuck in stage one, but should you make it to the later stages of the game, you'd be at the mercy of the man, waiting for him to pop the question."

"Yes."

"Seems a little unaccountable on your part, Ms. Farrow. You'll never get what you want if you're too afraid to ask for it."

Her mouth framed an objection, but she took a

moment to collect her thoughts. In a calm voice, she argued, "Traditionally, men propose."

"Yes, but not always."

"Regardless, I'd have to have a relationship in order for that to happen. Instead I'm sitting in a mysterious place, blindfolded, discussing my personal failures with a stranger."

"Does the topic bother you?"

"I don't think anyone enjoys discussing their shortcomings."

"It depends how one views their shortcomings. Failure isn't always a bad thing, Ms. Farrow. Many times it helps people better apply themselves and overcome adversity, climb those proverbial walls, if you will. I think it's a matter of determination."

"Are you saying I'm single because I wasn't determined enough?"

"That's not for me to decide. Let's discuss your sense of failure. I want you to focus on your current predicament of being single, and contemplate the feelings it provokes."

Her mind immediately shied away from all those gross feelings of inadequacy. That was it. *Inadequate.* "Failure makes me feel inadequate."

"We must accept failure as a humanistic trait, otherwise it will control us. Perhaps your fear of such inadequacy has become a handicap."

"I'm here."

"Under my conditions, for fourteen nights. Hardly enough time to promenade, fall in love, get *me* to propose marriage since you aren't accountable for that step, have a long, drawn out, tedious engagement, enjoy married life, and create life."

Her brow tightened behind the blindfold. "Are you making fun of me?"

"Only a little. I want you to understand the true nature of failure. Mistakes are part of the natural growing process that helps us reach success. You must embrace your failures in order to better recognize success."

"You want me to accept that I'm incapable of finding a husband?"

"Let's not be so dramatic, Ms. Farrow. I'm merely suggesting you embrace your mistakes and apply them to your success. Every failed experience with a man has taught you something about yourself. That's the angle of success. You must consider those lessons, not ignore them. Don't allow yourself to be emotionally hijacked by the intense emotions linked to failure. Rather, redefine failure as a useful tool, a device that delivers a fundamental lesson."

A bubble of laughter escaped her throat. This was no joking matter, but she found his personality humorous. "You sure you're not a life coach or a therapist?"

"I'm sure. Just someone who's had a great deal of success from failure. I see it for what it is, a driving force to do better."

"I could see that if I was talking about something simple, like, say, an exam." She pursed her lips in the direction of his voice. "But you asked for something personal."

"Did you hope to be kissed tonight?"

Her head drew back. Nothing like shining a spotlight on an already awkward situation. That quickly, she completely lost her grasp of what she was saying. "Um, I don't know."

"Would you object to me kissing you?"

Her stomach tightened as a jolt of excitement sent her nerves fluttering. "No."

"Will you consider it a personal failure on your part if I don't?"

She laughed, but only to mask her discomfort. "I don't think so."

"But you're not certain."

"I changed my mind. I don't want to be kissed tonight."

He chuckled. The room turned quiet with only the soft crackling from the fireplace. Her body lurched with awareness the second his hand touched the back of hers.

Her breathing immediately turned shallow and her tummy heated, causing her knees to press tightly together. When he spoke his voice was even lower than usual.

"Perhaps me kissing you would have nothing to do with you and everything to do with me. A kiss should be driven by passion, an expression of absolute need seeking an outlet through affection. Should we not kiss, it wouldn't be a failure. Rather, it would be a necessary component in the manifestation of something great. Every brick counts when building something impressive, Ms. Farrow. As I stated earlier, every action, every request serves a purpose. Never disregard my motive."

She hadn't been concerned with kisses, but having his lips on hers suddenly became her greatest desire. His hand drifted away, stripping yet another layer. This man was a genius with women. He had to have a background in psychology. His proficiency with rationed words twisted her thinking in a totally different direction. He was emotionally stripping her.

"Do you understand, Ms. Farrow?"

She swallowed back her plea that he kiss her and nodded.

A finger ghosted over her lips, mimicking the pressure of a kiss, and she sucked in a swift breath.

"Not your failure. My choice."

She wanted to lean forward and chase his fingers with her mouth, an impulse she'd never had with a man before.

"Your blush is back, Ms. Farrow. Tell me, is it because you're afraid or because you're aroused?"

Her face tightened. Arousal mingled with embarrassment. She whimpered and he chuckled.

"I'll assume it's the latter. Did you enjoy yourself tonight, Ms. Farrow? I know we had a bumpy start, but I found the evening pleasant."

She nodded. "I'm glad I came."

"Me too."

Were they finished? She didn't want to say goodnight as she was finally starting to calm enough to enjoy their visit.

She wanted... so many contradicting things. Home. The security of her house. His mouth on hers. His touch. To get rid of this damn blindfold.

"Good. I'll help you with your coat."

With a sound of fabric rustling, she sensed him standing. The second his hand closed around hers she turned her palm to his and squeezed. There was a moment of unspoken communication. She was thanking him, but still unsure for what. He clasped her fingers more firmly, the motion full of what she interpreted as affection.

He led her toward the door and she analyzed the change in her disposition. There was no hesitancy to her steps, no fear he might lead her into danger. Perhaps next time she'd demonstrate enough trust that the blindfold wouldn't be necessary.

"Lift your arm, please." He guided the sleeves of her coat over her shoulders. Her chest lifted as he carefully closed the buttons, grazing the curve of her breast ever so slightly. At the casual touch of his fingers she'd lost a bit of her composure, her body intensely responding to such a subtle caress.

"You left your purse on the chair. I'll go get it. Stay here."

She left her purse? Holy cow, her guard had lowered severely. She hadn't realized.

His steps drew nearer and her purse looped over her shoulder. "I'll need my phone back, Ms. Farrow."

What was wrong with her? She'd been holding the phone in a death grip this entire time and had totally forgotten its presence. Stupidly, she held it out and he relieved her of its weight.

A finger brushed over her cheek. The heat of his nearness seeped through her clothing, his scent intoxicating and implacable. She wanted to lean into him just to memorize it, finding the purposeful caress so much more meaningful than the accidental one.

"Goodnight, Ms. Farrow," he whispered, his breath tickling the hairs slipping past the blindfold.

"Goodnight, Mr. Stone."

The door clicked open and cool air coasted over her skin. In the distance a car door opened followed by the crunch of gravel. Pennyworth.

"Ms. Farrow's ready to go home now, Pennyworth."

"Yes, sir. Ms. Farrow." The chauffeur's hand curled

softly over the sleeve of her coat and Mr. Stone stepped back.

As she walked away, the increasing distance between them was cataloged with fundamental goodbyes of her past, moments so definitive they'd be impossible to forget or recreate—her parents driving away after moving her into her first dorm, her grandmother's final words, and watching her first class graduate middle school. How had he become so significant?

Frustration built as she was led down the stairs. Her eyes prickled as she fought back the urge to tear away the mask and see him. It was all very disconcerting and unprecedented. Perhaps it was best she was leaving.

Gravel crunched under her feet and the car door opened, the quiet purr of the engine enough to cut away all proof that he was still in observing distance. "Watch your head please, Ms. Farrow."

She quickly turned, unsure if he lingered or not. "Thank you, Mr. Stone."

"It was my pleasure, Scarlet." He was there. Validation he'd waited, looking on until she left, filled her with such comfort it gave her the courage to climb in the car.

She slid into the seat and buckled her seatbelt. Mr. Pennyworth took his place and they were soon on their way. Replaying the night in her mind, she shivered, knowing there would be many more. Pennyworth was quiet for several minutes and soon enough her wish was granted.

"You may remove the blindfold now, Ms. Farrow."

Odd, part of her didn't want to. Shaking off the confused desire to stay in the dark, she slid the mask off her head and blinked, as even the dim interior lit only by the night sky and dashboard lights, seemed too bright.

They were already in her neighborhood. Pennyworth looked exactly the same. She'd foolishly expected his appearance to be altered from the start of the evening.

When the car parked in front of her house, she smirked, thinking of Cinderella and the pumpkin carriage. "What time is it?"

"Ten to midnight," Pennyworth answered, opening her door. "I hope you had a nice evening."

She grinned. "I did."

There was such a rush of accomplishment. For all the danger she feared would come from taking such a risk, there was that much more pride. She'd done something reckless and she wasn't dead or trapped in basement full of skeletons. The sensation was so out of character for her, such an extraordinary high, she was actually sad it was over.

Her mouth hid a secret smile as she recognized the desire to go to him again. Of all her experiences with men, this one seemed to wake a part of her soul that had been still for a very long time.

She grinned and sighed. *Mr. Stone.*

8

EXPOSURE

"I can't believe you actually went through with it," Jet said as he sniffed the health shake Carla made for him. "I'm proud of you. What the fuck is this?"

"Kale. It's good for you."

Jet pushed the shake away. "How do you feel?"

Asher tilted his head in consideration. "Good. I'm still a little shocked. I mean, she did everything, got in the car, wore the blindfold, followed my every command. I never expected her to actually put that much trust into this."

"She's desperate."

His mouth tightened, not in agreement with that diagnoses. "She's disciplined," he offered, finding it a better-suited term. "It's weird. We have something. There's chemistry there."

"So why not cut the crap and level with her, maybe actually get the girl, Ash?"

He shook his head as he swallowed a bite of the grilled fish served for lunch. "Can't. We're too deep now. She'd see it as a betrayal if I showed her who I actually was. I need a guarantee this won't blow up in my face before I let her in."

"Love doesn't come with guarantees, my friend. And I know you. This isn't an act. Maybe this is part of who you really are, you just never looked deep enough to see it."

It did seem he was falling into his role with little difficulty. "I like taking an authoritative role with her. I never considered being that way with women."

Jet's dark eyes narrowed as he smiled. "You like *her*."

He shrugged. "I like what we're doing. It's different."

"I'd say."

"There's a rush involved," Asher explained. "It's a power trip. I'm in complete control. I've never experienced anything like it before."

His friend laughed. "You kinky little pervert."

"It's not like that. I didn't even kiss her."

"You didn't?"

"Nope. It's deeper than that. There's so much sexual tension just from prolonging the intimacy, it keeps building and building and she's getting drunk on need."

"How about you?"

Authority was definitely intoxicating. Between that and her sex appeal, there was a punch drunk lightness that hadn't existed before reintroducing himself to Scarlet. He'd almost backed out of everything last night when she'd started to panic, but then he'd calmed her down, and they found their rhythm and everything had jelled.

"I'm not sure how far I'll take things. I don't want to use her. I just want...what I never thought I could have. If I put too much faith in her this early on I'm afraid I'll end up hurt again. And this time it would be way worse than the first time."

"Things like this never end well." Jet stole an apple from the dish at the center of the table and took a snapping bite. "So long as you're keeping secrets, you're the villain of the piece and the second you get too confident, the rug will get pulled out from under you. Take the opportunity while you have it, Ash, and level with her."

"I don't think so. We're just talking. There's nothing villainous about having a conversation."

"Except your deceiving her. If she finds that out before you tell her, she'll see it as some sort of motive," Jet said, disapproval showing in the arch of his brow.

"I told her every word I say and every interaction we have has a motive. There's nothing wrong with having a goal." Right now his goal was to prove he could be what she wanted. His success was anybody's guess.

"Yeah, but she thinks you're interested in her. You've led her to believe your motive's are in the same realm as hers. If she remembers you from high school and knows you tried to hide who you are on purpose, she might see things a different way."

He was hiding who he was, but only because he wanted to be perfect when he finally introduced himself to her, not as Mr. Stone, but as Asher Roan. Still, Jet had a good point. He deflected. "Who said I'm not interested?"

"Are you?"

Asher wiped his mouth and pushed away his plate. He'd be lying if he said a lot of his old sentiments hadn't returned. She was as beautiful, if not more so than she was twelve years ago. Their strange encounter was revealing not only things about her, but things about him.

It was a daily battle to see past the pain she'd caused. Until he figured out how to do that without effort, their circumstances would remain unchanged. Besides, she'd likely face a similar battle if he asked her to see past the kid he was in high school, a kid he wasn't much different from now.

Physically, he was changing. Steve marked it in his charts, Hunter had made a comment about his physique, and Elliot noted that he was carrying himself with a bit more confidence. But Asher couldn't see a change yet—not a significant one at least.

Internally, *something* was happening to him. It was a potent tonic, authority. He was in control, a puppeteer pulling strings. It wasn't the power he had that effected him most, however—it was her compliance. It shocked him every time.

This woman, the same female still leagues ahead of him that he'd spent years fantasizing about, trusted *him*. Every time she allowed his words to guide her, there came a heady rush of awareness. There was nothing to compare it to. But he liked it and didn't want it to stop. Learning that he was Asher from high school might put an end to the game faster than anything else.

It was certainly a challenge to not take advantage of such trust. He'd never wanted to kiss a woman with the raw desire he felt last night when the topic was addressed. His main worry was disappointing her expectations.

"Asher?"

Returning his focus to Jet, he admitted, "I want to

get to know her more. She's still stunning. But now... there's a sort of innocence about her. I don't know how a person matures into a more innocent person than they once were, but she's somehow managed it."

"An innocence you could crush. That's not you, Ash."

He laughed without humor. "Yeah right. I thought I could do this and stay unaffected. I thought I could outsmart her wiles, be immune to her beauty, but I can't. And the way we've gone about getting to know one another...it's like an addictive game I tell myself I shouldn't play, shouldn't invest so much time and effort into it, but I can't stop."

He rubbed the back of his head and looked into Jet's concerned eyes. "I know she humiliated me in front of all of my enemies and then some. I shouldn't care what she thinks, Jet, but I care so much. *Too much.* Even when I thought this might all be a lesson in vulnerability, I never would have exploited her the way I was exploited. She saw so much of my shame, Jet. So much pain and weakness, I need to make an impression great enough to erase those moments from her memory. Or she'll always look at me and see that loser."

Jet shook his head. "You weren't a loser. Vulnerability and humiliation are private. Do you think those assholes remember you?"

"Yes, I do. Why do you think I skipped out on the reunion? Those jerks lived to torture us, especially me. She would've been sitting with them—just like in high school." As much as he couldn't imagine the sweet woman from last night doing that, he knew how things like a reunion went. People stuck with what they knew.

"I don't think you're giving her or yourself enough credit. She's a teacher, Ash. She has to have some level of compassion and understanding. I mean, my God, if we all believed what we believed twelve years ago Elliot would still be writing letters to Santa Clause and Hunter would still sleep with the light on. People change. They grow up. Let her see you so she can see the man you've become."

"I can't," he whispered, wondering if thirteen more dates would be enough to find his courage.

"Is she still friends with them?"

"Some. She's still close with Nicole, but she hasn't seen Westerman since graduation. I don't know who else she talks to." He tossed his napkin on the table.

"Just think about what I said."

"I will. I gotta go. Steve and I are going rock climbing."

Jet stood, his eyes creasing with worry. "Ash. You're not a bad guy. I get you're going through some personal evolution, and I'm glad you're finding some confidence, but don't let your insecurities win."

He nodded. "Thanks. I'm doing my best."

***

Scarlet whipped open the door and dodged Nicole's knuckles as they relentlessly pounded. "*What?*"

Her friend barreled inside holding a caddy of coffee. "What? What. *What* she asks. Um… you tell me."

Scarlet shut the door and followed her intrusive friend into the kitchen. Her gaze landed on her scribbled note from the night before. Snatching the paper she quickly crumpled it in her fist. Nicole narrowed her eyes.

"What's going on, Lettie?"

"Nothing."

"Nothing? What's in your hand?"

"Nothing."

The coffees landed on the table with a smack. "You better start spilling the beans about yesterday. Who did you spend the night with? Was it the guy from the picture? If so..." She paused and did a girly golf clap. "I want details."

"Myself. I was home by midnight."

"So you *didn't* go to Mr. Mystery's house? Spill. The suspense is killing me!"

She calmly slid a coffee from the caddy and pinched back the top. "I met someone."

"Where? Who? And why is this the first time I'm hearing about him?"

Scarlet sighed and walked into the living room where she plopped on the couch. It was too early for an interrogation. Nicole followed with a determined scowl.

She didn't want to disclose too much. First, because there was the whole danger factor, and second, this was her private business and she didn't want Nicole's cynicism to change her opinion. Scarlet had enough cynicism for both of them.

She chose her words carefully. "His name's Stone."

"Stone? What is he a soap opera character? Is that his first name or last?"

"Last."

She snorted. "That's what he goes by? Does he think he's Cher? What's his first name?"

"I don't know."

"You went to a guy's house and don't even know his first name? Who are you and what have you done with my best friend?"

"If I tell you his full name you'll just Google the shit out of him and come up with some lame excuse why I can't date him."

Nicole's expression softened. "That's not true. I want you to be happy, Lettie. It's my job to worry."

She put her cup on the table. "I know. But I don't want you worrying about this. It's new and I really like him. I don't want anything to ruin it just yet, because we all know it'll eventually end on it's own."

"And I'm the cynic? Who says it'll end?"

Fourteen nights—now thirteen. No promises. "Look at my track record. It will. We're just having fun and we both know what this is." *Sort of.* "I'm not going to get ahead of myself and label it as anything more."

Nicole's bleached brows lowered. "So, what are you, like, his booty call?"

She shook her head. "It's deeper than that. We're just talking right now. I'm not rushing into anything and neither is he."

Her friend groaned then whined, "Why won't you tell me about him?"

"I am."

"No, you're not. You're totally holding shit back. I can tell."

Her mouth twitched. There wasn't much to hold back. Mr. Stone was one big mystery. There wasn't much she could confess. "Nicole, it's brand new. Just give it some time. If it turns into more"—*big if*—"I promise I'll open up."

Disappointment pursed her friend's mouth. "Do you think Matt would get along with him?"

Scarlet groaned and flung herself back on the couch. "See? We are not double dating!"

"What? I'm thinking positive. You just yelled at me for being cynical."

"You're light years ahead of us, Nicole. I don't want to overthink things."

"A girl's gotta have a plan, Lettie. Do you think Matt would have tried out for the police force if I didn't push him? Do you think he would have proposed if I didn't persuade him?"

"I don't want to play games and neither does M—Stone." She had to be careful how she referred to him.

"There're always games. If there weren't games, the human population would drop and there'd be an overflow of men lost in a world of video games and stupid crap that's a waste of time."

She shrugged. "I like video games."

Nicole shut her eyes and slowly shook her head. "No wonder you're single."

"Hey."

Her phone buzzed and she was distracted. Scarlet had added the GeekPeek app to her mobile incase Mr. Stone tried to reach her when she was away from her computer. Her heart raced when she saw a text from 'restricted'. He'd never texted her before.

Her chest heated as she opened the message.

ood morning, Ms. Farrow.

. . .

"Is that him?" Nicole screeched.

Scarlet jerked her phone out of view. "Maybe."

"Oh my God! What's he saying?"

It was strange, having this much of Nicole's attention. Her dating life never really warranted such interest, but Scarlet attributed a lot of her friend's curiosity to the monotony of married life—or the fact that she'd preemptively asked her to call the cops if she didn't return from their first 'date'.

Enjoying the shift of gears, she said, "Mind your own beeswax."

She punched out a reply then quickly stuffed her phone in her pocket.

Nicole glared at her. "I tell you everything."

"No, you don't."

"Yes, I do! I even told you about the thing in the shower."

"I can't help it if you're a bragging pervert."

Nicole grinned and laughed. "That was some good sex."

"I'm sure. But the reality is, I haven't had sex in almost two years. I'm pretty sure my virginity's grown back and I'm dealing with some serious self-doubt in the performance department. I don't want to psych myself out any more than I already am."

Nicole smiled sympathetically. Maybe she'd back off—

"How tall is he? In the picture he looked tall."

Nope. Scarlet sighed. "Looks aren't important. Besides, that wasn't him."

Her friend's forehead crinkled. "Then who the hell was that guy?"

"His…friend. Penny—"

"Penny?"

"—Wise—*ly*. I mean *Wesley*. Wesley Penny."

"Well, what the hell did you send me a picture of him for? Next time I want a picture of Stone."

"Jesus, Nicole. I'm not saying anymore. Drop it."

They had their coffee and Scarlet's phone continued to buzz, but she ignored it, not wanting to provoke more of an inquisition. They discussed normal topics, like work, Nicole's incessant campaign to get a kid out of Matt, and their upcoming trip to her family's mountain house.

Nicole slipped in a few questions here and there, but Scarlet gave nothing away. There was a strange protectiveness regarding Mr. Stone. Or perhaps it was self-preservation. Either way, he was suddenly the biggest secret of her life and she desperately wanted to keep him to herself.

When Nicole left, she checked her phone. She should have known better than to expect a typical text message. Aside from the good morning, there were only instructions. Pennyworth would be picking her up that evening and she was expected to wear a skirt.

Interesting.

---

*A*sher paced the foyer and waited for the sedan to arrive. What if she didn't come? Her first text reply was immediate, but the following were delayed. He found himself doubting his ability to seduce her. Getting into her mind was doable, but he'd never had success with the human body. The familiar doubt made him bitterly aware of whom he really was.

He checked his phone, sure Steve—or Pennyworth, the surname of Alfred, Bruce Wayne's butler— would text him if there were any glitches in the plan. He should be on his way by now.

Everything was moving ahead according to plan, so why was he suddenly nervous? He glanced down at his attire. She wouldn't be able to see him, but his stylist had armed him with a sense of courage he never experienced. It was amazing what a designer suit could do for a man. The guys had made fun of him, but Steve and Jet dispelled much of his second-guessing by complimenting his new look.

Lights flashed in the distance and his gut tightened with anticipation. This had to be them. When the car pulled into the long, circular drive, he released a pent up breath, rolling his shoulders to relieve some of the tension.

The car slowed and Steve rounded to the passenger door. His gaze fastened to the dark interior as two slender legs came into view. She'd done it. She'd worn a skirt. "Amazing."

Taking a step back from the window he moved to the door. It took a few minutes for the driver to lead her up the stairs. As the knob turned, Asher drew in one last calming breath and dragged his moist palms down his jacket, chafing away the remaining clamminess.

The moment she stepped inside her delicate fragrance hit him like an aphrodisiac. Soft apple mingled with a scent extremely feminine and delicate. Pitching his voice low, he greeted her. "Good evening, Ms. Farrow."

"Good evening, Mr. Stone."

Her mouth twitched with the touch of a smirk. The atmosphere was markedly relaxed in comparison to the night before.

"Thank you, Pennyworth." He took her hand as the driver stepped away and exited the house.

Her tiny fingers fit around his and squeezed much like they had the night before and it was his turn to smirk, drawing a familiar comfort from the gesture. She appeared happy to return.

"Let's have a seat."

She nodded and moved her other hand to his forearm. Perhaps it was for balance, but there was curiosity hidden within her touch. Her palm curled around his sleeve and pressed into his triceps. The attention to his build would have made him uncomfortable a month ago, but since hiring a trainer his muscles had started to take shape and she was perhaps experiencing some evidence of his rigorous attempts at improving himself.

When they reached the chairs, he faced her and severed their touch. Without invitation, he unclasped the buttons of her coat, unwrapping her like a long awaited gift, savoring every part he slowly unveiled. She allowed him to slide the covering off her shoulders, enchanting him with the little shiver that trembled to her chin.

"Have a seat."

She lowered herself into the chair and he moved to hang the coat by the door. When he returned to his seat he took a moment to admire her outfit. "You look very pretty tonight, Ms. Farrow."

"Thank you." There was a slight quiver to her

voice, which made her blush even more charming than he usually found it.

"Are you nervous?"

"You always make me nervous."

She made him nervous too, but he wouldn't share that information. Unable to resist, he reached out and traced a knuckle slowly along the delicate bone of her jaw. Her frame leaned into the brief contact, her lips parting infinitesimally the moment he pulled his touch away.

"Did you have a nice day?"

"Yes."

"What did you do?"

"Nothing special. My friend stopped by. After that I cleaned and watched some television."

His gut clenched at the mention of a friend. "Tell me about your friend."

Her mouth curved down for a split second, the curious action catching his notice. Her friend was stimulating some emotion. He shelved the observation for later.

"Her name's Nicole. We've been friends since childhood."

His relief that her friend was female was instantaneous. He remembered Nicole—not fondly. She'd always seemed to boss Scarlet around. He wondered if her dominant personality still played a part in their relationship. "She's the friend that stole the mascot head."

A breathy chuckle escaped. "Yeah."

"Did you enjoy your visit with Nicole?"

"Sure."

"That's not a yes."

"She was asking me about you."

He tensed. Had Scarlet told her? "What did she want to know?"

"Everything. I didn't tell her much."

A surprising sense of camaraderie followed his relief. "Why do you think that is?"

She shrugged, but her play of ignorance wasn't genuine.

He had to reel back his need to know what she'd told her friend. There was a fine line between appearing curious and coming off needy. Asher wanted to fulfill the role of an assertive male. Turning the tables, he approached the subject from a different angle. "Tell me how you felt while she was questioning you."

She took a moment to deliberate as he poured two glasses of wine. As he guided her hand around one goblet, she thanked him and sipped.

"I felt annoyed."

"Describe feeling annoyed."

"Frustrated. Cornered. Slightly coerced."

"Nicole's a close friend of yours?"

"Yes, but she doesn't get it. She's the one that said my standards were too high."

"Ah, so perhaps you're holding back information because you're afraid of failing in front of her again, while *maintaining* those pesky standards."

Her head tilted and her mouth quirked. "Or maybe I was honoring your demand for privacy."

Her cocky response caught him off guard, but pleased him immensely. Interesting, that their relationship could tamper with her loyalties to a friend she'd had since grade school.

He reached for her free hand and brushed his fingers lightly over her knuckles. She immediately responded, turning her palm to his touch, seeking more. "I'm pleased, Ms. Farrow."

Her chest lifted as she breathed, a proud little smile on her mouth. She responded well to his praise.

His attention traveled to her attire. Brushing a finger over her stocking clad knee, her body drew to attention, her shoulders lifting another degree. "Let's discuss your attire tonight."

"O-okay."

"Are you anxious, Ms. Farrow?"

"You told me to wear a skirt."

"That's not an answer to my question."

Her throat worked as she swallowed. "I'm always a little jumpy around you."

"Good. I prefer you that way. It keeps your responses honest. Now, tell me why you chose *this* skirt."

Her breathing turned shallow. Her little pink tongue slipped over her lower lip. "I don't wear skirts often. This one seemed...safe."

The deep blue material reached to her knee while standing, but since she'd taken a seat the skirt had ridden up to her mid-thigh. Her shirt was a thin blouse he could see through if he looked close enough. His gaze fastened to her tight nipples. On her feet were black heels, but not the sort any man would appreciate.

"Why safe?"

"It's modest."

"Is it?" he asked, dragging a finger along her outer thigh, stopping only a few inches before her hip. There was no verbal objection to how freely he touched her.

Her breathing accelerated. Her body quivered, but she didn't move to lower the skirt.

"Does my touch offend you?"

"No." Her response was a mere rasp. Interesting.

"Are you aroused, Ms. Farrow?" Her cheeks flushed a deep shade of rose. That would be a yes. "Please answer the question."

The blindfold allowed him to scrutinize every part of her response. Through her thin blouse twin peaks formed at her breasts. Her excitement was evident in her physical reaction—something that triggered a physical reaction in him—but he still wanted her to confirm his suspicions. There was a potent rush connected to compelling her to vocalize a response. "Your nipples are hard."

She whimpered.

"There's no hiding from me, Ms. Farrow. I'm studying your every reaction, scrutinizing your physical responses. I like unnerving you. Sometimes your knees draw tight when I touch you. There's a slight lift to your posture when I address your hesitancies, as if you want to hide the truth and appear dauntless. Your breathing accelerates when we discuss sex. And then there's that telltale blush that implies your blood is pumping with adrenaline. So I'll allow you another chance to answer. Are you aroused, Ms. Farrow?"

"Yes."

"Good girl. Your honesty's imperative if I'm to help you." He wanted to push her. "Take off your shoes."

"My shoes?"

"Yes."

She hesitated then slid her foot from one and glided her stocking clad toe into the heel of the other. He swallowed. The move was entirely feminine and naturally sexy, ranking up there with the bra removal scene in *Flashdance.*

Her compliance impressed him. Removing the shoes triggered yet another effect. Vulnerability perhaps. One toe remained pinned to her shoe. "Tell me why you chose these shoes."

"I don't know."

"Typically, women pair high heels with skirts, yet you opted for a stout heel."

Her blush intensified.

"Are the shoes a defense mechanism, Ms. Farrow?"

"I don't know."

"Does removing them make you feel vulnerable? Take another sip of wine before you answer."

She did, sipping from the glass deeply. When she lowered the goblet she released a sigh. "Yes. I can't see and now my feet are bare."

"Not true. You're wearing stockings." He leaned forward and collected the shoes. "I'm going to place these out of reach."

Her body tensed. "Why?"

"Because your reaction tells me a bit more about your tolerance. I like seeing you unsettled. Every physical barrier represents an emotional one. Stripping them can be quite telling."

He stood and carried the shoes to the door, carefully and silently placing them on the floor. When he returned her posture was alert. "Are you still aroused, Ms. Farrow?"

"I don't know."

He glanced at her shirt. Her nipples still pressed into the fine fabric, but her core temperature might have reflexively dropped under the press of fear. He desired her aroused, but not afraid. "Forget the shoes. Tell me about your body."

She nearly choked, the subject clearly an uncomfortable one for her. "W—what?"

"I want you to imagine yourself sitting here naked." Her shoulders immediately lowered, as she appeared to curl into herself. "Does nudity make you uncomfortable?"

"I don't think anyone's comfortable being completely exposed."

"I beg to differ. There are times, in the privacy of one's home, that nudity goes without question."

She laughed nervously. "I'm not one of those people."

"Yet you live alone."

"Yes, but I have friends that stop by—and windows."

Yes, and every mention of outside friends reminded him of how precarious their situation still was. He wanted to intrude on that private side of her life, be there emotionally even when he couldn't physically. "It would please me if you started sleeping in the nude."

Her lips parted and there was a pregnant moment of consideration. Her voice was small when she finally agreed to his request. "Okay."

"When you go to sleep tonight, I want you to shut your eyes before you climb into bed and remove your clothing. Fold them neatly and don't open your eyes until you're completely nude. Then I want you to carefully walk the folded clothing to the farthest dresser and place them there. I want you to feel the air on your flesh, the floor beneath your bare feet. When you climb into bed, I want you to think of how softly the blankets weigh over your flesh. I want you to consider every part of your body and find comfort in its health and beauty. Do you understand?"

"Yes."

"And the next time I see you I want you to thank me for showing you this freedom of self, should you discover it. Coming to terms with our physical gifts and limitations can be quite liberating. I want you to reach a point of acceptance with yourself."

She nodded and he stood.

"Our time's up, Ms. Farrow. Please stand up."

Her palms pressed into the arms of the chair, her movements shaky as she rose to her feet. Catching her fingers, he soothingly rubbed them between his, bringing them to his lips. "Twelve more nights, Ms. Farrow. I believe we have a lot to anticipate."

Her lips trembled as he slid a delicate strand of red hair behind her shoulder. "Goodnight, Ms. Farrow."

"Goodnight, Mr. Stone."

He walked her slowly to the door and knelt, carefully sliding her feet into her shoes and helping her with her coat, taking his time fastening each button. When he opened the door, her grip on his arms tightened and he paused, deciphering her hesitation. Her posture was trusting, but her expression gave nothing away. Did she not want to leave?

Steve climbed the steps and her grip tightened another degree. Asher brushed a finger over the high arch of her cheek, careful not to disturb the mask. "Goodnight, Scarlet. I look forward to seeing you again."

"Goodnight."

Steve escorted her down the steps and guided her into the car. When they pulled away, Asher stepped inside and collapsed on the chair, letting his head fall back. Time was slipping away from them faster than sand through an hourglass. He should have suggested more than fourteen nights.

His face dropped into his hands and he groaned. She was *too* beautiful, *too* trusting. He'd set the bar too damn high and now dreaded her expectations would be out of his reach. This entire game was spinning out of control, despite his insistent claim to be the one in the power seat.

"Shit." He unknotted his tie and contemplated his options.

He could confess who he was, as Jet suggested, but his gut twisted uncomfortably at the thought. He *needed* those last twelve encounters desperately. He could stretch them out, use the remaining time wisely, but it would never be enough to truly change who he was inside.

The idea of staying away from her for any length of time also displeased him. She'd been gone minutes and he already missed her, wanted to call her, hear her voice again. Yet when she was present he was so nervous his natural impulse was to hastily wrap up their encounter. He was a disaster. With all of his planning, he was completely unprepared for how emotionally complicated this experience would be for *him*. It was supposed to be about her.

She'd continuously consented to put herself in a vulnerable position, yet he was the one feeling utterly defenseless against her lure. He'd been insane to ever think he could deceive her. Meeting her again, truly learning the qualities that made her tick, created an inescapable instinct to protect her.

But what if he couldn't protect her? What if there came a time when she needed protection and he didn't measure up? So many buried fears resurfaced. The more time he spent in her presence the more his deepest, festering insecurities returned. It should have been the opposite. She should have bolstered his confidence, but that wasn't what was happening at all, because the more he liked her the more he feared losing her again.

It became perfectly clear in that moment of personal truth. Her awakening had become equally his own. And while he commended her for facing her fears, he wasn't sure he had the balls to face his own.

*L*ater that evening, after returning to his primary home, Asher stood in front of his bed and considered everything he requested of Scarlet. Would she do as he instructed? Was she naked at that very moment?

Grimacing, he glanced down at his clothing. He was asking a lot of her, being that he was very uncomfortable with his own nudity. Turning, he went to the long mirror in his room and analyzed his physique through his clothing. His fingers unknotted his tie and slid it from beneath his collar. Slipping his jacket off, he draped it over the chair.

Toeing off his shoes, he stared at his reflection. His new haircut was nice, giving his face a more appealing shape and his visage a touch of much needed maturity. Drawing in a deep breath, he set to undoing the buttons of his shirt, not looking back at the mirror until he was unclothed from the waist up.

He scowled at the man looking back at him. His stomach, always a bit too concave, had begun to fill out with slight ridges of muscle. His chest was unremarkable. Turning, he admired his arms, noting the slight shape taking form in his biceps and shoulders.

"You got a lot of work to do," he mumbled to his reflection.

Walking to his bed, he stared at the coverlet. It was imperative he do this in order to understand the sensations involved, and to better question her the next time they met. Tipping his head back, he undid his belt buckle and shucked his bottoms, his heart reflexively racing as he quickly slid under the shelter of the covers.

He was a grown fucking man and couldn't face his naked self. Discomfort engulfed him. He could blame the reaction to his appearance on the precedent set by the few women that had seen him partially unclothed or the times he'd been made fun of in locker rooms, but deep down he knew it was his own fault. He'd never come to terms with who he was and that *had to* change. Who knew how much of a difference Steve could make?

In those quiet moments, alone with only himself, he realized it wasn't so much about changing his appearance as it was about changing his thinking. His low self-perception was perhaps his greatest weakness.

Playing with Scarlet boosted his confidence. But the truth was, he'd removed his kryptonite. Her blindness enhanced his courage, helped him become someone else, but it wasn't the antidote.

Their encounters unearthed a side of himself he appreciated. The question was, could he apply those qualities of self-assurance and poise to the outside world where everyone saw the real him? He wasn't so sure it was possible.

9

BODY LANGUAGE

"WHY DO we all have to be here?" Hunter asked, shifting awkwardly in his sweats.

Asher sighed, already exhausted with their questions. "Because Steve said it's more effective to take dance as a class."

Elliot remained in the corner, nose stuck to his phone obsessing over stocks. Asher sighed. This was never going to work.

He'd talked to Steve during one of their workouts about his feelings of inadequacy. Asher told him about his issues with confidence and Steve suggested he dance, which immediately had Asher laughing. Steve simply proposed he research the connection between dancing and sexual prowess. He did and now he was here.

"There's scientific proof that confident male dancers have a higher probability of delivering a female orgasm," he informed them.

Jet rolled his shoulders, appearing eager. "I'm an awesome dancer."

Elliot rolled his eyes. "I had plans this afternoon."

Asher rolled his eyes. His friend's plans, whatever they were, likely involved sitting in front of a computer by himself. "Just give it a chance."

Elliot lifted his face from his phone and gave him a disparaging look. "Asher, I understand you're on a quest to find your manhood, but some of us are fine with the sort of men we—"

His friend's lecture abruptly cut off as his expression turned to utter panic, his attention suddenly affixed to the other side of the studio. Asher turned and drew up straight. The instructor had arrived.

The four of them ogled as she bent and placed a small stereo on the floor. Long chestnut hair fell past her shoulders. Her hips were outlined in black stretch pants, her midriff completely exposed, showing an expanse of olive skin and the slight ridges of her spine. Petite buckle heels ensconced her feet and a tangerine blouse tied high around her ribs.

Unfolding her lithe body from the pose, she stood and faced them with a beaming smile. *Hello, breasts.* Wow.

"Hello, boys. I'm Nadia, your instructor for the next couple of weeks. Are we ready to dance?"

She held a remote in her hand and pointed it to the stereo. Pulsing music filled the studio as she tossed the remote to her bag. No one moved.

"Who's Asher?"

He swallowed and wheezed, "I am."

"Why don't you come to the front, Asher? The rest of you spread out."

Steve mentioned having a friend that taught dance. He never said anything about her being a woman. Asher should have assumed as much, but still... this woman was a force of nature.

Every awkward memory of huddling in the corners at school dances flooded his mind. That was before he gave up attending such ludicrous rituals. Jet moved beside him, but Hunter and Elliot remained frozen in the back.

"Let's start by warming up. Loosen your legs and let the music direct you. Let's see what you got." He detected traces of Hungarian in her voice.

She stepped from one foot to the other, a look of expectation on her oval face. He scrutinized her tiny feet. Jet mimicked her motions and she smiled. "Good. What's your name, handsome?"

"You can call me Jet, sweetheart."

Great. He'd seen Jet perform with the ladies before. He was about to hog all the attention and chances were the instructor would end up leaving with him and forget the reason she was there. Asher shifted and slowly distributed his weight from foot to foot. He had no rhythm.

Nadia stepped close, her hands pressing lightly on his frame. "Try to loosen your hips, Asher. Don't force it. Let the music take control."

Her hands-on coaching only served to tighten his muscles and make it more difficult to move.

"You boys in the back, I don't see you dancing."

Asher looked over his shoulder. Hunter took a few steps forward, his jaw slack, and gaze glued to Nadia. Elliot didn't move a muscle.

She chuckled and walked over to Elliot. Removing the phone from his hand, she placed it on the windowsill. Keeping hold of his hands, she turned so her back was to his front and pressed his palms to her narrow hips. Elliot's eyes widened behind the lenses of his glasses.

The song changed to one Asher recognized as the Dean Martin classic, *Sway,* only this version was sung by a sultry female voice. Elliot's shoulders visibly tensed as Nadia did as the song said and swayed.

Her hips slowly gyrated, brushing against his friend's rigid form. Her hands caressed her sides, traveling over the swell of her breast, through her long, dark hair, wrists twirling above her head. Asher's throat was instantly dry.

"You're not moving, boys. I can't teach you if you don't try."

One hand coasted down her extended arm as her hips made slow circles, her winking belly button playing a game of peek-a-boo. Elliot looked as though he'd seen a ghost and Asher actually took pity on him. Chances were he was hard as a rock and there'd be no hiding it in his loose sweatpants with Nadia pressing her curves against him as she was.

Hunter got a touch ambitious, throwing his hands into his exaggerated moves. Asher laughed. Any stereotypes about black men having innate rhythm was disproved the moment Hunter started to dance.

"Very good!" Nadia called, smiling at Hunter, which only encouraged the ridiculous display.

Asher fisted his hands and brought them to his sides, bending his elbows, trying to get more into the song. His chest lifted as he surveyed the others via the mirror. Nadia's palm drifted over her exposed belly and down her inner thigh.

She abruptly turned, her hair fanning out as she came face to face with Elliot, spreading her fingers wide over his narrow shoulder. Jerking him close, her breasts pressed into Elliot's chest and his friend made a choking sound.

"What's your name?" she asked.

"Elliot. Elliot Garnet." Was he sweating? He hadn't moved.

"Dance with me, Mr. Garnet." Her fingers caught Elliot's right hand as she lifted the dead limb. "Left hand on my hip."

Her smile remained in place as she swayed in a slight box step—if that's what it was called.

"A confident man leads, Mr. Garnet. And there's nothing more attractive than confidence." Shockingly, Elliot took a step. It was awkward and clumsy, but he was trying. Amazing.

She was drawing him out of his shell. Her mouth pressed into a tight smirk and she leaned close to his ear. "Confidence and intelligence," she amended.

Taking everyone off guard, she did a quick spin and left Elliot's arms, leaving him looking a bit devastated. Elliot's cheeks darkened and he stilled, slowly folding his hands in front of his crotch.

Nadia walked like fluid seduction, her eyes drilling into Asher's. He swallowed tightly as she held out a hand expectantly. Asher placed his hand in hers, painfully aware of how clammy his palm was. A throaty laugh tickled the air like soft bells as she pulled him close in a sort of tango pose. He stiffly complied.

"Such large hands, Mr. Roan. There's something intoxicating about having a partner who is clearly stronger than me."

His chest filled with heated breath, as he stood a mite straighter.

"Very good. Keep your hold firm, but your hips

loose." She continued to move her feet and he feared accidentally tripping her.

Glancing down, he ventured a step.

"Eyes on me, Asher. Eye contact is perhaps the strongest tool our bodies possess when it comes to seduction. Look at your partner as if you can see inside of her soul, every desire, every need. Look at her with the unspoken promise that *you will* satisfy her every craving and eventually you *will* be inside of her." She winked. "You must show enough confidence that it removes any questions as to whether you're capable of delivering such pleasure. You are, Mr. Roan. And your eyes tell her so."

He stared into her dark eyes and noted how they dilated, black eating up the brunette flecks of brown. He wished she had blue-green eyes like Scarlet. He also wished he could look into Scarlet's eyes without her looking back at him. For the first time, he resented the damn blindfold.

Distracted, he stepped on Nadia's toes. She flinched, but didn't get upset. Rather, she giggled.

"Sorry," he quickly apologized, only to botch the next step and crush the toes of her other foot. "Sorry."

She grinned softly. "You'll get used to it."

"I'm not very good at this," he admitted, perspiration gathering from his nerves.

"You don't have to be good, Mr. Roan. You only have to be comfortable. Even terrible dancers can be sexy if they're comfortable enough in their own skin to dance. Confidence."

He nodded and tried to relax without mangling the dance or her feet.

"Your grip's loosening. Hold me like you mean it."

He tightened his fingers over the warm skin of her

exposed hip and her gaze smoldered. Maybe he wasn't such a tragic student.

"Thanks for the dance," she whispered and spun over to Jet. "You're trouble," she laughed, as Jet immediately took the lead.

Next she went to Hunter who found his own groove and left Nadia in a fit of giggles. "That's it. Have fun."

When the song changed again, she returned to the front. The mood had lightened for everyone, it seemed, except for poor Elliot who appeared more guarded than ever.

An Argentinian beat picked up and Asher waited for what would come next. He was anxious, but enjoying himself, feeling safe to make mistakes and already intending to thank Steve for introducing them to Nadia.

"Keep moving. Don't worry about losing the rhythm. Let it find you," she said, as she slowly bobbed at the front of the class.

The mirror on the front wall provided a place to observe everyone. Through the reflection, she spoke to them, awarding an additional view of her ass. "Dancing isn't always about seeing. Eye contact's important, but not as important as the feeling of intimacy dancing can provoke. Mr. Roan, why don't you come join me at the front."

He took a couple steps forward and waited for direction.

"Who's in charge, Asher? You or me?"

"You?" He hadn't a clue what she expected.

"Wrong. You're in charge. Take charge. Let the music flow through you and guide your motions.

Dancing's a contact sport. First step is making contact."

He palmed the air outside of her hips, unsure if this was what she meant. Her hands slapped over his, bringing them to her hips and pressing them firmly in place as she wiggled. "Don't be afraid. Fear is the opposite of confidence."

"Sorry."

"And don't apologize. Act as though every action is intentional. You boys in the back, keep moving."

The composition intensified with the whine of violins and soft clicking cymbals. It sounded like a tango, but he wasn't sure.

"When you dance with a girl, you leave her feeling like a woman. For those brief moments you make her the focus of the room, the owner of your attention. And when you part, she should feel as though she handed over self-possession, not because you asked, but because you demanded it, and she should be grateful she did."

She made a swift turn and came face to face with him. Her hold fierce. "Connect with the music. Look at me. Pretend you're in love with me. See the woman of your dreams in your arms and hold me like I'm her."

His mind wandered. Nadia's dark eyes transformed into soft pools of blue. Her skin lightened and glowed like the belly of a blushing cloud. Her body became Scarlet's and his entire posture changed, taking hold of her as though he'd never let go.

Her voice lowered as she shifted her feet. "The tango is a love story between a man and a woman, Mr. Roan. It's passionate, dramatic, and at times even driven by anger. You must become a character of sensuality."

His steps turned bold as he led her back from the mirror. Her smile was its own praise. "You're going to dip me back. Don't let go. Keep your hand firmly on the center of my back, dragging down as if you're seeing me naked for the first time and preparing to make love."

She arched in his hold and he sucked in a breath as her abdomen lengthened, stretching far over his arm until her dark hair pooled at the floor. "Now walk, slowly dragging me with you."

Chances were, he looked like a complete fool, but the music grew in tempo and he no longer cared if he was on display. The dance provoked intense emotions—excitement, lust, need—and he was enjoying the experience, all the while imagining Scarlet.

Nadia lifted and her eyes met his. "Now, lead, Mr. Roan. Love is a battlefield and you are fighting to convince your lover she belongs with you. You don't need all the moves. Show me your confidence and fight to seduce her like no other man could. Look into my eyes and mean it."

Gone was his fear of stepping on toes and embarrassing himself. He led Nadia around the studio, locking his gaze with hers, intention clear in his hold. She twirled and he pulled her back to him as if they'd choreographed the move. It was vital he not let go of her hand.

When her calf latched over his hip his eyes widened. There was no space between them. Even her mouth was a kiss away from his. Taking several slow steps backwards, he drew her with him, as she conceded to his lead.

He hadn't realized the others had stopped dancing until the music cut away to silence. With a labored breath, he glanced around the room and found all three of his friends staring at him. His neck heated and he released Nadia.

"Well…" she said, a bit breathlessly. "I think, with a little practice, you will prove quite the capable dance partner, Mr. Roan."

Jet met his gaze and smiled widely. His friend's slow clap echoed through the quiet studio. "You're a hound, Ash. Who knew?"

Taking a self-conscious step back, Asher tugged at his hair and shrugged. Hunter laughed, "It must be all that Jedi training we did as kids. I never knew you had so much grace."

"Shut up," Asher said, his skin heating under their mocking.

He glanced at Elliot, who was scowling, but he wasn't looking at Asher. Rather, he was glaring at Nadia.

Taking a sip from a water bottle stashed in her bag, the expanse of her throat drawing their attention, she screwed the cap on tight, and tossed it away. "So I'll see all of you next week? Same time, same place?"

Asher nodded. He couldn't promise his friends would continue to accompany him, but he would definitely return. When he eventually danced with Scarlet, he intended to treat her to an unforgettable experience.

***

Scarlet hadn't heard from Mr. Stone in four days. Eighty-nine hours to be exact. Her anticipation of his next move had dwindled into frightened frustration. As the workweek carried on, the excitement unfortunately turned into unwelcome and decidedly insecure worry.

Her mood took a turn for the worse when she checked her phone, email, and GP messages while her students silently read. How could he wait this long to contact her? Not a single good morning or even an inquiry as to how her day was going.

The phone in her classroom buzzed and she quietly answered it. Keeping her voice low, so as not to disturb her students, she whispered a hello.

"Ms. Farrow, you have a package. Just letting you know so you can pick it up during your prep."

It was probably the new dry erase markers she'd ordered, which she could use for her next class. No sense in waiting. "Thank you. I'll send someone now." She hung up the phone. "Lori, would you like to run to the office for me? I have a package."

"Sure, Ms. Farrow," the girl said, enthusiastically dropping her book, which she didn't seem to be reading anyway.

The interruption caused a few whispers and she tapped on a few desks to regain control of the class. "We're still *silently* reading."

As she waited, she returned to her own desk and pulled out her eReader. Losing herself in romance, she cleared her throat when the class broke into a sudden rush of whispers and gasps. Glancing up, prepared to correct them again, she gulped. Lori was carrying an enormous flower arrangement down the center aisle of the classroom.

Nearly dropping the eReader, Scarlet sat up. "Are those for me?" Stupid question. They were obviously for her. But who were they from? Mr. Stone didn't know where she worked, did he? Another stupid question. The man apparently knew everything.

The scent of lilies filled the room. Sprays of exotic blooms burst from the bouquet like fireworks freeze-framed in the sky. It was the most majestic gift a man had ever given her. There was no question where they came from. Mr. Stone didn't do anything less than grand and these were simply magnificent.

Her students, no longer interested in the books they held, craned their necks and giggled, while the girls crooned sweet sounds of envy. Even the boys appeared impressed, making comments about the cost of a corsage and noting the crystal vase that held her flowers.

"Are they from your boyfriend, Ms. Farrow?" Lori asked, and Scarlet's face flushed.

"No, honey. I don't have a boyfriend."

"He must be rich," one of the boys in the back announced.

Flustered, and a little embarrassed, she said, "Back to your books, please."

"Ms. Farrow, you gettin' married or something?"

"What's your new name gonna be?"

She couldn't compete with the distraction. "Back to work." They lifted their books, but every gaze was aimed to the front of the class. "Thank you, Lori. You may sit down."

Carefully pulling the flowers apart she located a small sealed envelope. Her stomach flipped when she recognized the wax seal. Mr. Stone. Her fingers tore open the flap and held the card out of sight.

.   .   .

I assume your day is improving, Ms. Farrow. I want to see you tonight. Expect the unexpected.
Yours,
Mr. Stone
A.R.

Her chest lifted, filling with a breath of excitement. No matter how she tried for discretion there was no hiding the joy in her smile. The students snickered and she quickly stuffed the card in her pocket. "Back to work. I mean it."

All of her worry was gone, replaced with potent curiosity on the tails of much relief. He was still interested and she was going to see him tonight! Well, probably not *see* him, but she'd be with him, and he did say to expect the unexpected.

The last few hours of school dragged. It was as though all the clocks stopped the moment she had something to look forward to. When the faculty bell rang an hour after student dismissal, she closed up her classroom and booked it to her car.

Her strides came up short when she spotted Pennyworth and the sedan parked in front of her car. "Good afternoon, Ms. Farrow."

"Mr. Pennyworth. I wasn't expecting you."

He grinned. "I believe Mr. Stone advised you to expect the unexpected."

"Yes." She should have known better than to assume things would go as usual when he'd taken the time to warn her they wouldn't. Did this man even have a usual setting? Probably not.

"Care to join me?" Pennyworth asked, opening the passenger door.

"What about my car?"

"I'll return you to it later."

She supposed that would be okay. This wasn't as late as their usual encounters. She didn't think she'd be out until midnight. Nodding, she slid into the sedan. "Wait. What about the blindfold?"

"No blindfold today, Ms. Farrow." Pennyworth smiled and shut the door.

Oh my God! I'm going to see him!

She reached in her bag and pulled out a small compact. Why had she not put more effort into her appearance today? Fussing with her hair—hopeless—and applying a fresh layer of gloss to her lips, she huffed at the minor improvement she'd made.

Tossing the compact into her bag, her eyes devoured the world passing by. What did his home look like? Would his face be as sensual as his voice? There were so many questions to answer.

"Are you anxious?" Pennyworth asked.

She blinked in surprise. He didn't usually question her. It was usually the other way around. "I'm always anxious when I go to him. Why do you ask?"

"You seem a little high strung. Would you like some water?"

"No thanks."

They drove for a while. She tried to calculate the distance from her house to Mr. Stone's and factor in the distance from school, but nothing was adding up. She was too excited to think.

When the sedan pulled onto a highway she frowned. "Do we usually go this way?"

"Today's route is a bit different, Ms. Farrow."

"Oh."

The car sped along the busy interstate, past the next several exits, until the city came into view. Maybe they were going to a restaurant. Having dinner or cocktails—an actual date.

Pennyworth pulled into one of the nicer sections of the city. Tall skyscrapers blotted out the horizon and the paved roads varied from blacktop to smooth brick dating back to the development of the municipality. They had to be getting close.

When the car pulled in front of a long awning, she glanced up, trying to find the name of the establishment. A doorman in a sharp suit approached the car and Pennyworth exited the vehicle.

A gloved hand offered her assistance as she stood, taking in the mingled scents of the city. "Where are we?"

"The Belleview. Follow me, Ms. Farrow."

She took Pennyworth's offered arm and allowed him to lead her into what was the most luxurious lobby she'd ever visited. "Is this a hotel?"

"Yes, Ms. Farrow."

Her steps faltered. Wait. Was this a booty call? Oh no. She hadn't prepared for anything like that. Hold on. Who said she'd even *consent* to anything like that? The minutes leading up to Mr. Stone lasted far too long for her liking, but the second his presence was imminent, everything seemed to move way too fast.

They approached a tall marble counter. "I'm here to pick up any messages for a Ms. Scarlet Farrow," Pennyworth told the concierge.

Lo and behold, another crisp white envelope was produced, again, sealed with a drop of red wax. He handed it to her.

"Open it?"

"Yes, ma'am."

Plucking open the seal, she removed the small velum card.

I have a treat for you, Ms. Farrow. Let's hope you've done what I've asked and it wasn't too distressing. I've arranged a suite for you in the penthouse. You will be the only guest, so fear not. Dinner shall be provided as well as attire for tomorrow. Mr. Pennyworth is at your disposal should you choose to leave at anytime. Otherwise, he will be delivering you to work in the morning.

See you soon.

Mr. Stone

A.R.

She scanned the lobby, hoping he would stand out to her.

"Are you ready, Ms. Farrow?"

"Where are we going?"

"You have an appointment at the spa."

"I do?"

Pennyworth grinned and nodded. "Allow me to escort you."

She took his arm and they walked through the lobby, down a long corridor decorated with lavish flower arrangements, and entered a lobby on the other side of the building. A divine glass elevator was the centerpiece of the cathedral foyer. They stepped inside and Pennyworth instructed the attendant as to where they were going.

As the elevator rose, she glanced at all the finely

dressed guests wandering around below. This was insane. Things like this didn't happen to people like her. She fought the urge to call Nicole and play a game of *Guess where I am!* But who would believe her?

The bell softly chimed and the doors opened. The soft aroma of herbs and incense met her nose as they pressed through the opaque doors to the spa. Pennyworth touched a hand to her back and guided her inside.

"What are we doing here?" Was she getting her hair done? Her nails? It was impossible not to let the girlie lobe of her brain go nuts and twitter like a princess at the idea of being treated to such a luxury.

"A massage, I believe."

A massage! The last time she had a massage was just before Nicole and Matt's wedding. She was suddenly grateful she'd shaved that morning.

Giddy, she waited beside Pennyworth as he spoke to the woman behind the counter. "You can come with me, Ms. Farrow," the woman invited.

Scarlet glanced to Pennyworth who assured, "I'll be waiting here when you're finished. Enjoy."

There was no hiding her smile. Flowers, and now this? She was in heaven.

The spa attendant showed her where she could keep her belongings and instructed her to change into the fluffy black robe provided. As she undressed, she giggled, her mind painting Mr. Stone as the witch from *Hansel and Gretel*, fattening her up in a very schmoozing way.

Once in her robe and slippers, she exited the dressing room and found the masseuse waiting. The woman led her to a private room with a table and dim lighting. Tinkling chimes played from hidden speakers.

"You can hang the robe there and lie face down on the table. Cover yourself with this sheet and place the gel mask over your eyes." She quietly left the room.

Scarlet took a few seconds to appraise the room. This was a lot nicer than the place she'd taken Nicole. Beside the table was a small shelf with potions and lotions she didn't recognize.

Her slippered feet shuffled to the hook on the wall and she untied her robe, identifying that nervous moment of exposure when she feared someone might burst in and catch sight of her naked body.

Luckily, this week had enriched her audacity in that department. She'd done as Mr. Stone asked and slept nude. The first night was embarrassing, even though no one was there to witness the display. The second night she stripped hadn't seemed as outlandish.

She was far from becoming an exhibitionist, but she realized there was a sort of extravagance to sleeping without any clothes. The blankets became a bit softer and her slumber seemed a tad more restful. It was an extremely freeing and comfortable way to sleep once she got over her fears of being caught in the buff.

Slipping off the robe, she quickly moved to the table and awkwardly climbed onto her belly. Her heart raced, sensing the masseuse would return any second. She jerked the sheet over her body. It was larger than she suspected, covering everything between her back and her ankles.

Leaning up on her elbows, she found the gel mask

at the head of the table and slipped it on. Blindfolded again. She had a silent chuckle.

Sacrificing her sight was no longer as scary as it had been. The gel in the padded mask was cool. Settling her face in the hole at the top of the table, she waited.

Her heartbeat slowed, as the threat of someone walking in while she was uncovered no longer existed. The gentle melody piping from hidden speakers took her to a place of relaxation and her muscles gradually unclenched as she settled in for some first rate pampering.

The door opened with barely a sound. Scarlet's mind had drifted and she was reaching a very Zen place where even the slightest intrusion seemed miles away.

"Good afternoon, Ms. Farrow."

Zen gone.

Every muscle in her body drew up tight and she jerked. What was he doing there? A hand pressed gently into her rising shoulders.

"Easy, Ms. Farrow." Mr. Stone whispered, applying a touch of pressure until she lowered her face back into the opening.

"What are you doing here?" Her voice was oddly high pitched, but muffled. She was *naked!* Covered, but naked all the same.

He chuckled. "Do you like your gift?"

She did a second ago. Now she wasn't so sure. Where the hell did the lady go? How did he get in there?

He tsked. "You don't seem very grateful."

"What? I am—but—*you're in here!*"

"Shh, take a breath. I'd offer you wine, but I didn't bring any. I assume you received your flowers?"

She couldn't relax. Forcing a grateful tone to her voice, she mumbled into the table, "Thank you. They were lovely."

"My pleasure. Now, I have two options for you. Listen carefully, Ms. Farrow." His finger trailed over her shoulder. Tense muscles danced beneath his touch. "I can send Helga back in and she can give you a very relaxing massage or we can have a chat while I do the job. The choice is yours, but keep in mind, one would please me very much over the other."

She couldn't breathe. She was naked. *Naked!* And Mr. Stone was touching her! It was obvious he didn't want Helga to do the job, but he wouldn't force her to undergo his touch without being certain it was invited. What the hell kind of place was this?

All she could think about were those dodgy happy ending places the cops were always busting on the news. Was this one of them?

"Scarlet, I sense you're working yourself into quite a panic. Take a breath and make a decision. Either way, all you're getting is a massage. No one is planning to behave in an untoward manner."

Untoward? Seriously? He was in her massage room! She whimpered.

"I'm afraid I didn't catch that. Was that a 'Helga' or a 'Why, yes, Mr. Stone, I'd be delighted if you were the one to touch me'?"

She shivered. How did he manage to take her decisions and flip them on end every single time? She'd been fully convinced she wanted him to touch her, hoping and praying he'd soon kiss her. Every time he grazed even the knuckles of her hand she melted. Yet, now, here he was, offering to run those powerful hands all over her body and she was debating telling him *no*?

Would saying no be like declining Pennyworth's escort? Would it end the game? She didn't want that. She could do this. Instinct told her if he crossed a line, all she'd have to do was breathe the word *stop* and he would. Besides, there were people out there and no one was speaking above a whisper. She could always scream if she was in danger.

"I choose you, Mr. Stone," she mumbled.

"Pardon?" His clothes rustled as he leaned close. She smirked. The son of a bitch had managed to get her blindfolded this time too.

She sighed. "You." She was never going to see him.

A soft caress ghosted over the back of her hair. "I'm pleased, Ms. Farrow."

At least one of them was. Throat tight, she anxiously waited for him to begin. All of her peaceful musings disappeared. Every nerve was on high alert, every muscle suddenly tensing.

"Try to relax, Ms. Farrow."

She laughed. "I can't."

"Try."

The whisper of hands chaffing together tickled her ears. As the sheet lifted off of her shoulders and was folded back, she shivered. Warm hands, coated in oil pressed into her upper body. "You're very tense. Why is that?"

"Um... I'm *naked*."

"Have you done as I asked?"

He was referring to her going to bed without clothing. Her skin heated—not from the oil. "Yes."

"Good girl." His palms glided over the slope of her

shoulders, fingers pressing gently into the locked muscles and working them loose. "How did you feel, taking off your clothes in the privacy of your bedroom?"

She sighed. His touch was incredible, but also nerve racking. Trying to relax and accept the situation, she confessed, "Silly."

"Why silly?" His low voice was a needed distraction from his touch.

"I'm not used to being naked."

"You're naked now."

I know.

A few minutes passed without talking as he presumably allowed his assessment of her nude state to settle in. Her body mildly relaxed, as she slowly grew accustomed to his touch. The pressure was good, not too hard, yet firm. His large hands were warm against her flesh.

The sheet drifted over her shoulders as his fingers cradled her arm, extending it away from the table as he rubbed his palms past her elbow and massaged the joints of her fingers. "You have very dainty fingers, Ms. Farrow."

She'd never survive an hour of this. Would it be an hour? Wasn't that how long massages typically lasted?

Lacing his large fingers between her "dainty" ones, he jiggled and tugged until the muscles in her hand went lax. Tucking the arm back under the sheet, he repeated the process on her other side.

"I'm curious." *Shocker.* "When you make love do you remove your clothing?"

Her eyes squeezed shut behind the blackness of the mask. *I'm not here. I'm not here.*

The sheet lifted, exposing her calves to the cool air

of the room. His palms encircled the skin beneath her knee and stroked downward. Oh, God. He was touching her feet. Her mind calculated how long it had been since she'd had a pedicure.

A sharp giggle slipped past her lips as her toes twitched and his touch stilled, hovering just over a sensitive spot in the center of her foot. "Ticklish?"

"A little."

He stroked a finger swiftly over the same spot and her foot twitched again. He was teasing her.

"Are you familiar with the ten erogenous zones of the female body, Ms. Farrow?"

No. She was profoundly ignorant when it came to that sort of thing. She was lucky if she climaxed at all during sex and she'd never had a vaginal orgasm. Always requiring special attention, it was usually too much to voice direction, so she'd make some noises and hoped the guy found her performance believable.

Still, she lied. "Yes."

He pinched the soft skin behind her knee. "Liar. You took too long to answer. Allow me to enlighten you."

He moved to her other foot. "The feet are said to be a highly sensitive part of the female body. Some women enjoy the tickling sensation of having their toes stroked or even licked."

Dear God. She didn't think she was one of those women. Spending most of her workday on her feet, she found the area purely functional and would be more comfortable if his attention was elsewhere.

The sheet folded over her legs softly. A finger remained, lightly pressing to the base of her spine, dragging it slowly toward the nape of her neck as he rounded the table. His finger trailed over her shoulder and down her arm. He'd already touched there so the contact wasn't as jarring.

"There are the wrists." The pad of his thumb rubbed over the delicate veins there, making soft circular motions as he lifted her arm. Soft lips pressed into her sensitive flesh and she nearly combusted, mistakenly believing that area was safe.

His lips are literally touching you! Dear God, they were soft.

She moaned and he replaced her arm under the sheet. His finger caressed her arm, both hands making a slow climb until they curled around her shoulders, pressing and soothing the deep tissue. Coasting his fingers upward, he slowly dragged the backs of his nails up and down the column of her neck until her nipples pebbled against the table.

"The neck is of course an erogenous zone, so sensitive and feminine. I like watching your neck when we're together, seeing the telltale blush deepen your ivory completion, noticing when you swallow nervously. And then there's that fluttering pulse of yours. You have a very beautiful neck, Ms. Farrow."

Did he feel her pulse now? It was trembling with the subtlety of a jackhammer. Her breath shook as she slowly exhaled.

The rasp of his fingertips was enunciated as he caressed the shell of her ear. Her body shook as shivers traveled down her spine. His clothing brushed over her back as he leaned close and whispered, "And let's not overlook the ears. Such a delicate little lobe, perfect for nibbling."

He gave it a gentle tug with his fingers and she gasped. His breath heated, leaving a dew of inconsequential moisture in the hollow area.

"Ears are fascinating things. While it can be quite erotic having them kissed, nibbled, or sucked, they're also pathways to that principal sex organ I told you about—the brain." His voice lowered. "Every word can be processed as erotic when the ear is stimulated. I could whisper math equations and make you wet."

Mission accomplished.

He backed away, as her belly tightened with her thighs, and her folds grew damp. The situation catapulted to the next level. She'd never survive this.

His hands worked over the sheet, pressing into her lower back. As he glided his palms over her covered rear she tensed. The sheet again lifted off of her legs, this time really exposing her. Its folded weight gathered just beneath her bottom and she was excruciatingly aware of her uncovered thighs.

Words associated with unkind emotions fluttered through her mind. *Cellulite. Stretch marks. Freckles. Pudgy.*

He tickled the inner part of her knee, that soft flesh no one ever noticed. "There are an astounding amount of nerve endings in the backs of the knees. I wonder...what would it feel like to have a man drag his tongue from here..." His finger dragged slowly upward. "...To here?"

Her breathing had passed regulated ten minutes ago. Now she was panting, quick, shallow breaths as her body begged for him to do something more brazen than he was already doing and her mind feared the same. It was the same tug of war he always produced in her, but this time it was more intense than ever before.

Her body was aroused to a degree she'd never

known. She wanted him to touch her in places no one had touched in several years.

His fingers rode over her skin, making gentle whorls and easing the tired muscles at the backs of her thighs. *Keep going. Please. Oh God,* he's getting closer. *Don't go any farther! Don't stop!* Her mind fell into needy hysteria.

"The inner thigh, so close to heaven, is an obvious erogenous zone. Easily teased, but highly sensitive. Those tantalizing nerve endings are the prerequisite to fulfillment. This is the land of unspoken promises," he said, softly massaging the tender flesh. "Once here, a woman will likely beg for you to continue."

Just as her begging was about to burst forth in a way she'd never pleaded before, the sheet was lowered. Her lips tightened as she silently groaned in frustration.

Her irritation was abruptly distracted as the covering lifted from her shoulders and slowly dragged downward. Down, down, down, until she was sure he'd leave her bare. He didn't. The soft fabric folded just past the base of her spine.

Her body calmed, contrary to the alert state of her brain, as he carried on massaging as if he were a professional. Special attention was given to each vertebra of her spine and she almost forgot *he* was the one playing with her. *Almost.*

She should have known better. It seemed to be a special joy of his to give her a false sense of comfort thereby having a more potent effect when he next did something outlandish like—*expose her ass!*

His nails gently scraped over the sensitive flesh and her entire body convulsed. "*This* can be a highly erogenous zone, Ms. Farrow. The flesh is highly sensitive, yet padded, allowing all variations of play. Some women simply like their bottoms fondled, while others enjoy having it groped, licked, penetrated, and even spanked. I look forward to learning your preferences."

That's it. She couldn't take anymore. She groaned and he lightly swatted her ass before covering it. "Problem, Ms. Farrow?"

So many words to say, but in the face of his inquiry she couldn't voice a single one. "No."

"Then I'll continue."

Of course you will. Maybe he was a sadist and this was the introduction to torture. It sure *felt* like torture. Every part of her body was so sensitized, so stimulated, each twinge of pleasure had the strange effect of pain. She wanted... she wasn't sure. *Something!*

With her back still exposed, he skimmed his fingers up her side sending chills prickling in the wake of his caress. Her breasts were pressed against the table, which was oddly providing some form of relief until he trailed a finger over the side of her ribs.

"Of course we mustn't forget the breasts. Out of respect for modesty I won't ask that you turn over. I'm sure you're well aware of the sensitivity in this area, perhaps even coping with the symptoms of arousal there now."

She hated him. Hated him, but really, really liked him. It crossed her mind that any man this attuned to a woman's body had to have some sort of sex record. His name and that picture of him she was searching for, was probably in the *Guinness Book of World Records* under world's greatest player. She should really consider this as their relationship developed, because there were a lot of diseases out there a girl had to watch out for, and a man who likely had as many part-ners as Mr. Stone could very well possess one.

Great. Now her mind had drifted to an unwelcome place and she was imagining labs and all sorts of un-sexy things. This was why she sucked at sex. *Head in the game, Lettie!*

"Stay with me, Ms. Farrow. There are two more."

He massaged her back and hips, allowing her to drift and return to that lovely subspace. Her mind un-raveled, relinquishing all forms of paranoia. If they ever got to *that* point they'd address their histories and proceed accordingly. There was no sense in worrying about that stuff now—

"The ninth erogenous zone is what, Ms. Farrow?"

Huh? What? Did he tell her and she missed it? "Umm..."

"I believe you know. Think. It's what most assume is the most important place on a woman, but they would be wrong."

Oh, that...

"Tell me what it is, Ms. Farrow."

She swallowed. She could say it. She was a grown woman. Her chest tightened. Forcing out the word, she rasped, "The vagina." Biting her lips between her teeth she stifled the threat of any nervous, juvenile laughter.

"Is that what we're calling it? Very well. Technical it is."

He didn't change position or attempt to reach any-where near that zone. Rather, he kept his voice low and even, as he massaged her lower back.

"The vagina," he said, a note of humor in his voice. "There are numerous nerve receptors in the female genitals, but most tend to favor clitoral stimulation or having the elusive G-spot fondled. You know, I do believe describing it technically can be arousing as well. I wonder what your reaction would be to exposing this part of your body, allowing a man as much time as he desired to explore and see such an intimate part of your anatomy."

She was drenched. Not only that, she feared her next gynecological exam. He'd altered her thinking on the entire practice and she'd likely recall *this* moment at every annual appointment for the rest of her life. Wonderful. Not only was she naked, he was effectively stripping away her composure with each encounter.

"I'm afraid our hour is almost up, Ms. Farrow. Before I leave you to dress, I'll tell you the last erogenous zone on a woman's body, the most important of all."

There was more?

"The lips," he whispered. "The lips of a female are incredibly sensitive. They can be licked, toyed with, teased, and above all, kissed. They breathe out gasping sighs, pleas, and express a woman's need. But beyond all, the lips invite a man to kiss other places. A kiss is perhaps the voice of permission given to a lover before he possesses all else a woman can offer."

She'd never wanted a man to kiss her as much as she did in that very moment. *This* man. Fear that she'd embarrass herself because she was so eager to maul him was the only thing holding her still, that and her face shoved in the hole, breasts smashed against the table.

His lips pressed to the very center of her spine before the sheet covered her trembling body. "It's been a pleasure, Scarlet."

Her lungs released a pent up breath. Every part of her body gushed with need as her name whispered past his lips. He applied it like a reward, only given at the conclusion of their time, and with those two familiar syllables came the sense of deep earned praise followed by the sting of his farewell.

The door closed and she suspected he was gone. She wasn't sure if she wanted to scream or cry, but she had no regrets.

---

*A*sher shut the door and threw his weight against the wood. His cock was so hard he needed a moment before he could take another step. His intention had been to get deeper into her mind, but he seemed to be the one to receive the mind fuck here.

There had never been a more intense need for a woman. What he suffered in those ticking moments was raw and brutally human. Everything in him demanded he make love to her, but he'd somehow managed to keep his composure, not letting his fierce desire spill out in his voice or touch.

Swallowing hard, his head tipped against the door. His fists trembled as he denied himself the right to burst through the door and take her once and for all.

He could hear her moving around on the other side. Reaching in his pants, he quickly shifted his erection as much as possible. He needed to get out of there.

Stifling a whimper, he winced and slowly paced away from the door. There was a bottle of champagne in his room. He'd be icing down his balls with it as soon as he relieved some of the tension.

He couldn't survive much more of this.

10

REFLECTION

SOMETIMES THE HUMAN brain could be so thoroughly entertained, all connection to reality can be severed, and the return to the real world took a bit of adjusting. Scarlet referred to this as the movie theater effect. She was suffering the results of such at present, only a million times worse.

Her reflection in the dimly lit dressing room was not anything she recognized. How had her hair turned into such a wild mess of tangles when he hadn't touched her there? Her face was flushed and she looked as though she'd been through the rinse cycle—that or thoroughly fucked.

Her body acted as though a foreign cloak rested on her nerves. Every bit of flesh tingled with awareness and parts of her she couldn't identify begged for more of what was now gone. If this was desire, it wasn't like any sort she'd experienced before. She felt raw, needy, and, well...horny.

Shutting her eyes, she tried for steady breathing. No longer blindfolded, she again experienced a strange longing for darkness, finding the obscurity oddly comforting. Unexpectedly, what she originally opposed, she now yearned for, associating the sensation with him. It was as though she were forming a sort of Stockholm's fondness for blindness.

Her clothing uncomfortably covered her frame, abrasive in a way it hadn't seemed before. Her appearance should have slowed her exit, but puzzlingly she didn't care. Her mind was too numb, too distracted to pay attention to what others might think of her ragged exterior. All thoughts consumed by what was happening inside of her, what he'd done to her.

Exiting the room, she blinked at the unwelcome light. Discovering it was only late afternoon disoriented her even more. Her mind wanted it to be evening.

Pennyworth stood as she entered the waiting room of the spa, placing a fitness magazine on the table. "Did you enjoy yourself, Ms. Farrow?"

She nodded tightly, certain he was aware Mr. Stone had come into the room. Approaching him, she whispered, "Is he here?"

"I can't answer that. Would you like to go to your suite now?"

He'd arranged a suite for her, she'd nearly forgotten. She had no experience with this sort of spoiling. "Okay."

Pennyworth took her arm and escorted her through the hotel. They took the elevator to the top floor and he handed her a keycard. "I'll be in room three o'seven if you need me. Otherwise, he's left you instructions."

Her heart fluttered at the suspicious hope Mr.

Stone would return again that night. Sliding the key into the door, she thanked Pennyworth before he left.

Her jaw unhinged as she took in the space. Holy mother of luxury. She giggled. This had to be a dream. Stepping into the room, as if she were trespassing, she studied the space.

A large bed dominated the far wall. Plush pillows and blankets—all the color of snow—added several inches to the mattress. The furniture was darkly polished wood and the curtains were drawn. In front of the window were two high back chairs angled around a small accent table. A glass and a bottle of Merlot sat on the table and her stomach flipped at the sight of a wax sealed envelope.

She rushed forward and tore open the seal.

Ms. Farrow,
In the closet you will find two outfits. I assume it will be clear which was chosen for work. Take a bath, have a glass of wine, then dress and go to the Imperial Room for dinner. Reservations are under Stone for eight o'clock.

Mr. Stone
A.R.

She darted to the closet and found two garment bags hanging, and a small boutique bag resting on the floor next to two shoe boxes. Her fingers reached for the bags and stilled as awareness took hold.

This was it. This must be the sense of adoration she'd been waiting for. Every nuance, every detail, it all added up to total attention, yet, the more he gave the more prominent the still hallow spaces became. There was one thing she wanted beyond all the luxury, one thing she'd exchange for everything—*him*. She wanted him.

Suddenly overwhelmed, she backed away from the closet and perched on the edge of the bed. He made sense of her, understood her wants in a way that made them just and appropriate, but there was a great fear linked to his presence in her life. What would she be if he disappeared? She didn't want to go back to just Scarlet. She much preferred the Scarlet she became when with him—free and brave.

Her vision blurred as a tight and painful realization clamped down on her heart. She wanted to call him, but couldn't. She didn't have his number. Sniffling, a tear slipped from her lashes and fell to the floor.

"Thank you," she whispered, hoping he realized how much all this attention meant to her, told her that someone believed she was worth such focus.

It was so surreal, she wouldn't be surprised if at the end of their encounter she were slammed with an enormous bill. What could he possibly be gaining from all of this? She hadn't even kissed him.

Strange, the indebted feelings reminded her of all she could offer and one thing stood in the forefront of her mind. Sex. Earlier she'd worried that he might have health issues, but now that didn't seem as troublesome as it did heartbreaking.

She'd ask him. She had to. Not because she intended to pay for his kindness with sexual favors, but because if something were to happen to him... She couldn't even finish the thought. She just hoped he was healthy.

You're falling in love with him.

No. That couldn't be right. Her mind played over their encounters and conversations. To an outsider their relationship and the desires she was battling might seem contrived and superficial, but the emotional gifts far outweighed the material.

He made her feel things she had no reference for. Take away the hotel suite, the clothes, and whatever else lay in that closet, and her feelings for him remained the same. If he were ill, her affections wouldn't change. She'd take care of him, nurture his needs the way he did hers. One question echoed in her mind, drawing more worry than any other. While Mr. Stone was taking care of her, who was taking care of him?

Wiping her eyes, she attempted to stave off her tears and failed. She needed that chance to show him how much she cared and worried she might never have it.

A new sort of terror introduced itself. No longer was she afraid of a possibly dangerous man. Now she was terrified of what said man might do to her heart. He'd never demanded anything of her. He'd merely requested she trust him in order to give her everything she desired. At this point, she whole-heartedly believed he would succeed, because he'd already given her more than she'd ever dreamed.

Should she continue on this path, she'd never be the same. Ignorance had allowed her to assume and wish for something more in her love life. Now, she knew that *more* existed, but feared it might soon end.

Drawing in a deep breath, she released it slowly.

How did the saying go? *Better to have loved and lost?* Or was it *better to love for a day?* No, that was *live* a day. Whatever. Her mind was made up. She was doing this. For better or for worse and all that jazz, she was giving in to temptation and letting the chips fall where they may.

No more games. She was going to give him everything she had. Hopefully it was enough for a man like him.

She wanted to settle in for the full ride and treat herself to the experience of a lifetime, certain the man in charge was capable of taking her to places she never dared to imagine even in her wildest fantasies.

Blotting her eyes on her sleeve, she stood and returned to the closet. Unzipping the first garment bag she found a red wrap dress of the softest material. It was lovely and the color would compliment her hair nicely. Draped over the padded hanger was a strand of pearls.

Smiling, pleased, she bent to the floor and lifted the lid off one of two shoeboxes. Glittering black pumps with long heels rested in a bed of tissue. Holy crap they were fancy.

She opened the other shoebox and found beautiful brown leather dress boots. They would look perfect with the dress. It was a very nice outfit.

Biting her lip, she contemplated the fancier shoes and the other garment bag. The red dress was very elegant compared to what she typically wore to work, but those shoes were definitely too formal for it. Something formal had to be in the other bag, which meant she was likely dressing up for dinner.

Smiling, she pulled open the zipper and gasped. Deep emerald lace flowed out of the carrier and she quickly unearthed the dress. It was stunning. She'd never owned anything like it.

Pulling the hanger out of the closet, she appraised the garment. Beautiful didn't accurately describe how pretty it was. Long lace sleeves reached to the A-line waist. The neckline was wide and she wondered if her shoulders would be exposed.

She quickly checked inside, finding the bodice lined with the softest silk as she searched for a tag. There wasn't one and she panicked thinking it might not fit. How would he have guessed her size?

He did see her coat during the times she visited his house. Oh! And he had her remove her shoes. Sneaky man. Grinning, amazed at his attention to detail, she hung up the dress and went to take her bath, anxious to put on her new clothes.

As she entered the bathroom, she was again overwhelmed by the extravagance. A basket full of specialty items like handmade soaps and lotions rested on the counter. Her smile seemed tattooed on her face.

When she met her reflection's gaze she squealed like a little girl. "This is too freaking cool!"

She bathed quickly then emptied the contents of the boutique bag on the bed. She found panties, earrings, both pearl and rhinestone, lace stockings, a small clutch, and some other unmentionables.

No blindfold! Her heart raced.

As she slid into the strapless bra she faced the mirror and laughed. How much time did he spend staring at her boobs? The fit was perfect.

Next came the stunning emerald dress. It fit like a glove. The only thing she didn't have was makeup. She went to her bag and dug out her compact. Applying a dusting of powder over her freckles, she wished she had mascara. After slathering her lips with gloss she appraised the final product.

Wow. She looked really beautiful, almost to the point where she didn't recognize herself. Reaching into her bag, she found her phone. This sort of thing needed to be recorded. Snapping a few selfies, because when she woke up from this dream she wanted the souvenir, she took a deep breath and grinned. Never had she felt so content.

She stuck her phone, debit card, room key, and gloss in the clutch and checked the room for anything she was forgetting. Her nerves were snapping in every direction and she couldn't think straight, so she left, deciding the only thing she needed was him.

She was outside of the Imperial Room with exactly one minute to spare. Glancing around, she waited for Pennyworth or the man of her dreams to announce himself. Strangers bustled by, some formally dressed couples heading into the restaurant. He could be any one of the gentlemen in the vicinity.

Her pulse raced as she anticipated seeing Mr. Stone for the first time. It was already clear his looks were irrelevant. Gone were any vain needs for physical attributes. Fat, bald, skinny, scarred, she didn't care. The only thing that mattered was being able to finally look him in the eyes.

Assuming he was already there, she slowly approached the hostess station. A woman in a formal black cocktail dress greeted her. "Good evening. Welcome to the Imperial Room. May I have your name?"

Scarlet swallowed. "I have a reservation under Stone."

The woman typed a name into the discreet computer embedded in the podium. "Yes, here you are. Right this way, please."

She followed the hostess, doing her best to keep her breathing as even as possible. Her smile faltered when she saw he'd yet to arrive at the table the woman selected. She pulled out a chair for Scarlet and she thanked her.

"Your server will be by momentarily," the hostess announced, removing the other place setting.

"I think I'm expecting someone?"

She paused. "The reservation was made for one. Is that incorrect?" she asked nervously, no longer removing the extra dishes.

One? He wasn't coming? Such sharp devastation filled her, she lost her appetite as her mood deflated and her smile fell.

"Oh." Disappointment clamped tight around her heart. "No, you're probably correct," she forced out, trying not to show that she was upset. Of course she sounded crazy and was now on the verge of tears. Any sane person would know they were eating alone.

She internally winced at the thought of eating alone, something she loathed to do in public. The hostess, a bit confused, left the other place setting and made some comment about sending the server directly to her table.

Scarlet didn't know what was worse, openly eating alone, or eating across from an empty place setting and looking as if she'd been stood up. For as excited as she was about the evening, she suddenly wanted to leave.

The waiter arrived with a cheery smile she couldn't reciprocate. "Good evening, Ms. Farrow." She drew to attention the moment he said her name. How had he known her name when the reservation was under Stone?

"Good evening."

He poured fresh water in her glass. "My name is Xavier and I'm here to make sure you enjoy your experience as our guest at the Imperial Room tonight. Have you ever dined with us before?"

Her eyes scanned the restaurant. "No."

"Then you're in for a lovely treat. Mr. Stone has taken the liberty of ordering for you this evening. He's asked that we start you off with a bottle of our Imperial Red 1947. Will that be acceptable?"

Nineteen forty-seven? She really hoped he was picking up the tab, because a bottle of such aged wine might overdraw her bank account.

Stop being bitter. Embrace the experience for what it is. A treat and something no one else has ever come remotely close to doing for you.

Sighing, she pressed on a grin and said, "That would be fine. Thank you."

When the server disappeared to retrieve the wine, she was extremely self-conscious. Sitting alone in a dining room filled with other patrons had a way of making her feel on display. She glanced around the room and noted who was talking with company and who wasn't.

No one seemed to be watching her, so she tucked away all expectations, and tried to embrace the moment.

sher noted the moment her happiness flipped to disappointment. The hostess had begun to clear the additional place setting and Scarlet's happy expression wilted. He had to fight the urge to join her. It wasn't time.

His heart was still racing from that afternoon. He'd spent days researching the human body and decided he wanted to touch her. Over a conversation with Jet the idea for a sensual massage came to him. It was tricky, but he'd pulled it off, making arrangements with the hotel and convincing them he had a surprise for the woman in his life. After throwing a little money their way, they'd been more than agreeable to his terms.

Had Scarlet asked him to leave, he would have. He had no intention of violating her privacy any more than necessary and he had touched her only after her consent. It took a solid hour for his body to recover from seeing her so beautifully exposed. Her skin was silk under his fingers, traces of the memory still a threat to his composure.

With her stunning appearance this evening, he was again struggling to mask his body's reaction to her presence. She was divine in the emerald dress his stylist had suggested.

The waiter returned and filled her glass with wine. Something in her downtrodden expression shifted as she took a sip. *What changed?*

Keeping his expression blank, he continued to sip his cocktail at the bar, studying her through the mirrored wall. She fascinated him. When the waiter returned, she grinned, the gesture appearing genuine. Perhaps she'd come to terms with his absence.

As the meal progressed he enjoyed observing her. An evolution of confidence took place right before his eyes. He'd assumed it would be a touch distressing, dining alone, all dressed up in a five star restaurant. But her adjustment to the circumstances was impressive. They both appeared to be evolving in that department. Pride and shared understanding filled him, strengthening their connection in an unexpected way.

The meal concluded with a beautiful chocolate soufflé. Every bite she took was erotic. Her eyes fluttered shut as her lips closed over the tines of the fork, her expression pure delight as she savored the last nibble.

When the waiter returned, Asher noted her surprise that there was no bill. Did she think he'd invite her to dinner and not handle the tab? What sort of lowlifes had she dated? He tucked that question away for another time.

As she stood, he diverted his attention, not wanting his position made obvious. His body tensed when his stool was bumped and the clatter of her little purse fell to the floor, her soft whispered apology only an arm's reach from his position.

"I beg your pardon."

Not thinking, he bent to pick up the clutch and slowly handed it to her. Their eyes met for the briefest moment and she smiled, her blush most likely the result of her clumsiness. His heart thundered as she took the clutch, his gaze fastened to her striking eyes, the eyes he'd carefully avoided until now.

"Thank you."

He nodded, cautious not to speak and the moment was broken. An unexpected fury burned through him. Had she seen nothing remarkable in him? He breathed roughly through his nose as she left the restaurant without even a second glance.

What should he expect? Gratitude? She had no way of knowing he'd been the one responsible for her meal or the luxurious suite. Still, unpleasant and oily doubt coiled in his gut. Just as she always had, she saw right through him as if his presence was inconsequential while he'd spent every minute trying to see her soul and memorize every detail of her personality.

Paying his tab, he left the bar and returned to his suite. It was only as he slid his key into the lock that another thought crossed his mind. Perhaps it wasn't that she hadn't seen him. Perhaps it was that she only had eyes for Mr. Stone. That theory managed to repair a bit of his hurt.

Could she be that invested in the charade of Mr. Stone that she would only react to his known introduction? Asher contemplated this for several minutes as he drew off his suit and started the shower. There was no way of knowing how devoted she was to the mysterious Mr. Stone without asking.

Settling onto the bed, he pulled out his phone and hit send.

11

VULNERABILITY

Scarlet carefully zipped the dress back into the garment bag and touched the packaging affectionately. So she hadn't gotten the chance to meet him face to face as expected. The evening was still one she'd remember forever.

They had nine encounters left until the next phase began—whatever that was. She wished there was some sort of future guarantee, but there wasn't.

It was bizarre. Her entire day had taken a one-eighty at the hands of this man, yet she missed him. Sure, he'd been at the spa, but she was so taken off-guard by his presence she'd barely managed to utter more than a few syllables.

Her stomach suddenly swooped as though dropping into her feet. What if she'd made a fool of herself and he'd intended to join her for dinner, but then changed his mind after seeing her naked? Her belly clenched and she struggled not to lose her delicious meal.

A soft chirping came from the bed. So distraught over the course of her thoughts, she almost didn't recognize the muffled sound of her cell phone. Maybe it was Nicole. She was strongly considering confiding in her friend, if only to chase away her ridiculous paranoia.

She unsnapped the clutch and gasped when she read the word "Restricted." Quickly accepting the call, she brought the phone to her ear, hoping this wasn't a courtesy goodbye. "Hello."

"Good evening, Ms. Farrow."

Her voice shook with trepidation. "Good evening, Mr. Stone."

She silenced the compulsion to apologize for all of her awkwardness. It seemed the aftermath of her exposure was a lot more difficult to cope with than the actual moment she was exposed. Vulnerability and inadequacy were living-breathing things inside of her, strong enough to destroy everything.

"Why do you sound upset?" The sharp tone of his voice caused her to wince.

Because I'm overanalyzing the crap out of everything like I always do until I squander any hope or confidence I have left. "I'm...I'm not upset."

"Lies, Ms. Farrow. I assumed we were past that."

She swallowed. Earlier she'd decided to bare all. It was time to practice that concept—as difficult as that was for her. His clipped tone didn't make it any easier. "I am upset. But first I have to thank you for everything you did today. It was amazing. No one's ever treated me to such an experience."

"The pleasure was mine. Now, tell me why you're upset."

Her throat constricted as she confronted her greatest fear. "Is it over?" Tears rushed to her eyes, blurring her view of the pretty suite.

"I beg your pardon?"

"You...you didn't come to dinner."

"Who says I wasn't there?"

Her body drew up tight and she looked around nervously, wishing she were back at the restaurant. In a breathless whisper, she asked, "You were there?"

"You looked exquisite, Scarlet. Emerald suits you well."

Her insides melted at the compliment followed by the use of her first name. However, par for the course, there came a great sense of grief. He'd been there and she'd missed him. Right before her eyes and she hadn't known he was there.

Her mind played over every other patron at the restaurant. "Were you alone?"

He chuckled. "Where would the fun be if I answered that?" Still he answered her anyway. "I was sitting with others, Ms. Farrow."

Her body shivered as chills chased over her arms and legs. "I wish I had known. I was hoping to finally see you."

"And what if I turned out to be beneath your expectations, Ms. Farrow?"

"Impossible."

"Interesting. So have we changed our emphasis on physical appearance?"

She lowered herself to the chair and her phone beeped. Crap. Her battery was running low. Discreetly digging in her purse, praying she'd packed her spare charger, she explained, "It doesn't matter what you look like. I want to meet you."

"In time, Ms. Farrow. What are you doing? It sounds like you're rummaging around for something."

She huffed, not finding the charger. "I'm looking for my charger. My phone's not going to last long."

He was silent for a minute. "Do you have a charger with you?"

Dumping the contents of her bag on the bed she flung the items around, not finding it. Voice laced with distress, she said, "No. It's not here."

"What kind of phone do you have?"

"What?"

"I'll have Pennyworth run out and pick you up a charger. What kind of phone, Ms. Farrow?"

She laughed. Why was she surprised? "It's the new iPhone."

"Very well. Hold on please."

She was placed on mute and wondered if he was in the same room as Pennyworth. She considered paying the chauffeur a visit, perhaps running into Mr. Stone.

"My apologies. Your new charger should be there soon."

"Are you sharing a room with Mr. Pennyworth?" she blurted.

"Full of questions this evening. No, Ms. Farrow. I called him from the landline. Now that we have that straightened out, let's move on to more important things. Tell me how it felt to eat alone this evening. I trust the fare was to your liking."

She sighed and eased back on the bed. "Everything was exceptional. I wish you'd have joined me, but I'm beginning to think you like making me wait."

"Very much so, Ms. Farrow. There's something quite intoxicating about stimulating such longing that it becomes physically evident. Now, once you realized I wouldn't be dining with you, what did you feel?"

"Hurt."

"Why hurt?"

It was difficult to put her emotions into words. "Because I thought you'd be there."

"I was there."

Her lips tightened. She didn't want to think about him being there and her being too blind—might as well have worn the damn blindfold—to see him. "I thought we'd actually have a date."

"Is that what you'd prefer, a typical date? I assumed the way we were doing things was a touch more interesting."

He was right, of course. A collective look at her dating history absolutely paled in comparison to her experiences with Mr. Stone. Even without all her senses, he was safe and securely holding the title of best rendezvous partner ever. "No, I like the way you do things. I was just hoping..."

"We have time, Ms. Farrow. Now, after your surprise settled in, what did you feel?"

"Like I was on display."

"Was that a pleasant feeling or an uncomfortable one?"

"Uncomfortable."

He chuckled. "So no little exhibitionist hiding inside that body of yours?"

She blushed and then scowled as her phone beeped, informing her she had five percent battery life remaining. "I'm afraid not."

"Yet, you managed to enjoy the meal anyway."

"I had to get over it or I wouldn't have been able to eat at all."

"It pleases me that you made the best of an unexpected situation. Today you were very exposed. You dealt with your circumstances rather well."

She smiled at the compliment, but flushed again at the attention to how exposed she'd actually been. "Thank you."

"I enjoyed touching you this afternoon."

Her body immediately called to attention, her sex contracting and heart racing. "I enjoyed it too," she whispered.

"Did the massage arouse you, Ms. Farrow?"

How could it not? "Yes."

"Are you aroused now?"

"Yes." She swallowed.

There was a sharp knock at the door and she jolted off the bed.

"That will likely be Pennyworth with your charger. Thank him and tell him goodnight."

She went to the door and opened it. Pennyworth handed her a package. "There you are, Ms. Farrow."

"Thank you."

"Goodnight, ma'am."

"Goodnight, Mr. Pennyworth."

She shut the door and placed the latch over the bolt for extra measure. She quickly slipped open the box, grateful Apple didn't package things in a way that required a chainsaw. Finding a plug at the base of the lamp, she quickly hooked the phone to the outlet.

"Better now?"

"Yes. Thank you so much."

"You're quite welcome. I believe we were discussing your arousal."

The interruption had been a distraction, cooling her body, but the moment Mr. Stone mentioned anything sexual she was right back in a state of excitement. Sucking in a breath she waited to hear what he'd say.

"Are you still aroused, Ms. Farrow?"

"Yes," she confessed quietly.

"What is it that's arousing you?"

"You."

He paused. "How can you tell you're aroused? Describe it to me."

"I feel it. My heart's racing and I'd do anything to have you here."

"Anything?"

She tried to think of something she wouldn't do. Nope. She was pretty desperate in that moment. "I'm pretty sure anything."

"Interesting. Do you masturbate, Ms. Farrow?"

Her eyes closed as humiliation choked her. Creeping carnal delight provoked her answer. "Sometimes. I think everyone does."

"Does it arouse you to know I've masturbated while thinking of you?"

"Oh, God." She couldn't recall ever being this turned on. "Yes, very much so."

"Are you still in the dress, Scarlet?"

Her name. She savored it, but couldn't help the panic that it hinted to a goodbye. "No. I hung it up because I didn't want anything to happen to it."

"Describe what you're wearing."

"The hotel robe."

"Anything else?"

"No."

"Where are you sitting?"

"On the bed."

"Good. I want you to follow my directions. Are you ready?"

Her sex pulsed with need. She was beyond ready. "Yes."

"Lie back and extend your legs. Keep your knees together."

She scooted onto the pillows and slowly moved her ankles down the mattress. "Okay."

"Don't let go of the phone. Use your free hand to untie the robe and then carefully spread the lapels wide, exposing your body."

Her fingers trembled as she fussed with the knot of the tie. Her own breath ricocheted through the receiver and she winced. Once she had the knot undone, she separated the lapels. "Okay."

"Is the room cold? Did exposing yourself make your nipples hard, Ms. Farrow?"

Biting her lip she clenched her thighs tight, needing the pressure. "They were already hard, Mr. Stone." She smirked when she sensed she'd discomfited him. Maybe she could be sexy after all.

His voice turned gravely. "Touch your breasts, but you are not to touch your nipples. Move your hand slowly. Take your time and feel every caress. I want you to shut your eyes."

Her lashes lowered and she arched as her fingertips slowly traveled between her breasts, over the slope of chilled flesh, circling close to the areola, but not touching.

"Whose touch are you imagining, Ms. Farrow?"

"Yours. Mr. Stone." His name came out as a second thought, as if he were a lover holding her and she were pleading his name.

"Good Girl. Now drag your hand lower. You are not to touch your sex, but tease the skin closest to your clitoris with your fingers."

Her belly filled with liquid heat as she trailed her fingers lower. Her knees remained closed, but her bottom lifted off the bed.

"Describe what you feel."

"Soft hair."

"Red," he breathed the word, giving away a bit of the effect the conversation was having on him.

"Mmm, yes, red."

"I bet you're very pink there, Ms. Farrow."

She moaned. "I wish you were here."

"What would you want if I were there?"

"Your hands on me, your mouth, everything."

There was a slight rustling over the line and she wondered if he was touching himself as well.

"Part your thighs for me, Ms. Farrow. Show me all those glistening pink folds."

"Oh, God." Her knees slowly parted and cream trickled from her sex.

"Take your finger and circle your opening. Do not penetrate yourself, just tease your outer layers and do not lay a finger on that clit."

Her digit circled her sex and she moaned.

"Are you wet?"

"So wet. I've never been this wet."

He groaned with appreciation. "Now sink your longest finger into that wet pussy and keep it there until I tell you to remove it."

Her finger plunged deep and she arched, her shoulders digging into the bed as she let out a guttural moan. "Mr. Stone..."

"Is it hot?"

"Burning."

"And wet. Swirl your finger around without withdrawing it."

She did as he directed. Her body was so stimulated every slight motion caused her to twitch and moan.

"How close are you to climaxing, Ms. Farrow?"

"So close."

"Remove your finger."

She whimpered, but did as he instructed, immediately missing the presence of her little digit.

"Tell me what your fingers look like."

"They're wet and coated with my arousal."

"I want you to take a picture of your hand with your phone. Later, when you look at it you'll remember what I do to you. Do that now."

Lifting her phone from her cheek, she trembled as she keyed in the command for her camera. She focused the lens and stilled. This was the raunchiest, hottest thing she'd ever done in her life. *Click.* She definitely wanted a keepsake. "Done."

"Good girl. Now put that finger back in your pussy and fuck yourself to orgasm."

She panted, literally panted as her finger plunged into her wet sex. Her moan filled the room as she rolled to her side. "May I touch my clit?"

He cleared his throat meaningfully.

"Please," she amended.

"Touch everything, Scarlet. Those beautiful breasts, your strawberry nipples, your throbbing clit. I want to hear you come."

She arched and carried on like a skilled harlot. Never before had she behaved so carnally, not alone, not with a lover, not ever. Only for Mr. Stone. "Mr. Stone. Oh, God. Oh, God!" Her cries turned into whimpers as her body rocked under the quickening pulse of her sex. "I'm coming—"

All sound disappeared as the most intense orgasm of her life ripped through her. Her spine tingled, sending shivers to her scalp, fingertips, and even the soles of her feet. Her fingers rubbed and pressed, prolonging the pleasure as her body continued to quake. As the waves slowly subsided, she squeezed her eyes shut and caught her breath. It was then she realized she wasn't the only one with labored breathing.

Her face heated to a deep burn as she became aware of what she'd just done. Contemplating hanging up and hiding under the covers, she swallowed back her self-consciousness as Mr. Stone whispered, "Beautiful."

Reassurance flooded her and she sighed, pressing her heated face into the pillow. Softly, she confessed, "I've never done that before—with someone else listening."

"Well, I'm pleased you shared your first time with me."

So many unspoken words wanting to be said rushed through her mind. She didn't want to freak him out or scare him away, so she bit down on her lip, forcing herself to remain silent.

"Your wake up call is scheduled for tomorrow at six. I trust that's enough time for you to get ready for work and have Pennyworth drive you in."

No! She didn't want him to go, but recognized he was preparing to say goodbye.

"Ms. Farrow?"

"Yes. That's enough time."

"Then I'll wish you a goodnight. Sweet dreams, Scarlet. Eight encounters left."

Her chest constricted as she grieved his withdrawal. "Goodnight, Mr. Stone."

The line silenced and she felt him leave her, suffered his departure. Dropping the phone into the twisted blankets, she groaned. How could she get him to open up to her?

12

———

"O"

"WHAT DO you think of the word pussy?"

Elliot looked up from his sandwich and dropped it into the paper wrapper. "There goes my lunch."

"Because I said pussy?" Asher asked skeptically. "What would you like me to say, vulva?"

Elliot marched his lunch to the trash and dropped it in the bin. "I'd like to get through one day without having to discuss your personal life." He left the room.

Asher glanced at Hunter and Jet. "What's up his ass?"

Jet shrugged and continued devouring his meatball sub.

"He's been in a mood since dance class," Hunter mumbled.

Jet snorted. "He's been in a mood since sophomore year."

Shaking his head, he eyed the guys. "What do you think of the word pussy?"

Hunter shrugged. "Sort of demeaning."

"I. Love. Pussy." Jet hummed, sounding an awful lot like Bill Clinton.

"How is it demeaning? Other words sound silly."

"I guess it depends what context you're using it in. I mean, you aren't offending me, but you clearly offended Elliot. I wouldn't use it in front of a woman."

Hunter's opinion surprised him. "What if I already did?"

"Did she slap you?"

"Nope. She had an orgasm."

Hunter stilled. "What?"

Jet chuckled. "Atta boy! Get some!"

Asher smiled, the reverberation of such a victory still astonishing him. "Yup. A real one. At least I think it was real. Either that or she should get an Academy Award."

"Wait," Hunter said, plopping his soda on the table. "You gave *Scarlet Farrow* an orgasm? How?"

He stretched back in his chair and grinned. "On the phone."

"No way." Hunter argued, now rapidly shaking his head. "She faked it. You can't even give a girl an orgasm in person. There's no way you did it without touching her."

He brooded. "I can give a woman an orgasm in person."

"Have you ever?" Hunter challenged, raising a dark brow.

"No, but I also never lit a building on fire. That doesn't mean it's outside of my ability."

Hunter laughed. "Lighting a building on fire is a lot easier than lighting a woman on fire."

"Man's got a point," Jet agreed.

"Well, I did it. *To* Scarlet Farrow."

"Did what?" Elliot asked returning to the room.

"Ash gave her the big O."

Elliot ruminated. "You gave Scarlet Farrow a character from Game Boy Advance?"

Hunter burst into peals of laughter and Asher crumpled the trash from his lunch and tossed it at him. "No, you one dimensional moron! I gave her an orgasm, not the freaking automaton from Super Robot War Destiny!"

He shrugged. "I'd rather have the action figure."

Hunter's laughter turned into a roar of hysterics.

"You're so full of shit. Who wants toys when they could have orgasms?"

Elliot rolled his eyes. "I don't know. Maybe someone not obsessed with sex."

"Bet you'd give up a whole collection of action figures to watch Nadia come," Jet said and Elliot scowled.

"Don't...you shouldn't talk about her like that."

Wait. What? The side of Asher's mouth kicked up. "You have a thing for the dance instructor?"

"No."

Hunter and Jet simultaneously said, "Yes!"

Elliot's face turned bright red. "Shut up. You're all idiots."

"Why don't you ask her out?" Asher wondered.

Elliot scoffed. "Are you kidding? Have you seen her? Unlike you, I have no interest in baring all my flaws or fraternizing with women *way* out of my league."

Asher shrugged. "Who says she's out of your league? She could be interested. Steve says she's really nice."

"No, thank you. And do me a favor and keep your

mouth shut. I don't need her pitying me." He stormed out of the room.

"He really needs to get laid," Jet mumbled.

Asher's lips twisted with disappointment. He hated seeing Elliot so down on himself.

"So how much longer are you gonna carry on this Mr. Stone bit?" Hunter asked.

He shrugged. "I promised her fourteen encounters, but I have months to follow through."

"Why not just do it all at once?"

There was a lot Asher had learned in his research. Some universal truths he considered the ten commandments of women. "They always want what they can't have. The longer I make her wait the more eager she is to have me."

"That's fucked up," Hunter commented, but there was no missing the snort of laughter.

Jet crumpled up his wrapper and arced it across the room, sinking it into the trash bin. "I think you should just tell her it's you and get on with the sex."

"I'm not having sex with her."

Both men looked at him, clear misunderstanding on their faces. Asher already decided sleeping with Scarlet Farrow would be very bad for both of them. He was there to seduce her, grant her everything she thought she'd never have, not give her something that might be a great letdown.

Knowing personal things, like how Bobby Westerman stole her virginity and fumbled the entire aftercare portion of such a fundamental moment, made Asher certain he shouldn't have sex with her. If he did anything dishonorable it would cloud the whole purpose of their relationship, destroy the fantasy.

He wasn't sure how it would end, if he would tell

her who he was or keep it a secret forever—something beautiful that ended before it turned ugly. Maybe one day he'd strip the blindfold away and she'd beam and throw her arms around—wait. No. That wasn't going to happen. He had to be careful, because his emotions were starting to confuse matters the more he came to care about her. He had to be realistic. There was only so much a man could pretend.

This was meant to be something she'd enjoy. His inexperience was too much of a risk and chancing any sexual let down on his part might ruin everything he'd worked toward. Glancing at his friends, he said with resoluteness, "No. I'm definitely not going to have sex with her."

Asher was so aggravated with his desire to call Scarlet just to hear her voice, that he denied himself the privilege of speaking to her for an entire week. The following Friday he started his morning with a demand that Steve push him harder than usual.

When they finished, Asher was dripping with sweat and guzzling one water bottle after another.

"I see a major difference," Steve commented. "And I'm not just talking about your abs."

Asher chucked the bottle in the recycling and mopped the sweat out of his eyes without comment.

"Are you going to see her tonight?"

He should. She was likely wondering where he was. Or maybe she wasn't. "Yeah. Send flowers to her class and tell her to be ready at seven."

Steve hesitated. "You aren't going to write a note?"

The fucking notes. He grit his teeth. No matter

how hard he tried to treat it as a liaison, part of him just wanted their relationship to be normal. He'd have to buckle down. No more delusions. No more pretending this was anything more than what it was. He had to keep his head and had to constantly remind himself this would eventually end.

There was fantasy and then there was reality. The more time that passed the closer he stepped to that uncomfortable threshold. "I'll write it."

The workday dragged and Asher's mind was caught up in one distraction after another. By four o'clock, he accepted he wasn't going to accomplish anything productive and researched some things on-line—sexuality to be more exact, but unsure where exactly one found the answers he needed.

The wisdom he sought wasn't there. The Internet proved nothing but a pit of opinions, when what he needed was hard-core facts, guarantees. What made one source more knowledgeable than the last? He needed answers, advice, a guru of women that could teach him how to pleasure her.

Somehow he'd managed to gain her absolute compliance, and in doing so, something dark and needy was unleashed inside of him. He wanted to push her sexual appetites and push her hard, but he first needed to know how to satisfy her hunger.

"Shit." He sat back in his chair and stared at the computer.

His dick throbbed in his pants as he replayed their last conversation. He wanted her naked and no matter how much that was rushing things, good judgment didn't seem to intercede.

How could he get her naked? He could simply ask,

but that seemed a little weak. Women didn't just take off their clothes for strangers.

Frustrated, he closed his laptop and grabbed his keys. He was done for the day.

When he got home his body demanded a measure of self-control, so he headed for the shower. As the heated jets doused his sensitized skin, visions of Scarlet rushed through his mind. Eyes closed, he fisted his erection and breathed roughly through his teeth. His hand tugged as his lungs worked. Steam coated his body as his blood pumped hard.

Her eyes. Her soft body. The long line of her spine. The scent of her hair. The gentle rasp of her voice. He was so close. His mind devoured the memory of her breast in the blouse that practically showed her nipples. He wanted to see, taste and tease them, kiss, suck and mark them.

"Oh, God..." He stroked harder, bracing his arm on the damp tile wall. If only he could hear her say his name the way she whispered Mr. Stone. His imagination went wild, visions of her head tilting back, her throat elongating as her soft lips curved around those undisclosed syllables... *Asher.*

A guttural moan left his chest as his balls drew up tight and pleasure shot through his spine. Come splashed against the tile as he hissed and panted, pressing his forehead to his arm.

His fantasies were changing, evolving, maturing, detailing every specific truth he now knew and hardly had to improvise. She was no longer just a beautiful fantasy. She was flesh and blood and he wanted her to be his. For years he'd been imagining the taste of her skin, but now he wanted to truly know.

He selected his clothing carefully, knowing she

wouldn't see him, but needing the boost of confidence. When he reached the mansion it was six. They had eight meetings left and though he feared the end, the intentional procrastination was growing tiresome. He was running out of ideas. Oh, he had plenty of things he wanted to do with her, but he had to maintain control and keep his eye on the prize.

After lighting the fires and choosing a bottle of red, he waited for Steve to arrive. Fuck, he was anxious. Their last encounter—actually hearing her come— triggered a dark animal inside of him he wasn't prepared to unleash, a side of him so unfamiliar it shifted his bearings and planted seeds of great concern. What was happening to him? Desire, greater than he'd ever felt for her or any woman, was now an obstacle.

At the sound of a car pulling onto the drive, he stood and went to the door. Steve escorted her up the steps and he took her arm without greeting. Leading her inside he set about unbuttoning her coat.

Her lips were parted and her breathing shallow. "Good evening, Mr. Stone," she whispered, her voice trembling.

Fuck, he was botching this. He needed to pull it together. "Good evening, Ms. Farrow."

Her brow wrinkled, small divots showing above the lace of the blindfold. Her hand softly closed over his fingers working the last of the buttons. "Are you upset with me?"

He silently sighed and stepped back, needing to remove her touch before he got careless. "I've had a difficult week, but I'm happy you're here." Taking back the command of his actions, he stepped around her and removed her coat.

She shivered and he stilled. She was wearing the

red wrap dress he'd gifted her. She looked incredible, the garment accentuating her figure in all the right places. Even the boots were perfect.

While her beauty threatened his composure, if he shut his eyes and breathed her in, a sense of calm settled over him. Her mere presence soothed him, yet her beauty intimidated him to a degree that was troubling. Sometimes he wished he were the blind one.

But he could not fault her for such things when the issue was his inability to process the sensory overload her mere proximity wrought in him. Tracing his fingers lightly over the pearl necklace, he whispered, "You look stunning, Ms. Farrow. Let's sit and catch up."

He ushered her to a chair and she sat. Her hands fidgeted then found a home in the lap of her dress. Her ankles crossed and uncrossed until finally she seemed to settle.

He surveyed her for several minutes, speculating what she was thinking. She surprised him by stating, "You're not talking."

"I'm watching you. Does the silence bother you?"

A flush tinged her flesh from the pearl necklace to her cheeks. "No."

"What are you thinking, Ms. Farrow? You appear agitated."

She began to fidget again and he considered offering her a glass of wine, but something had him holding back.

"I haven't heard from you in seven days."

And the time apart did nothing to quell his desires. "Does that upset you?"

Her lips compressed.

"Answer the question."

"Yes."

"What is upsetting about my absence?" He was honestly curious about her answer. Was it the attention she missed? Or perhaps the delight of being spoiled?

"I missed... you."

Asher stilled. Could she have really missed him? No, she missed Mr. Stone. An odd quarrel took place in his mind, his alter ego seeming to steal his glory. "I see. And what exactly did you miss?"

"Your voice. Your nearness."

He contemplated her answer. His voice was his, though he altered his tempo and tone when speaking as Mr. Stone. How much of what she craved actually had to do with—

"Can I ask you something?"

His shoulders tightened with reluctance. "Yes."

Her blush intensified. "I... I've been thinking about us and I need to ask you something for my own peace of mind."

He waited for her to go on, already having given her permission to ask what she needed and not trusting his voice at the moment. Her lips were a distracting temptation and she was currently nibbling them in a sign of nervousness.

"Are you healthy, Mr. Stone?"

"Pardon?"

"I don't know where this is going and I like that you're the one deciding. But the other day it crossed my mind how little I know about you as a person. Every time you contact me I debate less and less the risks of coming to you. It seems I have no will when it comes to following your requests and I'd be remiss not to inquire about your health, considering what happened last time we talked. But more than that, I care about you and I worry about you. I wanted to make sure you're all right."

I care about you and I worry about you...

Jaw slack, he slowly grinned, taken aback by her confession. It was quite telling of where she imagined this going, but more than that...she cared and worried about him. Such personal interest on her part was unexpected.

His throat contracted with unexpected emotion. "I assure you I'm quite healthy. The last time I was near a hospital I was a boy suffering from dehydration after a nasty bout of the flu. I have my blood work done regularly and have never heard any concerns from my doctor."

She let out a deep breath she seemed to be holding for quite some time. This had obviously been weighing on her mind, which aided his confidence, touched a very vulnerable part of him. It might also confirm she'd considered crossing certain lines of intimacy, but he wasn't sure.

The physical was second to the emotional in terms of how much her confession jarred him. Did she truly care about him? He focused on the more manageable implication. "For health to be brought into question, one would assume you'd been thinking about intimacy."

She smirked. "I have. Ever since the hotel. I've decided to trust you and fully experience whatever it is you have to teach me."

His shoulders shook as her confession left him speechless. She couldn't possibly know what she was agreeing to. Even he couldn't predict what such a thing might entail.

The startling confession pushed his desires ahead

of his common sense. "Interesting. And what if I told you to remove an item of clothing? Be careful what you say, Ms. Farrow. I've spent a lot of time thinking of you this week."

"You did?" She smiled, surprising him again. This female was slowly disproving every assumption he had about women.

He waited for her to address his question. Her breasts pressed against the front of her dress as her breath quickened.

Finally, when she realized he was still waiting, she asked, "What did you want me to remove?"

His mouth opened. *All of it.* What was happening here? Swallowing hard he stood and reached for her hand. Her fingers curled around his with acceptance. "Stand up, Ms. Farrow."

Her jaw trembled as she was guided from the chair. Asher pulled her a step forward. Releasing her hand at her side, he appraised her. Two tight points formed under the thin material of the dress covering her chest. She was stunning.

His hands danced over her collarbone, tracing several of the tiny pearls, and her neck lengthened. Ghosting his fingers over the swell of her breast, he touched the loop of the tie that held the dress together. "May I?"

Her body shook with a delicate tremble. "Yes." Her voice was a rasp.

His cock throbbed in his pants, pressing hard into the zipper. Carefully, he unknotted the belt, taking care to control his breathing. The sash went lax and she sucked in an audible breath.

"Tell me to stop and I will, Ms. Farrow."

"Don't stop."

He stilled. Every fiber of his being wanted to kiss her in that moment, but he clamped his jaw tight and refused. Dropping the sash, the dress gaped. His fingers trembled as he reached for the silky fabric.

"Last chance," he warned.

She made no objection, so he slowly parted the folds. His lungs burned as he breathed deep. Satin flesh, white as snow, flashed as the material parted. Her breasts were encased in a chocolate lace bra matching her panties.

"You're exquisite," he whispered, conscious he was giving himself away.

Her shoulders lifted as he slid the silk dress off of her frame and let it whisper to the floor. Seeing her standing there, in her bra and panties and those sexy heeled leather boots was incredibly titillating.

Goose bumps covered her arms as her hands fisted at her sides. The hair on his arms rose as well. His throat became bone dry as his unblinking eyes devoured her beauty. He recognized signs of nervousness in the way her muscles appeared to tense and her lips twitched.

"Do you have any idea how sexy you are, Scarlet?"

Her lips trembled. "Thank you. Only you see me that way."

Bullshit. He wanted to worship at the altar of Scarlet Farrow, peel back those lace cups and gorge himself on the sharp nipples poking against her bra.

"You're quite tempting."

She sucked in a long breath and released it quickly. "You...you can touch me, Mr. Stone. If you want to." Her lips pursed as she quietly admitted, "I want you to."

His heart thundered as his hands trembled. It was

nearly impossible to maintain his calm façade. "Do you now?"

This was quite a predicament. With her permission, he was given free range to pet and caress her as he pleased. But doing so might be his undoing. He'd be wise to proceed with caution.

"Do you like being told what to do, Ms. Farrow?"

"I like when you tell me what to do, because…" She seemed to be as surprised by her words as he was. "I like how it feels."

He chuckled. If she only knew all the things she made him feel, emotions outside of his vocabulary. "I'm very pleased."

She licked her lips nervously as a slow smile curved her mouth.

"Are you aroused, Ms. Farrow?"

"Yes."

"Are your panties wet?"

"Yes."

And so was his cock, precome already seeping from the engorged tip. He took her hand. "Come with me." Leading her to the center of the room, he turned her to face the chairs. "I want you to stand here while I pour us each a glass of wine and enjoy the view."

Her motions were shaky, likely due to her arousal, but she nodded. As he walked slowly back to the chairs he adjusted himself, trying to find some measure of comfort.

Uncorking the wine, he enjoyed the echo of liquid trickling into the glasses. He turned, taking a seat, and sipped. "Spread your legs, Ms. Farrow."

Her stance slowly widened. Yes. He liked having this sort of authority. The heady sense of having a woman he prized bend to his will was incomparable to all other sexual experiences. He'd never imagined anything beyond traditional coupling—*vanilla* was what the Internet seemed to call it. But with Scarlet, he always had the upper hand, guiding her slowly into a poetic state of arousal that seemed to trigger so many hidden peculiarities inside of him.

Sexual release never failed to satisfy a human need, but what they shared went beyond natural reflexes. It was a new level of endorphins, an untold secret creating so much more than simple gratification. The perplexity of their interactions radiated sexual tension *because* of the limits they created, and he felt the high every time she surrendered to his command.

"Do you feel it, Scarlet? Do you feel the way our needs compliment each other so completely?" She'd surrender and he'd take control, every time, fitting as concisely as music fit to air, filling the silence that didn't seem lonely until one understood how incomplete it was without sound. She was the music that filled the hollowness inside of him.

Appraising her carefully, he focused on the apex of her thighs, fascinated by the darkened spot of fabric. "I can see where your arousal has seeped through the silk of your panties."

Her throat worked as she swallowed. Her command of herself was truly impressive. What would make a woman relinquish such control? But she wasn't really relinquishing it, was she? No, she was voluntarily entrusting him with all the authority.

"Let's discuss your past relationships. Tell me about your longest relationship as an adult."

Her mouth parted as she slowly licked her lips. "I dated a man for eight months when I was in my early twenties."

"How often did you fuck?"

She jerked back at his crass choice of words. Perhaps that term didn't apply to her, or have the same effect as when he spoke the word pussy. He quickly covered his tracks. "Do you prefer the term making love?"

"With him, it was neither. We had sex."

"Interesting. Explain the difference."

"Um, I think making love refers to a special bond shared between two people, which he and I didn't have." She cleared her throat. "Fucking...I think of as passionate. We weren't very passionate."

"I'm curious how you define sex."

"Sex is sex. There's a man and a woman, part A goes into part B."

"Did he bring you to orgasm often?"

"No."

"Ever?"

Her face lowered and her voice turned small. "No."

"Why are you lowering your face, Ms. Farrow? If a man fails to bring his lover to orgasm the failure's his, not yours."

"I guess."

"Back to my original question. How often did you two have *sex*?"

"In the beginning, once we got to that stage, it was about once a week. After that it sort of dwindled. Then sex seemed the only thing we'd get together for so I broke it off."

"Tell me about one particular memory of having sex with this man." Her nose crinkled. "Is the idea of sharing such personal anecdotes distasteful or is it the actual memory that has you making that expression?"

"Both."

"I want to know."

Her posture wilted and she sighed. "He was always on top. It was always faster than I would have liked. And it was so unremarkable I can't think of any memory in particular."

So honest and so easy to transfer to his own fears. "I see. Tell me about the last time you had sex. Or was it fucking?"

Her feet shifted. She was likely growing tired of standing.

"He was the best man at my friend's wedding. I was a bridesmaid. We both had too much to drink and I don't really remember much more than we never even got our clothes completely off."

"How long ago was that?"

She bit her lip. "Two years."

His brows shot up. Two years? Scarlet Farrow had been celibate for *two* years? He tried to recall the last time he'd had sex. He'd received a decent blowjob from a woman at the last ComicCon. Did that count?

"Does it bother you going so long without sex?"

Her face lifted. "It didn't..."

"Meaning?"

"That changed when I met you."

He sat back, letting her confession sink in. Holy shit. How had he done this? They'd been talking for less than a month, only been in each other's presence five times. It was too tempting not to explore her confession, see where the evening might lead.

"Do you need release, Ms. Farrow?"

Her breast slightly jostled as her breathing turned labored. "If that's what you want, Mr. Stone."

Never in his wildest dreams did he imagine them reaching this point. The more commanding he became the more she seemed to bend—and willingly. It was as if they were feeding off each other, him needing the authoritative role and her requiring his dominance, their opposing preferences creating a sort of perfect symmetry.

He placed his glass on the table with an intentional click and made a mental note to conduct more in depth research regarding dominance and submission. Perhaps that had been what he was searching for earlier that day. Though he'd read novels grazing the subject, he needed information from non-fiction sources if he truly intended to explore this dynamic.

Standing, he took slow steps to the center of the room. Her body appeared to draw tight the closer he came. "Do I make you nervous, Ms. Farrow?"

"Yes, but in a good way."

Standing only a few inches across from her, he brushed the waves of hair behind her shoulders. She shivered and he breathed in the soft scent of her skin.

Carefully observing her, he brushed the backs of his nails along her jaw and down the side of her throat. "You're pulse is accelerated, Ms. Farrow. That tells me you're either excited or scared. Which is it?"

"Excited."

Her breasts filled out the cups of her bra, heaving with every slow breath and stealing his attention. Dancing his fingers down her shoulder, he carefully traced the strap, and her breasts seemed to swell more.

His other hand repeated the motion to the other strap, this time dragging it off her shoulder. The elastic hung loose over her narrow upper arm. He slid the other strap down, leaving her breasts quivering inside of those delicate lace cups. Several freckles sprinkled along her cleavage and he wanted to taste every single one.

"Scared yet?"

"No."

He removed his touch and studied her for a solid minute. Her patience and restraint was extraordinary. Glancing down, he blanched at the enormous bulge in his pants begging for attention. There'd be no relief there. Not here at least.

Time to get serious. Reaching both hands forward, he slowly traced the scalloped edging of her bra and yanked the cups down. She gasped as two perfect strawberry nipples pointed sharply forward—better than he'd ever imagined.

Her breasts were extravagant, her nipples tight and dark mauve with the flow of blood, quite a breathtaking contrast to her ivory skin. The aureoles were perfect petite circles.

"Fold your hands behind your back, Ms. Farrow."

She complied, her motions a bit shaky, but still graceful. Her nipples lifted as the space between her breasts widened. Leaning forward, he crowded one tight bud with a slow open mouth kiss. Her knees jerked, lowering her body for a split second as she moaned.

His gaze went to her face. Lips quivering, she silently panted, definitely aroused. His attention went to the other nipple, tight and begging for attention. His mouth closed over the ruby tip and he sucked.

Her throaty sigh of relief was music to his ears. Gently applying pressure with his teeth and teasing the very edge with his tongue, he continued to suck her nipples, testing various methods of pleasure.

"Oh God."

His hands never touched her, but he wanted to. He was so close to losing control he should stop, but she had him under some sort of spell.

Returning to the other nipple, he again closed his mouth over her, this time engulfing the whole areola. The harder he sucked, the fiercer she moaned. When he pulled back, he admired how the strawberry shade had darkened to a deep crimson. "Your nipples are almost red, Ms. Farrow. I wonder if that's from all the wine you drink."

She laughed and smiled. She had a beautiful smile, shy, but pretty.

"Are they sensitive?"

"Yes."

"Do you like having your breasts fondled softly or do you prefer to have the tips pinched?"

"I... I don't know."

It was inexplicable, discovering she wasn't much more knowledgeable about sex than him. Unfolding his posture he slowly strode to stand behind her. "Fist your hands at your side and don't move them until I say so."

Her fingers unlaced as her arms draped loosely at her side, her palms curling into tight balls. He traced a finger down her spine and she shivered. "I enjoy your freckles, Ms. Farrow."

As his finger dragged from one sprinkling of marks to the next, her shoulders twitched. He stopped when he reached the twisted clasp of her bra. "May I?"

"Yes."

Briefly shutting his eyes, he prayed he didn't fumble. He undid the clasp on the first try and let the garment fall to the floor. Sliding his hands through her arms, he caressed the swell of her hips and ran his palms up her quivering belly. She was soft there, feminine. Some might see her as a woman who carried a few extra pounds, but he saw her as perfect.

His erection brushed the curve of her ass and he nearly came in his pants. "I'm going to touch you now, Ms. Farrow. Keep your hands still."

Turning his wrists he cupped her heated flesh and she sagged into his hold. Without thinking, he stepped closer. Her bottom pressed into the ridge in his pants as she sighed and he squeezed her breasts.

From this angle he could smell her sweet apple scented shampoo, which only added to his arousal. Whispering in her ear, he asked, "Do you like my hands on you?"

"Yes," she nearly cried.

He stepped closer, savoring the friction of her body crowded against his. His fingers went to her sharp pink nipples and pinched and plucked. She began to keen with every breath. "Mr. Stone... Oh...please..."

He ground his cock into her bottom, needing the relief of friction. Her cheek brushed his and his eyes briefly shut. The pleasure of holding her weight in his arm was so exquisite it bordered on pain. "Tell me what you feel."

Her voice pitched with each exhalation. "Pleasure. Pain. You. You're tall. And I can feel *you*. Please let me touch you."

He pinched her nipples a bit harder. "Do you like the pain?"

She was practically sobbing out her words, delirious with pleasure. "Yes. Sometimes. But it's the desire that hurts more than anything. I want you."

He rolled her nipples between his fingers and thumbs. "Tell me what else you feel."

"Wet. I'm very wet. All I can smell is you. Your touch is almost too much, your hair tickling my throat and your breath in my ear. I don't know how much more I can take."

"Can you come this way?"

"I don't know. I never have."

Releasing her quickly, he took her hand. "Follow me." He led her to the wall, pressing her back into the antique paper. She gasped, likely from the chill of the wall. It was suddenly imperative that *he* make her come—at his own hand.

"Lift your arms over your head. Keep them on the wall." She did as he commanded, her aroused breasts lifting like twin pieces of succulent fruit. Her head tipped back as her mouth opened.

Cupping her roughly, he bent and sucked a nipple deep in his mouth. She cried out, her raspy voice filling the room. His other hand plucked at her nipple, pinching tightly, twisting, and then allowing the blood to flow back to the tip only for a split second before moving his mouth there.

Her knees gave out and he shoved his frame against her, holding her in place, as his pelvis dragged deliciously against her body, separated only by his clothing. His attention became hyper-focused, his mouth, tongue, and fingers solely dedicated to her pleasure.

"Oh my God, it's happening!" her body trembled in his hold as he continued to tease. Her motions turned erratic as she cried out his name over and over again. Fastening his mouth to the ivory swell of her breast, he sucked, intentionally hoping to mark her porcelain skin as he pinched down on her nipples and tugged hard.

The most feminine, guttural moan filled the hall as she melted in his arms. She trembled as he breathed hard against her shoulder.

Fuck Hunter. I knew I could give a woman an orgasm in person.

Pulling himself back to the present, he slowly stepped back. "You can lower your arms now." They dropped immediately reaching for him and he gripped her wrist to assure she didn't fall. He cleared his throat. "I think you've earned that glass of wine."

She giggled, a bit breathlessly, and he slowly escorted her back to the chairs, helping her find her seat. When he pressed the goblet into her hand, she guzzled it. Her breathing remained choppy for several minutes which he spent admiring her nearly naked form.

Her belly naturally creased at her belly button. Her breasts weighed heavily against her ribs. She appeared completely unnerved by her nudity, which was unexpected.

Refilling her glass, he said, "I see you're coming to terms with your nudity."

She chuckled. "That's a first."

"I'm staring at your body. Does that worry you?"

Smiling, she leaned back in the chair and lifted her arms, putting her breasts on display. "Believe it or not, I love knowing you enjoy looking at me, Mr. Stone. It's a sort of attention I've never had." Brazenly, she reached for the table and slid her glass onto the surface.

His jaw unhinged. Later, when she returned home, she'd find the souvenir he'd left on her body. The plum blotch his kiss had left showed beautifully against her pale skin. He decided he wanted to leave her with many more, liking his mark on her flesh.

Grinning, he experienced deep satisfaction. He'd claimed her, in a way. *Mine.*

His smile faltered as reality came hurtling back to his sex-addled-brain. Fuck. None of this was part of his plan. It was far too personal. Artificial, despite the truth of his affection. It wouldn't be real until she learned who he truly was. And Asher Roan could very easily pale in comparison to Mr. Stone.

"It's time to say goodnight, Ms. Farrow."

Her grin fell and her arms slowly closed over her chest. He sensed the moment insecurity took hold. He could easily reassure her, but he didn't trust his own words at the moment. He needed to get her out of there, before he said or did something they'd both regret.

Standing, he collected her dress and bra. "Please stand up." She did, keeping her head angled down as he slid the garment back into place and worked to clasp the tiny hooks. Damn bras. Why did they have to be so complicated?

Once her breasts were covered he slid her arms through the sleeves of the dress. Docilely, she allowed him to tie the front, her posture guarded. Once he finished dressing her, he took a moment to fix her hair, and inspect that everything was covered.

"I'll get your coat."

As he stepped away he heard her sniffle and stilled. Glancing back, he scrutinized her face. As much as the blindfold protected him, it also protected her. Without seeing her eyes it wasn't always easy to ascertain her emotions.

Forgetting the coat he stepped in front of her. "Scarlet?"

She sniffled again and nodded.

"Why are you upset?" His chest constricted. What had he done?

"I'm fine."

She *clearly* was not fine. "Don't lie to me," he snapped, surprised at the lash in his voice. His frustration was with himself. He'd pushed too far and crossed a line.

She flinched. "Did I disappoint you?"

What? He shut his eyes and silently sighed. His need to conclude their evening wasn't an attempt to be coldhearted in the least. On the contrary, he was trying to reel in his control before things spun out of hand, save her from disappointment, but he was fumbling everything.

Brushing a hand over her cheek, he assured, "No, sweet Scarlet, you pleased me very much. I'm merely reacting to the awareness that we have seven nights left."

Which was also true. They were running out of time. He didn't disclose that he was panicking about what would happen over the course of those nights—mainly, to him. The more she gave of herself the less control he had over his restraint.

She was breaking down every boundary he'd purposefully built to protect himself. He'd been so worried about playing a part he'd overlooked the fact that this woman was the same woman who basically owned him and thrown him to the wolves twelve years ago. He hadn't thought he'd fall for her again, but he had. And now the fall, should she toss him away, was so much greater he doubted he'd survive.

Stepping away, he went to retrieve her coat and carefully fastened the buttons, as was their routine. Like the last time, she caught his hand on the last button. "Thank you, Mr. Stone."

He smiled forlornly. "You're welcome, Scarlet."

This time when he watched Steve drive her away there wasn't the familiar sense of accomplishment. Rather, there was cold worry. He decided their next encounter he'd reassess the woman. He'd find out more about her personality—there had to be some guarantee available, something great enough to give him the confidence to end this tiresome charade and trust her enough not to reject him again.

13

CONTROL

AFTER THREE DAYS of contemplating the uninvited emotions regarding Scarlet and their liaison, Asher decided the solution rested in maintaining absolute control—of himself and their situation. He'd let his own desires distort his motive to make this all about her and he needed to refocus. If he continued to please her in a way no other man had, her gratitude might overshadow any shortcomings he hid and perhaps there could be something more in the end.

Control was not necessarily taking what he wanted because he simply had the authority to do so. No. It was a tool used to unravel the many wants and desires that made Scarlet Farrow, thereby presenting the answers to her prayers. In order for his intentions to bear fruit, he must be able to deliver. Serving his own needs and desires should not be part of the immediate plan. She should always come first—literally.

"Tell me about your home," he asked late one evening as he had her on the phone.

"It's small. Yellow siding, a small garden in the front that can't grow more than weeds."

The image of her tiring from planting flowers that refused to bloom amused him in a tender way. He could so easily picture her toiling over the stubborn bed, sunhat protecting her fair skin. His amusement wasn't facetious. The image of her frustration, how her cheeks would likely flush and her mouth would purse, was merely another appealing part of her charming character.

"Do you like to garden?"

"I love to garden, but these thumbs aren't the least bit green. I'm lucky if I can keep a cactus alive."

He chuckled. "Tell me about the inside of your house. Walk me through it."

"Well, my front door leads into a small foyer." As she spoke he visualized the space, curious about her daily surroundings. It struck him as unfortunate that he couldn't witness it first hand—another drawback of their untraditional relationship.

As she detailed each space, he quietly coveted what she could see and he couldn't. How she'd tolerated their relationship blind this far was beyond him.

Her voice silenced. His mind had drifted. "Tell me about your classroom."

His heart wasn't in it tonight. The limitations were growing tiresome. He wanted to remove the veils between them, but doing so might end everything. As she described her classroom, he considered the remainder of their time.

At first, the freedom to stretch their relations over a length of time was appealing. Now it was daunting. Six encounters left and he wanted it over so they could begin something genuine. He required confidence, something he'd always been short of, and didn't possess the patience needed to wait for it's time-consuming arrival.

"Do you trust me, Scarlet?"

He'd interrupted her, but she quickly answered, her tone heavy with concern. He wasn't acting himself tonight. Or perhaps he was, but not as Mr. Stone.

"Yes," she answered.

The will of his restraint was fraying. "I want to see you tomorrow night."

"Tomorrow's Thursday."

Yes, and they usually only met on the weekends, but it was becoming abundantly clear the longer their association went on, the more difficult dragging things out would become. "We will still have the weekend."

"Oh."

She sounded disappointed. "Do you not wish to see me?"

"No, I do. It's just... tomorrow would be our sixth encounter and this weekend, five. I don't like sensing we're reaching an end. But maybe..."

She, too, seemed irritated with the counting of days. But she wasn't the one calling the shots. The unexpected could frighten her as much as it excited her, and for good reason. But the reality was, he wanted the secretiveness to end. The more he emotionally invested himself in this woman, the harder it would hurt when she eventually cut him down—*if* that was the way of things, and he found it impossible to imagine a better outcome. There were too many scars of his past emotional wounds marking his experiences with people in general—including her.

"One day at a time, Ms. Farrow. Let me worry

about how and when the days pass." Something he was doing a shitty job of at the moment.

"Okay."

He'd have to think of how they'd spend their evening and being that they were in the last stretch, he'd have to make it count. "Then I think we should say goodnight. Since it's a school night, I'll have Pennyworth pick you up at six instead of seven. Have a light dinner and wear something comfortable."

"Okay. I can't wait to..." She laughed at her slip. "Well, I guess I won't be seeing you, but you know what I mean. I look forward to it."

"Me too. Sweet dreams, Ms. Farrow."

"You too, Mr. Stone."

He ended the call. It was time to get serious. Cracking open his laptop he searched suggestions for romantic dates. When one recommendation caught his eye, his brain went to work, piecing together a list of everything he'd need. It would be challenging locating certain items on such short notice, but his friends were eccentric enough to point him in the right direction.

Unfortunately, despite Scarlet's parting wishes, his dreams were far from sweet that night. Kaleidoscopes of images from his past bled into his nightmares, mixing with hallucinations of the present. The disorienting memories built a vivid tapestry of what suffocated him.

"What are you gonna do, faggot?" Westerman's meaty paws shoved him into the wall of the locker room as his towel fell to the ground, tripping him.

Laughter echoed from those witnessing his shame. "Look at his little dick!"

"How do you even see something that small?"

"Here, give him his glasses!"

Westerman laughed and reached in his pocket. His fat fingers fumbled with his glasses and a small vile. "Hold him down," he snapped.

Two of the guys on the football team grabbed his arms, pegging them to the lockers. Asher jerked with panic as Westerman shoved his glasses on his face.

Tears immediately burned his eyes as his vision blurred under the intense fumes of superglue. He struggled, but their hold wouldn't budge. Within seconds the rims of his frames were painfully fused to his face and hair, the chemical burn immediately blistering his sensitive skin.

He stumbled as they released him, his head jerking quickly as Westerman grabbed a fistful of his hair. "Can you see your little dick now?"

He reached for his lenses and winced as he agonizingly tried to remove the glasses, but the plastic might as well have been welded to the soft flesh below his eyes.

He'd been there, saw the moment so clearly in his mind, relived the pain and humiliation, but his dreams added a new layer of cruelty. The images of his past tipped, colliding with visions of the present, embellishing realities to a brutal point of degradation.

. . .

"*Look at him, Lettie. This* is *what you want?"* Westerman taunted.

Asher's gaze lifted as his terrified eyes met hers. She was an adult, developed and perfectly beautiful in the emerald dress he'd given her, but this time it was a gown. There was no recognition in her expression, no empathy, or anything close to the warmth she showed Mr. Stone.

She laughed. It wasn't the chill of her voice that gutted him, but the pity in her eyes. "Poor little Asher Roan. Did you think you could impress me? I can't even look at you." Her hands lifted and there was the blindfold—

*A*sher bolted upright, jackknifing out of bed, his skin drenched in a cold sweat as he shivered and panted. His heart raced as he frantically identified his room and the familiar objects that marked present day.

Adrenaline rushed through his body like an icy avalanche in his veins as his breath echoed in the silence. It was a dream. Part of it had been real, a flashback he'd never forget, but the parts about Scarlet were purely a nightmare.

Shutting his eyes, he let out a reassuring breath that did little to calm him. In the darkness he saw Westerman and the rest of his alumni taunting him. His fingers went to his cheeks, just beneath his eyes, as if he could still feel the torn flesh their brutality had left, and still scent the vitamin E his father insisted he apply for a solid year to the burn.

He'd never forget the look in his father's eyes the

day he tried to painlessly remove the glasses from Asher's face. His mother had been resting after a grueling reaction to the chemo and that was what his father had to deal with on top of everything else.

The sickening tear of sensitive flesh brought tears to his eyes, but his greatest worry was not the scars he might bare or the pain great enough to cause him to vomit. Applying a cool damp cloth to his face he grit his teeth as his father's hands shook with the necessity to be gentle.

Asher stilled his father's hand and whispered, "Don't tell Mom."

His father sighed and shut his eyes. "Someone needs to stop this, Asher. It's getting out of hand. I need to tell someone."

"No. If you do then Mom will find out and I don't want her to worry about me with everything else going on. I'll stay away from them from now on. I'm good at hiding."

He saw it then, in his father's eyes—disappointment— not in the son he'd raised, but in failing to protect his son from the world. It wasn't his job, but his father saw it as his responsibility.

"I'll be okay, Dad. It'll heal."

His father's mouth was tight with tense rage and Asher needed to relieve his worry. "It doesn't hurt," he lied.

Asher had never been strong and had no interest in fighting. He simply wanted to be left alone. He'd learned long ago, telling on people like Westerman only led to a worse fate. He wanted to avoid further retaliation.

As much as his face hurt, as much as the marks and chopped away hair humiliated him, nothing was as painful as seeing his father take responsibility for others' cruelness.

. . .

*A*sh pushed the painful memory back into the hidden corners of his mind. It had been years since he'd had nightmares. Thinking his habits with Scarlet were bringing such memories back was not something he relished.

His father had begged him to take boxing or karate, but it all seemed too little too late. There was nothing quite as heartbreaking as those moments when his parents became aware of how brutal school could be for him and knew there was nothing they could do to save him.

One evening he'd heard his mother crying, berating herself, saying if not for her weakness caused by the cancer that she might have been able to save him with homeschooling. He'd never hated cancer more, believing homeschooling would have been his saving grace.

But the reality was, his mother was fighting her own battles and didn't have the strength to fight his as well. He'd made a promise never to let on how bad it got at school after that. Sometimes he even lied, saying he had a great day just to see her smile.

It wasn't as easy to fool his father, being that he was the active parent when his mother was sick and he noticed a lot more. As the bullying got worse, the telltale symptoms of playing the victim became harder to hide. There were moments his father could simply place a cereal bowl on the table and Asher would flinch.

One day during Asher's junior year, his father broke into tears. Perhaps it was the overwhelming fear of losing his wife, or the immense pressure to stay hopeful, but it was the most startling sight Asher had ever witnessed. His fear amplified Asher's, paralyzing him in a daze, an awareness that his mother might actually die.

He understood the statistics of breast cancer, knew what the chances of survival were, but he'd never once considered that losing his mom might very well kill his dad. It had been a very difficult year and Asher wasn't sure how much more he could take. He'd selfishly begun to make arrangements, plans to escape— the only way he could assure the pain and pressure would end.

Seeing his father break was the wakeup call he needed. They were in this together. Family. That week, he went to his computer and opened up his history— so many searches revolving around methods of suicide. He deleted everything, knowing his father needed him there. Finishing school might kill him, but he'd somehow survive it. He had to, because there was no room for any more sadness in their home.

Leaning forward in bed, he scrubbed his palms over his face and reached for his glasses. What had he been thinking, reopening all these doors to his painful past? She'd worn the blindfold, but he was the unseeing idiot. How foolish to think he'd grown enough to face down those demons. Thirty years old and still just a scared little boy pretending he possessed the constitution of a man.

I can't do this.

The thought jarred him, chilled him, and propelled him into action. So frightened if the pressure continued that he'd back out and lose her forever— something he didn't want to happen—he reached for his phone and sent her a text. He needed to know she was still there, still with him.

Are you there?

$\mathscr{H}$er response came in less than a minute.

I'm here. Just getting ready to walk out the door to work. How was your night?

$\mathscr{H}$e exhaled and shut his eyes, drawing immense comfort from her emotional presence. He wasn't used to depending on other's reassurance.

If I asked you to come to me—right now—would you?

$\mathscr{S}$end. Her response was immediate.

Yes.

*H*e breathed a sigh of relief. Then his phone vibrated again.

Is something wrong?

Mr. Stone? Did something happen?
Do you need me to call out of work?

*F*alling back into bed, he sighed and held the phone to his chest. Realizing he was likely scaring her, he typed a response.

Everything's fine. I just wanted to
wish you a good day at work. I look
forward to seeing you soon.

*H*is phone chirped a moment later.

Soon can't come fast enough. xo

*H*er reply left him with a renewed sense of competence. Six encounters left. After tonight it would be five, he could survive that. He just had to keep her interested and wanting him.

When he and Steve finished his morning workout, he picked the other man's brain. "What do you think women want?"

"In general, or are you referring to Ms. Farrow?"

"Both."

Steve wiped down the machines as he deliberated. "Flowers, but you already did that. Some like to cuddle, others like chocolate and teddy bears. Once I dated a girl and had her car detailed. She blew my doors off that night. Never expected a chick to be so grateful about a little Armor All and wax."

Scarlet had a car. "What kind of car does Ms. Farrow drive?" Steve had picked her up enough to know.

"It's a little blue thing. Maybe a Dodge or a Chevy, I'm not sure. Why, you gonna fix it up for her?"

He didn't know the first thing about cars, but he could pay someone to do it. He quickly located his phone and sent her a text.

Hope your first class went well, Ms. Farrow. On your next break, please leave your car unlocked and the keys under the mat. Don't worry. I'll have it back by four. Have a pleasant day.

. . .

his would be a test of trust. Asher was well aware of Scarlet's salary, not that it was a deciding factor in anything. He knew where she worked and salaries in the public school system were communal knowledge. If her modest income didn't often lead her to spas and hotels, the chances of her car getting a little TLC were unlikely as well.

"Is it a new car?" he asked Steve.

"Nah, probably about ten years old."

His phone chimed and he grinned. So easy, but always a refreshing surprise to hear back from her.

"She's going to leave the key under the mat on the driver's side. I want you to take the Mercedes, park it out of sight, and pick up her car."

"Where should I take it? Do you have a garage in mind?"

He thought for a moment. They had Gus, the guy who worked on KITT and the ambulance, but he worked slowly. Asher still had to make the arrangements for that evening and make an appearance at work, but the temptation of peeking into her space was too much. "Pick me up once you have the car and we'll take it to a dealership. They'll likely have everything we need in stock."

---

teve drove the small blue car that turned out to be a Ford, as Asher busied himself snooping through compartments. She was very organized. Her inspection was up to date and her registration and proof of insurance were neatly clipped together in the glove compartment.

In the backseat he found an umbrella and a travel trash bag holding only a receipt for produce. Disappointed there weren't more telling hints of her hiding in the car, he gave up his search.

When they pulled into the garage at the dealership, an attendant wearing an expected jumpsuit stained at the cuff with grease greeted them. Steve handed over the keys as Asher selected from the menu of services. He gave his credit card to the attendant. When everything was finished, Steve would return the car to the school, key inside.

———

Scarlet was on cloud nine. Once again, Mr. Stone had done something no one had ever come close to doing for her before. When she'd left the keys that morning, only curiosity had her heart racing. There was no worry regarding his care of her property, as Mr. Stone seemed to define responsible.

Never had she expected returning to the parking lot to find what he'd left. Her little blue Ford sparkled in the sunlight. There were no traces of the dent from a runaway shopping cart and all those tiny scratches by her bumper and door were gone.

Four new gleaming tires rested under the frame and the windshield glistened. She expected the surprises to stop there, but, of course, they didn't. In the dash was a new stereo with an updated auxiliary hookup complete with a tiny red iPod all ready to go. She giggled. He. Was. Amazing.

The scent of polished leather jarred her. He'd had

her seats replaced with luxury ones, boasting electronic controls and the much-coveted heated settings she'd always longed for. How would he know she'd always wanted such things?

He couldn't know. The gift was so extravagant it left her breathless and slightly intimidated. She'd already surmised Mr. Stone had money, but to throw it away on her and her old car... how limitless were his funds? Some women might find that attractive. But for her it was slightly frightening. How would she ever measure up or compete with such openhandedness?

Who was this man and why had he chosen her, of all people? When she located her keys she spotted more additions. Her Ford had an automatic start control now, which would be lovely when winter really took its toll. But, oddly, the most touching gift of all, was the small keychain dangling from the ring.

It was a beautiful silver sword with a garnet stone embedded in the hilt. She turned the jewel, admiring the way the sunlight gathered in the crests, forming reflections of scarlet deep in the stone. Why had he chosen this?

Of course, the sword reminded her of him and his silly profile picture. Was he the sword in the stone? Somehow locked in place, while she was the scarlet light? There was a reason she taught math instead of literature. She sucked at symbolism. Still, this was better than anything he'd ever given her because she could hold it every day, like a secret her heart would always protect.

As she drove home she noted other improvements. Her fluids were full and the car had a new set of windshield wipers. When she turned on the radio the iPod illuminated. She shouldn't have been surprised, but she was when music slowly strummed through the car.

It was a remake of an old song, quite familiar, and relevant. Curious about the pretty vocals, she glanced at the artist's name displayed on the screen. It was Amanda Seyfried singing *Little Red Riding Hood*.

The quiet thrumming of strings paired with her husky vocals cut right to her heart as the words sank into her soul. Had he purposefully selected this song? Of course he had. There was such desperation to the song. It was romantic, yet ominous. She wasn't afraid, not of him. No matter what happened, she truly believed he'd never intentionally hurt her.

When she got home she fed Thor and changed into jeans and a soft sweater. He'd instructed her to wear something comfortable, but her feminine side forbade she go to him in grungy sweats and sneakers. He deserved her efforts.

She carefully brushed out her hair, and clipped it into a twist. Reaching into her jewelry box, she selected the thin pearl necklace he'd given her, pairing it with twin pearl earrings her mother had gifted her with on her sweet sixteen.

On the drive to him, her mind remained busy, turning over possibilities and disqualifying the sense that he was rushing to the end. Maybe he was, but maybe that was in order to get to the next stage, a stage where blindfolds didn't exist and she could finally look into his eyes.

"Did you like all the improvements to your car, Ms. Farrow?"

Pennyworth's question jarred her attention away from the lingering apprehension. Their short conversations over the mysterious drive had become familiar, never carrying the weight of her and Mr. Stone's dialogues.

"I love them!" She smiled in the enforced darkness. "I never expected anything like that when he told me to leave the keys."

"He was happy to do it for you."

She silently grinned, finding it peculiar that Pennyworth had divulged any information regarding his employer's motives. "He's incredible," she whispered.

The driver didn't miss her appraisal. "Inspiring," he amended, bringing her back to their first meeting when he'd used that same word.

Mr. Stone certainly was an inspiring man. He'd inspired her to attempt things she never dreamed she'd have the courage to dream.

I love him.

Her mind jolted at the silent confession. Did she love him? Knowing she shouldn't—not yet—she reprimanded her fanciful heart and remained quiet for the remainder of the drive.

"We're here." The car slowed and her stomach turned over, a pinch of excitement folded into nervousness, but as the door opened any worry was replaced with euphoric joy.

"Good evening, Ms. Farrow."

Tension escaped her as she sighed. "Good evening, Mr. Stone. Thank you for my incredible gift today. I loved it." There was that pesky word again. She'd have to be careful tonight.

Taking her hand, he surprised her by leaning close, his warm scent breathing into her soul, as warm lips pressed at the corner of her jaw, just beneath her ear. His breath was hot, tickling her throat. "You're very welcome."

Her body shivered, drawing to attention and revving up faster than ever. He escorted her inside and slowly unbuttoned her coat.

Overcome with so much longing, she wanted to maul him before he got to the second button. Her body shook with effort to restrain her desire. His fingers deftly stripped her of her jacket. Her ears followed his footsteps as he placed the coat in the usual area. She was coming to recognize her surroundings, but tonight, over the sweet scent of wood burning nearby, there was a new smell.

It was fragrant and calming. The delicate traces of a scent unarguably feminine penetrated her senses and her mind went wild with guesses as to what he had in store. She forced her mind not to linger on the sense of trepidation that another woman might be there.

His finger traced over the side of her throat, the action drawing her like a feline into a caress. "Your hair's up," he observed.

Stepping behind her, his hands slowly combing over her arms, touching her hips, and tracing up to her shoulders, he seemed to breathe her in. She loved the liberties he now took to touch her, loved feeling the weight of his caress on her skin. He'd become so bold with her and she treasured every bit of contact.

Shoes softly scuffing over the floor in gentle steps, the heat of his body warmed her front. His finger played with a fallen lock of hair by her ear and she shivered. Creeping closer, she sucked in a breath as his chest grazed the tips of her breasts pressing through her clothing.

"I find..." he whispered gently, his lips tracing over

her thundering pulse, "it's becoming more and more difficult to keep my hands to myself in your presence."

"Then don't." Would she ever stop being breathless around him?

He chuckled and licked at her exposed throat, throwing her heart into double time. "I have a treat for you this evening."

Every moment with him was a treat. He didn't have to continuously orchestrate things. Simply being with him was a gift in itself. "You already did something extraordinary for me today."

"You're worth spoiling," he said, sliding his hands down her back, he drew her to his front.

He was hard. Evidence of the effect she had on him took her arousal to a new level. Boldly, she reached for him, her hand curling around his hip, fingers firming as a thousand volts of erotic energy shot up her arm.

He stilled.

She breathed through the frozen moment, silently begging him to allow the contact.

"What are you doing, Ms. Farrow?"

Shallow breaths panted past her lips. She wanted to slide her palm over his thigh and cup him, bring them each a modicum of relief. She couldn't bring herself to apologize, so she said nothing. He wasn't the one who was blind. He could see what he was doing to her, feel her need. Hell, it was thrumming through the air like a collapsing star.

He stepped back and her face lowered. "Not tonight."

Her tongue refused an apology. "Why?"

His voice gave nothing away. "Because I have a different plan."

She waited. Though she desperately wanted to touch him, he had yet to disappoint her. Perhaps his plan was better.

Without knowing exactly where he stood, she sensed he'd moved out of reach. "Please remain still."

She shivered as he lifted her arm, pulling the sleeve of her sweater slowly. "I'm afraid your clothes need to come off. Do I have your permission, Ms. Farrow?"

"Yes," she rasped.

He carefully fed her arms through the sleeves of her sweater, cautious of the blindfold and her hair as he lifted it over her head. Her breasts lifted as her breathing accelerated at the moment of exposure.

Caressing fingers traced over her hip, and unsnapped her jeans. The zipper lowered with torturous slowness, each tiny tooth enunciating its parting in the quiet room.

"Step out of your shoes, please."

She toed off her shoes, one by one, and he lowered her pants. She detected him lowering to his knees as he slid the denim from her calves. Warm breath bathed her naked thighs for an extended moment.

He was looking at her. She could feel his gaze weighing on her sex and the tickle of his breath. Gentle fingers teased the hem of her panties. "These too."

Jaggedly, she nodded as anticipation left her trembling. Slowly, the silk of her panties pulled away, loosening at her knees and eventually dropping to the floor. Her body went on high alert, a thousand jolts of sexual tension wreaking havoc on her brain.

Barely there, like the brush of a small breeze, his fingers grazed the fiery curls covering her sex. Her fingers twitched and her hands balled into fists as she struggled to remain motionless.

Again, his breath teased her flesh, this time tickling her lower belly. "I've changed my mind," he said.

Why? Panic took hold of her patience, slamming her heart into palpitating apprehension.

He stood and took her hand. "Come with me."

Objection quivered on her lips as his fingers laced with hers and he towed her across the room. "Sit."

She lowered into the seat, the fabric cool on her naked bottom. His clipped steps did nothing to calm her nerves as he suddenly walked away. Something clicked and there was the clank of glass, not shattering, but carelessly knocking. He returned and the plug of a cork popped in the silence. Liquid tinkled into a glass and she scented the flowery fragrance of Merlot.

His fingers lifted her wrist and guided the glass into her hand. "Have a sip of wine, Ms. Farrow. I'm going to touch you."

Sucking in a deep breath, she found it impossible to sip from the goblet. Her hands shook so tumultuously, she feared spilling the staining liquid. Forcing the glass to her lips, she wet only the tip of her tongue then felt for the table, sliding the goblet onto the surface carefully. She loved wine, but she loved his touch more.

"Very good," he said. "Place your hands on the arms of the chair and don't let go until I give you permission."

Eagerly, she did as she was told. Fabric whispered. She wished she knew what he was wearing as he was clearly removing an item of clothing.

Finally, his touch returned, a slow trace of his finger running from her upper thigh to her knee.

"Scoot forward for me."

She shimmied lower on the seat, careful not to let go of the arms of the chair.

"Good girl." Her body flooded at his praise. The rustling of his clothes and her excited breathing blurred out any telltale clues as to what he was doing.

Warmth covered her knees as his hands crept over her flesh, parting her thighs. He was kneeling before her. "Open for me."

Dear God, every command was an aphrodisiac to her starved libido. Though it was dark under the blindfold, she had no idea if he was seeing her in blinding or dim light. Exposed didn't begin to describe how on display his actions made her feel.

He sucked in an audible breath. "I knew you'd be pink," he whispered as her outer thighs pressed into the upholstered chair. "Your pussy's glistening. You're very aroused, Ms. Farrow."

Rapidly breathing through the unparalleled experience, she fought back all insecurities. *Please* ... She couldn't remain silent any longer. "Please touch me," she begged.

"I will. I want to look at you first."

The brush of his sleeve caused her to jerk as it tickled her thigh.

"You're so wet it's trickling from your slit like a little drop of dew. I can see your body trembling for my attention. Describe what you feel, Ms. Farrow."

"Throbbing. Wanting. Need."

The heat of his hands closed over her inner thighs, dragging slowly to her center. She held her breath, awaiting the moment he'd actually touch her there. The first graze of his finger jarred her, ripping a moan from her throat as her hips jerked, lifting her rear from the chair.

"Stay still, Ms. Farrow."

Her fingers tightened over the upholstery as he parted her folds. Delicately pulling back her drenched layers, he whispered, "And you're even more pink inside. So delicate and feminine, so sexy."

Her clit pulsed with unequivocal need. He held her open for several seconds, presumably examining her like no one, not even her doctors, had ever done. Meticulously.

"I can scent your arousal. It's sweet and beguiling. Do you want more, Ms. Farrow?"

"Yes," she begged.

Pulling the flesh of her sex, his thumb grazed her clit and she shivered so violently it was as like a miniature orgasm, quickly transcending into the thrums of something greater.

"Are you close, Ms. Farrow?"

She was there. He'd barely touched her and she was already hanging on the cusp of what would undoubtedly be the most intense orgasm of her life. Words were impossible; syllables were hard, she moaned in the affirmative.

"Would you like to come?"

"Please."

"Good, because I very much want to taste your pleasure." His finger sank into her, lifting her body off the seat as the digit drilled deeply into her core. She cried out, begging him for more.

His shoulders forced their way between her thighs and his hot mouth covered her weeping sex, his tongue penetrating her opening as his fingers teased her clit. The orgasm needed no time to build. At the first brush of contact he'd released a knot of hunger inside of her begging to be undone.

Her body arched into him as his mouth devoured her. Back bowed, fingers digging into the arms of the chair like talons, she was practically standing over him. Muscles tensed and rocked her bones as she shattered. He groaned, licking at her slit, his mouth latching onto her sex as his fingers filled her. He stretched her, adding another digit, fucking her with his hand as his lips closed over her throbbing clit, prolonging the rushing waves of ecstasy racing through her.

There was no waning. The stubble of his jaw chafed deliciously at her tender flesh. The pleasure mounted and mounted, ripping down layers of pent up need as he drove his fingers into her pussy. Dragging out new sensations he pleasured her until her strength depleted and she collapsed in the chair, her body twitching with each caress.

His attention slowed, his tongue tasting every fold, licking at every spent trace of arousal. The blindfold had become irrelevant. Her eyes rested in the darkness as he tended to her pulsating body.

When he finally eased back, he blew over her heated sex, cool air tickling and sending more shivers up her spine.

His voice was hoarse. "Now you're even more beautiful, Ms. Farrow, because I can see evidence of my touch on your already stunning body."

She shivered. Last time he'd touched her he'd left a hickey on her breast. At first it had concerned her, but when she reminded herself no one but her would see it, she cherished the mark. It left her feeling connected to him even in his absence. The idea that she'd likely wear scratches from his five o'clock shadow was a welcome and erotic souvenir. "Thank you."

His knuckle brushed over her tender sex and she gasped. "Are you sore?"

She shook her head. Sore wasn't a fair description. Sore carried negative connotations and there was nothing negative about the way she felt in that moment.

"Your sex is swollen, slightly chafed, and your hole is contracting by the tiniest degrees. That's your body asking for more."

Breathing fast, she wondered if *more* was on the menu. She couldn't have sex with someone without seeing him, without even knowing his first name, could she? Dear God, he had her under such a spell. Anyone else would call her crazy for letting things get this far.

His lips pressed to her knee and he stood. "I think you'll really enjoy your surprise now, Ms. Farrow." Taking her hand, he slowly helped her rise. "Let us not forget this." His fingers unclasped her bra, sliding the material away from her sensitized flesh.

Like a newly born fawn, she walked jaggedly, her limbs languorous as he led her deeper into the house. She'd never been this far in his home and her curiosity awakened a bit of her drifting senses.

The flowery fragrance intensified with the sound of babbling water under a low hum of machinery. "I hear water," she announced.

"Very good. That's because I've arranged to give you a bath. I think you've earned it after the last hour." He took two more steps. "It's a tall jetted tub, so I'll help you in. The water's heated."

She hesitated when he gave her fingers a tug.

"Ms. Farrow?"

Her lips pursed. This had never happened before. "Um... Before I get in the water...I need to..."

Silence.

She waited for him to comprehend what she was inelegantly trying to bring to his attention.

"Of course." He cleared his throat. "Right this way."

She followed his lead through the house. Winding turns disoriented her and her steps became sluggish. "Here we are." A door opened and he escorted her inside, her feet brushing over cool tile, the polished sort without grout lines.

He turned her and she stood dumbly as the swift flutter of tissue unraveling from the roll filled the room. Wadded up paper filled her hand. In a trance, she waited for him to step away.

When he made no move and her body demanded prompt release, she whimpered. "I'll be right out."

The silence turned heavy. "My back is turned. I can run the faucet to drown out my presence, if that will help."

She frowned, the pressure in her bladder making it difficult to speak. "I need privacy."

He cleared his throat. "I'm afraid this is all the privacy I can offer, Ms. Farrow. It's only human nature." The soft rush of water from the faucet masked the silence and added to her uncomfortable predicament.

Was he afraid she'd snoop? "I won't peek."

"I'm afraid not." His words hit her like a bucket of ice, reality's cold truth breaking her sense of comfort.

He didn't trust her. It hurt. She trusted him so profoundly and he couldn't trust her enough to leave her alone for two minutes. "I can't go in front of someone."

"Would you like me to get your clothes and Pennyworth?"

Her lips parted as she sucked in a breath. Anger at his easy solution, which would cut their night short, sliced through her. "No, I'd like you to leave me alone for a minute." If she didn't sit soon, she was going to embarrass herself.

"Sit on the seat, Ms. Farrow, and stop being so modest. I assure you I'm not watching."

Out of time and without physical choice, she rapidly dropped to the seat. Her muscles reflexively slackened as the humiliating tinkling broke the silence.

He'd never upset her until that very moment. Feeling outmaneuvered and deceived, she scowled into the darkness. Mouth tight, she cleaned herself up and slowly stood, refusing any silent offer of help, should he offer one. The blindfold made it impossible to tell.

"Would you like to wash your hands?"

Nodding tightly, she allowed his palm to hover at her lower back as he directed her toward the sink. He placed her fingers on the cool lip of a counter as the slushing sound of water continued to fill the room.

Blindly, her palm patted the surface until she located the soap. She silently cleaned her hands and felt for the faucet, shutting the water off.

He escorted her back to the room. "Wait here. I want to grab the wine."

"No." Her body shook with disbelief, anger, and the sting of her stripped vanity.

"Ms. Farrow?"

"I'd like my clothes."

Silence.

"Please," she insisted, her voice a quiver away from tears.

"Scarlet..."

"I wouldn't have looked," she snapped. "You don't trust me at all."

He remained quiet.

"May I please have my clothes? I want to go home."

"I didn't watch you, Scarlet."

It didn't matter. All she'd asked for was a minute of trust after weeks of granting him blind faith.

His voice was low. "I don't want you to leave yet," he said slowly.

She'd felt so close to him only minutes ago, so certain they were moving forward. This unwelcome step backward had her mind in turmoil. He'd taken advantage of the situation.

"Either give me my clothes or I'll find them myself —*without* the blindfold."

"Scarlet—"

"You humiliated me. *Please.*" Tears choked her. In a small voice she begged. "Don't make me ask again."

His reply was quiet. "I'm sorry."

He might regret that she was upset, but she didn't believe he'd act differently if the situation were repeated. His apology didn't change the fact that after everything, he still didn't trust her.

His steps returned. "Put your arms forward." Her bra slid over her shoulders and she brushed his touch away as he attempted to fasten the clasp. She hated that her body still responded to his nearness, prickling from the slightest contact, even after he'd hurt her.

As he helped her dress, her mind replayed the day. So many emotions packed into such a few hours. She recalled the song he'd chosen for her, the subtle warnings of the singer, warnings she couldn't align with him until that very moment. The truth was, when Mr. Stone hurt her feelings, it hurt badly.

Why was he so afraid to expose himself to her when she'd disclosed all to him? Her brow pinched beneath the blindfold. Something had happened to this man. His aversion to being seen went beyond a need for privacy. She detected his underlying fear, an insecurity that didn't suit the strong, capable man he was with her normally. But that's exactly what his behavior was—fear.

There was nothing else keeping this blindfold between them but his worry that she might somehow react negatively to whatever he was hiding. No one was perfect. If he could accept her flaws, she could accept his. She didn't care about the packaging. It was the man on the inside she wanted to be close to.

Despite her upset, she needed to get through to him. "It doesn't matter," she whispered, lightly grasping his hands as they buttoned her jeans.

"I beg your pardon?"

Her head slowly shook. "What you look like, it doesn't matter to me. There's nothing you could show me that would change my feelings for you, Mr. Stone. I'd never hurt you."

He was quiet for a long moment. "That's not why you're blindfolded."

He was lying. If he refused to be honest there was nothing she could say. They were already treading delicate ground and trying to get an inflexible object to bend often ended with broken pieces.

She took a different approach. "Tell me your first name." If he could just give her something personal—

"No."

Her face lowered. "I've given you everything you've asked for and you refuse to give me anything."

A derisive sound pierced the air. "I haven't given you *anything*?"

"Nothing of meaning."

"Really?" His tone was affronted.

"What's the value of things when I can't have your name? You've showered me with luxurious gifts, when all I'm asking for is something you grant everyone else that crosses your path. I just want your name, to know what color your eyes are and to see how they change when they look into mine."

Though he remained silent, his breathing accelerated. He was irritated and she didn't savor possibly making this powerful man feel cornered.

"Perhaps you should have put that in your letter then, Ms. Farrow. I've given you everything you've asked for, uninhibited adoration, attention, intellectual conversation, and pleasure. I promised you fourteen encounters, but nothing more. My name is mine and I'll share it when I'm ready."

"You're forgetting one important thing. You've also given me the courage to increase my standards. This blindfold is a wall between us and it doesn't have to be."

"If you intend to revoke your trust in me, say so now and we'll end this." He breathed raggedly as he waited for a response. "The blindfold stays. Accept that or this...this will be our last encounter."

All windows of compassion slammed shut as a cool chill crept up her spine. "I want my coat." Who was he to speak to her like that? She might accept his conditions, but she drew the line at ultimatums.

"Scarlet..."

Although dressed, she felt more exposed than she had all night. "Goodnight, Mr. Stone."

With clipped steps he walked away. The door snapped open, introducing a cool breeze to the room. He returned with her coat and slipped it over her shoulders. A throat cleared in the distance. Pennyworth.

As he fumbled with her buttons, she swatted his hands away and took over the task, not having much success. "Mr. Pennyworth will see you out."

With that he walked away, leaving her desolate and confused, her anger subsiding into panic.

"Ms. Farrow?"

Her head tilted in Pennyworth's direction as he took her arm, slowly escorting her to the car.

When she was buckled inside and they were on their way, trepidation choked her. She wanted to rip off the damn blindfold and race back to him, forcing him to confront whatever held him at bay.

Music clicked on interrupting her chain of reckless thoughts. They never listened to music in the car, but perhaps the driver had picked up on her distress and this was his attempt to offer her privacy, should she want to cry.

"You can remove the blindfold now, Ms. Farrow," he said after they'd driven a ways.

Sliding the covering off her eyes, she blinked, her cheeks moist and tingling under the press of cool air. Glancing out the window, she stared at the unfamiliar landmarks rushing by, coming to recognize some of them the closer they drew to her house. But there would always be the mysterious part of the route she was never permitted to see, the portion that led to *him*.

"Tell me something, Pennyworth. If I put a gun to

your head would you take me to him *without* the blindfold?"

He chuckled. "You wouldn't do that, Ms. Farrow."

"How do you know?"

His grin flashed in the rearview mirror. "Do you *own* a gun?"

"No, but I could get one."

"I highly doubt you would."

She tsked and rolled her eyes. "Just answer the question, Pennyworth."

He sighed, his smile turning considerate. "Mr. Stone has been very good to me. He's my friend, Ms. Farrow. I'd find it very hard to go against his wishes. I wouldn't want to betray my promise to a friend."

Sighing, she crossed her arms and admitted, "Then I won't shoot you."

"Good to know." The rest of the ride passed in silence.

Unrequited wanting had her questioning her sanity. What if it never ended? What if the end was just an end? She didn't know if her life could tolerate such an unsolved mystery of never knowing who he was. What if *this* was the end?

They should have five days left, but what if tonight was their last? He'd given her an ultimatum and hit a major cord. He should realize everyone had limits and, if he wanted this to work, he needed to respect hers. If anything, she wanted the chance to talk to him about her boundaries, make him understand that a relationship consisted of give and take and she wouldn't take that sort of treatment from anyone, let alone someone she loved.

If not for him, she might not have had the courage to put her foot down tonight. But he'd encouraged her to keep her standards high and it was his own fault she no longer considered lowering them an option—not even for him.

Couples evolved together, requiring both partners to be open and honest, something he couldn't seem to manage at the moment and something that eventually had to change if their relationship continued.

Her stomach tipped sending nausea tunneling through her. It couldn't be over. Like an addict, she knew the risks were getting dangerous, but the truth was, she lacked the strength of will to stop. But she had enough self-respect to call him out on his bullshit, making it perfectly clear he was just as accountable as she in this relation. He hurt her and until he apologized, there would be no moving forward.

14

COMPREHENSION

There was no relief in the passing days. The tension in her chest contracted until every bit of her strength was devoted to holding back the tears choking her. It was over.

It had been eleven days and she'd not heard from him. When the withdrawal became unbearable, she'd messaged him on GeekPeek, but he hadn't replied or even opened her message, not that it said much, just a simple "Hi."

He claimed the blindfold was an instrument in developing her trust, enunciating each experience, which it was. But it was also a form of protection for him and whatever secrets he had to hide. His rules existed for a reason. She'd never comprehend the rationale behind them until she understood the man. And she wanted—very much—to understand him.

She was angry at his inability to bend after she'd followed his lead around every curve. But she was also sad, sad for whatever happened to him in order to make him so closed off. He clearly had trust issues. It was something to work on, something many couples struggled to overcome. Unfortunately, as time went on, she feared such a chance was unlikely.

When another weekend rolled around, bringing another Friday to pass, she'd forced herself to accept the fairytale was over. Wandering through her house, she cleaned as Thor maneuvered around her ankles, crying for some attention.

As she cleaned out her closet, she gathered all of his letters, tying them carefully with the prettiest ribbon she owned. Nora Jones sang softly from the CD player on her dresser about nightingales and wishes to be carried away on songs of love that once belonged.

Closing the box over the dried flowers and letters, she softly wept. Thor butted his head at her hand and curled onto her lap. Rolling to her back, she let her tears slide through her hair to the carpet. There wasn't anything she could do.

The sound of her front door opening startled her. Sitting up, she quickly blotted her eyes.

"Lettie?" Nicole's voice called up the stairs.

"In my room," she answered, clearing her throat.

Her bedroom door opened and she met her friend's scowl. "You don't pick up the phone anymore?"

"Sorry. I've been busy."

Nicole glanced at the pile of unwanted items tossed on her bed and Scarlet toed the box holding all memories of Mr. Stone deeper into her closet.

"What are you doing?"

"Just cleaning out some old junk."

Her friend sighed and dropped to the carpet. "What happened?"

"Nothing happened," she lied. "I've been meaning to declutter—"

"Scarlet," Nicole interrupted, her scowl replaced with an expression of concern. "Level with me."

She sighed and the tears quickly returned. "I think we broke up."

"You and Stone?"

She nodded.

"Oh, honey, what happened?"

There was only so much she could tell without making a mockery of how deep her feelings ran. "I think I pushed for too much too soon."

Her friend gave a sad, but comprehending smile. "Yeah, guys are stupid with stuff like that. Most of them have mommy issues and find it hard to face real commitment."

She was way off, but Scarlet allowed Nicole her own interpretation. "I knew what we had. I shouldn't have tried to make it more before he was ready."

Nicole scoffed. "Men are never ready. You have to be stealthy when pushing for more, make them believe they're in complete control, otherwise they get defensive. Have you talked to him?"

"No."

"They're such pussies. Why don't you write him a letter, then he has to listen to what you have to say."

"That's a possibility."

"You could even deliver it in person, then when he reads it you guys can have great makeup sex."

Yeah, *if* she knew where he lived. "I don't want to crowd him. I'll probably just email him or something." She didn't mention messaging him on GeekPeek because then Nicole would insist on seeing his picture, which didn't exist.

Nicole glanced around the room and sighed. "Come on, I'm getting you out of here. Even Thor looks depressed. Let's go shopping and out for coffee."

"I don't feel like it."

"I don't care. You can't stay in your closet rolling down memory lane all day. It's nice out. You don't even need a ski mask."

She laughed. Winter was upon them and she was already looking forward to the coming spring, hating the bitter cold that bit through even the thickest coats. "Fine, but we're going to the mall. I'm not walking around the outlets in thirty degree weather all day."

"Deal. But coffee first."

"*Asher!*" Hunter hissed from across the small café table.

Ash entered the last few commands, skimming off the coffee shop's Wi-Fi and glanced at his friend.

Hunter's dark eyes were wide, his head tilted to the left, drawing Asher's attention. Every muscle tensed as he recognized Nicole Pickerelli sitting with Scarlet.

"Is that her?" Hunter whispered.

Asher's breath turned jagged as every muscle locked with the paralysis of a feeble animal within a predator's reach. Clearly, he wasn't making as much progress as he hoped. His heart was racing as if he'd just run a marathon. Every instinct he had told him to stay perfectly still, but his heart begged to go to her. It was as if the mere closeness of her pulled him into her orbit, a magnetic force his common sense couldn't out-maneuver.

Silently, he nodded. His mouth was suddenly bone dry, his gaze locked to her sitting only ten feet away in the small café. He never came to this place, but after their meeting that morning with the youth group OddSquad, he wanted to finalize the app so Eugene could take it viral. The kid had been really excited to see his work come to life.

His heart pounded, as he feared she'd recognize him. She looked...tired. It had been well over a week since he'd seen her and the slight purple crests under her eyes told him that time apart had taken its toll.

He hadn't pulled back to punish her. Rather, he'd withdrawn from her life to protect them both. Things were moving too fast and getting too complicated. Somewhere in the midst of holding all the control, he'd lost control of his purpose and hurt her. He never meant to upset her that night, but he panicked when something unexpected happened. Then she threatened to leave and he reacted badly, feeling cornered and unsure. She started flinging demands at him and asking things he wasn't ready to answer.

But worst of all, as she begged him to tell her his name, he saw a shift. The anger seemed to ease and she appeared to make sense of something. Then he sensed her pity.

He didn't want her pity, hated the idea that he might give her reason to believe he needed any such thing. There was simply too much emotion between them and until he thought of an explanation for his behavior—beyond his own cowardliness—he decided time apart was best.

But as he watched her now, he noted, not only exhaustion in her appearance, but the sadness in her eyes. Damn him and his foolish inexperience. He should know better. Women were sensitive, his mother always reminded him of that. How could he even think what he did was okay? She'd been vulnerable and asked for two minutes of privacy. It was completely narcissistic for him to believe she wanted anything more than a few moments alone.

God, I've fucked everything up again.

As he studied her, Nicole talked and she nodded along despondently. He wished for the courage to go to her and introduce himself, but he couldn't stir even the slightest nerve to lift his coffee to his lips, afraid she'd notice him and at the same time not notice him at all.

"Go talk to her," Hunter whispered.

He shook his head. He couldn't. Swallowing tightly, he continued to analyze her. A waitress delivered drinks to her table and she smiled.

Her eyes, so chameleon like, shined bright in the sunlight. They were as stunning as always, varying shades of blue and green. His breath caught as it always did when her glance cast in his direction. The last time he saw her eyes was at the Imperial Room and the restaurant had been too dim to truly appreciate their beauty.

Her hand tucked a ruby strand of hair behind her ear as she carefully took a sip of her beverage. Her full lips touched the brim of the mug and his body reacted. Flashes of their last encounter played through his mind, a torturous kaleidoscope of fantasies brought to life for a fleeting moment. He needed to get out of there.

When Nicole handed her a napkin, he frowned.

Scarlet shook her head and blotted her eyes, laughing in spite of her clear distress.

She's crying...

His attention zeroed in on her mouth, trying to make out what she said. He caught the words "*stupid*" and "*pathetic*".

Was she referring to him? She couldn't be talking about herself. She wasn't either of those things. He was. Those tears were his fault and he couldn't let her go on blaming herself for his personal shortcomings.

Minimizing the app page on his laptop, he signed into GeekPeek. He knew she'd messaged him, but he didn't want to encourage her. Luckily, the preview showed the note in its entirety. A simple "Hi" was all she'd written.

Opening the message finally, he quickly typed out a response.

> Sweet Scarlet, I've been thinking about you and hope you're doing well. I'm sorry my insensitive actions hurt you. That was never my intention. Perhaps the distance between us is wise. Please don't take it personally. It was me that was wrong. Missing you. ~Mr. Stone

He sent the message and waited. Her dialogue slowed as she reached into her pocket and pulled out her phone, but she continued to converse with her friend, her eyes on Nicole until she had the device in her palms.

Her words cut off, her mouth opening as her shoulders lifted on a slow breath. *"Oh my God."* He read her lips. She glanced nervously at her friend. *"It's him."*

Nicole's voice was loud as she gasped, "What did he say?"

Asher frowned, questioning how much Nicole actually knew of he and Scarlet's relationship. Scarlet's lips compressed and her brow knit as she read her phone. When Nicole stretched to snatch the phone Scarlet quickly jerked it out of reach and scowled. His chest filled with pride. Glad to see Scarlet had established some boundaries with her pushy friend.

Leaning back in the booth, she thumbed over the screen and his gut clenched as expectation thrummed through his veins. She was writing back. Quickly muting his laptop, his eyes volleyed from her to the screen, awaiting her reply. She lowered her phone to the bench and grinned at Nicole.

The message appeared and he quickly opened it.

> I miss you more than words can say. I think we both said and did some things we shouldn't have the other night. You hurt me, and I pushed back. I can be patient. I don't want to rehash it. Can we please get together soon? Your conditions, my trust. XO, Scarlet

. . .

There were wiser things to do than place himself right back in a situation he was quickly losing control of. "Shit."

"What'd she say?" Hunter whispered.

"She wants to see me."

"So see her."

He shook his head. "It's complicated."

His friend sighed. "Only because your letting it be. Get out of your damn head and do what your heart wants, Ash. She's clearly upset and misses you. This isn't difficult."

As he glanced at her table, she was smiling, her eyes no longer weary, but full of hope. It felt good to restore a bit of what he'd taken from her. Maybe Hunter was right, but he couldn't just walk over to her —especially not with Nicole there.

He typed out his reply, glancing quickly at the time. It was four-thirty.

I've missed you too. Pennyworth can pick you up at six. I'm sorry I hurt you. Yours, Mr. Stone

He waited as the message traveled to her phone. Her face illuminated, an expression of pure joy banishing all signs of worry. She stood and Nicole sulked over her unfinished coffee. As she gathered her belongings, he lost sight of her face and any chance of reading her lips.

She tossed some money on the table and left, her friend wearing a look of abrupt confusion as she trailed behind.

He grinned. He'd have to plan their evening quickly. He only had a little over an hour. He quickly shot Steve a text. Shutting his laptop, he paused as he noted Hunter's expression of shock.

"What did you say to her?" his friend asked, a look of pure awe in his eyes.

Asher shrugged. "I just told her I missed her, said I was sorry, and she asked if we could get together tonight." His phone chimed and he grinned. "Steve's picking her up at six."

Hunter's head shook slowly. "Just like that?"

Asher smiled, surprised as well. "Just like that."

He stuffed his laptop into his shoulder bag and dug out some money. As he tossed the cash on the table Hunter continued to stare at him. "What?"

"If you mess this up with her, you're an idiot."

Drawing in a slow breath, he confessed, "I'm reevaluating my concerns."

"Good, because I gotta tell you, no matter how many secrets you two have, something there is real for her to go running off to you like that. Don't mess that up, Ash."

He swallowed, deciding that was the biggest goal, not to mess this up. "I'll try."

That night, as he paced by the window awaiting her arrival, it became apparent how much he'd actually missed her. When the lights of the Mercedes cut through the limpid twilight his stomach knotted with eagerness.

The dizzying effect of her nearness rocked him as he opened the door wide. Steve helped her from the car and he stared unblinking as she approached.

"Thank you, Pennyworth," he whispered, his voice a touch husky under the bulk of his appreciation. "Good evening, Ms. Farrow."

Her chin trembled as she stepped over the threshold. He reached to unbutton her coat and she surprised him by throwing her arms around his waist and squeezing him tight.

Warmth filled him as he allowed her genuine show of affection, needing her touch as much as she apparently needed his in return. Slowly, his arms wrapped around her and he simply held her for a moment.

Her hair smelled of sweet apples, bringing nostalgic comfort to his senses and easing his tension.

"I missed you," she whispered.

He pressed a light kiss into her hair. "I missed you too."

They slowly drew apart and she beamed. He unbuttoned her coat and hung it beside her scarf. He bent to remove her boots. Placing them by the wall, he also removed his shoes.

He hadn't worn a suit today. Rather, he kept his clothing casual, jeans and a soft sweater he'd recently purchased. "I thought we'd do something a little different this evening, Ms. Farrow."

"Okay." He walked her to the ballroom, his fingers

laced with hers. She continuously gave his hand subtle squeezes. He'd missed those tiny gestures. When they reached the bed, she smiled and said, "You're not wearing shoes."

Supposing she usually tracked his movement by the sound of his footfalls, he grinned at her cleverness. "Not tonight. I want to hold you. I have a bed. Nothing sexual will happen. I just want to give you the experience of being held. You're welcome to nap and perhaps when you wake, you'll finally know what it is to wake up in a man's arms, something you've confessed to never experiencing."

Her appreciative smile was slow, displaying her straight pearly teeth. "I love that idea."

He placed her hand on the bed. "It's tall, so I'll guide you to the pillows."

She carefully maneuvered her way onto the mattress. Feeling around for the pillows, she turned and lowered herself to her back.

"Comfortable?"

"Mmm. Very."

Rounding the four-post bed, he sat beside her and drew the covers over them, settling in to her side.

She sighed, the sound full of contentment. Observing her, he said, "Tell me about your week."

"I worked, cleaned out all my pantries, and reorganized my cabinets. Got rid of some stuff I no longer use."

Was she purposely not mentioning how his absence made her feel? "Is purging something you do regularly?" His fingers picked up a lock of her hair, admiring the fiery highlights of red and rubicund gold.

"When I'm stressed."

"Other than our relationship, is something stressful happening in your life?" She had friends and family. It was arrogant to think her behavior only resulted from his actions.

He'd also been under a lot of stress lately, but nothing out of the ordinary was happening in his private world. His levels of tension had dramatically lowered since deciding to see her again.

"No. I was upset and couldn't reach you. That's stressful."

His fingers traced the freckles along her brow, teasing the edge of the blindfold. Guilt was a great responsibility he momentarily shied away from. "Tell me about your favorite time of day."

Her voice was pitched low in a hypnotic tone as he stroked her face, softly teasing each delicate arch, learning the curves of features he'd committed to memory long ago.

"I like the morning. Not waking up—I'm grumpy when I first get up—but once I'm awake, I love long, quiet mornings."

"What do you love about them?"

The corner of her mouth curved as she drew in a slow breath through her nose. "The stillness, the scent of coffee, how lovable my cat is because he wants food." She laughed.

"What's your cat's name?"

"Thor. He's a white Persian, but thinks he's a part Doberman. His goal in life is to steal all my socks and knock over as many lamps as possible. He also steals food, but that's my fault. I feed him from the table."

He liked imagining her with her cat. "Do you have any other pets?"

"No. I was thinking about getting a dog, but... you came along."

He laughed. "Should I take offense to that?"

Her cheeks darkened. "I just mean I haven't had much time. Puppies require a lot of attention and my life's been busier than usual since meeting you."

"I'll accept that. How do you take your coffee?"

"At home I just take cream and sugar, but my favorite's the white biscotti they sell at the café near my house." She snuggled closer to him, her hands curling by her chest as she fit her body against his and rested her face in the niche of his shoulder. "You smell good."

"So do you," he rasped.

His lips rested on her hair, breathing in her warm scent. She felt right in his arms. His body recognized her nearness, but he quelled his lust for this woman, wanting tonight to be peaceful.

"Tell me something that makes you happy," he asked.

She hummed. "You know what makes me happy."

"Aside from a man's esteem. Tell me something tangible. Something quantifiable that the mere sight puts a smile on your face."

"Like a sock monkey?"

Her answer was unexpected enough to make him chuckle. "Sure. Do you have a thing for monkeys?"

"No, but I like sock monkeys."

"What's a *sock* monkey?" he asked.

"It's a monkey made out of socks. Haven't you ever seen one?"

"No. Are they new?"

She shook her head. "I think they date back to the Victorian era."

"Do you collect them?"

"No," she said, her brow slightly kinking. "I should. I think they're adorable. I don't even own one."

He'd have to remedy that.

Their conversation dwindled as a sort of restful peace settled between them. He never stopped watching her, knowing the exact moment she fell asleep as her breathing softened and her head slipped slightly to his chest.

It was tempting to shut his eyes and join her, but he couldn't do that. Her soft mouth so close to his was another temptation. He could so easily trace his lips over hers, but he'd waited too long to simply steal a kiss now, without the pleasure of looking into her eyes.

As the hour passed his mind contemplated how they'd spend their last few nights before he would bravely remove the blindfold. He still feared disclosing who he was; worried his past could botch his progress. But if he never tried he'd never know, and he feared missing out on something spectacular with her more than anything else.

Not only was his past a hindrance, he wanted her response to be sincere. Women often acted differently when they learned he was a co-founder of GeekPeek. There was wealth, and then there was a level of comfort even he had trouble measuring. He didn't want his success to influence her decision in the end. Neither did he want her memory of him—if she had one—to deter their future.

When it started getting late, he traced a finger over her jaw. "Scarlet."

Her chest lifted as she drew in a long breath, her hand fluttering to the mask covering her eyes. Gently catching her fingers, detouring them from the blindfold, he placed a kiss on the back of her knuckles. "Did you have a nice nap?"

She hummed and curled into his side. "I passed out. I didn't mean to."

Holding her fingers, he rubbed the pad of his thumb over her knuckles. "It's okay. I told you to nap if you wanted."

"But now the night's over."

"We have more nights ahead of us."

"Promise?"

He placed his hand on the curve of her hip. "I promise."

She twisted closer to him, her chilled nose rubbing along his throat. His body tensed as she pressed a kiss under his jaw. Each encounter left her a bit more brazen.

"Thank you," she whispered.

It took everything he had, not to roll her to her back and kiss her then and there. Passion tunneled through him, leaving him in a state of need so intense it bordered on agony. "You're welcome," he rasped.

"When will we be together again?" she asked, her hands making a casual detour over his arm, putting him on high alert.

She hadn't broached the subject of their last departure and he was grateful. If anything, Scarlet was unpredictable and for the most part he found that refreshing. But that night... His carelessness had fractured a bit of their foundation. Nothing was severed, but he'd taken the lesson to heart.

Scarlet was more delicate than he'd realized. She had strong boundaries surrounding her tender emotions, much like him. "I need to tell you something, Scarlet."

She stilled and he sensed her worry. "Okay."

"What I did the other night was wrong. I made you feel cornered and...I wasn't thinking." His mind traveled to moments when he'd been vulnerable, naked, and cornered. "I had no right to impose on your privacy like that and I'm so sorry I hurt you. I never want you to feel bullied into doing something you don't want to do. I should have trusted you and I... I made a mistake. I won't violate your privacy like that ever again."

Her hand rested on his chest as her lips curved with a soft smile. "I accept your apology."

15

———

HUNGER

THE FOLLOWING Monday Scarlet dressed carefully. Though she and Mr. Stone had fallen on that one rough time that made their future seem questionable, their last encounter had banished all doubt.

Rushing home from work, she quickly showered and donned a long green sweater-dress paired with the brown leather boots he'd gifted her. Pennyworth arrived at six and she appreciated Mr. Stone's attention to detail, in that he always made their weeknight encounters a bit earlier in respect for her early mornings.

As they drove, she and Pennyworth fell into easy conversation. The car slowed and she grinned, recognizing the approximate time it took to get from her place to his.

"We're here," Pennyworth announced, stepping from the car.

She reached for the door just as Pennyworth pulled it wide and took her hand. The walk up the steps was bitterly cold, the temperatures dropping into the teens. She hated winter. As the door opened, heat from the interior of the house beckoned.

"Good evening, Ms. Farrow."

"Good evening, Mr. Stone." He took her arm and guided her inside. "I liked my note tonight."

He never failed to surprise her. Tonight's note had been especially sweet. She'd memorized every word.

Ms. Farrow,

You once expressed an envy for couples, the sort where the man watches the woman and smiles even though she has no idea he's studying her. I smile all the time when you don't know I'm looking. You also expressed an interest in simple conclusions to ordinary days, the simple act of sharing a meal becomes extraordinary. Tonight we will be dining together. I look forward to hearing about your day as well as your deepest desires. There is much to cover.

The choice is yours, Ms. Farrow. Should you choose to continue, it will be on my terms and your trust. If you consent, place the mask over your eyes and my chauffeur shall deliver you into my care. I hope to see you soon.

~Mr. Stone

A.R.

He removed her coat and scarf. "You're hands are freezing. Where are your gloves?"

"I forgot them," she confessed.

The air smelled of roasted meat and spices. She wondered if he cooked. "We have company in the vicinity tonight, Ms. Farrow, my personal chef. She's in the kitchen and will not disturb us, but you should know we aren't alone."

"Oh." At one time, company would have made her feel safe. She no longer needed that added security. Oddly, the outsider troubled her. She didn't want to be seen blindfolded—because, really, who did that? And she also worried having someone nearby, aside from Pennyworth who never interrupted, might keep Mr. Stone at a distance.

"Let's have a seat." A chair scraped heavily along the floor. "The table's been set, nothing too fancy. We have roasted chicken, potatoes seasoned in fresh rosemary, basmati rice with mushrooms, steamed broccoli, dessert, and of course wine. Everything's here, so we shouldn't be disturbed, but the chef is near in case there's anything we forgot."

She was still processing that he had a personal chef. The menu, though he said it was nothing too fancy, sounded extravagant. Had she been home she'd be dining with Thor on a crappy microwavable dinner. "Everything sounds delicious."

He placed a napkin over her lap, swiping a hand under her hair and placing a kiss on her neck. Her shoulders lifted as a shiver went down her spine. "Not as delicious as you, Ms. Farrow."

He tucked her chair into the table and the trickle of wine filling a glass echoed. "The chef selected the wine tonight. I hope you don't mind that it's white."

"All wine is good wine," she joked.

When he sat down, she was taken off guard. Rather than sit across from her, he sat directly beside her. "Have you ever dined in the dark? Tell me what you'd like to start with and I'll assist you."

She selected the chicken and he actually cut her

meat. Her hand felt for the fork, her fingers traveling up the heavy stem until her fingers pressed into the identifiable tines.

As it turned out, eating blind was a lot harder than she'd expected. Without sight, she found it difficult to accurately locate her mouth. She hadn't anticipated having so much trouble. It wasn't that she couldn't get food into her mouth. Her fingers knew where the hole was, but the fork was messing her up. She likely looked ridiculous, missing the target and chasing down food with her tongue.

"Let me help you, Scarlet," he said, humor in his voice.

She placed the fork on the table. "It's harder than you'd think."

He chuckled. "Open. This is chicken."

Feeling ridiculous, she parted her lips. The meat was warm and tender. Savory juice burst over her tongue as she chewed.

"How about a piece of broccoli?"

He fed her throughout the entire dinner. She felt infantile and sort of like a bird, but in the end, when it came time for dessert, things didn't seem so juvenile.

"You're lips are red from the strawberries, Ms. Farrow."

The wine had gone to her head. Smiling she licked her lips and hummed. "I bet they taste like strawberries too. Wanna try?"

He chuckled. "In time. I want to discuss those deep dark desires of yours. Care to share one?"

There weren't many, though the fantasies she used to entertain now paled in comparison to the ones including Mr. Stone. "Right now my biggest fantasy is kissing you."

He tapped her nose with a berry. "Not yet. Let's make this a bit easier. I'll say a word and you tell me how it makes you feel in a word."

"Sort of like the first night we talked."

"Yes, but this will be like the childhood game Hot and Cold. You remember that game, right?"

She nodded.

"Very good. The first word is, kissing."

"Hot."

"Good." He paused for a moment. "Breasts."

"Mmm. Warm."

"Pussy."

"Wet."

He tsked. "I'm sure, but you're supposed to tell me the degree of the effect. How hot is your wet little pussy, Ms. Farrow?"

"Burning." She giggled.

He grunted, the sound masculine and carnal. "Biting."

Her head tipped as she thought about biting. No one had ever bit her. "Curiously warm."

"Fair enough. Oral sex."

"Who's receiving?" she asked.

"You."

"Hot."

"Me."

"Hotter."

"Really?"

She lifted a shoulder and smirked. "Give me a green light at this point and I'm not sure you're safe, Mr. Stone. No one's ever made me want them this badly."

He made a sound of understanding. "Next word. Fucking."

"Steaming."

"Spanking."

"Burn."

"Good burn or bad, Ms. Farrow?"

"Good."

"Interesting. Hair pulling."

Her mind filled with images of Mr. Stone behind her, fucking her hard, his nails scraping over her ass, rosy from his palm, as his other hand tightened in her hair, forcing her back to bow. She needed another sip of wine. "Scorching."

"You have quite a kinky side to you, Ms. Farrow."

She shook her head. There really wasn't anything this man couldn't do to her at this point. "That's only because I'm imagining you doing all those things. With anyone else I'd be cold."

His voice turned hoarse as though her words shocked him. "Is that true?"

Slowly, she nodded. "I think I've made it clear what you do to me."

"What if I wanted to tie you up?"

Pausing, she analyzed the slight vulnerability hiding behind the question. He was honestly asking, no longer playing a game of Hot and Cold. She detected curiosity in his tone of voice.

"Do *you* want to tie me up, Mr. Stone?"

There was a moment of utter silence. When he didn't answer she reached for his hand, but he pulled it away. She stilled, not sure why he was suddenly withdrawing.

"I know you like control," she whispered. "It's okay. I sort of like when you take it."

"I think our evening's come to an end, Ms. Farrow."

She frowned. "Please don't be embarrassed. I've confessed so much tonight. I'm not judging you."

"I should get your coat."

Lowering her head, she questioned why he was so uptight about some topics, when at other times he seemed almost shameless. "No."

"Scarlet?"

"I...I want you to talk to me. I try to honestly answer everything you ask me, but a conversation takes two points of view. You agreed with that when I told you about the one-sided dates I had to suffer, but now you're leaving me in the dark. Why can't we just have a conversation about this?"

His clothing shifted as he lowered to his seat. "Fair enough. Go on."

"Do you want to tie me up or do any of those things we just mentioned?"

He drew in an audible breath and hesitated. "I... don't know."

Blindly, she reached for his hand and squeezed. "I didn't say no, Mr. Stone. I don't know either. I know seeing you, looking into your eyes would help. It's perfectly fine for two adults to discuss their desires. But when you push me away every time the tables turn and you get a little uncomfortable, I'm left exposed in the dark."

His hand turned, his fingers lacing with hers as he squeezed. "I'm sorry. I don't mean to do that. I suppose it's a reflex of mine I need to overcome."

She smiled. "Look at me. I'm sitting here blindfolded—probably with food on my face. Who am I to judge?"

He lifted her hand and kissed her knuckles. "You're

right. But it is getting late and you have school tomorrow."

She grinned and released his hand. "Then I'll take my coat now."

He was very quiet as he guided her to the door and buttoned her coat. It occurred to her they had three nights left. Only three.

"When can we be together again?" she asked, fishing for reassurance, as he gently tucked her scarf around her throat.

"That depends on a few things. I may have to go out of town for a few days."

"Oh." This took her by surprise. She never knew where he was anyway, but always assumed he was nearby. "Where are you going?"

"Milan."

"Tennessee?"

"Italy. Give me your hands. You can wear my gloves."

Italy? Why was he going to Italy? Was he going alone? "Is anyone going with you?"

"My partner."

She made a choking sound and stepped back. "Your...*partner*?"

"*Business* partner, Scarlet. It's a business trip. We're flying over, signing papers, and flying right back. It's not a vacation."

"Oh."

Well, good, because the last vacation she went on was at some hokey campground in upstate Pennsylvania. If he was flitting off to Milan riding gondolas or whatever people did there, they clearly didn't belong together. Business was different. She frowned, the vast difference in their social class once again made apparent.

"I'll call you when I get back."

She nodded.

"Good night, Scarlet."

"Good night, Mr. Stone."

On the ride home she worried that part of his reluctance to let her in had to do with her position as a simple middle school teacher. For all she knew, Mr. Stone could be some obscure version of American royalty. The car Pennyworth drove was a very nice Mercedes Benz. She had no idea what a car like that cost, but it was probably more than her annual income.

As the Mercedes hummed quietly along the drive, she worried what he must have thought when he saw her sad, diminutive Ford. He was probably repulsed. "Has Mr. Stone ever been to my house, Pennyworth?"

"I don't believe so. Has he ever left you a gift there?"

"No."

"Then I don't believe so."

"Have you ever described it to him?"

"Yes."

Her lips pursed. "How did you describe it?"

"I can't remember my exact words, but I didn't say anything negative, Ms. Farrow. You're house is a lot nicer than mine."

She grinned, liking Pennyworth more and more each time she talked to him. "I'm just being paranoid I guess."

"I give you a lot of credit, Ms. Farrow. I don't know if I could do what you're doing—blindfolded and all. By the way, we're almost to your house. You can take the blindfold off now. Mr. Stone left you something on the seat."

She quickly removed the mask, wincing as the tie snagged in her hair. Her eyes blinked in the darkness, adjusting to the dim interior of the car. To her left, sat a gift bag, gold tissue fluffing out the top.

She smiled and snatched the bag, ripping the paper from the opening and rummaging until her fingers closed around something plush. She pulled the present from the bag and gasped. It was a sock monkey!

The brindle pattern was classic brown, his eyes little black buttons, his mouth vibrant red. She laughed quietly, knowing exactly where she'd keep him—right on her bed, next to her E.T. and Yoda doll, two of her most prized toys from when she was a child.

Sifting through the bag, she found what she was hoping for—a note. Breaking the seal, she quickly scanned the familiar handwriting.

He told me his name is Caesar. Treat him well.
~Mr. Stone

Caesar, appropriate and reminding her of the character from *Planet of the Apes*. Her hand ran over the stitched detail of the monkey, fondly admiring the gift.

With only a few blocks to her house, she returned her attention to Pennyworth, asking the question that had been weighing on her most of all. "Pennyworth?"

"Yes, Ms. Farrow?"

"Did something bad happen to Mr. Stone?"

The driver sighed. "I honestly can't answer that."

"Because you don't know?"

"Yes."

And if he did know, he wouldn't be able to tell her anyway. She'd get to the bottom of it eventually, with or without his help.

Typically, Asher left the mansion soon after Scarlet, but tonight he needed to face some demons. Their conversation had been uncharted, leading him into some very dark realizations. When she'd so brazenly asked about *his* desires, the resounding *yes* ringing in his head shook him to the core. Incapable of answering, he'd tried to cut their evening short.

Finishing a bottle of wine, he breathed in the lingering scent of her perfume. His mind painted pictures of Scarlet's naked body tied before him, not cowering, but full of pride.

But the question was, how far did he want to take his attention? Over the course of their relationship he'd researched various fetishes, never finding any specific proclivity overly appealing. However, when Scarlet posed the question of tying *her* up, the game changed. That idea held an unfathomable amount of appeal, none of which he was prepared or confident he could manage.

So many times he'd been restrained against his will and suffered pure terror. If she trusted him enough to voluntarily surrender to such limitation, without the fear he associated with restraint, it would be a true breakthrough, a testament to how far they'd come. It would also place him on the other side of the paradox, a position he'd never imagined.

He was coming to discover that control wasn't always tied to abuse. Sometimes a restraint led to freedom. It could be a liberating experience for both of them.

He'd never been the authoritative type—per say—at least before meeting Scarlet again. Sure, he managed million dollar accounts and ran a fortune five hundred company, but those experiences were generic. Dealing with Scarlet was acutely unique.

Hoisting himself off the chair, he slowly walked the bottle to the trash. This new conundrum required more thought than he was able to give at the moment. There was no denying his desire to act out his surfacing fantasies. The allure was there. The question remained, would he be a good lover?

It seemed an enormous responsibility. He never wanted her to feel like he wasn't enough to meet her needs—ever. As if the thought of mere sex wasn't enough to worry him, *great* sex was creating new levels of anxiety. He needed to do more research. Never in his life had he studied something requiring more investigation than women—this woman in particular.

16

GRATIFICATION

Ms. Farrow,

I could not feel your heartbeat in Italy, which means you were too far away. Looking forward to holding you in my arms again.

The choice is yours, Ms. Farrow. Should you choose to continue, it will be on my terms and your trust. If you consent, place the mask over your eyes and my chauffeur shall deliver you into my care. I hope to see you soon.

~Mr. Stone

A.R.

Tucking the note in her purse, she grinned at Pennyworth. "I'm ready when you are."

Her eyes voluntarily shut as she placed the blindfold over her face, and gently tied the ends. Once the chauffeur assisted her into the car they were on their way.

"Did Mr. Stone have a nice trip?"

"You know the rules, Ms. Farrow. All personal questions go to the man in charge."

"Did you enjoy your time off?"

"Actually, I went with him."

"You did? He said it was only him and his partner going."

"Elliot had a last minute change of plans."

"Elliot?"

Silence filled the car. After a long moment passed, music came on. "No more talking, Ms. Farrow."

Who was Elliot? Was Elliot his partner? Or was that Mr. Stone's name? *Elliot Stone.* No, he didn't strike her as a Elliot.

When they reached Mr. Stone's place, she was still pondering who Elliot was. Pennyworth escorted her up the ten steps and the door opened.

"Good evening, Ms. Farrow."

"Good evening...Elliot."

"I beg your pardon?"

Shit. "Never mind."

"I'll be in the car," Pennyworth announced, making a fast retreat.

"Were you interrogating my driver, Ms. Farrow?"

"Just the usual small talk."

"You talk to Pennyworth?" This seemed to strike him as odd.

"It gets lonely being shuttled around in the dark. I have to do something to keep myself occupied."

"I see."

"Who's Elliot?"

"A colleague of mine."

"Ahh. So this Elliot...what's his last name?"

"Nice try. Let me help you with your coat."

She giggled. "I missed you."

His fingers stilled over the button. "I missed you too, Scarlet."

As he removed her coat, scarf, and gloves, he made no comment about her not returning his gloves. He wasn't getting them back. They were too big for her, but they smelled like him and she was just weird enough to hold onto them as a constant source of his scent. She may have even gotten carried away one night while he was away, sniffing the gloves with her eyes closed as she did bad things to herself. Thor hadn't been able to look her in the eye in days, but it was worth it.

He escorted her past where they usually sat and into a room that echoed. "Is this the room with the bed?"

"Yes, but we're not using the bed tonight."

"Oh."

He stepped close, his finger dragging over her collarbone and down her back. "Does that disappoint you, Ms. Farrow?"

"I just assumed...your note said you'd be holding me in your arms tonight."

"Correct. Stay here please."

His steps echoed as he walked a distance away. Her body pulled to attention as the hum of soft strings filled the room. Music. She beamed.

He returned to her and lifted her hand. "We're going to dance, Ms. Farrow."

Her breath caught. Oh, dancing. She loved dancing, especially slow dancing.

The composition was lovely. Her mind worked to place the familiar melody as it picked up pace, but she grew distracted as Mr. Stone pulled her close.

Lifting her right hand, he fit his left hand to her

hip and slowly led with evident experience she lacked in the dancing department. Her heart fluttered, so many girlie emotions coming to life inside of her, as vocals harmonized like angels softly in the background over the gentlest plinking of bells.

The orchestra tempo picked up and—why was she imagining snow? He spun her as the symphony peaked, vocalists taking her breath away as the masterpiece built. She was dizzy from the sensations provoked by the stunning compilation as much as she was dizzied by his competence as a dance partner. No men danced this well in her world.

Building and building, to the highest crescendo, he pulled her back to his front and she smiled from the thrill of being twirled around like she was in a fairy-tale world. It was perfect.

She knew this song. What was this beautiful song? It made her want to cry and at the same time she could not get the image of snow and ice out of her head. The melody slowed and she tried to place the piece one last time.

"Do you like dancing, Ms. Farrow?"

"Yes," she answered breathlessly. "You're a very competent partner. I've never danced to classical music like this before."

"These are some of my favorites."

The next song began, clarinets pitched low, their soft melody climbing then drawing back. Her brow crinkled under the blindfold. This one was familiar too. It triggered a sort of pent up euphoria inside of her leaving her with traces of longing and too much time gone by.

Violins and flutes joined the clarinets as a far away

trumpet quietly announced a sense of hope and new beginning. "I know this," she whispered.

His steps slowed, losing a bit of the rhythm, but quickly recovering the cadence. "Pardon?"

Harps plucked and she could perceive an image clear as day in her mind, imagine the birds chirping and water babbling. The words soft and smooth came to mind. She gasped. "Are we dancing to *Attack of the Clones*?" These were movie scores! No wonder she recognized them. "What was the one before this? I knew that one too!"

"Ms. Farrow, you're distracting me. Stop trying to play name that tune and enjoy the moment."

"Oh, sorry." She quietly gasped, placing the previous song as *Ice Dance* from the movie Edward Scissorhands. Was Mr. Stone somehow involved in the movie business? Oh my God! Was she dancing with Danny Elfman?

He cleared his throat. "Ms. Farrow."

"Yes?"

"Where are you? I feel your body in my arms, but I sense your mind has gone elsewhere."

"Sorry...Danny."

"No."

"Damn it."

He chuckled, his palm traveling up her back as they swayed. Leaning closer, she rested her head on his chest, breathing in his scent.

She hummed, her heart content. "This is nice."

They danced for a long time to some of the prettiest ballads ever composed. It was unlike any other experience she had with dancing. Mr. Stone did that a lot, took something familiar and made it new and exciting, different, so it couldn't get lost in the shuffle of similar memories. No. The memories of him would always stand a bit taller than the others in her mind.

He'd created an incredible compilation. The problem was, as she recognized each score, she remembered the movies—and the love scenes they accompanied.

Her mind was a medley of memorable kisses and passionate acts. Mr. Stone had done exactly as he promised and held her in his arms all night. In short, her body was on fire.

"Mr. Stone," she asked, her fingers trailing over his collar. He'd worn a dress shirt.

"Yes, Scarlet?"

"I want to kiss you."

He stilled. The music continued, building to crescendos that were written for making love. Lifting her cheek from his chest, she tipped her face upward. His hand left her hip, his finger tracing softly over her lower lip.

Pressing up on her toes, she leaned into him, only to have him place his hands firmly on her upper arms and take a step back. "Ms. Farrow."

"Please."

"Not yet."

"When?" She'd never been so sexually frustrated in her life. Being celibate for two years was nothing in comparison to the two months of knowing this man.

"When it's time."

Frustrated, she stomped her foot in a despicable display of immaturity. "What's wrong with now?"

"It isn't time."

"Why?"

"Don't be tedious, Ms. Farrow. Because I said so."

She scowled. "I'm not being tedious. I'm telling you how I feel."

He stepped closer, his hand cupping the side of her face, as he whispered, "How do you feel?"

"Like I'm going to die if I can't touch you soon."

Holding her breath for a pregnant moment, he finally took her hand. "Come with me."

He moved at a clipped pace and she panicked as he towed her blindly behind him. "I don't want to leave."

"You're not leaving."

"Where are we going?"

"You ask too many questions, Ms. Farrow. Get on the bed."

Not realizing where they were, her legs crashed into the mattress. Bed was good. She eagerly climbed onto the soft covers.

He took her hand. "Sit on the edge."

Scooting quickly to the edge, her feet dangled over the end of the mattress not quite touching the floor. Her hands folded in her lap as excitement rushed through her.

He stood before her, his legs taking up space between her knees. "Which hand do you write with, Ms. Farrow?"

"My right."

"You may use your left hand to touch me, but nothing else and you may not move from your seat on the bed. Any questions?"

"Is there a time limit?"

"Until I tell you to stop."

"Can I take off the blindfold?"

"No."

This was a mistake. He knew it the second he walked her toward the bed, but...she knew the score from *Attack of the Clones*—not the main theme, either.

Sucking in a deep breath he stared as her hand slowly lifted. Fanning her fingers wide, she gradually reached for him. The first contact was to his stomach. Her palm pressed into the buttons of his shirt, heat searing through the fabric. He was suddenly grateful for all the medicine ball crunches he'd bitched about every morning.

Her breath sucked in as her lips parted. Could touching him really mean that much to her? Her hand traveled up to his chest, grazing his nipple and causing him to suck in.

His cock lengthened as her thumb teased through his shirt. Her fingers curled, traveling slowly to his throat. The backs of her nails traced his jaw and he swallowed. The soft pads of her fingertips dragged over his lips, following the small divot beneath his nose.

Her brow creased the moment her fingers made contact with his glasses. "Glasses?"

"Do they bother you?"

"Not at all, I just wasn't expecting them."

He'd removed them the day he'd pleasured her in the chair.

Her fingers slowly grazed the shell of his ear, muffling the music for a few seconds. Stretching, her touch teased his sideburn and hair. "Your hair's so thick." She smiled.

She spent a long time running her fingers through

his hair. It was intoxicating. When her touch returned to his face, she inspected his glasses, tracing the rims. The side of her mouth quirked, and he suspected that meant she liked discovering this identifying trait about him.

She brushed over his shoulder, squeezed his bicep, and traced each one of his fingers. His breathing turned irregular when she returned to his lower belly. As she caressed along his hips her chest lifted, her breasts pressing into her shirt. He could see the pucker of her nipples.

Shocking him, she swiftly moved her hand between his legs and he grunted as she cupped him. She sucked in an audible breath as the bulge of his pants filled her palm. "Mr. Stone."

Moving quickly, he bent, snaking his hand under her hair, cupping the back of her neck. His mouth closed over her exposed shoulder, kissing and sucking her sweet flesh.

Her grip firmed, massaging through his pants as he climbed on top of her and yanked her shirt to her chest. Her supple breasts plumped as he held her and sucked on the succulent ivory skin. She moaned, her fingers tugging at his belt.

Landing open mouth kisses along the curve of her throat, he quickly undid the buttons of her blouse. Once he had her shirt open, he jerked the lace cups of her bra and fastened his mouth to her nipple.

She arched into him and cried out, her hips grinding into his thigh. His belt came undone and the heat of her palm scorched his cock, flesh to flesh, nothing in between. Jerking back, he caught her wrist.

"Please," she begged.

He glanced at their position. Her bare breasts were

red with traces from his stubble. Her nipples were engorged and wet. His belt was hanging undone and his cock was ready to explode. None of this was supposed to happen.

Quickly, he climbed off the bed and she eased up on her elbows. As she panted, his attention returned to her breast. Dear God, he wanted to keep going.

"Why are you stopping?" she snapped.

"Scarlet," his voice was a mere rasp. "Scarlet, we can't do this now."

"Why?" Her brow was pinched, her lips tightening in frustration. "I want you. Don't you want me?"

"Yes, but—"

"But what? This is getting impossible!" She reached for the blindfold.

"*No!*" He caught her hand, startling her, and she froze. Softening his tone, he said, "No, Scarlet. Not yet."

"Why? You're *killing* me. I don't know how you can keep denying us."

"Discipline," he whispered.

"But what's it worth if it's making us miserable?"

It was worth his pride. Who knew how she'd react in the end, when all veils were removed? Showing himself to her might be *the end.* "Just a little longer, Scarlet, and then all the waiting will be over."

She plopped back on the bed. "I don't know how you're doing this."

"You felt me. I'm not immune to you."

She mumbled something he didn't catch.

"I beg your pardon?"

"Nothing." She mumbled again.

"Scarlet, are you talking to yourself or talking to me under your breath?"

Shaking her head, she muttered, "This is why I'm sniffing your gloves and masturbating."

He stilled. "You sniffed my gloves and masturbated?"

Her cheeks flushed. "Only once. Fine, twice, but they smelled like you and you were off in Milan doing God knows what."

His mouth stretched in a cocky grin, wishing someone were there to hear such confessions. "Did you orgasm?"

Her mouth pinched tight.

"Ms. Farrow?"

"No," she snapped. "I...I can't do that without... you."

Interesting. A slow burn began to smolder in his veins. "Do you need to come, Ms. Farrow?"

"Are you offering?"

"Perhaps."

She slowly lifted her arms over her head and spread her legs. "Yes, Mr. Stone, I'd *very much* like to come."

He'd never survive this woman. "Then you shall. Tomorrow."

"*Tomorrow?*"

"Yes, and you are not to touch yourself until then. Do you understand?"

"I hate you," she grumbled.

"Don't pout."

"I'm sexually frustrated!"

So was he.

17

———

CAPITULATION

"I HAVE TO TELL HER." Asher plopped down on the couch at the Think Tank. Elliot, Hunter, and Jet stared at him. "What?"

"Well, yeah."

"Told you this wouldn't work."

"It's about time."

They all spoke at once.

Ash huffed. "She's...amazing."

"So tell her who you are and get on with a normal relationship," Hunter said.

"I'm scared. So much is riding on this. She...we were dancing and *Across the Stars* came on. She knew it was from *Attack of the Clones*."

"Is that Star Wars?" Jet asked, and they all snapped a unanimous, *"Yes!"*

"Maybe she just watched it," Elliot said.

"Or," Hunter cut in. "Maybe she's got a little nerd girl in her after all. Imagine that, all this time, Lettie Farrow was a geek."

"She's not a geek. She hasn't shown any signs until last night."

"Sometimes geeks look like ordinary people," Elliot said.

Asher eyed his tie. It had molecular formulas on it. "Is that a new tie?"

Elliot glanced at his chest and smiled. "Yeah—" He frowned, registering the point Asher was making. "Whatever."

"I think it's great," Jet said. "She likes you. You like her. Sounds simple enough to me."

"She almost ripped off the blindfold last night."

"Why? Did you piss her off?" Hunter asked.

"Not exactly. She was...frustrated."

"With..." Jet asked.

"Our lack of sex."

"Wait." Elliot held up his hands. "She hasn't seen you yet and she wants to *have sex* with you?"

"Badly," Asher confirmed.

"That doesn't make any sense!"

"I know," he agreed. "But if I don't give her some relief she's going to snap."

"Just get rid of the blindfold and do her," Hunter said.

Jet shook his head. "I say keep the blindfold and do her. A little kink never hurt anyone."

"I don't want to get rid of the blindfold yet and I don't want to have sex yet. It's too soon. I can't sleep with her until I'm sure she's okay with sleeping with *me.* The only way I've been able to build up my courage is by giving myself the time I need to prepare. I'll show her who I am soon enough, and when I do, I'll see if it matters to her. Only then, if she's still interested, will we...make love."

Jet arched a brow. "You sure you want to throw around that four letter word?"

He wasn't sure of anything at the moment, but he knew if they got to that point it would be a hell of a lot more than sex.

Elliot stood. "Then why are we talking about this? You aren't an animal. Just don't have sex. Find something to distract yourselves."

"Nah, Ash wants the sex. I can tell," Jet said.

"Not blindfolded sex," he repeated. "I want her to see me—the *real* me. I want to look in her eyes and..." It was difficult, exposing his honest feelings to the guys. Everything he felt for Scarlet ran deep. "I'm just not ready yet."

"But she's all fired up," Jet recapped.

...For Mr. Stone. "So what do I do?"

His friends contemplated his predicament. Jet shrugged. "You fake it until you make it, Ash."

"I've been faking it all along."

"No, you haven't. All of this is you. This is just the first time you've unearthed your hard-ass setting and played a dominant role. So far the mystique seems to be working for both of you. Just keep doing what you're doing."

"Can't you just think of it as role playing like in *World of Warcraft*?" Elliot suggested. "We know it isn't real, but we also know we can't walk away. Fantasy's addicting."

Hunter nodded and pointed to Elliot in agreement. "Yeah, give her a fantasy, Ash. You have a masterful mind, master her in other ways without crossing that line."

Jet's dark brow arched, the side of his mouth hooking in a half-smirk. "What gets her hot?"

Lots of things. The question was, could Asher deliver such things once he was no longer Mr. Stone and simply Asher? "I need to think about this. We have two more encounters and the last one's the big reveal. This is my last chance to show her I can be what she needs." Because once she was looking him in the eye, he wasn't sure how *Mr. Stone* he could be.

While fantasy play was appealing, he didn't want to live his life in a fantasy world. He wanted something *real*, something he could openly share with others. He wanted a place in her heart.

Sitting back, the truth sank in. Scarlet was giving him hope and hope could be a very dangerous thing. For the first time in over a decade he was risking everything and opening himself up to what could be the best thing in his life or the worst. Only time would tell.

Not only was he stressing about meeting her expectations as a man, he was now worried she might prefer his alter ego to the real him. Never once did he imagine he'd be in competition with himself.

He sighed and faced the guys. "I just want her to like...me."

Jet blew out a slow whistle. "Look at you, admitting your feelings and showing your human side." He slapped a hand on his back. "My boy's all grown up!"

"It'll be like watching Batman remove his mask and learning it was Bruce Wayne all along," Hunter said, his face poised in awe. "It's always a bit of a shock, but after a while, you realize he's the same person, no matter what name he goes by."

Elliot finally smiled. "And so the Padawan becomes a Jedi. *Already know you that which you need.*"

"Thank you, Yoda," Ash joked.

Elliot shrugged. "Yoda's my hero."

Drawing in a steadying breath, Asher nodded. One last evening of secrets, then...he'd tell her exactly who he was and hope with all he had that she could care for him as much as she cared for Mr. Stone, realizing they were one in the same.

There was something fundamental coming. Scarlet sensed it in the tone of Mr. Stone's voice, the quelling silence of her dark surroundings, and by the way her heart beat rapidly in her chest.

Her coat was removed, as were her shoes. Every touch was refined yet reverent. Integrity bled from him as he guided her to the room with the bed. His words seemed reserved for direction, each carefully chosen directive baring an acute effect on her senses.

"I want you to remove your clothing, Ms. Farrow."

Would he not help her?

"I'm going to watch."

His words gave her pause. After discovering his glasses and piecing together many scenarios in her head regarding the mystique of their relationship, the state of his vision crossed her mind. She'd considered perhaps he was blind and this was all a lesson in empathy. It would have explained why Pennyworth always drove.

Quietly, she asked, "You can see me?"

He chuckled. "You make it hard to blink, Scarlet."

Good enough.

Her skin tingled as she slowly unsnapped her jeans and slid the zipper down. Peeling back her socks, she placed them on the floor then carefully folded her pants. Her shirt bore six buttons and she counted each one, her fingers trembling over the tiny pearl disks.

Slowly disrobing, he never interrupted her process, and she had no doubt he watched every move. There was no music tonight. The echo of her breathing played as a backdrop to each rustle of fabric and even the rasp of her fingers tucking her hair.

She imagined him sitting a distance away, leg casually crossed in some sophisticated manner, long fingers veiling his mouth, glasses masking all telltale reactions her performance evoked.

Swallowing tightly, she savored all the assumed reactions he might be suffering as she stripped down to nothing. When she stood, baring her soul to the man who had embedded himself there, she interlocked her fingers behind her back and waited for his direction.

"Please kneel."

Jarred by his command, her lips parted in question, yet she uttered not a sound. Her body throbbed, every point of her senses awakened by her intense need. Slowly, she lowered her body to the ground with as much grace as she could manage.

The floor was chilled, despite the passing warmth of the room. Drafts of heat flowed from the nearby hearth and she found comfort in the familiar crackling of the burning wood.

"Have you touched yourself, Ms. Farrow?"

"No."

"Good girl."

"The next time we're together, it will be the last time you wear the blindfold."

Her shoulders sagged with relief. Knowing the end was near gave her a new hope. She would finally look into his eyes and know exactly who this incredible man was.

His words were paced, drawing her attention to each syllable. "Blindfolds are used for a myriad of reasons, Ms. Farrow. Historically, theories claimed if a man did not see who wielded a sword, the accountability of his death becomes fully his. You're in no danger, Ms. Farrow, but I believe, over the course of our liaison, the blindfold has allowed you to take accountability for yourself, emotionally, physically, and sexually. Would you agree?"

Her shoulders rocked, cool air kissing her skin, as she remained kneeling. "Yes, Mr. Stone."

"Blindness also promotes a level of courage in place of natural instinct. Animals, such as horses, are also blindfolded. It allows them to be easily led. It also protects them, often used during barn fires, when such skittish animals would balk and stubbornly endanger themselves. Blindness provides the courage to move forward. Do you feel that you've gained courage from blindness, Ms. Farrow?"

"Yes, Mr. Stone."

"Lady Justice also wears a blindfold. It keeps her impartial. She's not influenced by money, fear, power or weakness. She's blind to everything but the experience being conveyed to her. You may relax, Ms. Farrow."

She lowered her bottom to her heels, searching for the most comfortable position while remaining on her knees. He wasn't specific, but she liked the image of her naked form kneeling before him, enjoyed imagining herself as a sort of offering to the man that brought her to life.

Once she settled he continued. "When the gift of

sight is eliminated, all other senses are heightened. We hear more acutely, scent more clearly, tastes become more defined, and touch is beyond sensitized. Anticipation proliferates dramatically the longer we're blind, as we're no longer granted the visual cues that tell us what to expect."

Her chest expanded, as she digested his every word, tasted it, savored it, let each comment sing to her need until she experienced the blossoming anticipation he so eloquently described.

"When I chose your blindfold, Ms. Farrow, I took care to select the softest fabrics. The lace accentuates your delicate complexion, yet the velvet lining is dark enough to block out all light. When you first came to me, you suffered acute fear bordering on claustrophobia. Are you still battling such fears?"

Licking her dry lips, she answered, "No, Mr. Stone. The darkness doesn't scare me anymore. Sometimes I crave it. It reminds me of you."

"You've embraced the darkness, Ms. Farrow. It's liberated you to share secrets you've kept from even yourself. In a strange way, I believe the darkness has brought your true self to light."

He was absolutely correct. Their courtship was a masterpiece of emotions only a true artist of human nature could create.

Delight grabbed hold, tightening every organ, asphyxiating every hope as his clothing rasped and steady footfalls approached. She waited for his affection, breathed for it, and anticipated it more than any tangible gift.

The gravelly scrape of his deep voice seeped into her, anesthetizing any nervousness. "You look beautiful, Ms. Farrow."

Her hair ruffled slightly as he drew closer. His finger ghosted down the side of her throat, drawing her off her heels and to attention. His phantom touch shaped a manifestation, blacking out the details she didn't know—didn't *need* to know. So long as it was he touching her, any superficial details were irrelevant.

His patient manner only intensified her wanting as it always did when he drew out their intellectual discussions, pushing her another degree. But she would wait as she'd waited through every prior encounter, tortured by curiosity, aroused to a point of near lunacy, because the end would mark the beginning—a future with this incredible man.

He aroused her on a cerebral level no other person had ever come close to, stimulating her, pressing her, and undoing her until she craved his total possession. He exposed her in a way no one else could.

He adored her so devotedly, her only worry that remained was the difference in their social class, but she sensed no pity from him. Although she sometimes surmised the blindfold played a part there as well. She shoved the troubling thought away, not wanting it to interfere with their precious time together.

"I've placed four gifts before you, Ms. Farrow. Reach out and familiarize yourself with them."

Her hand shook as she steadied her balance, fingers creeping into the abyss of darkness until her fingers stumbled over something cool and smooth. "May I lift it?"

"You may. Use your senses available to familiarize yourself."

It was heavy, like glass. Lifting the item in her palms, she carefully ran her fingers over it. Sleek and phallic. Her cheeks heated as she fondled the blunt end and compared it to the smooth rounded tip on the other side.

"What are you holding, Ms. Farrow?"

Breath escaped in a choppy exhale. "I think it's a… phallus?"

"It's going inside of you tonight."

Her shoulders lifted as she silently panted and placed the glass piece on the floor.

"You're blushing, Ms. Farrow. Are your embarrassed or excited?"

"It excites me, Mr. Stone."

"Have you ever used such an item?"

Her lips were again dry. Swiping her tongue, she confessed, "No. I've never used anything but my own fingers."

"Keep in mind, nothing happens without your consent, Scarlet. Do you want to stop?"

"No."

"There are more items. Keep going."

She nodded and reached for the next item almost passing over its delicate presence. Her fingers crept over the ground, tracing the long curved shaft running down the center, no wider than a thread. Finding the edge, she lifted the feather and smoothed the downy barbs over her cheek.

"How does it feel?"

"Soft. Teasing."

"Good. Two more items."

Replacing the feather, she reached forward. String caught her passing pinky. She gathered the slight filament, identifying it as soft elastic. As she elevated it, something weighted dangled from the end. It was flexible, covered in a jelly like skin. Two flat sections connected to a kind of thorax of sorts. Small ridges and bumps were molded into the design. "I don't know what this is."

"It's a butterfly. The straps go around your legs so the vibrating element rests over your clitoris."

Her lips twitched as she considered if that appealed to her senses. She was still having trouble picturing it, so she remained undecided.

"Identify the last item, Ms. Farrow."

She replaced the butterfly with the other items and stretched for the last. Her fingers grasped something thick and flimsy. Using both hands, she held one end as her fingers traveled over its length. It was long and smooth, braided. "Rope."

Her smile stretched. He'd told her something personal about himself with these items, shared a bit of his own desires.

"Do you wish for me to remove any of these items, Ms. Farrow? Say the word and they disappear. Your decision won't disappoint me. I'm trusting you to be honest."

"I'm curious."

"Are you afraid?"

Was she? With anyone else she would be, but not with him. "No."

"Would you like to play?"

Those words should have carried a juvenile effect, but there was nothing childish about what they were considering doing together. His hands would be touching her. Their breath would mingle. He would tease and torment her and she would likely leave here a different woman.

Raising her chin she distinctly vocalized her answer. "Yes."

Silence.

After a long beat he slowly stood and approached. Her heart thundered with each nearing step he took. Something cool dragged over her shoulder, not his hand. "The rope is to keep your hands occupied. The blindfold must stay on, Ms. Farrow."

She nodded, a touch proud of him for seeing where his own cravings might lead. The other night when he'd mentioned tying her up she sensed something in his voice, some dark yearning to explore such desires, a sort of innocence that told her he'd never done this before with anyone else and she liked that very much. It put them on even ground.

"Take my arm. I'll help you stand."

Her legs protested as he gingerly pulled her from the floor. Pins and needles rushed to her feet. His palms chafed her outer arms and she breathed in his scent, taking it deep into her mind.

"Give me your hands, please."

She slowly held her wrists in front of her. His touch was gentle. His lips pressed to each proffered hand, placing a kiss over her thrumming pulse.

He wove the rope around her bones, making a series of knots until her palms were tied into place in an unbreakable clasp. "You look pretty wearing nothing but rope, a blindfold, and a rosy blush."

His praise slithered into her, warm, coiling and heating her insides to near scorching. "Thank you."

His thumb traced over her lower lip. "Such a beautiful mouth. I love how naturally pink your erogenous zones are."

Brazenly, she closed her lips over his thumb, tasting him for the first time. A groan ripped from his throat, full of shared yearning, but he quickly plucked the digit from her mouth.

"I'm going to put the butterfly on you now." He stepped away and returned a second later. Taking her tied hands, he placed them on his shoulder. "Balance yourself and step. Right foot first."

Lifting her leg, he slid the elastic over her calf and up her thigh. Once he fed her other foot through, he adjusted the straps over her hips. The moment the butterfly touched her clit, her body awakened.

Standing behind her, his finger slowly traced down her spine, not stopping until he grazed the crease of her behind. "Have you let a man tie you up, Ms. Farrow?"

Her lungs filled to near bursting. "No," she rasped.

"Have you ever contemplated it?"

"Not until tonight."

"Do you find the idea tempting or unpleasant?"

"I find it... erotic." So many sensations stimulated her in that moment. Her body was on overload and her brain was losing ground.

"I'm going to walk you to the bed now."

The heat of his hands covered hers, sending shivers and goose bumps over every exposed inch of flesh. She walked slowly, the presence of the butterfly awkward, yet granting her a bit of modesty.

He turned her so they stood face to face. Sliding his palms up her waist, he lifted her onto the bed. The simple act was incredibly sexy. She'd never been lifted up or carried by a man, and knowing he possessed the strength to move her so effortlessly triggered something in her.

He adjusted her on the bed, resting her head over the fluffed pillow and tracing his hands down her tapered legs as if he were sculpting a priceless work of art. Lifting her foot, he placed a kiss on the arch. "Perhaps I'll tickle these feet a bit tonight," he whispered, placing her sole firmly on the covers.

He did the same with her other foot, leaving her thighs spread and her sex exposed. She realized he was looking at her there. He'd done it before. This time had the same exciting effect. Her body wept for him, arousal trickling from her folds, evident of how deep her craving for this man ran.

"You're wet, Ms. Farrow. Dripping."

"I'm sorry."

"Don't apologize. It's the most erotic sight, so pink and glistening. Ready for me."

Oh God.

"Shall we begin?"

"Please," she begged. If he didn't touch her soon she was going to shatter.

"Your wish is my command, Ms. Farrow."

The first touch of the feather drew her nipples to attention. Her body arched, her back lifting off the bed as he dragged the soft plume over her breasts and down her sternum. The seductive tease of each caress fed her arousal, as soft, pleasant moans slipped past her lips.

"Your nipples are very hard, Ms. Farrow." His finger flicked over the turgid tip and she whimpered. "Shall I play with them for a bit?" He seemed to be posing the question to himself. "My mark's gone. Did you enjoy finding the souvenir I left you?"

"Yes," she confessed breathlessly.

"Then I'd be remiss not to give you another."

His mouth closed over her left nipple, his lips tightly holding the bud as his tongue teased the tip. Her heart beat rapidly as his other hand cupped her flesh, massaging roughly, his thumb treading over the sensitive skin.

She moaned and arched into him. Her tied hands pressed into the pillows as her feet dug into the mattress. His mouth switched to the other breast, his own moans of pleasure beating at her senses as his breath cooled her dampened flesh.

Closing his mouth over the supple curve of her breast, he sucked hard. "Yes!" she cried, savoring the image of him marking her.

He groaned and sucked harder. His hands squeezed, plumping her breasts, as his tongue dragged over the slope of her cleavage to her nipple. Her hips lifted, seeking his weight. Climbing between her thighs, his erection pressed through his clothing.

She ground her body into his and he became a man possessed with lust. His lips dragged across her stomach. His tongue traced each rib as his mouth closed over the sensitive skin below her breasts. He marked her again. And again. She'd likely look like a bruised piece of fruit when she left him, but she didn't care. On the contrary, she relished it.

"Mine," she thought she heard him growl.

Yours.

He moved, reaching briefly for something nearby. When he sat back, his weight was no longer on her. His clothing tickled her calves as he sat between her parted legs. Cool glass touched her wet sex and she jerked.

"Stay still, Ms. Farrow. I don't want to accidentally hurt you."

Forcing her body to calm, she breathed through her excitement. Warm fingers traced her slit, parting her and delving deep. She moaned as he quickly fucked two digits deep into her core.

Removing them quickly, she caught the succinct sound of him tasting his fingers. "Delicious."

Her body trembled, his erotic words washing through her like lava. The sleek phallus, slightly warmed from his handling, pressed at her opening. Her lungs sucked in a hard breath. It was wide and unbending.

"Do you want me to continue?" he asked, a note of concern in his voice.

"Yes." The only thing she wanted more was the *real* him.

"Then I need you to open for me, Ms. Farrow."

She widened her knees, relaxing her hips. The glass phallus made gradual progress. Her breathing increased as he worked the piece deeper with shallow dips.

"Does it hurt? You're very tight."

"It's big."

He paused and she wasn't sure if her observation pleased or upset him.

Quietly, he said, "It's the same size as me."

Air rushed from her lungs as she blinked under the blindfold. He was *big*. The implication was not lost. As a matter of fact, it made her determined to take the large piece. She opened her legs a bit more, her folds parting. "Then I want all of it."

His breathing echoed between them. "Tell me if it's too much."

She wouldn't. She'd take it, because she was determined to take him. He pressed forward, the glass gliding into her opening and stretching her neglected tissue.

"Oh God."

He withdrew the piece and pressed it deeper. Her arousal removed any friction. "A couple more inches," he warned.

"More," she demanded. "Do it."

Pulling back, he inserted the phallus deep, filling her. She moaned, never feeling so complete. The only thing better would be him.

"What do you feel?"

"Full. Tight. On the verge of screaming."

"In pain?"

"No pain."

"Good. Let's continue." Abandoning the glass phallus wedged inside of her, he leaned to his side. There was a click, but she barely noticed as her body was suddenly under attack. Tiny vibrations spun from the butterfly on her clit. Her shoulders pressed into the bed, her back bowing from the mattress as she cried out a string of broken obscenities.

Her body tumbled into a vortex of shock as she broke, her orgasm stunning her with its sudden arrival. The pulsing on her clit didn't cease, leaving her pleasure no chance to wane.

The glass phallus hitched as he grasped the end and started pumping it in and out of her. The pattern of vibrations from the butterfly changed, two short and one long, ripping several screams from her as her mind blanked and her body went on sensory overload.

His weight shifted. His clothing tickled her trembling tummy as his mouth closed over her nipple, sucking and pinching her sensitized flesh as he fucked her hard with the glass dildo. Every time she reached for him she was reminded of her restricted hands and her arousal doubled. Yes, she definitely liked everything he was doing.

Her body became possessed, thrashing and undulating into his ministrations, as her pleasure intensified to the point of no return. An orgasm unlike any other broke through her, soul shattering and mind numbing. Her thoughts scattered to a serene place of darkness, so tranquil everything appeared blinding white.

She shivered as the phallus withdrew completely, leaving her sex contracting and hollow. She moaned, too tired to vocalize much else as he loosened the butterfly and peeled the straps off her legs.

"You're swollen. Your clit's very dark, Ms. Farrow." She hummed, acknowledging his observation, finding his strange fascination with her body's reactions fascinating in itself. "I'm going to kiss you there. I'll be gentle."

Unsure how much more pleasure she could take, she whimpered. His hair tickled her thighs as he scooted between her legs, his shoulders wedging into the slight space. Her legs could no longer remain stiff. Her knees lightly collapsed over his broad sides.

The first touch of his soft tongue had her gasping, but he was extremely tender in his ministrations. He sipped from her, worshipped her, his touch so delicate and loving she drifted into some unvisited corner of her mind where everything was soft and quiet.

Her mind traveled outside of herself, untethered on some dreamy plane where only they existed. Drawing back slowly, the mattress dipped as he stood. His arms slipped beneath her knees and shoulders and she was cocooned in warmth. He held her on his lap, balancing her cheek carefully against his chest.

His shirt was gone and she wished she had the mental awareness to appreciate the warmth of his bare skin pressing against hers. She was physically depleted, yet more satisfied than she'd ever been in her entire life.

"Take a sip of water, Scarlet." A glass pressed to her lips and she drank slowly.

Where he'd taken her, time no longer existed. He held her for what seemed like days, long bouts of uninterrupted rest having the effect of extensive restful nights.

When he laid her on the bed again, she was on her front, her upper arms forming a pillow for her face. The covers had cooled and she sighed into the softness of the mattress. He lifted her hair, gathering it beneath the tie of the blindfold and twisting it over her shoulder. His mouth kissed down her spine, bringing her slowly back to reality.

He moved and the bed shifted. His lips tickled the curve of her behind, tracing a path for shivers to follow. His palms pressed into her shoulders. His hands were warm and slick with oil. Strong fingers massaged her tired muscles, revitalizing her bones as her mind was drawn back to the present. Curiosity gave way to new desire as his hands worked lower down her spine.

He cupped her behind, kissing each rounded cheek as he continued kneading. His thumbs pulled at her fleshy bottom, exposing parts of her she'd never shared. Sliding his palm lower, he hooked his finger into her sex, slick with new desire. "Your responsiveness to my touch is amazing."

She was thinking the same thing. No one else could draw out such physical reactions so unfailingly.

Until him, she hadn't known her body *could* respond in such a way.

His mouth pressed into the curve of her ass as he pulled her cheeks apart again. She should be mortified that he was inspecting her so closely, examining her body so intimately, but she wasn't. Her bottom pulsed as he continued to hold her open, his fascination with her body's response evident in the excited way he exhaled.

"Your come's on my pants, on the sheets, my fingers. You're everywhere. I can still taste you on my lips; scent you on my skin and in the air. There's never been anything more magnificent."

He gently released her bottom and came to rest beside her, his fingers lightly playing with her hair. It was as if he couldn't keep his hands off of her. He stayed.

An intangible scar inside of her slowly began to heal as he held her. *He stayed.* Unlike others had done, he would not leave her side after such an intimate experience. His presence touched her deeply.

As he continued to run his fingers through her hair she made a soft sound of pleasure.

"Are you awake?"

Twisting, she pressed her face to his throat and breathed him in.

"How do you feel?"

"Incredible."

He was quiet, seemingly in a contemplative mood. "We have one night left, Scarlet."

Her heart stuttered, wavering between trepidation and relief. So many questions ran through her head. Would he reveal himself from the start or give her the blindfold and then remove it when it was time? Would he finally share his name? Would they make love and plans for the future? She wanted all the answers, but at the same time, after making it this far without knowing, she wanted to experience the moment without spoilers.

Rather than ask for clues regarding his intentions that likely wouldn't come, she asked, "When?"

"I think we both need time to reflect. Fourteen nights."

Her face lowered. He couldn't mean starting all over again. Before she could ask for clarification, he explained.

"We'll take two weeks, fourteen consecutive days, to process the journey we shared and what expectations we developed along the way. On the fourteenth night I'll send for you. Should you decide to end our association, I'll understand. The choice will be yours, Ms. Farrow."

She recognized his words as the parting line from every note he'd ever sent, only this time there was no mention of blindfolds or terms, only choice.

"I'll be there," she promised.

He let out a long breath. "Either way, I'll be waiting."

18

DESPAIR

Asher entered the Café near Scarlet's home. Being that it was the eve of their meeting, he wanted to pick up a bag of her favorite coffee. *White Biscotti.* His hope being that she would be spending tomorrow night with him if all went well.

As he waited in line, he thought about all his careful preparations. They'd have dinner, discuss her reflections over the past fourteen days, and then...he'd remove the blindfold. What happened after that depended on her, but he hoped she'd join him, returning to his primary home where they could officially begin their relationship.

Stepping to the counter, he waited as the new server bent over the register, struggling to get the screen to clear. When the clerk looked up, everything in Asher froze as stark panic snaked deep in his gut, coiling around his lungs, choking him.

Westerman.

The man glared, a cocky arch to his brow. "You gonna order or what?"

Breathing jaggedly, Asher stared at the tyrant. Westerman's body was no longer the hard build of a high school linebacker. Flab hung over his belt. His complexion was ruddy, vouching for rough living or perhaps too much indulgence. Memories of his uncountable cruelties came flooding to the forefront of Asher's mind like a tsunami, knocking out all other thoughts.

"Dude, you gonna order or just stand there?"

Chest heaving, he said, "Sorry." His throat was bone dry so he swallowed. "I'll take a pound of your white biscotti."

Rolling his eyes, Bobby Westerman turned and filled the bag with grounds, the grinder buzzing loud. He tossed the clipped bag on the counter. "Seven ninety-five."

Asher's fingers gripped his credit card, but he hesitated. Placing the card with his identity emblazoned on the plastic back in his pocket, he withdrew a ten. Westerman made change and handed two ones and a nickel back. "Next."

Taking a retreating step out of the way so the next customer could order, he sidled over to the condiment station. Retrieving a small cup, he blindly filled it with sugars and creamers as he watched his nemesis serve coffee to strangers. It should have brought him some measure of triumph, knowing this was where the animal ended up, at a job he clearly detested, but it didn't.

The only thing Asher processed was familiar, cold-blooded terror. As the line snaked to the counter, he observed silently, noting the way Bobby's hair had thinned, trying to find some measure of joy from his downtrodden appearance, but he couldn't.

Why were people cruel for no reason? Blinking, his mind was assaulted with memories. There were so many harsh moments of brutal humiliation, he wished he had the balls to say something, but was frozen with fear. Then he thought about Scarlet, remembered how broken she sounded the night she confessed the way Bobby treated her. When he'd asked if it got better with time, she'd said no, that sometimes it got worse.

His hand fisted over the grounds as his jaw clenched. Why she ever dated someone like that would forever be a mystery. She could have had anyone, yet she'd settled for the worst person of all.

Cold rage settled over him. Everything inside of him wanted to march back to the counter and rip his throat out. Hit him until he begged and tell him that was everything he deserved for mistreating her. How dare he—

"May I have a medium white biscotti with cream and sugar?"

Asher's attention snapped to the person ordering and he nearly stumbled into the group of people crowding him at the condiment station. Creeping back toward the booth at the window, he dropped into the seat, eyes wide, as Scarlet waited for her coffee.

"Hey, I know you," Westerman said.

You better fucking know her, you piece of shit. You stole her virginity. Asher's teeth clenched as he willed the other man to stop looking at his woman.

"Lettie, right?"

Her face was turned so he couldn't read her expression. "Bobby? Bobby Westerman?" Why did she sound so pleased?

"Well, I go by Rob now. How you been?"

"I've been...great actually."

"You look incredible."

Asher's fist slowly crushed the cup in his hand.

"When, um, when did you start working here?" she asked.

Westerman shrugged it off. "Oh, this is just a temporary thing. I'm switching jobs and the guy I'm replacing doesn't leave for another month. This is just to keep me busy."

He was such a lying sack of shit.

"Oh, well I guess we'll be running into each other a lot over the next few weeks. This is my favorite café."

Asher scowled, as this revelation seemed to please her as well.

Westerman smiled at her, his regard crawling over her body in a way that made Asher want to rip his seedy eyes out of his fucking head.

"Let me get your coffee."

"Thanks."

As Westerman made her coffee, Scarlet glanced around the shop. Asher ducked lower in the booth and quickly pretended he was busy with his phone.

"Here you go, Red."

"Thanks, Bobby."

"Why don't you let me take you out sometime, for old time's sake? If I recall we always had *fun* together." His eyes continued to devour her as his tongue slithered over his teeth making a disgusting sucking sound he could hear halfway across the café. "I'd love to see you again, Red. All of you."

She slid her card across the counter and picked up her coffee. "Sure."

Sure? Sure? What the fuck?

"You're looking good, Lettie."

"So are you."

"Can I hit you up? Get your number? I'm free Saturday night."

Westerman slid her a slip of paper and Asher's heart stopped as he watched her jot something down. "Sure. Message me. I'm on GeekPeek."

"Still Farrow? Never married?"

She laughed. "Nope."

"Lucky me. Why did we ever break up, anyway?"

"I'm not really sure. College, I guess."

Leaning over the counter he whispered something in her ear. Her face flushed, her smile undisturbed.

"Yeah, I remember." She laughed. "But, hey, I gotta run. I have an appointment."

He grinned, his seedy eyes full of self-satisfied egotism. He waved the slip of paper and nodded. "Okay. I'll be in touch, Red. Saturday night."

Still smiling, she adjusted her coffee and purse. "You bet."

His gaze turned lascivious as he tacked on, "Can't wait to see more of you."

Asher stared unblinking as the door closed behind her. Pure fury boiled inside of him. How could she?

Clamping down his molars, he stood. As he passed the trashcan he threw the bag of grounds inside, interrupting the nearby conversations of the patrons. Shoving his way out the door, he yanked the collar of his coat high and marched to his car.

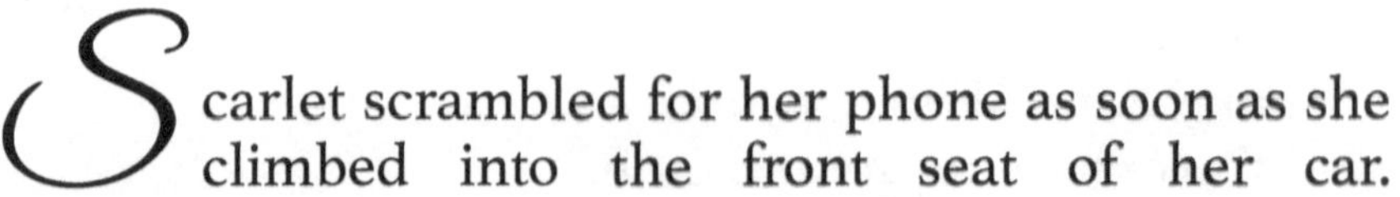

Scarlet scrambled for her phone as soon as she climbed into the front seat of her car.

Thumbing over Nicole's contact info, she quickly dialed and started the car.

"*Yello!*"

"You will *never* guess who I just ran into at The Stomping Grounds!" Shaking off the lingering sensation, as though an eel just swam threw her legs, she squirmed and gagged.

"Who?"

"Bobby. Westerman."

"Nooooooo...." Nicole bellowed. "Ew!"

"I know! He *works* there."

"Oh no! Who hired that asshole? Now we're going to have to find a new place to get our caffeine fix."

"I know! This sucks! The only thing worse would be if he worked at the liquor store."

"Bite your tongue!" Nicole laughed. "So what does he look like?"

"Old. Wanna throw up?"

"Not really, but tell me anyway."

"He asked me out."

Nicole made a gagging sound into the phone. "Did you say yes?"

"*Ew! No!* How desperate do you think I am?" Sticking her coffee in the console, she pulled onto the road. "He asked for my number and everything."

"Did you give it to him?"

"Hell no! I told him to hit me up on GeekPeek. If he sends me a friend request I'll just leave him in purgatory."

"Better yet, block him. He's so creepy I can totally picture him whacking off to your profile picture."

She gagged again, this time tasting vomit. "Gross, Nicole! Now I'm picturing it."

"What? You slept with him."

"Shut. Up. I've never regretted anything more in my life. He's so disgusting. Oh, and get this, he can't figure out why we ever broke up."

"Are you serious? Did you explain it's because he was a selfish brute?"

"No, I didn't want to get into all that in the middle of the coffee shop, so I just nodded and smiled, pacified the asshole, and got the hell out of Dodge. Now I have to go shower, because even looking at him makes me feel filthy."

Her friend giggled. "Damn it. I was going to stop there after the gym. Now what am I gonna do?"

They talked as Scarlet drove home. She'd needed the distraction, being that she was making herself crazy obsessing over every passing second until she finally got to *see* Mr. Stone.

Over the past two weeks she'd done every possible thing she could to keep from ripping out her hair. She missed him desperately, wanted him with all her heart, and no amount of reflection would change that. She just had to survive the last few hours.

---

*A*sher paced by the window waiting for the car to appear. When Steve finally arrived, his gut cramped painfully. He should just lock the door and never think about her again.

He didn't call her last night like he'd planned and all day he'd been wondering if Westerman had contacted her, if they talked, set up that Saturday night date he suggested.

She emerged from the car and he couldn't bring himself to look at her. He'd severely overestimated her feelings, thought she honestly cared enough about him not to see other people, but what did he know?

Nothing. He knew absolutely nothing beyond the fact that this was too much for him. He'd allowed himself to care and now it felt as though his heart was being ripped from his chest.

Steve escorted her up the steps and placed her hand in his. "Thank you, Pennyworth."

Asher escorted her inside, quickly removing her scarf and undoing the buttons of her coat.

"Good evening, Mr. Stone."

"Good evening." His eyes blinked furiously as his throat constricted, making it difficult to speak. After tonight, he'd never see her again, never know the touch of her skin to his or the scent of her hair. Dragging out any sort of goodbye seemed cruel, but he needed one last glimpse of her before everything she shared disappeared to a memory.

"I missed you."

He made a disbelieving sound.

"Should I undress?" Every muscle tightened, making it harder to breath.

"Please..." The word escaped as some sort of prayer for strength, but she interpreted it differently. Her fingers quickly unbuttoned her blouse and he balked. Why was she doing this?

He paced away, not venturing to watch her or stop her. Pouring a glass of wine, he drank heavily. When he turned, she was slipping off her panties. As she stood, her ivory form shone under the light thrown from the hearth.

Taking her narrow arm, he instructed, "Come with me." Refusing to go into the ballroom with the bed, he led her to the chairs in the foyer. He needed to take control of the situation fast. "I'd like you to kneel, Ms. Farrow."

She lowered herself to the ground, her motions shaky. Her breasts no longer wore his markings. Small raspberry nipples pointed outward. Her chest heaved as she waited. His eyes went to the thatch of red curls between her legs and he turned away.

Get it over with. "Are you comfortable?"

She nodded.

Jesus, she was stunning. Her delicate beauty arrested his common sense, stole his logic and made his task more daunting than it already was. Face tight, he slowly approached, his arm reaching for the only woman he'd ever felt a connection with. His fingertip ghosted over her larynx, barely touching her smooth skin. As overwhelming as her beauty was, he'd fallen for the woman behind the grace and elegance.

He'd thought time would bring courage, believed changing his exterior might strengthen the interior, but he couldn't do it. He couldn't bare himself the way she so exquisitely bared herself to him and believe he'd someday be enough.

The return of his nightmares, the paralyzing fear in the face of his nemesis, it all still existed and would never go away. She deserved better. He was a fool to think he was in control, in any way, shape, or form. Despite the joys of love, there would always be the immobilizing truth of how badly she could hurt him.

Her breathing was labored, her cheeks flushed. Sensing she was getting ahead of herself, he said, "I need you present, Ms. Farrow."

"I'm here, Mr. Stone. Always here."

For him, he thought coldly. She was here for some fantasy man he'd created and could never measure up to in real life. Her posture shifted as she shivered and drew her shoulders back. He needed to take a step back.

Even now, she stoically waited for a promise he couldn't deliver. The slight curve of her lips gave him pause. It seemed impossible that he'd unearthed this confident side of her. Initially he believed she was unbreakable, but as he got to know her, he discovered the fragile secrets she had and the responsibility to protect such vulnerability became more and more daunting.

To see her now, so tranquil and at peace with her exposed self, it gave him a modicum of pride. At least he'd helped her recognize a portion of the value she held. If only she knew how much more she had to offer. Knowing she'd someday realize how special she was and how understated her standards actually were, he regretted his own inability to meet them.

He needed to make her see that this was not the end. She would someday find everything she wanted and it would be real, better than any short-lived fantasy he could fabricate for her.

Her mouth quivered with the sweetest hint of a smile. "You're pleased."

"I am."

His eyes closed as he reciprocated her smile as best he could, but inside his heart was breaking. "And so you should be. It's been quite a journey."

Her shoulders trembled delicately and he wanted to calm any fears, but knew he couldn't continue to make her promises he couldn't keep. Gently cupping the side of her face, he ran his thumb across her soft lower lip. "Be still," he whispered.

Turning his wrist, he dragged the backs of his fingers slowly over her jaw and behind her ear. He should stop now.

Drawing in a slow constricted breath, he whispered the only truth he knew. "It isn't fair for a woman to hold such beauty."

His thumb coasted over the soft curve of her throat, tripping slowly over each ridge of her larynx, teasing the slight curve of her collarbone. Every freckle, every soft curve was so perfectly feminine. No other woman compared, which was why he'd likely return to his world of work and redundant meetings, banishing any hope of ever finding a partner in this life.

He couldn't think about that now. He needed to do what had to be done and let her go. His own desolate future shouldn't concern her or cloud his judgment. This was the right thing to do.

Keeping his voice low, he spoke carefully. "When I read your letter, I knew there was something special about you, Ms. Farrow. While there was courage in your words, I sensed the absolute desperation of your plea. True, you did not ask to be found—only to be heard—but I found you all the same. Genuine courage is not borne of fear. True courage takes action, despite the fear. You, my lady, feared what?"

Her lips parted as she softly whispered, "I feared always being alone."

"Correct. Yet, you've given months to a complete stranger, trusting me to show you something that changes nothing of your predicament outside of these walls. Why?"

The realization that this was not the end but the means to an end needed to come from her. She'd been the one to meet every challenge and face down her fears. He wanted her to recognize that courage came from her and belonged to her, his presence was merely temporary, an attempt to prove how powerful passion could be.

Her head lowered. "I wanted to know what it felt like to be adored, cared for, placed at the top of someone's priority list, Mr. Stone. You said you could give me that experience."

And he believed he had, for a time. He'd given her everything he could manage. It simply became too much and he couldn't give any more. "Do you feel you've achieved your goal, Ms. Farrow? Have you felt those very things?"

"Yes."

"And do you have any regrets, Ms. Farrow?"

"I have no regrets."

He smiled sadly. She'd been so easy to adore. Despite what her friends said regarding her standards, she should never lower them. She shouldn't have to settle. Exactly why he decided to remove himself from the equation.

"And is the fear gone, Ms. Farrow?"

He understood fear. The fear of not measuring up, the fear of bleak loneliness, the fear that everything will stay the same or might drastically change. He suffered every version there was, still continued to struggle with overcoming his fears. It was an almost impossible thing to outgrow, but he believed she'd overcome a great deal of her own.

"Yes, Mr. Stone."

"Very good."

And so there was nothing left for him to show her. He reached for her hand. "Allow me to help you stand."

"Very good." He'd said the words as if finding her progress agreeable, but there was something hidden in his tone, as if her achievement wounded him in some way.

Blinking in concern, Scarlet's lashes softly brushed behind the dark mask.

A gentle hand brushed down her arm. "Allow me to help you stand." There were always hints of chivalry behind his actions, even when his intent was unclear.

Placing her hand in his, she carefully rose from the cool floor. The front of her body shivered as the heat of his frame encroached on her personal space. Excitement filled her chest. Without placing a finger on her, he leaned close. His scent intensified as his lips delicately traced hers.

Breath stilled in her lungs as she cherished that long awaited caress, his mouth pressing softly to hers, an innocent brush of affection, trembling with restraint. He'd never kissed her there. It had all been building to this moment, this one point in time.

"You're a beautiful woman, Ms. Farrow," he whispered, his warm breath teasing her parted lips.

Leaning into him, she frowned as the soles of his shoes scraped over the floor and he pulled away, leaving cool emptiness in the place of his warmth. With his withdrawal came the prickle of fear, fear she'd believed she'd buried.

"However...our relationship has come to an end."

The finality of the word *end* echoed like a gunshot through the air. Shock knifed through her, hard, jerking her nerves to an unpleasant point of attention as denial suddenly had her shaking. They couldn't simply *end*. This was the beginning they'd been waiting for...

She'd clearly heard him incorrectly. Unable to hide her worry, a chirp of nervous laughter slipped past her lips. "Mr. Stone—

"This is no laughing matter." He'd never cut her off before.

Her eyes burned at the sharp arrival of tears, the tart injection taking her aback. "I...I don't understand."

He became so silent she panicked, loosing her grip on her surroundings, unable to identify where he was. When he finally spoke, his words chilled her soul. "This is over."

"What—"

"My driver will take you home now." His edict stabbed through her, each syllable slicing into her heart. Where had this come from? What caused such an abrupt change? This wasn't what was supposed to happen.

Boiling indignation had her scrambling for words. Her limbs trembled as utter bewilderment took hold. Desperate to stop this nonsense, she threw away his rules, her unsteady fingers rushing to the blindfold.

"Do not." Catching her slender wrists he snatched them back.

Her voice broke somewhere below its natural octave. "Why are you doing this?"

"Life isn't a fantasy, Ms. Farrow. You need to leave now. And the blindfold stays."

She yanked her arms, but his grip only tightened. *"What are you afraid of?"* she snapped, her patience fraying too fast for her to salvage her composure.

He stepped closer, his clothing brushing her exposed breasts. "I'm not afraid. I simply know what I want and what I don't need."

Her. He didn't want or need her. She'd had enough of the games. Her mouth compressed, betraying her poise, as she begged, "Let me see you."

"No."

She jerked her arms in an attempt to remove the blindfold once more, but his strength and control outweighed hers.

His voice lowered as he carefully enunciated each word. "Careful, Ms. Farrow. You've come here of your own free will. You *will* honor my wishes not to be seen if you expect me to respect your privacy. There's no end to the ways I can exploit you."

Beyond her anger was the reality of earth shattering, humiliating betrayal. She'd foolishly trusted him. Former concerns rushed to the forefront of her mind, stealing any false sense of security she'd imagined. Had he recorded their encounters? There was so much she risked in order to be with him, trusting him not to harm her—a total stranger. God, she was a fool!

Blinking in the darkness, she finally understood. This wasn't about *her* trust. It was about *his,* his inability to trust anyone other than himself!

Her voice cracked, hating the powerless position she held. "Why can't you trust me?"

"Because at the end of the day, I'm still me. This is best for both of us. You'll move on."

Her chest constricted as if her heart were actually breaking in two. "Don't do this."

"It's done."

Every bit of unrequited affection flipped into indignation, equally as intense, but altogether different.

Jaw locking, she wheezed from the pain and whispered, "I hate you."

He wouldn't even touch her. "You have every right. I'm so sorry. Goodbye, Ms. Farrow."

Reaching into his pocket, Asher removed his phone. His hands trembled terribly as his vision blurred. Sweeping his thumb over the screen, he sent an already typed text to Steve telling him to come get her. Shutting his eyes, trying to block out her gasps, he raced to the door as it opened and Steve entered, a look of shock taking over his face as his eyes jerked away from Scarlet's naked form.

He couldn't meet the other man's eyes. He was too ashamed of what he'd done. He should have never involved himself in her life. This entire attempt to be someone else ended in another disgraceful failure, his inadequacies driven home with the force of a meteor.

Steve caught his arm as he shoved past him, his eyes searching for some form of explanation.

"Please," Asher wheezed, finding it impossible to hold his emotions inside. "See that she gets home safely."

Disbelief flashed in Steve's eyes as Asher shook off his hold and raced down the front steps. The cold cut through his clothes as he hurried around the side of the mansion to his car. Pressure built in his chest so tight he worried he was having some sort of attack. He climbed inside, jamming the key in the ignition and missing completely as his shaking transcended to a full body tremor. "God damn it!" he shouted.

When the keys finally slid into the hole he overturned the motor and sped away from the house. He took the turns furiously, breath panting through his teeth as the consuming pain in his chest tightened.

His fingers gripped the wheel as his jaw locked. His vision blurred.

Go back to her. You can fix this.

With every passing mile he begged himself to turn around, but the coward inside of him held its ground on a continued escape. The further he went the more permanent his decision became.

He couldn't imagine her calling for him. She'd likely already made up her mind to hate him forever. That was best. He blew out a harsh breath. He'd always be less than what she deserved and the sooner she realized that the better off she'd be.

*S*carlet's knees softened and she collapsed like a broken doll to the floor, a marionette cut loose from its strings. For several minutes she cried blindly on the cool tile. What sort of a mind fuck had she consented to? This wasn't what she'd asked for, hoped for, and nothing close to what she assumed they'd shared.

Her chest shook with each gut-wrenching sob. *Why?* It was the only word she could think in that moment.

A throat cleared and Scarlet stilled like a small creature in the presence of a great, unforeseen preda-tor. She reached for the mask—

"I'm afraid the mask must stay on, Ms. Farrow, or there could be consequences." It was Pennyworth.

"Why is he doing this?"

"I don't know, Ms. Farrow." The weight of her coat whispered over her shoulders.

Who *were* these people? Dropping her trembling hands, she bitterly denigrated herself for not taking that question more seriously until now. Her ignorance was frightening and her own stupid fault.

It was all fake for him, but so very real for her. The pain consumed her and she shook with the effort of containing it.

"If you'll allow me to help you... The rest of your clothing's in the Mercedes and once we're a few miles out you'll have permission to remove the blindfold. I'll deliver you home, safely, as promised."

His voice was always soft and kind, now spoke of barely contained rage, which made her reluctant to go with him. But what other choice did she have. Reluctant to trust anyone, she begged, "Please don't hurt me." Her disgrace bloomed into crippling humiliation.

"Never, Ms. Farrow." Her feet left the ground as strong arms lifted her to a warm chest. "I have you. The cars only a few feet away."

Beneath her confusion rested gratitude for his assistance. Cold wind bit into her exposed skin as he quickly carried her down the steps. He fed her into the warm leather-scented car idling and shut the door.

As soon as he reached the driver's seat the car swayed into motion. Her head rolled back, her body weak from the emotional assault she still couldn't fathom. Debased. It was the only reoccurring word that made sense in that moment. He'd debased her without even fucking her. He'd betrayed her, tricked her into loving him, while knowing full well that nothing would ever come of her wasted heart.

She'd likely be waiting a long time for the fallout

of their experience to stop resonating. It traveled beyond hurt, reaching to such depths, filling her with such angst the pain gradually transcended to numb agony.

For as lonely as her world had been three months ago, returning to it—cherished, then rejected—made her perfectly aware of just how vacant her future would be. Nothing was worth such anguish.

Suddenly furious, she wanted no trace of him left on her body. "I'm taking this off. Go ahead and tell him."

She ripped the blindfold from her face, peeling back the lace moistened by tears. The chauffeur sighed, but didn't object. He appeared quite distraught for an outsider and she took comfort in their fragile alliance—unsure how it compared to his loyalties to Mr. Stone.

Needing the shelter of her clothing, she ignored her surroundings and hastily dressed, her survival instincts kicking into autopilot. Spontaneous words laced with anger came barreling from her lips.

"You can tell him I never want him to contact me again. He's not the man I thought he was. No *man* would do this. He's just a scared little boy and you can tell him I said so."

The driver remained silent, his eyes modestly avoiding the mirror, but his brow creased with what she assumed was uneasiness. While he didn't verbally agree with her assessment of his employer, he also didn't disagree.

She saw more than anyone realized—blind or not. She'd read Mr. Stone and sensed his vulnerability. She loved that gentle part of him that seemed to need what they shared as much as she did, but he'd destroyed everything.

He lacked the courage to see the person he truly was. But Scarlet saw him. Blind or not, she saw the real him and knew one day he'd come to see his mistake.

---

*A*sher didn't return home for several hours. When he finally entered the house, the sky was deep mauve announcing the oncoming light of a new dawn. Arms weak and shoulders burdened, he staggered into the den.

"You're back." Steve's words interrupted his assent to the couch.

"Hey," he rasped. "Why are you sitting in the dark?"

Steve rested his elbows on his knees, his brow pinched as he shook his head. "I'm leaving, Ash."

"What?" He was so tired.

"I quit."

Asher turned. "Why?"

"I can't work for someone who does whatever it is you do."

Knowing he'd asked a lot of the other man, but unable to take any more criticism than he'd already drilled into himself, he defensively asked. "And what is it I do, Steve?"

"You're a bully. And I made you stronger."

He scoffed. Knowing full well what a bully was and that he wasn't one. "You don't know the first thing about bullies."

"No? When I was a kid I had terrible acne. I was

scrawny and short and always picked last in gym. I wasn't always the man I am now. But at least I can claim to be a man. A real man knows his strength and doesn't flaunt it. He takes responsibility for his actions. A real man doesn't do what you did to that woman."

I am not a bully! He ended things because he couldn't handle what they had. "Do you think I hit her, Steve? I'd never—"

"No. What you did was worse. You dishonored her, humiliated her, and used her in a game to satisfy some sorry part of yourself with no intention of taking responsibility for your actions. And I helped you."

He swallowed. "You don't understand." He couldn't explain his decision. He was exhausted and mentally drained. "If you love someone, you let them go. You do what's best for them. That's what I did."

"You don't get it, do you? A bully doesn't have to use his fists to hurt someone. He's just a coward passing off his pain to someone that doesn't deserve it."

Asher swallowed painfully. "I never meant to hurt her."

"Then you seriously lost control of the situation, Asher. I had to wrap her naked body in a coat and carry her to the car. You killed her."

No. He didn't want to hear this. "She'll recover." She was strong.

"You left!" Steve snapped, jumping to his feet. "You didn't see the look in her eyes or hear her sobs! How could you think your actions wouldn't hurt her? Have you ever even talked to her?"

"Have you?"

"Yes!"

Asher stilled. Scarlet had mentioned she and Steve

talked, but Steve had strict instructions not to reveal any of his personal business. "You weren't supposed to."

"She talked, I listened. Jesus, Asher, that woman loved you. Every damn note you sent, she'd hold it to her heart and try to scent you in the paper. She gladly tied on that stupid blindfold just to go to you, to spend one measly night in your presence. Do you know how lucky you were to have a woman that dedicated to you? And you destroyed it. You destroyed her."

He couldn't breathe. Steve was wrong. He had to be wrong. "She didn't love me," he rasped, desperately waiting for Steve to confirm. "She loved a fantasy."

"She loved you, you shmuck. It doesn't matter what name you go by, she fell for the man she *thought* you were. That man was *you, Asher.*"

He didn't know that! How was he supposed to believe in something when there was no tangible proof? *"Then why didn't she tell me?"*

"Love isn't something you say. It's something you feel. You're a smart guy. Don't be naïve."

Breath jagged, shoulders tensed, he tried to understand. The episode in the coffee shop raced through his head like a steel train, shaking him to the core. Westerman asked for her number and she wrote something down. She smiled and acted agreeable to seeing Westerman again. People in love didn't make dates with other men. She should have told that prick to get fucked—

He suddenly saw himself hiding in the shadows; too afraid to even pass the bully his credit card in the chance he might recognize his name. Why was it okay for him to hide, but he expected her to confront someone three times her size who'd hurt her in the past? He was a hypocrite.

Credit card...

He slowly panted as he replayed the moment in slow motion. She didn't give him her number. She signed the receipt. Chills chased up his spine and down his arms. Could he have misread her response? Maybe that was how she dealt with people like Westerman, humored them, pacified them with a smile in order to escape unscathed as quickly as possible.

A cold sweat blanketed him. *What have I done?*

His face dropped to his palms as Steve's feet crept into his view.

His mind worked, rapidly trying to recall everything he'd said. Maybe she wasn't as upset as Steve imagined. Maybe there was still time to fix this. "I need to talk to her."

"You destroyed her. I picked up a woman full of life and returned a hollow shell of the girl she was. She doesn't want you to contact her anymore."

"I thought..." He couldn't breathe. "I didn't know she cared that much. I didn't trust..." He exhaled harshly. "I don't know how to *trust* people. How was I supposed to know how she really felt?"

"Did you ask her? Did you tell her how *you* felt? Did you offer the slightest respect of actually *talking* to her?"

He swallowed. "I was too afraid."

"In the beginning, you said we'd talk about further investments down the line *if* I could make you like the man you saw in the mirror. Do you like him, Ash? Because tonight, I'm not sure I do. If you're really that much of a coward, she *is* too good for you." He dropped an envelope on the table. "There's my resignation."

With every step Steve took, Asher's pain became more pronounced. His treachery bled into every aspect of his life until he felt like the life had been ripped out of him. And he had no one to blame but himself.

The door closed. Alone again. Denial choked him. Falling to his side, he pulled at his hair. He wanted to scream and hit something. Maybe there was still time.

Scrambling to his feet, he reached for his phone, frantically patting down each pocket. It wasn't there. He ran to the door, knocking into furniture as he raced out of the house and skidded into his car. Flipping forward the seat, he searched.

His heart thundered with a sense of urgency. Twenty-four hours ago he had everything he'd ever wanted. Now he had nothing. She was his everything and without her—

The screen of his phone glinted from the shadows. Snatching the device, he willed his fingers to stop trembling as he quickly dialed her number. He'd beg if he had to.

Breathing fast, he waited as it rang. Each unanswered ring was another stab in his bleeding heart. Voicemail picked up and he dialed again. *"Fuck!"*

On the fifth attempt a voice finally answered.

"Hello?"

"Scarlet—"

"Who is this?" a female voice hissed, deep loathing in her tone.

"I need to speak to Scarlet."

Silence. "Well, well, well, if it isn't Stone."

"Nicole?"

"Scarlet doesn't want to speak to you."

"I need—"

"I don't care what you fucking need you sick, twisted son of a bitch. Who do you think you are? You're lucky she can't tell me who did this to her because I'd hunt you down and crazy murder you, you perverted fuck."

"You don't understand!" he pleaded.

"I understand. She told me everything. Leave her alone or I'll call the police. Do you understand me? Leave. Her. Alone."

His chest constricted. This couldn't be it. "I was wrong."

"Too late. Come near her again and my husband will throw your ass in jail." The line went dead.

19

———————

HINDSIGHT

"Asher?"

"Ash?"

"Ash—shit," Jet said as he, Elliot, and Hunter stumbled to a halt inside the ballroom. It wasn't good.

Jet approached slowly. "Hey, bud. How you holding up?"

He glared at them and tipped back the bottle filling his hand. His sense of flavor disappeared somewhere around bottle nine, so he couldn't be sure what he was drinking. Hopefully, it was poison and the pain would soon end.

Elliot noticeably analyzed the room. "You have a bed in a ballroom."

He ignored him.

"So it's been quiet at work. When you thinking about coming back?" Hunter asked, appearing as if this was all quite ordinary. "We, uh, miss you."

"Yeah," Jet nodded. "Maybe coming into the office for a few hours would get your mind off things."

"Scarlet," he mumbled. "My minds not on things. It's on Scarlet."

Elliot rolled his eyes. "I told you this was a bad idea—"

"Leave him alone, Elliot," Jet warned.

Hunter read the label off one of the many bottles piled on the table and placed it back with the others. "So you're staying here now? Wouldn't you rather be home, where your stuff is?"

"It reminds me of her." It was all he had left.

Asher was supposed to be a smart guy, but there had never been a greater jackass. Proving himself to Scarlet was supposed to be an exercise in redemption. It was supposed to make him whole, take away the sense that he'd never be enough.

Clearly he failed. Since bringing her back into his life, the memories were relentless, his failures inescapable. The nightmares were so vivid and traumatic he hadn't slept in days. Everything was safer when he'd shut off his emotions. He'd give anything to have that peace back now.

"Why not go to her if you're this miserable?" Jet asked.

"I can't. She hates me."

"You made a mistake. You're human," Hunter said.

He shook his head. "No, I hurt her. I wanted her to love me and I was too blind to see I succeeded. Too fucking scared to trust it. After asking so much of her she'll never forgive me for not trusting her enough to open up." He laughed coldly. "Ironic, she wore the blindfold and I was the one that couldn't see what was right in front of me."

"So tell her that," Jet pushed. "Maybe she'll hear

you out. If you hurt her, she had to care on some level."

"The man she wanted, the man she believed I was, would have never hurt her. The moment I stopped thinking like Stone and started acting like Roan I fucked everything up."

"How long is this gonna go on?"

"Elliot!" both Jet and Hunter snapped.

Ash waved away their defensiveness. "It's okay. I know I'm shirking off a lot of my responsibilities. I'm sorry. I didn't expect this to spiral so far out of control like this." If only they knew this inexplicable pain, this constant worry for someone he couldn't reach.

"I'm just asking because we have the Technology in the Classroom approval coming up and you said we'd all be a part of the decision process."

He laughed. That was Elliot, always playing by the rules. If only his friend could be passionate about something else for a change. But who was he to hand out advice. "I'll send for the paperwork tomorrow and read through the proposals. I'll make a selection by the end of the week."

"The deadlines in a month," Hunter announced. "You have some time."

It didn't matter. A week, a month, a year, eventually he'd have to get back to reality and accept that this was his life.

In the back of his mind he hoped that if he could recover in time, so could she. There was some cockeyed formulation convincing him that the sooner he did that, the sooner she'd be whole again. More than anything, he wanted her whole and happy, as if he'd never interrupted her life at all. He loved her enough to wish that for her, even though the thought of her forgetting he existed killed him.

"*S*carlet, can I talk to you?"

Her body naturally tensed, every little encounter with others seeming to throw her off balance these days. It didn't matter who approached her. While the rest of the world continued to spin, she was falling apart on the inside and would rather be left alone.

Calvin Armstrong, her superior and principal, wasn't a bad guy, but after the most unfortunate turn of events in her personal life, she'd made the educated decision that all men sucked.

As he approached, her mind analyzed him like the computer of an underworld spy.

*C*alvin Armstrong:

Mid-thirties; dark hair, attractive, likely a briefs man, recently divorced, no children, possibly an early ejaculator.

Qualities of Mr. Stone: Less than 30%

Likelihood of being a scum sucking man with commitment phobias...

Calculating...

9,875% probable.

ABORT!

. . .

*D*id she mention she was back to being jaded and cynical?

She tucked away the last of her students' paperwork and pasted on a fake smile like she always did in uncomfortable situations—grin, bear it, and get the hell out. He was her boss, after all. "Sure, Calvin, come in."

His clothing confirmed his higher salary as he strode into her classroom, his tailored slacks sculpting perfectly to his lean thighs. She, on the other hand, had rapidly packed on sixteen pounds and developed a dangerous addiction to Tasty Cakes. It was pretty bad. She was even licking the wrappers in private.

Every day she swore off sweets and takeout, but every day she came to the utterly depressing realization that she really didn't give a fuck. She was going to die a spinster. *Que sera, ser—fucking-ra.*

"Can you believe spring's finally here?" Calvin sidled up to her desk at the front of the classroom and perched on the edge.

Dear God. Bathing suit season was coming. Yet another joy...

No. She couldn't believe it. Thirty-four days since her world came crashing down and her life had not moved. Some days the jolting reality of the hollow, decaying heart inside of her chest was staggering. Other days, it was just life. She'd dig her spoon into another pint of fattening comfort and truck on. God, she hated men.

"Yup. It's been a long year."

He grinned. "You had a pretty good group of kids this year."

Everything inside of her wanted to scowl. *What do you want?* "They're wonderful."

He hesitated and scooped up the small wooden apple a student had given her during her first year of teaching. "Scarlet..."

He was really struggling. He didn't typically have that look of worry—oh shit! Was she getting laid off? Forcing out a slow breath, she tried for cajoling. Losing her job would simply push her over the edge. She smiled and tipped her head thoughtfully. "Calvin, is there something you need to tell me?"

He placed the apple on the desk and appeared to refocus. "Yes." His throat cleared. "I want you to know that—what I'm about to ask you—you have every right to say no and I won't be offended if you do."

"Okay," she answered slowly. What the hell was this?

"I wanted to see if you'd be interested in having dinner with me."

Her brows lifted betraying her shock. That was not at all what she expected. "Oh."

"I understand this isn't the most brilliant invitation, but I've been meaning to ask for a while now and I just figured, to hell with it. I'm single. You're single— oh, God, you *are* single, right?"

Her lips pursed as her eyebrows returned to their customary position. "I'm single." *Always single.*

"Like I said, if you say no, I'd totally understand."

"I'm flattered," she admitted. She was on some level, behind all the shock and relief that she wasn't getting bad news. Calvin Armstrong had thought about asking her out? For a while? A sharp pinch jolted her heart.

But it's not him.

Per usual, whenever she thought of him, the world turned quiet and seemed to float away. *Mr. Stone.*

He'd crushed her, lifted her up higher than she'd ever been, worshipped her, and then... Nothing. She'd given him every piece of her soul, and it wasn't enough. He didn't want her, didn't need her. There really was nothing more frustrating than still wanting him to a degree that seemed like need. It was some sick fantasy to him, but to her it was real. Nothing fake could ever hurt so much.

"Scarlet?"

She shook her head. "Sorry. I drifted for a minute."

"So it's a no then?" He grinned politely, but what seemed genuine disappointment shown in his eyes.

Nothing about him is genuine. He. Is. A. Man.

He's also your boss.

Crap. "Can I think about it?"

His shoulders perked up under his tweed jacket. "Of course. I understand—what, with us being colleagues and all—that it's a fairly big decision. I want you to know, our association outside of school would be completely private. No one else would need to know."

Her mouth tightened. *More secrets. See? They're all sneaky. Go ahead, Scarlet, be another man's dirty secret.*

Attempting to disguise the trembling of her hand, she smiled. "I'll let you know. Now, if you'll excuse me. I really have to finish these papers."

"Of course." He stood, a hint of premature victory to his step. When he reached the door he paused. "Oh, and Scarlet, I forgot to tell you. We got the approval for the OddSquad grant. Next week a shipment of three hundred tablets are coming in and some of the CEOs from GeekPeek are coming in for the launch."

They won? Her proposal won? Her chest filled with deep satisfaction, an almost forgotten emotion. "That's fabulous news!"

She'd worked so hard on writing the material for that grant program. Their students would benefit hugely from having such tools at their disposal. While her life outside the classroom was in the gutter, moments like this made her proud of the things she accomplished in her field. "This is huge."

Calvin nodded. "You did good, Ms. Farrow. We're going to need a few teachers to take the training course. Should I put you on the list?"

"Definitely!" She had no doubt the future of learning rested in technology. She wanted to be as savvy as possible when it came to helping the kids and other staff understand.

"Perfect. I'll see you tomorrow. Have a good night."

"Goodnight, Mr. Armstrong."

Once he left she was too excited to focus on the papers she should have been grading. Although she typically returned assignments in record turnaround time, her students would understand. For the first time in weeks, she was truly happy about something.

When she got on the road she dialed Nicole.

"Hello?"

"Hey. Guess what!"

"Well, aren't you in a chipper mood? What?"

"We got the grant!" Her feet stomped on the floorboard of her car as she squealed. She wished she could honk her horn and let the world know how big of a deal this was.

The company that managed OddSquad, also the founders of GeekPeek, the largest, most lucrative social network on the planet, was only offering the tablet program to one school in each district. Scarlet had obsessed over the grant writing, desperately wanting their school to be chosen.

"That's great, Lettie. Did you just find out?"

Of course her friend didn't share her enthusiasm, but that was fine. "Yeah. Calvin came into my office to —get this—ask me out, and then he told me and—"

"Wait, wait, wait, *wait!* Who's Calvin and did you say he asked you out?"

"He's my principal and yes, but I don't think I'm going to go—"

"Of course you're going."

"No, I'm not there yet, Nicole. I'm still fragile and way too cynical. If I saw a penis right now I might snap it like a pencil."

"Scarlet, listen to me. I know you've been hurt."

Her friend didn't really know the whole of it. It was too much to tell, too personal and private, too deep.

"But you have to get back out there. Stone is gone. Over. Let him go and move on."

Nicole didn't know how much she'd fallen for him. Scarlet didn't have the courage to tell her friend all the mortifying details, though she'd told her enough.

"I know," she whispered, her elation giving way to deep sorrow.

It was clearly over. He hadn't contacted her just as she asked and that was for the best. There was no point in wanting someone who didn't want her. But it would still take time to heal. He wasn't hers, but she also wasn't ready to let him go.

She pulled into her driveway. "I just need a little more time. I'm home now. I'll call you later."

Nicole congratulated her one more time on the grant and Scarlet slid her phone into her purse. She entered the empty house, greeted only by a silent brush of Thor's tail.

The familiar crush of loneliness seeped into her shoulders, weighing her down as she fell heavily on the couch. Her gaze drifted to the shelf beside the blank television. There, within the mahogany box, were his letters.

She sighed as the ache inside of her bloomed and burst into palpable heartbreak. She needed to let it out at night. Every day she struggled to hide the agony of losing him, to keep it together in front of others and not fall apart. But at night, when she was all alone in the deafening silence, that was when she'd let down her guard and let the pain swallow her whole.

The following Friday Scarlet was giddy with expectation. The delivery was coming that afternoon and the front office was going to buzz her the moment it arrived.

She'd done a wonderful job of avoiding Calvin and evading his invitation to dinner, but chances were he'd have the unfortunate opportunity to ask her again today.

She was torn. Part of her wanted to say yes and force her recovery, the other part wanted to save him the torment of dating someone as scarred and screwed up as herself. Both reasons were selfish and exactly why she had to tell him no. Not a single part of her was remotely considering the possibility of romance. Such things no longer existed in her world.

When the call came, she requested coverage and speed-walked to the front office. She spotted Calvin through the glass wall speaking to a man in a burgundy shirt and striped tie. A large box sat on the counter and her fingers itched to set up the devices.

Taking a calming breath, she turned the knob and entered the office with an air of professionalism.

"Ah, here she is," Calvin announced. "Ms. Farrow, I'd like you to meet Mr. Garnet, CEO and co-founder of GeekPeek and OddSquad. Mr. Garnet, this is Scarlet Farrow, our sixth grade math teacher and grant writer extraordinaire."

"It's an honor to meet you, Mr. Garnet." She shook his hand with two of her own. This guy was like a celebrity genius.

"Likewise."

Her armpits were starting to sweat, so she tried to reel in her exuberance. Also, the guy looked a little skittish. "Thank you so much for choosing our school."

His smile was tight. "I wasn't responsible for the selection. You'll have to thank my partner for that."

Noting how uptight the man seemed and finding it strange, she dropped her energy another notch. Maybe he didn't visit the schools often. "Would that be Hunter Turay?" He'd come to introduce the kids to the OddSquad program in the beginning of the year. She hadn't met him personally, but the teachers running the program raved about him.

Why was he looking at her like that? Did she have food in her teeth?

Calvin cleared his throat, obviously sensing the weird vibe in the room. "Yes, Mr. Turay was wonderful. Please send him our thanks."

"The selection was made by my other partner. Asher Roan."

Why does that name sound familiar? She must have heard it on CNN or read it somewhere. "Oh, well please express our gratitude. We're very excited to have such an incredible opportunity—"

"You really don't remember us, do you?" he suddenly interrupted.

"I...I beg your pardon?"

"We went to school together."

Her social inadequacies exploited, she bravely excused her short-sightedness. "I'd heard that your company was local, but I didn't realize you graduated from—"

"Not just me. All of us," he corrected. "We all went to school right here, me, Hunter, Jet, and Asher. You were in my homeroom."

"You'll have to pardon my forgetfulness. I'm terrible at remembering names and faces."

"Not a problem...*Lettie.*"

Her heart jolted at the familiar term only people from her past used, but he hadn't said it endearingly. He spoke the nickname as if to prove a point she wasn't seeing.

Feeling like an outsider looking in on a project she'd initiated, she tried to refocus the conversation. Maybe she was being overly sensitive. "Well, it must be neat for you to see all the changes to the building." What else could she say? This guy was crabby.

He turned to Calvin. "Asher and Jet will be here first thing Monday morning to do an orientation. Hunter will set up the sound system and overhead before they arrive. We ask that students be in the auditorium by nine-thirty sharp so everything can be wrapped up within two hours, leaving room for plenty of questions. The teacher orientation will be the following two Wednesdays."

"Perfect," Calvin agreed. "Thank you again for selecting our school. I think you'll find you made a great choice."

Mr. Garnet nodded and turned, his eyes narrowing as he glanced her way. "Scarlet."

She frowned as the door shut behind him. Did they not get along in high school? She was nice to everyone. And who remembered stuff like that? They graduated twelve years ago.

"Are you excited?"

She turned, shaking off all thoughts of the confusing man. He was a wealthy CEO of a global company. That had to make a person eccentric and slightly awkward. Smiling, she faced Calvin. "I'm thrilled. Let's open one up and play."

"Come into my office." He lifted one of the boxes and stashed the others behind the counter.

Once the door was closed and the box was cut open, she crowded in. Individually wrapped tablets stacked neatly in tight little rows. "Wow. Do you think they're charged?"

"They should be."

They each removed a tablet and unwrapped the protective foam paper. Everything was so shiny, not a single fingerprint on the screen. They powered on easily and she laughed, still finding it surreal that a company had made such an incredible donation.

"Have you thought any more about my offer?"

And there it was. Lowering the tablet as it booted up, she smiled regretfully. "I'm flattered, Calvin, but I just don't think I'm in the right state of mind to..."

"Eat?"

She laughed. "What?"

"I asked you to dinner, Scarlet. You don't have to promise me your first-born. Just have a meal with me."

"But I don't want to lead you on."

"I'm a big boy. I think I can handle it." When she didn't answer, he said, "Come on, we can celebrate the grant. Let me buy you food in exchange for healthy conversation and maybe a few laughs."

The offer was tempting. Thor was disappointingly unenthused about the grant when she told him. Plus, she had a really hard time disappointing others. "Okay, but just as friends, Calvin."

His smiled expanded. "Deal. How about tonight? We can go from here."

"That works." The teachers often had happy hour on Fridays, though Scarlet usually passed, but this was good. Maybe they'd run into other members of the staff there and it would actually feel like a small gathering of co-workers instead of a date.

"I'll meet you in the parking lot after detention."

"Sounds good."

When the last bell rang and the last student left, Scarlet grabbed her tote and locked the classroom. The building was always peaceful and somewhat changed on Friday afternoons, more so than any other evening. It was as if the school was finally able to exhale.

The click of her heels echoed down the long corridor as she walked toward the exit. The office door opened as the light flicked off as Calvin came out, wearing his shoulder bag that likely contained his laptop.

They stilled as they spotted each other, a twinge of awkwardness setting in with the hint of expectation.

"Perfect timing," he said, turning the key in the office lock. "How do you feel about Italian?"

"Italian's just fine."

They remained close but not within accidental touching distance on the walk to their cars. "Should we drive together?" he asked.

Her mind rejected the offer immediately, not wanting to complicate a simple thing. "That's okay. I'll follow you. That way you don't have to drive me back to get my car at the end of the night."

"Okay."

Stowing her belongings on the passenger seat, she started her car and stilled, her fingers curling delicately around the sword keychain with a garnet stone. *Mr. Stone.*

What was he doing at that moment? Did he ever think of her? Had he forgotten her? For all she knew, he had multiple women he toyed with and fucked over. What made her think she was something special?

Her phone buzzed when Calvin texted the address of the restaurant. "Isn't this disappointingly normal," she mumbled, shifting the car into reverse and following his Volvo east.

As she drove she carefully listed all the reasons why it was illogical to continue loving a man that didn't want her. Not only had she never laid eyes on Mr. Stone, she didn't know his name. She couldn't describe how he kissed, had never known his mouth against hers for more than a whisper. She wouldn't recognize him if he were standing beside her.

But that wasn't necessarily true. She could identify his scent from a mile away, recognize his voice in a crowded room. She could sense his presence by the way the hair on the back of her neck lifted whenever he was near. But he was no longer near and her hair had no reason to rise.

She pulled into an empty parking space and gripped the steering wheel. "There's something wrong with you," she mumbled.

Calvin was a nice, attractive man. She should be flattered he'd shown any interest at all. Six months ago she would have killed to have a guy like him ask her out. Her head fell back on the headrest. Why couldn't she just be normal?

The sharp knock at the window had her shelving all matters of self-doubt. "Sorry," she said as she opened the door and stood.

Calvin politely closed the car door and opened all other doors between there and the table. Once they were settled into a booth with cocktails on the way and well associated with their perky waitress Jennifer, she took a deep breath and embraced the awkwardness.

God, she hated this. Mr. Stone plowed through any barriers, jumped right into the most personal details. She'd loved that about him. There were no secrets—well, at least not on her end. Maybe that was the trick?

All the social boundaries and superficial niceties made it impossible to really get to know others. People toed the surface and expected some deep relationship, but never really connected. It was impersonal bullshit and she was sick of it. So she decided—with nothing left to lose—she was going all in. *Cannonball...*

"So...how long's it been since you had sex?"

Calvin choked on a sip of water and quickly blotted his chin with a napkin. He cleared his throat. "Wow. I wasn't expecting that."

She shrugged, more convinced than ever that she'd lost her mind. "Clearly you're ready to get back out there if you asked me out. You're divorce has been final since last spring. Isn't this the sort of thing friends talk about?"

Sex seemed to dominate a great deal of her and Nicole's conversations and Calvin said they were going out as *friends.* Maybe if she crossed certain lines so their association could no longer fit in some neat and tidy box they'd actually be friends and not some posturing courtship. If he had a secret motive she was intent on destroying it. She didn't like secrets anymore.

He cleared his throat again and Jennifer delivered their cocktails, which Calvin seemed delighted to taste. "I wasn't asking you out as an attempt to get laid, Scarlet."

She sipped her vodka cranberry—Merlot no longer sat well—and tossed him a coy smile. "Oh, come now, Mr. Armstrong. You're a man. If this were truly a man's world there'd be no call for dating at all. We'd just run around like animals mating on some geographic special. How long?"

He tugged at his collar, setting the knot of his tie askew. "Six months."

She chuckled, slowly tipping her head back. Life was a continuous learning experience. "How silly of me to assume I was the first woman you'd asked out."

"Did I miss something? I feel like what was a friendly engagement ten minutes ago has turned into an aggressive scrimmage."

Her drink was empty. "Sorry," she said without much sincerity as she hunched deeper in the booth. Maybe she didn't want to go deep after all. It seemed, with people, she would always have something to learn.

Calvin looked at her for a long moment, studying her until she had the urge to pull the collar of her blouse tighter. "Who was he?"

She searched for Jennifer in the restaurant, wanting another drink. "Who?"

"The guy that broke your heart."

She chuckled, her finger flicking the edge of the paper placemat. "He was...no one."

No name to give. You're pathetic.

"That bad, huh?"

She couldn't look at him. Why were they even discussing this? The waitress returned and Calvin ordered another round.

"Want to tell me about it? I'm a good listener."

She laughed without humor. "I don't talk about it." *Him.*

"Okay." Their drinks arrived and they ordered. She quickly selected the ravioli without glancing at the menu. "Do you want to talk about sex?"

Twirling her straw through the ice and diluted cranberry, she mumbled, "Someone once told me sex is a hollow impression of love, an impression that can be conducted seamlessly without the main ingredient."

He frowned. "Meaning love?"

"Yup. Biggest four letter word there is, but totally unnecessary in the grand scheme of things." Their second round arrived and she took a hardy sip. "I'm not into impressionism. I also don't automatically believe sex is more than sex. It's not. It's just two bodies coming together and relieving a physical need."

"How very..." He laughed. "I'm not sure what that is, exactly."

"It's sad." Her drink wasn't strong enough, yet somehow it managed to bully the confessions out of her head and into her boss's lap. "He was a coward and I'm the idiot that let him in. At one point, I actually thought he was the strongest, most powerful man in the world. I don't really understand men at all. I'm sorry I said those things to you. I shouldn't butt into other people's personal lives when I hardly have a grip on my own."

"Look, Scarlet, we all make mistakes. I'm thirty-two years old and already divorced. Don't beat yourself up because you decided to trust someone and wanted love. We all do."

His empathy tormented her broken heart like shitty glue incapable of holding her together. She couldn't fathom ever feeling whole again and the longer this went on the more segmented she became from reality. "Please don't say nice things to me, Calvin. I'm a glommer."

"A what?"

"I glom. Even when common sense tells me I'm reading too much into things, I somehow turn into a stage five clinger that can't let go."

"I recently read one of those little postcard things people put all over GeekPeek. It said, *Being polite is so rare these days, it's often mistaken for flirting.* I'm merely being polite, Scarlet."

"Of course you are." Time for drink number three. She looked for perky Jennifer, but didn't see her. Maybe she could learn something from Calvin, help her own recovery in some way. He seemed so well-adjusted after a failed marriage. "So, when you had sex after your divorce, was it weird being with someone else?"

He shifted and rearranged the condiments. "It was with my wife."

Her head slowly lifted. "But you were divorced."

"I know, but sometimes..." He shrugged. "Old habits die hard."

That was the truth.

"We both knew it wouldn't change anything," he quickly clarified. "You're right, sometimes sex is just two bodies coming together to relieve a physical need."

Or an emotional one. For a moment she'd thought they were comrades, people of the same rejected fiber, but now... "Do you still love her?"

"I'll always love her," he answered quickly, as if there could never be another option. "But we aren't compatible as husband and wife anymore."

The waitress fluttered to their table. "Here we are, one ravioli and one steak, medium rare. Can I get you another round?"

Scarlet stared at her ravioli. She might as well rub it on her thighs. Calvin did some talking and the waitress disappeared.

"Hey."

What was she doing? Glancing at her dinner date she gave an apologetic smile. "I'm sorry, Calvin. You asked me out and I've been a complete brat, barging into your personal life and spewing my private business all over the table. I ruined what was a very sweet gesture. I'm sorry."

He smiled. "You didn't ruin anything, Scarlet. I sort of like the fact that we cut out all the bullshit and made it real. We already know each other on a professional level. It's nice to see such a different side of you."

Two more drinks were placed on the table. She should probably slow down.

"Let's eat," he said, scooping up his knife.

She picked at her ravioli and stared at the ice in her cocktail. Could she have meaningless sex with her boss? Maybe she should? *No. Think about Monday morning at work.*

"You're being quiet."

She studied him for a silent moment. He was attractive, bald by choice with a good jaw and handsome face, dark brows and five o'clock shadow that worked. "Sorry. I was just thinking."

"Anything interesting?"

Her mind wandered to images of Calvin pressing her up against the entryway of her den as her heel dug into his ass. He did have a nice butt. "Not really."

"How's your ravioli?"

She'd barely taken three bites. "Good."

They ate in silence and the restaurant crowded with a dinner rush. When their plates were cleared, Calvin ordered coffee and asked to see a dessert menu.

"I guess this wasn't exactly what you were expecting," she said as she sipped her coffee.

His shoulder lifted as he eased back in his seat, studying her. "You're a pretty woman, Scarlet. Smart too. Don't waste your charm on guys that don't appreciate everything you have to offer. I wanted to have dinner with you as more than colleagues and I think we accomplished that, even if I'm only gaining a friend. I have no regrets."

She'd thought the same at one time, but she regretted plenty now. "Thank you."

"Did you want dessert?"

"Oh, I shouldn't—"

"I'm ordering the black forest cake."

"But I will," she laughed. *I'll do the diet tomorrow. Fresh start.* "Make that two black forest cakes."

"Perfect." He snapped the menu shut and grinned.

Though they never breached any other personal topics, a sense of understanding established between them. She didn't know why Calvin and his wife split up, nor did she intend to ask. No matter what he said, Scarlet would never assume to understand his experience any more than an outsider could understand hers.

When he walked her to her car, he opened the door—a rather polite gesture she couldn't determine to be manners or flirting. "I actually had a nice time tonight."

"Imagine that," he teased. "I did too. Maybe we can do it again soon. I don't know about you, but the silence at home gets sort of old."

She chuckled. "I hear that." Silence was all she heard at home, apart from the occasional meow from Thor. "Thanks again."

She slid into her car and he gently shut the door. For the first time in a long time, she felt like she might stand a chance at beating the overwhelming depression blanketing her life—a *very* optimistic hope for her cynical mind. But seeing that other people managed after divorce told her she should be able to handle a breakup.

20

———

WHAT BIG EYES YOU HAVE

THOR HID on the bookcase as the vacuum roared and the stereo blared. Scarlet let her tears fall as she sung along with Three Dog Night. *"One is the loneliest number! Onnnnnnne is the loneliest number that you'll ever doooooo…"*

Shouting with the chorus, she bopped her head, her ratty hair sticking to her tears. Her mismatched socks tapped along to the beat. *"Onnnnnnnne....la la—"*

The power running to the vacuum cut off and the stereo silenced. She pivoted and found Nicole standing in her doorway holding the limp cords.

"No," her friend stated, deadpan. "No, no, no, no, no. You are not doing *this*."

Scarlet adjusted the vacuum to its upright position. "I was just cleaning."

"Bullshit. There's a fucking kitten on your shirt and those pants are from nineteen ninety-nine. There's nothing clean about—" She waved her hand in a very metrosexual circle. "This."

Taking inventory of her personal appearance, she gave up any argument. "Fine. I was crying."

"Scarlet," Nicole sighed. "You have to get out of this house."

"I went out yesterday."

"Where?"

"To the pharmacy."

"Oooh. And what did we buy on this big excursion?"

"Toothpaste and tweezers."

Her friend shook her head and plopped on the couch. She followed and Nicole took her hand. "Okay, listen to me, hon. I *know* what you're going through."

No, you don't.

"I know you're afraid to get back out there."

"I'm not afraid."

"But—wait, you're not?"

She shook her head. "No. I just don't see the point. I'm perfectly happy here, doing my own thing."

"Crying and listening to Three Dog Night?"

She shrugged. "I'm not going to pretend out there is any better. I've been out there. It's all fake."

"See? *Right there!* Honey, it's not all fake. What Matt and I have, that's real. You can find something real too—not necessarily meaning you need a man, but you need to rejoin the land of the living. You have to get out of the sweats and stop wearing clothing with animals on them, and for God's sake brush your hair."

"Why? So someone can see some polished version of the truth? Sounds like lying to me."

She dropped her hand. "Okay, how's this? You're turning into Debbie Downer and no one's ever going to see how beautiful you are if you mope around looking like an extra from *Thriller.* I know he hurt you, but you're not the first woman to go through something like this—"

"Yes, Nicole, I am. I'm absolutely the *first* woman to go through anything remotely close to what I've been through. It wasn't normal. What we did, the conversations we had—they were beyond intimate."

"You didn't even have sex with him!"

She jumped to her feet. *"So?* Some things are more intimate than sex! You'll never understand, so stop trying!"

"Fine." She stood and collected her purse. When she reached the front door she turned. "Just remember that I tried to get through to you and make you see there are things to be happy about, but you wanted to be sad more. Enjoy your misery."

The door closed. "I will."

Later that night as she lay in the bath she texted Nicole.

I'm a shit friend right now. I'm sorry. Please don't hate me.

Her response was immediate.

I shouldn't have yelled at you. I'm not trying to minimize what you've been through. I know you're heartbroken. But I miss my friend and hate seeing you this way. I'm sorry. Do you want him back?

She sighed, appreciating her friend's apology. Nicole's husband was a cop and more than once offered to run the minimal information they had on Mr. Stone to see if they could find him, but Scarlet didn't see that as a solution. She only wanted him if he wanted her, which he didn't.

No. I wanted someone to love me. He doesn't. I have higher standards than that.

She chuckled and hit send. Nicole, of course, got the inside joke.

THAT'S MY GIRL! YES!!! You hold on to those standards because you deserve someone who can reach them!

She smiled. It was nice to know Nicole at least changed her position in that department. If Mr. Stone taught her anything, it was to admit what she wanted and settle for nothing less. Though she didn't want a man in her life, she knew what she was worth, and any man incapable of fighting for her wasn't worth her time.

Sliding her phone away, she faced some uncomfortable truths. Her body was suffering from this depression. Her mood was unbearable. Her libido had shriveled up like an old...she couldn't think of something that shriveled. Maybe a hermit crab or an old mummy. Ew. The point was she was falling apart, literally rotting from the inside out. And Nicole was right. It needed to stop.

Maybe she should talk to a professional. Maybe she should see about getting on antidepressants. Exhausted by the mere thought of her options, she sunk deeper in the tepid water and shut her eyes. Maybe it would just go away and one day she'd wake up normal again.

The problem was, she didn't remember her normal before him. She hated him for what he'd done. Hated the idea that it was all just an act for him. She *felt* him, *connected* with him. But her honesty and trust wasn't enough to compensate for his lack of faith and it never would be.

It didn't matter. He was never coming back and she was never going to see him again or have the answers she wanted. Deciding enough was enough, she left the tub and focused on the things she could count on—herself, her friends, and her students. Tomorrow was a big day at school and she wouldn't let her happiness be overshadowed by what she could not change. There would be no more dwelling on Mr. Stone.

*L*ifting her hand, she waited for the students to settle. "Boys and Girls, I'm waiting."

Gradually, the noise in the auditorium quieted. "We have the luxury of meeting some very clever men today and I expect everyone to be on their best behavior."

The students weren't aware they were about to be gifted with ninety thousand dollars worth of technology and she was giddy with anticipation. "How many of you are familiar with GeekPeek—a show of hands?"

Every hand went up.

"How many of you use that social network?" Most hands remained lifted. Some younger students lowered their arms.

"Well, did you know the creators of that social network actually went to our school and once sat right here in this auditorium?"

The kids began to whisper and comment on this news. She grinned, sure she had their attention and grateful Mr. Garnet had shared that inspiring fact.

All four of the creators actually graduated with her class. She'd looked them up online, but didn't recognize any of them. She was going to dig out her yearbook this week and see if older pictures brought back any memories.

"That's right," she continued. "Not only did they attend the same school as you, they're here today with an incredible gift. I want you to put away anything distracting, give your full attention to our guests, and show them how much we appreciate their time. Please welcome two of the co-founders of GeekPeek, Mr. Jet Piazza and Mr. Asher Roan."

The students clapped as she stepped back from the podium as their two honored guests stepped out from backstage. Both were dressed in suits, one tall, dark, and dangerously handsome, the other refined and equally dangerous, but in an intellectually attractive way, the sort of sophisticatedly handsome look every woman fell for.

She smiled in greeting, wishing she'd had a chance to welcome them before the students arrived. "Thank you so much for coming," she whispered, handing off the microphone. "I'm Scarlet Farrow, the teacher that wrote the grant."

"Nice to meet you, Ms. Farrow. I'm Jet and this is Ash."

She shook his hand, surprised by her nerves. The other man, Ash, nodded and she didn't sense an opportunity to offer more of a greeting so she quickly stepped backstage where the curtains hung.

"How we doin' today, kids?" Jet shouted and the students again applauded. "How many of you recognize this?" He held up a tablet and every hand went up.

"It's a telephone, right?"

"No," the kids called.

"It's not?" Jet frowned at the device, creating an immediate rapport with the crowd. "Is it a typewriter?"

"No!"

"A computer?"

"No!"

"Then what is it?"

A bunch of hands shot up and Jet pointed to a girl in the front row. "It's a tablet."

"Can you type on it?"

The girl nodded.

"Can I take it online?"

"Yeah."

"Can I use it to video chat with friends in China?"

"Well, yeah…"

"So maybe it is a typewriter, computer, and telephone all in one."

"Yeah, but it's more than that," the girl said.

Jet nodded. "Interesting. How many of you kids have one of these at home?"

A few hands went up and someone shouted, "My mom has one."

"What if I told you Ash and I had a few to give away? Would you sit up straight and be the best audience we ever had?"

The chairs squeaked as every student suddenly corrected his or her posture. Jet laughed and Scarlet smiled. He had a wonderful disposition the kids immediately responded to.

"Before I go handing out tablets to the good listeners, I'd like to hand the mic over to my friend Ash who's going to tell you all how much these little things can actually do. See…we're sort of nerds like that. We like to invent toys that can always be upgraded and advanced. So while some of you might have seen similar tablets before, this one is brand new and not on the market until next month. I bet you'll learn something new today and maybe when you get home you can share your expertise with Mom and Dad. You ready to learn?"

"Yeah!" The crowd shouted.

He handed the mic to the man with the dark hair and glasses. He didn't seem to have the ease with public speaking that Jet possessed. As he approached the podium slowly, he glanced over his shoulder and she smiled, thanking him with a nod. This was such a wonderful thing they were doing for the community.

His shoulders lifted, as he appeared to draw in a deep breath. "Good morning. I'm Asher Roan, founder and creator of GeekPeek."

Her jaw slackened as every muscle in her face went lax. Her stomach sunk and her knees softened. Reaching out, she quickly caught something beside her as her entire body went weak.

"Scarlet?" Calvin stood, quickly catching her arm. Her nails dug into his sleeve as she fought to remain upright. "Scarlet, are you ill?"

On the stage and through every speaker in the auditorium his voice echoed. She shut her eyes, the familiar blindness tightening everything into acute perspective. Her last thought, before all sound cut out to a humming whistle and her body went limp was, it had to be him. She'd know that voice anywhere. *Mr. Stone.*

---

*C*ool moisture pressed against her brow and she snuggled into the couch. Her nose crinkled as she breathed in the unpleasant scent of plastic and body odor. Why did her sofa smell like the gymnasium? Her eyes shot open—because she was at school.

She gasped, totally disoriented, and tried to sit up a little too fast. "What happened?"

Calvin's face blurred into view. "You fainted."

She blinked as Nancy, the school nurse, dabbed her head with a cool cloth. "You've been out for almost forty-five minutes."

She looked around, no longer backstage. "This isn't where I was."

"We didn't want to make a scene in front of the whole school so once Nancy got there and said you were safe, we moved you to the gym."

"These mats smell like a twelve year old's armpit."

Calvin chuckled and helped her sit up. "Did you skip breakfast today?"

"No, I—" Her breathing turned choppy. "Where are the men from GeekPeek?"

"They're still here. You missed the big announcement. The kids freaked when they realized they were *all* getting a tablet."

"Here, have some water. Your color still looks off to me," Nancy said, handing her a bottle. "I'm going to get some hard candy out of my desk. Maybe your sugar's low."

She chugged the water and wished she'd had three more bottles. "Did anyone see me faint?" How embarrassing!

"I don't think so. It was quiet. I've never seen a person actually faint before. You just sort of wobbled and grabbed my arm then I felt your body go limp and eased you into a chair."

"Thank God you were there." If Calvin hadn't been there she would have hit the ground like a ton of bricks. "I've never fainted before."

"Maybe you should call your doctor."

She shook her head, dismissing his suggestion. She knew exactly what caused her to faint. Shutting her eyes, she listened carefully, trying to hear his voice through the speakers on the other side of the wall.

"I found some hard candy," Nancy said as she returned.

Scarlet took the candy and stood.

"Maybe you should sit a little while longer, Scarlet. You don't look too steady," Calvin advised.

Of course she wasn't steady. He was here in her school. Wandering to the entrance that separated the auditorium from the gym, she cracked the door a smidge.

"There are apps for all those things. If you have a science project and need to clock the rotation of the planets, all you have to do is download..."

Unbelievable.

It was him. She was certain of it. It was either him or she was having a complete psychological break and needed to take some time off.

Without thinking, she slowly pushed through the door and drifted into the auditorium. Teachers stood in the aisle beside their classes and watched the stage aptly as—*What was his name?*—Asher Roan took them on an in-depth journey of technology.

Awareness slammed into her with incredible force. A.R. He signed every single one of his letters with those initials. Breath sawed in and out of her lungs as she stared at him with unblinking eyes. This was not a coincidence. Slowly, she walked down the center aisle, appearing to be nothing more than a teacher acting as an usher.

He was young. Her age. Well, duh, he graduated with her. *Oh my God, he knew me!* Every thought was an epiphany, violating a new level of privacy and raking over her senses like irons over a bed of hot coals.

Every incident of their past flashed before her eyes. The times he'd surprised her at work with flowers... Of course he knew where she'd worked, they'd gone there as children together. Why didn't she remember him?

Her chest lifted as she slowly ghosted up the aisle, closer to the stage. He was handsome. Her deep hatred and hurt did nothing to diminish his natural appeal. His shoulders were broad and his posture assertive. *Mr. Stone.*

Her insides tickled and she worried she might get sick or possibly pass out again. Mr. Stone was the owner of GeekPeek? Mr. Stone was someone from her childhood? Mr. Stone was standing right in front of her. Maybe she should sit down. Her hands and feet were starting to tingle again.

She stopped only about twenty feet from the stage, her eyes drilling into his. Shock made blinking unnecessary.

"So you'll see," he said, directing his finger over the tablet, which showed its screen on the overhead. "With this application you can not only—" His eyes met hers and his words halted. Didn't he realize she'd recognize his voice? "You can not only..." he continued, but seemed to struggle with his statement. He blinked and pulled at the collar of his shirt, a show of nervousness she never imagined the impenetrable Mr. Stone to express. "...not only..."

Speak up, you pretentious son of a bitch. Go on, tell them what you can do, all the incredible talents you have.

Under the narrow silk of his tie she noted the

steady rise and fall of his chest. What was he thinking? Did he do this on purpose? Had he even read her grant proposal or was this just another game? He had no business coming into her school and speaking to her students with any other motive than to give these kids what they worked so hard to earn.

Abruptly, she turned and marched out of the auditorium, letting the door slam behind her. The school was vacant, every student and teacher in attendance for the big unveiling.

He'd done it. He'd managed to infiltrate the last sanctuary she had, violate every part of her life until there was nothing left unbothered by his presence.

This was *her* project. She'd written the grant. She'd poured her heart into the reasons why her students deserved this program. He had no right to take this away from her too. It was the first thing that made her happy and had absolutely nothing to do with him—or so she'd thought.

She returned to her classroom and shut the door. Maybe she should go home. Her mind spun as she stood in the center of the room surrounded by thirty empty desks. Her hand pressed to her queasy stomach as she caught her breath.

The cadence of heavy footsteps built down the hall, echoing through the barren corridor. Perhaps it was Calvin or Nancy coming to ask if she'd lost her mind. She'd politely thank them for their concern and inform them that, yes, she was officially bordering on insanity and needed to take the rest of the day— maybe week—off.

The door clicked and her head lowered. She had no excuse for her display or any of this nonsense. "I don't know what's gotten into me—"

"Scarlet."

The breath knocked out of her as he whispered her name. Not Nancy. Not Calvin. Slowly, she turned and glared at him, again, floored by how attractive he was. His brow creased in what appeared to be concern. So many times she'd considered what her exact reaction might be if she ever got the opportunity to talk to him again, if she ever got the opportunity to *see him* at all. Nothing prepared her for this.

He approached and everything in her demanded she run, but not a single muscle in her body seemed to be working. "Scarlet," he repeated, voice hoarse. His hands lifted as if to cup her shoulders and—

Her hand shot out from her side with no warning from her chaotic mind and punched him. His head snapped back the second her fist connected with his face. Her eyes went wide as pain radiated in her knuckles. She couldn't have just done that.

"*You asshole!*" she shouted, unaccustomed to the level of rage spewing from her. It was as though she'd lost every ounce of self-control.

His fingers cupped his nose as he bent forward and groaned. Blood, there was blood. "I know! I'm a complete jerk, but, *please*, listen to me."

"Listen to you? *Listen to you?* I spent months doing nothing but! How dare you come in here and act like some sort of hero! Did you even read the proposal I wrote?" Her hand throbbed and she regretted hitting him, almost certain she'd broken at least one of her fingers.

Horrendously shaking with adrenaline, she marched to her desk and used her unspoiled hand to open the drawer and dig out her purse.

He unraveled several paper towels from the dispenser on the wall. "Scarlet, please—"

"Don't talk to me. Don't even look at me."

"I love you."

She paused, her entire being trembling. Pain exploded in her chest as tears threatened.

Keeping her gaze on her desk she heard him approach. He handed her a paper towel. "Your knuckle's bleeding."

It literally hurt to look at him. Focusing all of her energy on her composure, she silently turned. "What's *wrong* with you?"

"So many things. But you were the one thing that was right. Please don't walk away again. I...love you."

Walk away? *He* was the one that walked away. He left her there in front of some driver, *naked* and shattered. Her jaw tightened. He didn't love her. "Stay the fuck out of my life...whoever you are." She shoved past him and let the door slam behind her.

21

MEMORIES

HER STUDENTS READ a lot of shapeshifter books. They all had the same theories about shifting. It was a painful process, stretching ligaments, contorting muscle, and snapping bones, all to become something else. Sometimes, recalling the person one used to be was equally painful.

Looking into her past was not a pleasant process. When she finally found her high school yearbook her recollections of the good ol' days faded into honest truths of a very confusing time in her life. Over the years she'd somehow wrapped up that part of her past with a pretty little bow, but the truth was, all those people she thought were her friends were not people she remembered fondly.

Nicole was the one exception. Her loyalty and dependability was the one souvenir she kept from her past and Nicole was the only person she'd ever really believed knew the real her. The jocks, the cheer squad, the people she passed time with, she'd only ever showed them an impression of the person she thought they wanted to see.

So many insecurities, so many moments of self-doubt and worry came back to her. Some days she'd hated the people that made up her social world, but knew it was easier to stick with them than find herself on the other side of the great divide. They chose her for whatever reason, but she could have just as easily been one of the ostracized pariahs sitting alone at lunch.

Graduating high school was like exhaling after the longest obstacle course of her life. She'd survived, which was the whole point. Minor moments and events chipped at her protective shell, but she'd made it out with hardly a scar and when she left she never looked back. Some weren't as lucky.

It turned out she remembered Asher Roan from high school.

It took a while. Her memories were shoddy at best, overwhelmed by creepy recollections of Bobby Westerman and his dominating presence over so many of her adolescent years. But Asher was in the background, a quiet little noise they seldom noticed and swatted away like an annoying gnat. Elliot and Hunter were there too. Jet, she vaguely remembered, but never as their friend.

Asher was definitely someone to her—or he should have been. She wasn't sure what exactly provoked certain events in her life, but looking back as an adult and a teacher who actively spoke out against bullying, she needed some answers. Which was why she waited outside the coffee shop at six o'clock in the morning on Wednesday.

A light flashed on from the inside and she

frowned, assuming the store only had one entrance. Peeking through the glass, she spotted Bobby turning on machines in the back. Her lungs tightened as she breathed deep. She could do this. She could face him. People would be arriving for coffee soon, so she wasn't necessarily putting herself in any danger—besides, she had pepper spray.

Her knuckles lightly tapped on the door and his initial scowl at being disturbed transformed into a welcoming, yet nauseating, grin. He rounded the counter and unlocked the front door. "Hey, Red. You here for your coffee? First cup's always the best."

"I was wondering if I could talk to you for a minute."

"Hell yeah. Come on in. You can keep me company while I get everything going."

She followed him into the store, but kept her distance. "Bobby, do you remember a guy named Asher Roan from high school?"

"Asher Roan, Asher Roan...Names not ringing any sirens, but I don't remember a lot of things from back then. Who was he?"

"I know you know him. Think. You used to pick on him, played a trick on him senior year before homecoming. I remember him showing up at my house and I know you and your friends lead him to believe something—"

"Oh yeah!" He laughed. "I remember that dweeb. Ha! He used to follow you around like a little lost puppy."

"He did?"

He laughed again. "Yeah. Everyone knew he was obsessed with you."

"I didn't."

"And why should you? You were with me. Speaking of…" He leaned over the counter. "You haven't accepted my friend request yet. When we gonna have that date?"

She ignored his question. "Why did he show up at my house that day?"

Bobby scowled. "Why do you care? It was twelve years ago."

Her reasons weren't any of his business. "I just do."

He shrugged. "He must have thought if he showed up you'd go to the dance with him. What a loser." He chuckled and busied himself filling a carafe at the sink.

She tried desperately to recall that night, but her memories were distorted. She'd been embarrassed. He'd said something or done something, but she didn't remember what. The entire night was a disaster, ending with Bobby clumsily taking her virginity. She'd tried so hard to forget the entire mess, but now she wanted certain details back.

Her eyes closed, the darkness making her other senses stronger. She'd worn her purple dress and Asher had shown up in an old suit—"You told him to come to my house."

"Nah," he denied with a smirk. "He was just stalking you as usual."

"Then why would he show up like that, dressed up with flowers?"

"You're not gonna let this go are you? All right." His smirk stretched into a grin. "I didn't invite him, Red. You did."

She frowned. "What?"

"All your sweet love letters."

"What are you talking about? I never wrote him any letters."

"Sure, you did. Why do you think he'd leave all those bouquets of flowers by your locker?"

She stepped back, recalling several mornings she'd been surprised with mix tapes or fresh flowers. "I thought they were from you." He'd acted like they were plenty of times and she took them as a sign of redemption.

He laughed. "Nah. I don't do that pansy ass shit. Only fags do that crap."

She shook her head, stumbling back another step. "What's wrong with you?"

He frowned. "What? Red, it was over a decade ago. I'm sure he's fine."

She laughed without humor. "You don't get it, do you? You've never been pushed around or manipulated, called names or forced to do something that makes you sick. You have no idea how horrible it feels to be the victim of someone else's cruelty."

He waved a hand. "Easy, Red. I've been pushed around plenty. Don't act like an expert on things you don't understand."

Recalling all the times she'd asked him to slow down and he didn't, she wondered if he had any concept of the monster he was. "I understand," she growled. But maybe he did too. Bullies weren't born. They were made. "Who picked on you, Bobby? Your dad? An older sibling? A kid in your neighborhood?"

"Hey, Oprah, figure out someone else. You want coffee or not?"

She swallowed. "Not." Stepping to the counter, she quietly said, "I want you to know, the first time we had sex, I wasn't ready. You were rough and took something I didn't want to give."

"Yeah, well, you never said nothin'."

"*I said plenty.*" There were other times too, moments she should have walked away and stayed away, but somehow he'd always found her again. "You can wait an eternity for me to be your friend, Bobby, but it'll never happen. People like you don't have friends."

"Get lost," he sneered, rolling his eyes as if her accusations were ridiculous. But she saw the moment the truth hit him. "You were never that good anyway."

"I feel sorry for you. And that kid, that guy that you called a loser..." she tossed a copy of *Time Magazine* on the counter where Asher, Elliot, Jet, and Hunter made up the cover. "That's him. He *is* doing just fine. You're the loser." Without giving him a chance to respond, she turned on her heel and walked out the door, not able to bear another second in his presence.

When her feet hit the pavement she was trembling. Her heart raced as she struggled to maintain her composure. She needed to find a new coffee shop and a place to sit down. Then she needed to think of how she was going to face the other ghosts of her past.

---

*D*isappointment didn't begin to describe her feelings when she realized Asher wouldn't be teaching the seminar for Technology in the Classroom. Running into him there had been her only hope of tracking him down, his social status making him impossible to locate. She thought—if he truly loved her—he'd return, but he didn't.

She waited until the staff cleared out and quietly

approached Elliot and Jet. When she cleared her throat Elliot stilled, eyeing her from under his glasses, but paying her little mind. It was clear he didn't like her very much. She turned to Jet. "Mr. Roan couldn't make it tonight?"

"Ash doesn't usually teach seminars," Jet said as he boxed up sample tablets.

Elliot paused and gave his friend a warning look.

"Do you have a contact for him? He said something the other day at the assembly and I wanted to—"

"We know who you are, Lettie. It's you who forgets."

She turned to Elliot, rather caught off-guard by his accusing attitude. "You're right, I do forget. I had to look in my yearbook to stimulate the slightest memory of any of you, but why is that so horrible? We weren't friends. That doesn't mean we were enemies. I remember you now. I also remember Asher and Hunter." She glanced at Jet. "Sorry, I don't really remember you."

"It matters, because you were a bitch," Mr. Garnet suddenly said.

"Whoa!" Jet drew back. "Elliot, not cool."

Taken aback, she scoffed, speechless. "What did I ever do to you?"

"Nothing. You did absolutely nothing. All the times your boyfriend locked us in uncomfortable places, stole our clothes, beat on us...you were always there, doing nothing. Like we were invisible. I guess you know what that feels like now."

His words hit too close to the truth and her throat suddenly closed as her eyes stung. Swallowing, she croaked, "I thought we could talk like adults, but I guess I was wrong." She cleared the emotional strain from her throat. "For the record, I didn't know what was happening, because I had my own battles to fight. But if I ever saw Bobby truly go after someone else, I would have done something." She had to believe that was true.

"That's a lie. I remember a time when I looked right in your eyes and thought, how does she walk away with him after he treats people like that? In my book you're just as guilty as every other bully."

No one had ever accused her of being cruel. Her mind shrank from the allegation. "That's not true."

He shrugged. "Doesn't matter now."

Her gaze lowered to the floor. She couldn't be a villain if she'd been a victim, could she? Backing out of the room, she collected her belongings and walked slowly down the hall.

"Scarlet?" Jet jogged after her.

Her throat was suddenly tight with restricting emotion and the need to cry. She shook her head. "I don't remember any of that, I swear," her words were clipped as distress seeped into her voice. "Bobby was horrible to me, always bossing me around, embarrassing me, forcing me to do things I didn't like. I was so worried about protecting myself half the time, I didn't think about anyone else. I swear, I'm not a horrible person. I was just a kid."

"Hey, it's fine. We were all kids. Elliot's just being a dick. Here."

She wiped her eyes and glanced at the card in his hand. "What is it?"

"My business card. I wrote Asher's cell number and address on the back."

The breath knocked out of her lungs. Just like that, everything she'd wanted? It was surreal. Slowly, her fingers closed over the card and his grip tightened, not letting her take it. She whimpered. Another trick?

"Do you love him?" Jet asked.

She stared at him, unsure how to answer such a personal question.

"It's a simple question," he said. "Maybe there could be a simple solution to all of this if people started telling the truth and being okay with who they are."

She swallowed, and rasped, "Yes. I love him." A tear tripped down her cheek as his fingers released the card.

"Then tell him. He's falling apart without you and we all want to see our friend whole again."

A chilling calm came over her as he walked away. *He's falling apart...*

Was that true? Did she really mean something to him? Had he been suffering the same as she'd been? Her fingers turned over the card and there was his contact information. Should she call? *Could* she forgive him?

She wasn't sure what any of this meant, but she was beginning to understand the man behind Mr. Stone. Just like her, he had insecurities weighing him down. It didn't excuse his actions, but it explained a whole lot.

What she couldn't comprehend was why a man like Asher would feel the need for so much secrecy at this point in his life. He'd proven himself to the outside world. Opinions from assholes like Bobby Westerman shouldn't matter anymore.

Asher was a very sexy man, so she couldn't imagine him doubting his desirability. There was a quiet magnetism about him that went beyond normal charm. So why hide who he was? She was exhausted with the guessing game.

It took her a minute--or twenty—to collect herself and put her car into gear. She'd typed his address into the GPS on her phone and there were only thirteen miles separating them. Thirteen. Miles.

Her heart pounded as she gripped the wheel and drove, teeth clenched the entire way. How many times had she traveled this road with Pennyworth? She laughed every time she spotted a landmark she recognized.

Their entire liaison seemed like an adventure in a far off fantasyland, but really they'd been in her neighborhood the whole time. How bizarre and... ordinary. They probably dropped their mail off at the same post office.

"You have arrived at your destination."

She frowned and slowed the car. Where? There was nothing there.

Edging along the shoulder, she looked left and right. Tall willow trees grew sporadically on what appeared to be some sort of park. Hedges thickened where a sidewalk would fit, but there was no walk.

The dusk made it difficult to see. Creeping slowly down the road, she spotted a cement pillar, only about three feet tall. There was a stone drive. Was this it?

She frowned and looked at the card Jet gave her. Her eyes scoured the property for an address, or more sensible, a house. But there was nothing.

Turning onto the drive, she coasted slowly. The narrow path twisted like a road in a cemetery. She wanted to shut her eyes to see if any of this felt familiar, but that wouldn't be wise.

Her car slowly climbed a grassy hill and the first

traces of a home peeked over the horizon—no, scratch that. That wasn't a house. She had to be on some sort of historic property the township owned. The castle like structure was impeccably maintained with plush gardens and freshly mulched beds.

"Is it a castle?" she mumbled as she followed the road onto a circular drive. Maybe it was a funeral home.

Two towers budded the enormous stone structure. The windows were old, detailed with metal glasswork. She slowed and stopped at the entrance, two wooden doors carved with great detail. Maybe it was a church.

She counted the steps. Ten. That's how many it took for her to reach him. Was this where they'd had their fourteen encounters?

She shut off the car and waited. No other cars were visible. It was nearly eight o'clock at night. Shouldn't he be home? If the place was vacant she might as well look around.

Climbing out of the car she shut her eyes and savored the familiar crunch of gravel under her feet. Her heartbeat quickened as she recognized the uneven press of the stones under her feet.

As she faced the steps she smiled. She hadn't imagined anything quite this lavish, but the steps were fairly close to the set she'd pictured in her mind. Her eyes closed as her fingers dragged lightly over the cement banister. One. Two. Three. Four. Five. Six. Seven. Eight. Nine. Ten. This was where he'd greet her.

Her heart sputtered as familiar excitement caught hold of her insides, tightening and tingling. Her lashes lifted. Alone.

Lowering her hand, she debated knocking. She thought about Elliot and the way he looked at her, despised her for things that happened twelve years ago, things she'd barely been aware of.

You knew. The admission came out of nowhere, dark and shameful despite the privacy of her mind.

Memory after memory slowly crept in. Bobby had been awful, not just to her, but to everyone. Worst of all, was his treatment of Asher and his friends. She couldn't tie the boy from high school with the man that called himself Mr. Stone. It was disorienting, trying to associate the two.

But there was the truth. They were one in the same. Her heart hurt every time she recalled a time she simply walked away as Bobby tortured some innocent bystander. She'd never know how awful he behaved in her absence. Thinking of Asher and Bobby now made her want to hit something.

Oh, God. I hit him. *I punched the wrong asshole.*

She contemplated her own students, so young and innocent, trying so hard to find him or herself, yet be like everyone else. Her heart broke whenever she caught a student being bullied or made fun of.

Mr. Stone had been made fun of. It was almost impossible to believe. Not only that, he'd been bullied, beaten black and blue by kids three times his size at the time.

Her fingers trembled to her lips as her vision blurred under unshed tears. She recalled the poems she often found in her locker. They were from *him*, not Bobby—though Bobby accepted her gratitude without objection. If only she'd known they weren't from Bobby she might have had the courage to leave him. But each one touched her heart and served as a redeeming indication that Bobby might possess some loving traits. She should have known he was incapable of such sweetness.

Her throat dried as she tried to imagine how many times Bobby had tricked Asher in order for him to make such gestures. He'd written letters under *her* name only to laugh in his face. Asher had shown up, walked right into the lion's den that day he set foot on her lawn.

Had she meant that much to him? Why?

She remembered her confusion and the girls laughing at her as the guys snickered. Asher was undaunted, prepared to escort her right into homecoming for all the school to see. How blind she was not to see what was happening then.

That entire day was horrible. She tried to understand why he'd come there, but then he'd said something and she only recalled being furious with the strange boy who never said more than two words to her.

He's using you.

His warning came back to her, now holding the prophetic wisdom she was too naïve to hear as a girl. Bobby *was* using her. Asher was right and he'd tried to save her. If only she'd listened, there could have been so many more happy memories to her high school years.

She didn't remember what she'd said after he'd upset her. She could barely remember looking at him again after that day. It was as if he'd purposely avoided her.

But now, understanding who he was and how their paths were tied, she suspected he had a plan from the start. Thinking Mr. Stone could have done all of this as some form of revenge broke her heart all over again.

Elliot was right. She'd done nothing when she could have possibly done something. Did Asher see her that way too?

Her stomach knotted painfully. Once the thought crossed her mind it wouldn't leave. That was why he didn't want her to see him. He never meant for any of this to go on longer than he'd planned. He wanted to hurt her.

"Well done," she slurred, stumbling away from the door. Jerkily fumbling her way down the steps she gasped through new tears of betrayal. She needed to get out of there.

Her head hung between her shoulders as she sat in her car—waiting. For what, she didn't know. Her chest ached. She wanted to curl up in a ball and shut her eyes until the world became a nicer place. Life wasn't supposed to hurt this way. *Love* wasn't supposed to cause this much pain.

Her fingers curled around her keys, her thumb slowly tracing the garnet stone of the sword. He should know she was there, know she'd pieced it all together.

Removing the sword from her keychain, she reached in her bag for a piece of paper and a pen. She wrote a quick note and folded it around the sword.

I remember you. I remember every flower, every poem, and every gift, but I never knew they were from you. For the record, I never loved anyone the way I love you. That you couldn't be honest about who you were when I was always honest with you...That, Mr. Roan, is my greatest regret. I understand now why you ended it.

Take care,

S.F.

She left the paper and sword wedged in the crack of the heavy double doors. Enough.

By the following week Scarlet had made some progress. She'd thrown away all the picked over junk food in her kitchen, forced herself to walk the track during her lunch break, and made a valid attempt to take pride in her appearance again. Working on the outside helped with the disaster dwelling on the inside.

Becoming aware of so many things in such a short time took a few days to process. It hit her late Saturday night that Asher first approached her on GeekPeek, the brainchild of his career. There were some ethical red flags there, but overall she was simply fascinated that someone she knew was smart enough to create such a thing. Part of her—the teacher in her—wished she could go back in time and nudge little Asher Roan and tell him everything was going to work out just fine for him in the end.

That was another difficult pill to swallow. Asher was going to recover. He was going to be just fine. He was gorgeous, smart, successful, exciting, and gentle. Soon enough he'd be rebounding with someone else and she'd be nothing more than a weird childhood memory gone awry.

She didn't want to be a tragedy, so she stopped comparing herself with others and turned all her attention to bettering herself. Her focus was work, her students, and finding hobbies she enjoyed. Currently, she was learning how much she did not care for knitting. But she smiled and did exactly what the instructor said, certain her seat would be open next Monday at the local stitch and bitch.

That following Wednesday, after the last teacher seminar for Technology in the Classroom, she again waited to speak to Elliot and Jet. For seven days she'd considered how to apologize for doing nothing rather than something. It wasn't easy.

Once everyone left the room she slowly approached Elliot. "Oh, good. You're back," he snidely said as she meandered toward the front of the classroom.

His nastiness was intimidating and, to her thinking, a bit undeserved. "You know," she started, losing sight of her purpose. "Not all bullies look the same. Some wear bow ties and glasses and can be real assholes."

He paused and glanced at her from the corner of his eye. "Are you calling me a bully?"

"No, of course not. I'm calling you an asshole."

He scowled at her then shook his head, rolling his eyes like she was beneath him.

She sighed. It really bothered her that he could dislike her this much without even knowing her. "I was coming up here to apologize, but you make that impossible. I don't know why I bothered."

He stacked the tablets in a box and faced her, arms crossed at his chest. "*You* were coming to apologize."

"Yes." She fidgeted. "It turns out—after taking some time to think—I remember a lot more than I thought I did about high school. I wasn't always nice and there were some times I stood by when terrible things happened to all of you... when I probably could have intervened. You don't have to forgive me, but I need you to know that I'm sorry for that. The person I am now would have done something."

"Why didn't you?"

She shrugged. "I was a kid. I didn't respect myself enough to expect it from others. Maybe I was scared if I stepped in that they would have turned on me. You should know I also wasn't immune to Bobby's cruelty. He bullied me in a different way, but it was enough to keep me quiet and too afraid to interfere."

Something changed in Elliot's expression as his entire demeanor softened. "I'm sorry. I didn't know he...was mean to you."

Her smile was regretful. "That's the thing about being an insecure little girl. I didn't know it at the time either. I just thought the way he treated me was normal."

"Well, I accept your apology and I'm sorry for being...an asshole."

She cautiously grinned, feeling like a modicum of damage had been repaired. "Thanks." Seeing he wasn't into discussing things further, she slipped away.

As she left the room, Jet, again, chased her down. "Hey."

"Hi Jet."

He shook his head, appearing a bit frazzled. "What's with you? You ask for a contact, I give it to you, and you never get in touch with Asher. What's your deal?"

Taken aback, she stiffened defensively. "Nothing is with me. I figured some stuff out and realized it might be easier for everyone if we just let the past go. Forgive what is and move on. I was trying to do what's right."

"What's right? Didn't you hear me when I said he's falling apart?"

She was getting a little fed up with everyone picking sides in regard to *her* and *Asher's* personal life. "And what, exactly, do you think I'm doing? It's a battle just to get out of bed each morning. If I don't stay totally regimented I fall completely apart. I went to his *castle,* Jet, and I saw just how unsuited we are. He contacted me and broke up with me for a reason. He may love me, but he doesn't like me. There's just too much hurt between us."

"You're wrong. He broke up with you because no one's ever wanted him before and he doesn't know how to believe someone—a woman he's always put leagues above the rest—might suddenly see something in him."

Her nerves were shattered. "I don't think I can handle much more of this."

"So that's it? You're just going to walk away?"

"I don't know what else to do."

"Talk to him!"

"I can't!" she snapped. "Don't you see? I fell in love with Mr. Stone. Your friend is Asher Roan. I can't ask him to be something he's not. He deserves someone to want him for the man he is."

"He *is* Stone."

She shook her head. "No, he's not. He's a genius that runs a tech company who happened to go to school with me and made a sizable donation to my students. Other than that, he's a stranger."

"You're wrong. Everything you guys shared was Asher. He never had the courage to be himself until he got to pretend to be someone else. When he was

Stone, there was no fear of coming up short. It was the first time he got to be real."

Frustrated and out of solutions she slapped her hands on her thighs. "If he's so miserable without me, where is he? It's been almost two months—"

"He's scared."

"The Mr. Stone I knew didn't get scared."

"You're wrong. Everyone gets scared. He's terrified he's broken your heart and he doesn't know how to make this right. He's afraid, Scarlet, afraid if he makes one more move he'll break the two of you to the point you're unfixable. He was so afraid you fell in love with the fantasy, he panicked about disappointing you with the reality."

She did fall in love with the fantasy. Everything was so screwed up and she and Asher seemed to be taking the same approach. Avoidance was safe. What was the point in making things worse?

Looking into his eyes, she asked, "Did he do this to get back at me?"

"No. He did this because he's always cared about you. I think part of him thought if he could prove himself to you he could let go of all his insecurities once and for all."

Well that helped, but it still didn't fix things. But if he couldn't confide in her she couldn't help him. "I don't know how to fix this. I can't make him do something he refuses to do and he *doesn't* trust me."

Jet looked down, his concern for his friend evident in his tight expression. "He doesn't trust himself. He's a great guy, Scarlet. He just...needs to believe in himself."

"What if I'm scared too? I won't survive being rejected by him again."

"He won't reject you."

She considered his words, debating if they passed as any sort of guarantee. "Why did he like me, in high school, I mean? What was so special about me? I'm plain, I don't wear fancy clothes, and my hair's never been anything more than boring red."

Jet smiled. "To him, you're perfect."

The word wrapped her heart in tender warmth, fulfilling little nicks of insecurity buried deep within her soul. *To him, you're perfect.*

"Perfect's a tall order to fill."

"That's the thing, Scarlet. Now he knows you're not perfect and he loves you more for all your little imperfections. He has imperfections too."

"He won't share them with me."

"I think," Jet said slowly. "If you give him one more chance to show you who he is, his honesty would surprise you. Relationships are about meeting each other halfway."

He'd tried to approach her and she punched him. She still couldn't believe she reacted like that. Sighing, she said, "I'll think about it. That's all I can promise."

It wasn't the answer he wanted, but he nodded. "Good enough."

When she got home that night she tried to distract herself but it was impossible. She wanted to believe he'd confide in her about his feelings if given the chance, but she was scared, scared of being hurt again.

She wanted a man that wasn't afraid to fight for her, but maybe she had to let him know he had a fighting chance. *Meet him halfway...*

She glanced at Thor as the credits rolled and *Return of the Jedi* ended. "I know. That one's my least favorite too."

Thor glanced her way and flicked his tail.

"You're totally selfish. Do you know that? Here I am, suffering through my endless emotional turmoil, trying to make the biggest decision of my life, and you're practically snoring."

His eyes closed.

"That's it." She slid him to the empty pillow. "I can't sit here anymore. I'm going out and you can't come."

She drove aimlessly for several miles until she wound up very close to Asher's house. Pulling to the shoulder of the road, she held the top of the steering wheel and pressed her cheek to the back of her knuckles. "What am I doing?" she moaned, lightly banging her head as she groaned.

Sitting back, she sighed. "Damn it." Cranking the car into drive, she turned onto the private road. Four windows were illuminated, but the rest remained dark. The sweet scent of burning wood filled the air so she suspected someone was home.

She should have changed, was her first thought as she slowly climbed the ten stairs. Maybe she should go home and come again in the morning, when she was wearing something a little sexier than black slacks and a dated emerald blouse covered in Thor hair.

You're just making excuses.

Gritting her teeth, she lifted her fist to the door and hesitated. What if he wasn't alone? Her confidence didn't return simply because his friends suggested it should. Rather than knocking, her fingers closed around the ornate knob and turned. The large door creaked and slowly opened.

Her breath left in a rush as the expansive foyer gaped before her. Towering walls and classically painted ceilings expanded to a soaring chimney made of the same stone used on the exterior. A flame flickered low in the cavernous hearth and recognition struck with the subtlety of an anvil.

There were two wingback chairs, tall and sewn of the darkest sapphire blue. A small, round leather topped table sat between them and in the corner of the enormous entryway was a wine fridge and an armoire of sorts. Where was he? Did he live here?

Shutting the door quietly, she slipped off her shoes and shut her eyes. The moment darkness surrounded her she remembered how to get to the other room and opened her eyes. Going left, she carefully walked toward a tall set of pocket doors, slightly parted at the center.

She breathed jaggedly, her nerves telling her to go back, but her will insisting she keep going. She deserved to see him, see this place of her past. If he got mad she broke in he could call the cops. *Let's hope that doesn't happen.*

Her heart thundered behind her ribs with dizzying force as she slid the doors apart, stepped into the massive ballroom and froze. As his face lifted his lips parted, a million words and accusations flung between them as the moment carried through time with cutting implication.

"Scarlet..." His gravelly voice ripped through her, countless memories of pleasure assaulting her senses. How many times she'd craved the sound of her name from his lips.

He looked terrible, clearly not expecting company. His hair was a mess and his jaw needed a shave. He looked so ordinary in jeans and t-shirt, yet he still looked beautiful.

He bolted to his feet and took an urgent step forward, as if intending to grab her in his arms. She flung out a steady hand and he halted. His eyes clouded with regret, but he didn't take another step. Slowly, she lowered her arm and drew in a shaky breath.

Her lips pressed tight as her throat contracted, fighting back a sob. "You hurt me." She hadn't thought about what she might say. The words simply fell out.

His gaze softened as his head lowered. "I know. I'm sorry."

Her head shook at the unnecessary pain. "Did you do it because of what happened in high school?"

He shook his head. "No."

"The truth, Asher." It was so strange calling him something other than Mr. Stone.

Throwing a hand through his hair, he dropped into the chair. "I didn't know what I was doing. At first, yes, it crossed my mind, but then I actually got to know you and realized high school wasn't a picnic for you either. I thought..." His hand brushed over his head again. "I thought I could help you, thought we could maybe help each other. If I could get you to see the good in me maybe I could see it in myself."

She did see the good in him. "Then why did you end things?"

He looked away. "Because you loved someone else."

"I loved *you*."

"You loved Mr. Stone."

"Yes."

He seemed to want to say more but hesitated. "I don't want to be someone else. I couldn't bare the thought of disappointment flashing in your eyes the first time you saw me. I've seen it before, Scarlet. It hurts."

"You never gave me a chance."

He held out his hands. "This is me." Shaking his head, he said, "All I see in your eyes is hurt and anger. I put that there." Glancing to the far wall, he rasped, "I never meant to hurt you."

He'd first been attracted to the idea of her, some girl she couldn't recognize as herself. What difference did it make if Mr. Stone was who first attracted her? At the end of the day it was this man sitting in front of her that she loved. "And this is me. Who do you love, Asher? Because I'm not perfect and I'm not some teenager. I'm just me. Do you see *me*?"

His head turned and he met her gaze, truly looked into her eyes, and the effect was potent. He was beautiful.

"I love *you*, Scarlet. I've always loved you on some level, but my feelings then were nothing compared to what they are now. I know you're not perfect. Being so only makes me love you more."

She drew in a slow, jagged breath. "And when you touched *me,* did you mean it? I didn't fall in love with a name. I fell in love with a man who made me quiver with only a caress, or a command. I fell in love with the man who managed to make me feel alive, the man who cherished me, and missed me when I was gone. I could live without ever saying the name Mr. Stone again, but I don't know if I can live without the man who made me feel all those things."

His face pinched with tension. "I meant every single moment."

"And the things you said?" She held her breath,

still unable to believe someone could see all those wonderful things in her.

"I meant every word. But Scarlet, I also meant the things I said on our last night." His hand pressed to his chest. "I never wanted to need something the way I need you. This pain...I never expected it. I have no idea how to handle the constant worry that you're all right or the unending desire to simply be by you. I just wanted to protect you, and the truth is I never could."

"I never asked for protection."

"But it's what a hero's supposed to do, Scarlet. A good man protects the woman he loves."

"And he let's his woman do the same. You never even gave me the chance to show you how much I cared, to prove how much I worried about your well-being too."

"I was going to, but then..." His eyes closed as if seeing a painful memory. "I saw you at the café."

"What?"

"Westerman was there. I wanted to kill him after the things you told me, but I couldn't move. I'm a coward."

"You saw me?"

"Yes, and while I was trying to figure out how to punish him for hurting you, you smiled and acted like you were old friends. Why?"

She swallowed. "Because he scares me too, Asher. I didn't want a confrontation. I just wanted my coffee. Life's too short to try to fix the assholes of the world."

His hand slid directly over his heart. "I thought you gave him your number. I didn't think you would, but then you wrote something down—"

"I was signing my receipt."

"I know that now. I was an idiot, but... imagining you choosing someone else—*him*—broke my heart."

"I chose you."

"Try to understand the life I led, Scarlet. No one ever chose *me*."

Her vision blurred as she spoke the truth. "Me either."

His mouth was bracketed with lines of stress. "I chose you. Everything I said came from my heart. At first I wanted to do this so I could prove something to myself, but then I just wanted to see you happy. When I saw you that morning, saw how confidently you handled a situation that left me paralyzed, I realized I gave you some of that confidence."

"You did. You gave me so much."

"But I didn't know how much I had left to offer. I figured cutting ties was the most selfless thing I could do for you, so you could find someone who could be all the things you wanted. I didn't see it as selfish until I realized how much I misread the situation. Then I tried to call you but it was too late."

She'd thought it was too late too. Maybe it was. "Do you still feel that way?"

"I know I love you enough to step aside if that's what you want. I never wanted to hurt you and if the mere sight of me causes you pain, I'll somehow deal with the mess I made and let you go. These last few weeks I've been sitting here trying to figure out how to do that so you could move on. But despite all the things I know, I don't know how to live without you."

Her vision blurred as his words seeped into her broken soul. "Then don't."

His head lifted, hope hidden in his eyes as his

chest expanded with each breath. "Do you mean that?"

"Asher, if you want me, then fight for me. Do you think I have the slightest clue what I'm doing? Your world is huge compared to mine. I haven't been in a relationship in *years*. Most nights I'm sitting on my couch, talking to my cat, watching corny sci-fi movies."

His lips parted as though this shocked him. What did he think? He'd read her letter. She told the world how bleak her life was, how lonely, and hollow. "Stop imagining some cheerleader from grade school and start looking at the woman in front of you. I've never hidden myself from you."

"You like science fiction?"

She frowned. "What?" Was he even listening?

"It's important, Scarlet. Are you making fun of people who enjoy sci-fi or is it something you honestly enjoy?"

Unbelievable. Shaking her head, she waved her hand and let it drop. "I don't see how it has anything to do with what we're discussing, but yes, I actually enjoy them. As a matter of fact, if there was a flight to The Shire, I'd get a one-way ticket and be gone."

He was silent. She rolled her eyes. Once again, she bared her soul and he just sat there. "I have to go. When you figure out what you want... I don't know." She turned and walked away.

At the front door, she blinked back tears as she slid her feet into her shoes. All the words in the world couldn't push him into action. She'd met him halfway and he left her hanging. If he wanted it fixed he'd have to make a—

Her body was abruptly grabbed and her back flung into the door. His mouth crashed over hers as he swallowed her surprised gasp. His lips pressed hard as his hands dragged up her body and through her hair, a thousand volts of electricity shooting up her spine.

"What are you doing?" she gasped. His hand glided up her thigh and hooked her leg over his hip as he ground his body into hers.

"I'm fighting for you. *Don't* go. I won't let you turn your back on this. On <u>us.</u>" His mouth dragged down her throat as her eyes rolled back in ecstasy, so many needs rushing at her at once. "I'll fight every day for the rest of my life if I have to. I don't ever want to let you go, Scarlet. I can't."

Her chest tightened as more tears filled her eyes. She gripped his face and kissed him with every ounce of passion she possessed. His scent filled her, familiar and rich. "You can't shut me out."

"I won't." He closed his mouth over hers as warmth bloomed in her chest, chasing out the cold. "I'll never shut you out again. I promise. It was the worst mistake of my life. No more secrets."

No more secrets. Had there ever been more beautiful words. "What's your middle name?"

"Michael."

Her hand tugged at his clothes, needing to touch his skin. His lips dragged over her flesh as their breath mingled and her need transcended into a form of madness. She'd never wanted someone so much in her life.

"Whatever you want to know, I'll tell you."

She panted as he grazed her breast, nibbled her ear, so many erogenous zones and her panties were already soaked. "Asher..."

He stilled and slowly met her gaze. Her mouth quirked shyly, as his deep blue eyes studied her through his glasses. She bit her lip, wondering why he'd stopped.

"Say it again. Say my name again."

"Asher."

His cheeks flushed as his hand slowly slid into hers, their fingers lacing as his other hand glided over her shoulder to the back of her neck. "I've fantasized of this far too long," he confessed as his mouth descended. She drew in a deep breath as he kissed her slowly, the passion building until her entire being trembled for more.

Her arms drifted to his shoulders, palms sliding over his thick shoulders and into his soft hair. His hips pressed to hers and she felt his desire full and heavy against her belly.

"Asher..." she couldn't stop saying his name, savored the knowledge that she could finally do so. His mouth was madness, coaxing her body open like a flower under his touch. It was the most passionate kiss of her life. "I want you."

His fingers pulled at her hair, mussing it as he ground his front into her. "We should wait," he whispered as his hands gripped her ass.

"Are you crazy? I'm pretty sure we've both waited long enough."

He pulled back and stared at her, eyes blinking through the lenses of his designer glasses. "True."

She gasped as he suddenly lifted her in his arms like a knight rescuing his princess and carried her back through the grand entryway to the ballroom. Even now he made her feel like she was in a fairytale.

They reached the enormous bed in the corner of the empty room and he carefully lowered her. She'd been there before, with him. What an indescribable relief it all was to be there again, only this time was better because she could look in his eyes.

He leaned over her and stilled.

"What is it?" she asked.

His mouth curved slightly. "I love you, Scarlet."

"I love you too, Asher Michael Roan. I loved you before I even set eyes on you."

His lips pressed to hers as he crawled onto the bed, his fingers slowly unfastening the buttons of her blouse. Her palms glided over his strong arms and back, cherishing that ability to finally touch him freely.

His eyes closed as he confessed, "I've died a thousand deaths waiting to feel your hands on me, your gaze on me. But I never imagined this."

"Me neither. You don't need to be afraid of me, Asher. I'd never hurt you." She quickly tugged at his shirt, wanting all barriers away. "Take this off. Hurry."

He eased back and swiftly stripped the shirt away. His mouth crashed to hers as his fingers slid beneath the strap of her bra and yanked it down. "Do you have any idea how many fantasies I've had about this moment?"

A euphoric trance slipped over her. People didn't fantasize about her. She wasn't exotic enough to build a fantasy around. "Really?"

"God, yes," he confessed, his mouth kissing down her chest as his hands plumped her breast. "I nearly died, every time you let me see or touch you."

He'd always made her feel so good during those moments. "Asher?" She arched into him as his hot mouth closed over the sharp tip of her nipple.

"Mmm?"

"How did you get so good at...pleasuring a

woman?" She'd always assumed he'd had countless lovers. How else could he have known everything he knew about the female body, like all the things he'd taught her when they'd visited the hotel?

His attention at her breasts paused as he rose above her. "I learned everything I know for you. I read, I studied, I interviewed people from all lifestyles, and I watched you carefully to determine what aroused you the most." His fingers traced her brow. "It's your mind, Lettie. As much as I love your body, there's nothing more erotic to me than your mind."

And oh, how he could seduce her mind. "I wish..." her words fell away. She didn't want to spoil their reconciliation.

"Tell me."

Licking her lips, she confessed, "I wish we could take back all the lost time."

His head shook slowly. "I wasn't ready. It took me a long time to admit there was something missing and do something about it, but all the changes I made didn't matter. It didn't matter how I dressed or what I wore. I needed a woman that could really see *me*. I needed you, Scarlet."

"But I was blind."

"No, you saw the parts of me no one else could."

"I see you now, Asher Roan. And I never saw anyone so beautiful."

He smiled. "Should I find you a mirror?"

She laughed, but then turned serious. "I mean it. You're a beautiful human being, not just on the outside, but on the inside where it counts."

His face lowered, hiding a sweet smile. Quietly, he whispered, "You don't know how much that means to me, Scarlet."

"It's true."

He smirked again. "I'm so glad, because…this morning my company went bankrupt. I no longer have a penny to my name."

Her lips parted. "Oh, my God. Are you okay?" She shook her head. Of course he wasn't okay. "What can I do to help? Do you need anything? I…I don't know what to say."

"I just wanted to let you know before we went any further. If that changes your mind I'll understand."

Here she was, dumping all this other stuff on him when he'd lost his *company* just that morning. "Do you want to stop?"

"Do you?"

She didn't want to be selfish, but she would understand if his mind was on more important matters. "I don't want to, but we can if you'd rather talk—Oh!" She gasped as he rolled to his back pulling her with him, his lips smiling against hers as he kissed her.

"Why are you laughing?"

He drew back and grinned. "I'm just playing with you. My companies are fine. But it's great to know that doesn't make a difference to you."

Her mouth gaped and she pushed him. "You jerk! I felt terrible!"

He laughed and rolled her to her back, kissing her again. "Which tells me how genuine you truly are, but I already knew that. Don't be mad. I like teasing you."

Pursing her lips, she pouted. "Jerk."

He nuzzled her ear as shivers tightened her nipples. "Forgive me?" he whispered.

"No. That was mean."

He bit her shoulder. "Please."

She sighed, knowing she'd of course forgive him

and actually liking this teasing side of him. "Fine. I'll forgive you...for a price."

He chuckled. "Okay. What will it be? A trip to the spa? A new necklace?"

"No way. I want your shirt."

He frowned. "My shirt?"

She nodded, glancing to the corner of the bed where it lay in a wrinkled mess. "Yup."

He blinked, his eyes a bit forlorn. "But that's an authentic 1989 Brainy Smurf classic."

"I'm aware. I tried bidding for one on eBay last year and got outbid somewhere around a hundred bucks."

He did a double take. "I got it on eBay."

"When?" There was no way they'd been bidding in the same auction.

"Maybe last June. I forget."

Her eyes went wide. "Oh, my God! Are you *TheRealMcFly99*?"

He drew back. "*Yes!*"

They both laughed. What a small world. "Oh, I'm definitely getting your shirt now! You outbid me!"

His gaze turned intense, lust darkening his eyes. "Would you really have paid a hundred dollars for a Brainy Smurf shirt?"

"Of course! Do you know how rare he is? It's not like a Papa or Smurfette. They're everywhere."

He gripped her arms. "I seriously need to make love to you. Right. Now."

Her giggle was silenced by a very serious kiss and she moaned.

His hands curved around her breasts, plumping and massaging as his mouth descended. Her thighs parted as he pulled her pants away. After so much patience it was impossible to passively lie there. She un-latched his belt and tugged it free of his jeans, tossing it carelessly to the floor.

Twisting the button loose, she unzipped his pants and reached for him, not stopping until her fingers wrapped around thick heat. "I've got you now," she teased and he groaned, his head resting on her shoulder, his breath beating against her flesh in a rush, as her fist slowly pumped over his impressive length.

"I'm afraid I have a confession, Scarlet."

She stilled. "What?"

"There haven't been many women. I'm not a virgin, but..."

She frowned and released him. "Asher... Please look at me."

His head slowly turned, his eyes apologetic. "I'm not sure if I can deliver perfect, but I want this to be right."

"It *is* right," she whispered.

"I might..." he swallowed and glanced away. "I've waited a *really* long time for this—for *you*—longer than fourteen encounters. It's closer to fourteen years. I'm afraid I won't be able to..."

Her hands cupped his jaw as she softly kissed his lips. "Asher, this may surprise you, but I've never been good at sex. You're the only man that's every made me feel sexy. If it's over quickly, we'll do it again. And again." She grinned. "And again."

He chuckled, his smile full of relief. "God, I love you."

"No pressure, okay? We're in this together."

His focus drifted over her shoulder and back to her. "Okay. You'll have to pardon my occasional doubts. It's a habit I'm trying really hard to break."

"I have those moments too. We can work through them together."

He kissed her, slow and deep until her toes curled. Gripping her wrist, he brought her hand to his cock. "Touch me, Ms. Farrow."

Her nipples tightened at the sudden commanding tone in his voice. She'd never expected to enjoy a demanding lover, but she loved it when he took control. With him, nothing was ordinary. Her fingers tightened as she slowly stroked him. His hips pressed into her as his mouth spread kisses across her shoulders and throat.

The feel of his skin against hers was indescribable and she sensed him getting close as he gasped and whispered her name. His body tensed and he tried to pull back, but she wasn't having any of that.

"Your touch is the most incredible thing I've ever felt. Please don't stop."

"I'll never stop." Her body flooded with arousal as his body trembled. Seeing him respond to her touch was incredibly erotic. "I've waited so long to touch you like this."

Her hand worked over his flesh as the most vulnerable, sensual sound left his throat and heat shot onto her belly.

His arms pulled her close as he shook and pressed his face to her throat. "I'm sorry."

He had absolutely nothing to apologize for. The fact that she could actually make him lose control was euphoric. She pumped her fist one more time and his body trembled. Releasing him, she lifted her fingers and stared into his eyes as she slowly licked them. She'd waited an eternity to taste him. "Delicious."

Eyes wide, he let out a slow breath. "Fuck."

"Yes," she agreed and smirked.

He glanced down. "I'm going to need a moment."

Stretching beneath him, she sighed. "Hmmm... whatever could we do to pass the time?"

His smile was slow and priceless. He laughed quietly and turned away for a split second, collecting himself and quickly cleaning up his release. When he looked back at her, he smirked and asked, "Ms. Farrow, do you need to come?"

Her breasts lifted as her gaze softened and lust breathed between them. "Yes, Mr. Roan, I'd very much like to come."

"Then you shall." He removed her pants with impressive speed. "Part your thighs and let me look at your pretty pussy."

His words were such a turn on her body immediately responded. Yes! This was the man she loved. This was the man that made every encounter stand apart from all the rest, gave her the courage to expose hidden parts of herself. Slowly, she drew her legs apart. "I'm very wet," she confessed, as his eyes dropped to her core.

He sat back and there were no words to describe how much it pleased her to watch him look at her with such hunger.

"Your panties are soaked through, Ms. Farrow." Her body pulsed as he spoke, his eyes focused on her core. "Pull the lace aside and let me see."

Her fingers slipped beneath the silk and she slowly exposed her sex. Cool air teased her folds as he stared at her and growled. Leaning close, he slid a finger deep and held. "Next will be my cock."

Her eyes rolled back as she gasped, his finger withdrawing and plunging deep again. She held her panties aside as he fucked her with his fingers, intently increasing her pleasure and stretching her with each added digit.

Her hands were suddenly pushed away as the lace of her panties tore and his mouth was on her, kissing, licking, and nibbling as his fingers continued to probe. Arching into him, she cried out as he teased her clit and her sex pulsed. "Yes!"

The scrape of his jaw dragged over her tender flesh as he bit her thigh. He drove two long fingers deep, hooking them at the perfect angle as his mouth closed over her clit.

Her toes curled as every muscle in her legs tightened and her back bowed against the bed. "Asher!"

Relentlessly, he sucked and teased until she could take no more and her control snapped. Her body pulsed and trembled irrepressibly as she came hard against his mouth, crying out his name. He didn't stop at one. On and on he went, plying one orgasm after another until she was wrung out and breathless, all thoughts drifting someplace sweet and peaceful.

Heat surrounded her as he climbed up her body and pulled her to him. Her curves fit against his sculpted form, molding perfectly into every crevice. He softly kissed across her lips and she tasted their blended arousal.

"Scarlet?"

"Hmm?" she pliantly stretched, beneath him.

"Are you ready?"

"Mmm-hhm." Words were too difficult.

The heat of his belly burned hers as wide hips fit between her thighs. Her tender folds parted under the direction of his gentle fingers and suddenly thick heat was filling her. Her eyes gradually opened to find him watching her. This was what she'd waited for.

"Tell me if I hurt you."

Using her minimal strength, she grinned and cupped a hand against his jaw. "You won't."

His pelvis pressed to hers, as he slowly he drew back and then filled her. Together they gasped. "We might have flaws, but this is perfect," he whispered, gently pumping into her as he stared into her eyes.

"Yes," she breathed in full agreement. This was perfect.

While there had been others, tonight was the first time either of them had made love. It went beyond sex and it was more intense than the most passionate fucking. It was intimate, a connection dependent on more than physical contact. Through every glance she felt more and more connected to his soul.

All of her life she'd felt invisible and then this man had come along and took away her sight. One by one, her flaws drifted away and all the pressure dissipated. By making her blind he'd helped her see who she truly was.

They'd fallen in love with nary a kiss between them. Seeing was easy. They saw every shortcoming they had, but it took each other to truly understand those inadequacies did not define who they were as a whole. Hearing the truth took effort, but together they found the courage to finally listen to reason. Fear could make a person blind to many things, but love left nowhere to hide.

Love exposed all.

Asher didn't love her as a child. He was merely infatuated with a girl he didn't know beyond what his mind wanted to see. But now, as he held her and filled her under nothing but the flickering flames of the fire-light, she showed him all of her, and he saw her flaws, her strengths, and even her deepest insecurities, just as she saw his too. There was truth to love, a truth which neither of them could deny.

She didn't want the fantasy, nor did he want the unattainable version of perfect he'd imagined. What they wanted was exactly what they got, something undeniably real, sewn from honest confessions and genuine promises to always do their best to love and protect the other.

That evening, Scarlet spent the night in a man's arms, as they whispered in the dark and confessed their deepest desires. It was incredible to know he'd be there, not just tonight, but tomorrow and the day after that, slowly unveiling the secrets inside their souls that they couldn't see on their own. The future was very bright indeed.

EPILOGUE

"She was amazed to discover that when he was saying 'As you wish',
  what he meant was, 'I love you.'"

~Grandfather
The Princess Bride

As it turned out, fantasy was underrated and living with a guy like Asher Roan drove that point home—and by home, she of course meant their kickass castle. Teacher by day, sex goddess by night, her life had become something incredibly close to a work of fiction. But it was *real*.

Asher loved to play and every day with him was an adventure. His creativity was endless, his sense of humor perfectly dry like a good martini, but also potent. He could be called to any task and took every role seriously. It didn't matter if they were gaming, working, or simply lounging around naked on a Sunday, he always was her knight in shining amour, her hero at the ready.

It turned out they had much more in common than either of them assumed. She was a closeted nerd and he was her perfect counterpart. When they realized how much they enjoyed the same things, they truly hit a euphoric point and let their geek flags fly.

Their wedding, of course, was Star Wars themed, being that the movie scores were unarguably the best. Their groomsmen, or troopers as Asher liked to refer to them, were wonderful. Elliot and Hunter got to know her adult side and forgot the child. Jet was a sweetheart she never stopped appreciating.

Mr. Pennyworth—or Steve, as she'd come to know him—was a welcome return to their lives and someone she would always share a special connection with. She adored the way he looked up to Asher and hoped one day her husband realized that the friends he admired so, loved him with a loyalty that could outlast time.

But still, there were limits to what she could tolerate. For instance their son, who was due to arrive in three months, would *not* be named Gandalf, Mulder, or Flash, but Anakin was not out of the question.

It was amazing, the sort of man her husband became as his confidence grew. It boggled her mind that he had insecurities at all. To her, he was remarkable.

The more he realized she was pretty much shockproof the more interesting their life became. The amount of fantasy play was endless and sometimes the blindfold even went on him. Asher loved role-playing and she loved seeing how many ways he could be her hero.

Escapism was something they all practiced, whether consciously or otherwise. There was simply something beguiling about being someone else for a time, it was liberating to test fantasies they otherwise wouldn't dare to admit.

It wasn't clear who possessed the more capricious side, her with her need to be rescued again and again by a dominant knight, or him with his call to duty and honor—that deep seated need to prove himself time and time again. Either way, their life never stopped being engaging and their desire never seemed to wane.

Scarlet was deeply in love with a man who was dedicated, loyal, and affectionate beyond the norm. Their hearts were indeed scarred, but all those imperfections made the beautiful moments of love and security extraordinary, and they never overlooked how lucky they were to find each other again. It was as if their destiny had been written in the stars.

As she waited on the grass before a table set with homemade bread, two apples, a dagger, and a bottle of cider wine, she turned the last page of William Goldman's classic, *The Princess Bride.* It was one of her favorite tales of true love and there was nothing quite as magical as reading a first edition copy from Asher's impressive collection.

His affinity for the obscure and impossibly rare enchanted her. There was nothing Asher viewed as impossible. If he wanted something, he did everything in his power to acquire it, which was exactly how he'd captured her heart.

She sighed as she read the words *The End,* wishing

the story could continue just a bit more. Her hand rolled over her distended belly disguised in the crimson gown. Asher had started quite a collection of costumes for female characters and she adored that any ordinary Tuesday could end with an evening in a far off land. Their love extended through space and time, a continuum that stretched to any fantasy and broached many mysterious circumstances.

The back door opened and she smiled as he appeared, sleekly dressed in black. He was so beautiful, so playful and fun. Jogging slowly down the stairs, his sword catching a glimmer of fading sun and flashing in the distance as he approached with a smile.

He appraised her gown and the picnic she'd prepared, his mouth hooking in a little smirk. "Is it Princess Buttercup then, about to be absconded by the Dread Pirate Roberts?"

She grinned, loving that he could not only identify the setting, but the exact moment of the plot. She slid the book to the grass. "It is, but I won't go easily," she threatened. "Not after you killed my Westley."

He adjusted the black mask he wore and smirked, that adorable dimple of his winking as he holstered his sword. "As you wish."

God, she loved him. Lowering her blindfold the world went dark and her hero rescued her once more.

THE END

Want more Mastermind?
Read Elliot's story next! Start *UNTIED* (*Mastermind 2*) now!

. . .

ALSO BY LYDIA MICHAELS

BOOKS BY SERIES

Many first in series books are FREE

Grab them here!

Free Books Here!

MCCULLOUGH MOUNTAIN

Almost Priest *

Beautiful Distraction

Irish Rogue

British Professor

Broken Man

Controlled Chaos

Hard Fix

Intentional Risk

JASPER FALLS

Wake My Heart *

The Best Man

Love Me Nots

Pining For You

My Funny Valentine

Side Squeeze

CALAMITY RAYNE

Calamity Rayne Gets a Life *

Calamity Rayne Back Again

Calamity Rayne Gets Hitched

BONUS: Calamity Rayne Veiled & Railed

Calamity Rayne Over the Moon

Calamity Rayne Knocked Up

THE SURRENDER TRILOGY

Falling In

BreakingOut

Coming Home

Ruthless Billionaires

One Billion Secrets *

Two Billion Enemies

MASTERMIND

Blind

Untied

NEW CASTLE

First Comes Love *

If I Fall

Shattered Vows

ADDICTED TO YOU

Crush *

Bang

Throb

THE ORDER OF VAMPIRES

Original Sin *

Dark Exodus

Prodigal Son

Immortal Bastard

Primal Kill

Blood Moon

STAND ALONES

La Vie en Rose

Simple Man

Sugar

Breaking Perfect

Hurt

Protege

ABOUT THE AUTHOR

To receive Lydia's Newsletter and 7 FREE Books, click HERE !

Lydia Michaels is the bestselling and award-winning author of more than forty novels. She writes heart-clenching, unpredictable romance with dark elements and high heat. Her work is character-driven and bursting with broken heroes and badass females. With a sweet spot for overbearing, territorial types, her deeply emotional books are spicy, emotionally satisfy-ing, and guaranteed to leave readers with many book hangovers.

Lydia is the consecutive winner of the *2018 & 2019 Author of the Year Award* from *Happenings Media* and the recipient of the *2014 Best Author Award* from the Courier Times. She has been featured by *USA Today*, *Romantic Times Magazine*, the *Women in Publishing Summit*, and more.

Michaels started her author career in 2007, becoming a recognized presence and advocate within the publishing industry. She is the CEO of LMC Consulting, a certified author coach specializing in character and plot development, and the founder of the *East Coast Author Convention*, the *Behind the Keys Author Retreat*, and www.LydiaMichaelsBooks.com.

She is happily married to her childhood sweetheart. Her favorite things include cooking Italian cuisine, hosting extravagant dinner parties, sipping espresso martinis, listening to her husband play piano, and escaping to her coastal home on the Jersey Shore. She's an LGBTQ ally, a BLM supporter, a firm believer that the patriarchy must end (women's rights are human rights), and an advocate for pediatric cancer research.

LYDIA

Follow Lydia Michaels on social media!
Facebook | Instagram | TikTok

THANK YOU FOR YOUR REVIEW!

Reviews help authors so much! If you left a review for this book, I greatly appreciate it!

Thank you,

Lydia

Click here to leave your review!